GLASS SLIPPER

A Retelling of Cinderella

Rebecca Fittery

Copyright © 2021 Rebecca Fittery

All rights reserved

The characters, places, and events portrayed in this book are fictitious. Any similarity to real persons, living or dead, is coincidental and not intended by the author.

No part of this book may be reproduced, or stored in a retrieval system, or transmitted in any form or by any means, electronic, mechanical, photocopying, recording, or otherwise, without express written permission of the publisher.

ISBN-13: 978-1-7361122-2-9

Cover design created using Canva.
Map design created using Inkarnate.

*To my brother, Mike. Truth seeker. Wise man.
Greatheart. Love you always.*

CONTENTS

Title Page
Copyright
Dedication
Map of Istoire
PROLOGUE 1
CHAPTER ONE 11
CHAPTER TWO 17
CHAPTER THREE 31
CHAPTER FOUR 40
CHAPTER FIVE 47
CHAPTER SIX 53
CHAPTER SEVEN 61
CHAPTER EIGHT 76
CHAPTER NINE 86
CHAPTER TEN 98
CHAPTER ELEVEN 109
CHAPTER TWELVE 117
CHAPTER THIRTEEN 130
CHAPTER FOURTEEN 144
CHAPTER FIFTEEN 152

CHAPTER SIXTEEN	169
CHAPTER SEVENTEEN	185
CHAPTER EIGHTEEN	207
CHAPTER NINETEEN	216
CHAPTER TWENTY	226
CHAPTER TWENTY-ONE	233
CHAPTER TWENTY-TWO	242
CHAPTER TWENTY-THREE	247
CHAPTER TWENTY-FOUR	263
CHAPTER TWENTY-FIVE	270
EPILOGUE	273
Books By This Author	277
About The Author	279

MAP OF ISTOIRE

PROLOGUE

Happiness reached Luca's ears, ringing laughter rising above the crunch of his boots on gravel. He had just finished his morning ride and was using the break before school lessons to stretch his legs, walking around the tradesman yard in the chilly winter air.

It was a large space; enclosed by high walls to hide it from the palace on one side, and the residential manors on the other. At one end of the yard were stables and a common hall, used by the tradesman during cold winter months. As you walked east, the yard became quieter, dotted with various shacks and pavilions that workers used during the heat of the summer, when indoor workshops could quickly become infernos.

Luca liked to wander around the quieter eastern space. The workers were generally too busy to notice as long as he didn't make himself conspicuous, and the quieter end of the yard was never used by courtiers and the like. If he walked in the royal gardens, nobles were liable to pop up and push forward their children, attempting to curry favor with the young crown prince. He enjoyed company, but sometimes he just wanted a minute to breathe. His personal guard was happy enough to let him wander in the safety of the yard, so Luca often surrounded himself with the noise of oblivious work while he stole a moment to think for himself.

Today however, his thoughts were being pulled apart by

laughter. It was a girl's voice. *One of the tradesmen's children?* Normally Luca would walk quietly on by, but the obvious joy of the sound was gravity to his feet. It pulled him around the end of the wall to a forge used in the summer by the blacksmiths. Slowly, hoping not to be seen, Luca poked his head around the gate, expecting to see one of the workers' grubby children playing some rustic game or another. He did see a grubby child, but daughter of a workman she clearly was not.

She looked to be around twelve or thirteen years old, close to his own age. Flame red hair spilled around her shoulders, escaping in long straggly waves from a netted hair covering that was popular with court women. Her blue cloak and dress were covered in soot and she was kneeling on the ground, laughing as a mangy dog licked her face, eliciting giggles as she tried to shove it away. The dog's kisses smeared some of the soot that was on her face, leaving gray swirls over her freckles.

The dog noticed Luca's presence and bounded over to him, barking hello and wagging his tail as Luca patted his head. The girl looked up in surprise, and Luca expected an embarrassed flush to appear under the soot and freckles as she recognized who he was. Instead she gave him a wide smile without a hint of self consciousness, watching as the dog jumped up at him in excitement.

"His name is Marbles," Luca offered, not knowing quite what to say and wondering who she was.

She giggled. "Hello Marbles." The dog bounded back over to her, making her laugh again, the sound loud and strong and free. "He came over to see what I was up to. Quite right since I suppose I'm an intruder. I'm sorry if I'm not supposed to be here, but I didn't mean any harm."

Luca blinked at the dusty girl in front of him. She had transferred her attention to the dog again, giving it a kiss on the head, which Marbles accepted stoically before pricking up his ears and running out the gate on the other side of the forge.

"Oh bother," the girl said, wrinkling her nose and looking back over at Luca. "If you were trying to catch him I'm afraid I've let him go."

"Oh no, I wasn't trying to catch him," Luca assured her, his brow wrinkling even as a smile at the silliness of the situation pulled at the corners of his mouth. "He belongs to the basket maker. They let him run free. He's friendly enough and he usually stays out of trouble."

"Oh yes, I could see he was a good boy right off. They must love him to bits. I would if he was mine. Only I wouldn't let him run free. I'd keep him with me to go on all my adventures. I'd train him so he would run alongside my horse. Do you work in the stables?"

"What?" Luca was bewildered by the change in conversation. He was still trying to find a way to ask what she was doing without seeming rude. As crown prince it was important to always be gracious in manner, or so his father liked to remind him at every opportunity. Part of him expected the girl's parents to spring out from behind the forge and solicit a dance for their daughter at his first official ball tomorrow.

"I asked if you work in the stables," the girl repeated, giving him a kind smile. "You have riding clothes on you see so it was easy to guess. I love horses. So do my parents. They're mad about it! I have to be too because it's in my blood. If I had to live at the palace, I think I should like to work at the stables. They have some lovely horses there."

"Yes they do," replied Luca, a grin stretching across his face. He pushed his nut brown hair out of his eyes and felt his feet tugging him a little closer. *She doesn't recognize me. She must be from the country. One of the minor nobles here for the ball.* The notion of being able to talk to someone, a girl no less, who didn't recognize him, was like a breath of fresh air.

"Are you allowed to exercise the horses? Well, I guess you're a bit young for that, but are you in training?" She looked at him curiously.

"My father exercises many of them himself," Luca replied truthfully, not wanting to lie but also not wanting to destroy his newfound anonymity. *It's lucky I'm wearing my older riding clothes, they're faded enough not to be obvious. Mother would be appalled if she saw me.*

"Oh how marvelous. Which ones is he assigned to? We saw someone out exercising Star Chaser yesterday, could that have been your father? He was handling the stallion wonderfully well."

Luca opened his mouth, but hesitated to go down the road to more specifics about the stables. Instead, he changed the topic, a maneuver his politics tutor had instructed was the first option when attempting to avoid difficult discussions.

"Did Marbles push you into the remnants of the forge fire? I'm sure I could find a maid to help you with your things."

The girl looked around vaguely, then seemed to notice the cinders and ash dusting her arms and coating her clothes. She chuckled again and gave him a rueful look, threaded with bursting amusement. "I must look a fright! I hadn't realized. No indeed, it wasn't Marbles fault. But don't worry, my parents are used to it. They won't stir up trouble for you, if that's what you're afraid of. They're rather nice that way." She tipped her head toward the cold forge. "Actually, I was testing out a theory I've read about."

Luca glanced at the smithy, then back to the girl. "What theory?" he couldn't help asking.

She rubbed her hands together in glee and Luca found himself taking a few more steps forward, drawn in by her single minded excitement.

"Have you read Vallens?" She paused but before Luca could answer, smacked her forehead, smearing yet more ash across her face and shot him an apologetic look. "Of course you haven't. Not exactly required reading for working with horses. I suppose it's not required reading for gently bred ladies either. That's what I'm supposed to be when I grow up you know." She gave him a prim look and Luca couldn't help laughing.

"Yes I know. I have a long way to go don't I?" They grinned at each other until she gestured back to the forge. "Anyway, I found his book in my father's study last summer. Most of it's bothersome and deadly dull. But at one point in the middle he's droning on about alchemy and - oh dear I can see I've shocked you."

Luca couldn't help starting in shock when she brought up the magical art of alchemy. No one would normally dare speak of magic to the royal family. *Of course she doesn't know she's doing so right now.* The Charmagnian royal family wasn't as notoriously anti-magic as the Pelerines or especially the Snowdonians, but magic was still wholly outlawed. Any chapel-going citizen would be familiar with the royal sanctioned sermons against it. This girl didn't seem evil, but it was a bit shocking.

"I shouldn't have brought it up, I know. Especially since I'm at the palace. Oh I do hope you won't say anything because then I'll get in trouble. Not that I know anything about it, just that this Vallens fellow liked to blather on about it and rail against the royal family. Not ours of course. Well I guess it was ours, except they all lived a hundred years ago."

Luca stared at her and she shrugged and huffed out a breath. "Well anyway, strike all that from your memory if you don't mind. The point is, he was droning on about all that and started berating some scientific chap who proposed that diamonds and the like were not the product of fae magic, but that they were all lumps of coal that were exposed to a lot of heat and pressure, which turned them into something else. Vallens thought it was all lies, but I did wonder about it. Because you have to mine gems don't you? They're all at the bottom of mountains. So maybe they're at the bottom of mountains because the mountains have been sitting on the lumps of coal all this time, putting pressure on them, and then they're turned to diamonds." Luca listened incredulously, half his attention attempting to follow her train of thought, the other half tracing the motions of her hands, which waived about in the air as she spoke.

"So this fellow, the scientist one, not Vallens, anyway he says that instead of fumbling about with alchemy, it's more likely for a blacksmith to produce diamonds, because of the heat of a forge acting in the same way that volcanoes and mountains and such do. I've been so curious to test out the theory every since I read it."

Luca shook his head and blinked twice. "If all that were true, don't you think the blacksmiths would have noticed by now?" he asked, drifting the final few feet between them and crouching down next to her to peer into the cold and dusty forge fire.

"That's the thing," she answered triumphantly, "I don't think so! They wouldn't really be looking for them would they? They're busy producing horseshoes and nails day in and day out. Unless the diamonds are huge, they wouldn't notice! Besides which, you don't find hot diamonds in the ground do you?"

Luca shook his head, trying to suppress a smile. The girl wriggled in her seat with excitement. "No, you don't! I would know because they do have mines near where I live. So *my* theory is that there must be a cooling off period for the diamonds to be transformed from coal. And have you ever known a blacksmith to let his forge grow cold for any length of time? Of course not!"

Luca nodded vaguely, not having the slightest idea how often blacksmiths allowed their forge fires to go out. They always seemed to be busy during his jaunts around the trade yard but he had never thought about it before now.

"Yesterday I saw this old forge sitting here when Nanny and I were out walking, and I've been scheming ever since to come back and check for diamonds."

Luca leaned forward to look further into the firing area. "And have you found any?"

The girl shifted forward as well, her shoulder leaning against his as they both searched for sparkles in the soot.

"No such luck of course. But just because they aren't in this one doesn't mean it's not true." She nodded her head once, then began pushing up off the ground. Luca rocked backward, offering her arm and helping her to her feet. She laughed her lovely loud laugh again at the sight of her skirts.

"Well, I'll definitely have to go straight home now! I'm supposed to be in the royal gardens, strategically placed to pop out at the prince, should he take his morning constitutional today." Luca stiffened but the girl didn't notice, preoccupied with halfhearted attempts to brush dirt off her dress and then wipe the same stuff off her hands. "Apparently it's one of the few appropriate pastimes allowed to young ladies at court. My mother is busy catching up with her friend, who's supposedly my godmother but much stranger than you usually think of godmothers. I slipped away to come here as soon as I had a chance. Science is so much more interesting than Princes don't you think?"

Luca frowned, defensive even though she knew she didn't mean to be rude. "I beg your pardon?"

She looked back up at him in surprise. "Oh, I've let my mouth run away from me again. I mean no disrespect of course. From all accounts he's marvelous and will make a great king one day. Except I always picture him moving from one stuffy lesson to another stuffy court function all day long. So he must be a very stuffy person. It's not his fault he needs to fill his head with all the boring things you need to know to be a good king. I hope he has someone who can help him have fun from time to time. There can't be much time for heretical books and poking around forge fires I wager." She gave him a disarmingly sunny smile, and Luca felt himself giving her one in return.

"No, he's not allowed to have heretical books or poke around forge fires, but he's not stuffy. At least I don't like to think he is."

The girl bounced on her feet. "Do you know him then?! Are you training to be one of his grooms? How marvelous. You seem a friendly enough sort, so if you're friends with him I'm sure you help him have a little fun between lessons." Luca's smile widened as the girl chattered on.

"What's he like? I'm to be presented to him and the royal family tomorrow at his coronation ball. I'm ever so curious to see them all. We went to the actual coronation yesterday of course, but we're not important enough to have been inside the main chapel. All I saw was a boy with dark hair in amongst the blondes."

Luca laughed at the image, remembering the interminable ceremony he had endured the day before. Today was meant to be a rest day between festivities. He hadn't thought about what the events of his coronation would be like for other people, focused as he was on getting the words and timing right, and not tripping on the hem of his state robes. He grinned at the cinder dusted girl in front of him, brushing off a few smears of ash that had attached themselves to his own clothes.

"Oh he's more like you and me than you'd think. You'll probably like him when you meet him tomorrow. No doubt he'll ask you for a dance at the ball."

The girl snorted. "Oh that is good! Dance with me? I hope not. I'd have all the other girls our age glaring at me." She chuckled and crossed her arms. "No, his dance card is probably assigned already, with only the most important people on it. He'll never remember me. And why should he? I'll be one of hundreds of girls there tomorrow."

Luca narrowed his eyes in contemplation, absentmindedly scratching at his neck where his fraying old collar itched his skin. She was right, his dance card was completely full of strategic partners, but he thought he could wrangle a dance with her if he played things right tomorrow. Giving her a speculative look he asked, "what's your name, by the way? Won't you tell me? I won't forget it, even if the Prince does."

She laughed and shook her head. "Here we've been chatting for ages and I never properly introduced myself. I swear I do have manners!" Dipping into an appropriately regal curtsy she replied in genteel tone, "You may call me Ella. And you, kind sir?"

"Luca," he answered, berating himself when he realized his name would be a dead giveaway. He relaxed after a moment when it became clear that she didn't make the connection.

"I should have known," she replied, her tone light and teasing, "you and every other boy our age are named after him. My birthday is three days after his. If I had been a boy, I probably would have been named Luca too. It's bad enough my own thirteenth birthday celebration has to be postponed just so we can come to his coronation as crown prince. I mean, of course I'm excited to take part and meet our future sovereign, but I'd rather have my own party quietly at home with my friends, wouldn't you?" Luca opened his mouth to reply but didn't know what to say. As Crown Prince, all of his birthdays were state occasions and involved lavish political functions. He had never had a quiet party at home, and didn't know whether he would like it or not.

Ella lowered her voice conspiratorially, not noticing Luca's hesitation. "Mother said I can pretend the coronation ball is in my honor tomorrow, since it's on my birthday. I think that will be fun for a bit, but there's only so much pretending one can do at the end of the day. Oh well. At least I don't have his name hanging over me. Is it irritating?"

"To be named Luca? I've never really thought about it, actually." He shrugged as she looked at him incredulously.

"Never thought about it?! I would hate to have the same name as everyone else! I've never met another person with my name," she stuck her nose in the air mockingly, then burst out laughing. "Although, now that I think about it, I was named after an Aunt, who was named after her grandmother, and so on and so forth, so I suppose I'm in the same boat after all."

Luca raised his eyebrow. "There may not be a lot of Ellas where you're from, but I know at least three." He mirrored her pose, crossing his arms and giving her a teasing smile.

Another clear, sparkling laugh tumbled from her lips as she answered, drawing forth another part of Luca's soul. He loved hearing it, especially since *he* had been the one to make her laugh.

"That may be true - no doubt you know many an Isabella, or Florabella, or Clarabella. But I'm *sure* you've never met someone with *my* name!" She gave him a triumphant smirk and raised her eyebrows in challenge.

Luca smirked. "Let me guess, is that because your name is Cinderella?" He teased, gesturing to the soot still smearing her clothes and face.

She looked at him in surprise and then burst out laughing, Luca following suit until they were both wiping tears off their face. Suddenly the sound of bells burst in on them, the castle clocktower chiming the noon hour. Luca glanced at it in horror. "It's midday already? I'm going to be late!"

"Me too!" Ella cried, dashing around him, shedding soot and trying to shove some of her flaming red hair back up into the netted snood that was supposed to be keeping it in place. She turned before she left the abandoned smithy yard. "Thank you for such a lovely morning. I'm glad I met you instead of the prince! You've been so kind about my mad theories and, well…" she gestured vaguely to herself and shot him a grin that warmed him down to his toes. She turned to go but stopped when Luca called out to her.

"Wait! Can't I escort you home?"

"There's no need! The house we're renting is just over there. Besides, if Nanny sees me with you she won't stop until she gets you in trouble with your master. I can't have that after you've been so kind!" She turned and started running toward the end of the trade yard. Luca jogged after her a few steps.

"But you never told me your full name!" he called, wanting to make sure he could prepare for her presentation tomorrow.

One more sunny, clear laugh floated back, and she slowed for moment, turning to shout back, "it's not nearly as interesting as the one you gave me. From now on, I think I'll just be Cinderella!" They shared one more grin before she turned to run again, disappearing around a corner, and taking all the sunshine with her.

The final notes of the bells disappeared, reminding Luca that he was late for lunch, which would make him late for lessons and earn a scolding from his tutor and his father. He turned to head back toward the stables, the memory of Cinderella's laughter floating around his ears. *Will she laugh like that tomorrow when we're introduced properly? Or will she be embarrassed that I caught her in such a state? Or worse, start to view me as a prize like all the other girls my age at court?* Somehow he thought the strange girl he had met that day might be the brightest thing about tomorrow's ball.

CHAPTER ONE

Ella - Ten Years Later

The clock chimed it's jangly announcement through the door to my office. Lunch time already? Somehow the morning had slipped away from me without much notice. I brushed my hands off on my work apron, smearing dirt on the already stained fabric.

"Luckily I've just about finished with these," I told no one in particular. Glancing down the long solarium, I took stock of the newly emptied row I had harvested. The radicchios that had been growing so nicely now lay in the large basket in front of me, their maroon and white leaves peeking up over the sides. There were more than enough to feed our small workforce at Lucedimora Castle for the New Year's celebration in a few days time. I loved the bitter flavor, especially when roasted and drizzled with olive oil and herbs like our cook, Aida, usually served. *It will be a well deserved feast.*

Grabbing the handles of my harvest basket, which was almost up to my hip, I dragged it over the dusty stone floor toward a long workbench, where they would be washed and sorted after lunch. Untying my work apron and hanging it on a nearby peg, I poured some clean water from a plain ewer into a nearby basin and scrubbed as best I could, scowling at the dirt that insisted on staying under my fingernails. My stepmother, Beatrice, would surely have some gentle remonstrance once she caught sight of them. She had made it her mission to ensure I was brought up a lady, just like my mother would have wanted. I appreciated her efforts, but since it fell to me to keep this entire estate running and a roof over all of our heads, most days I couldn't afford to act like a gentle Lady of the Manor.

There was no hand towel in sight, so I held my dripping wet hands away from my skirts, making sure I didn't get any watermarks on my pretty, but serviceable dark brown work dress. *The nice thing about this color is that it will hide any stray dirt,* I thought with a smile. A section of hair slipped down from the simple braided crown that my stepsister Aria had pulled it into earlier this morning, tickling my neck as it settled down my back. Despite my best efforts, my hand brushed along my dress as I reached for the door handle, leaving a dark patch of a water mark on the brown linen. "It's not *too* noticeable," I told myself, wrinkling my nose. Sighing, I turned back toward the door and stepped out into the courtyard.

Crisp winter air tingled on my face nudging away the warmth that still clung to me from the solarium. Hugging my waist tightly, I ran as fast as I could across the uneven pavers lining the courtyard, rushing past our ancient well and straight into the main door of the living quarters of our small castle.

Aria was walking into view from the direction of the music room just as I turned around from shutting the front doors.

"Ella!" She called, her smooth voice filled with concern. "Were you outside without a cape? You'll catch cold if you aren't careful!"

I smiled at my stepsister as she hurried toward me, pulling her shawl off her shoulders. "Don't worry, Aria, I was only running across the courtyard from the solarium. I didn't want to go through the servant's quarters and disrupt everything there."

She helped me settle her faded blue shawl around me, chiding me gently. "You should take better care of yourself. You know the servants wouldn't mind if you came through the kitchen to get to the dining room. We're all basically family anyway."

I smiled at her mildly revolutionary statement, dropping from her lips in such a confident and nonchalant tone. Aria had the face and temperament of an angel, and her mind was too pure for this plane of existence. Sometimes she reminded me of a scholar I had read about years ago, who insisted that all humans were equal under the sight of the Creator, and that our natural existence was to meet everyone we met with love. *You wouldn't catch that being taught in Chapel on a Sunday,* I thought sardonically. *Most people's natural state seems to be looking out for themselves. I'm lucky to have a family that isn't like that.*

"...Ella, are you even listening to me?" Aria's wide blue eyes were looking at me with fond exasperation.

I gave a surprised snort of laughter before linking arms and pulling her toward the formal sitting room. "I'm so sorry sister dear, but my mind wandered again. I suppose I'm hungrier than I thought!"

She shook her head, her tinkling laugh so much daintier than my own unavoidably loud one. "I've known you a long time, Ella. Somehow I don't think food will cure your absentmindedness."

I shot my step-sister a fond grin and led the way into the formal drawing room. My stepmother, Aria's mother, reclined on a light green sofa near the fireplace, wrapped in a shawl and two blankets, even though the room wasn't terribly cold.

"Beatrice!" I exclaimed, dropping Aria's arm and walking over to her. "Are you all right?"

"Yes, Ella dear, just a little cold. These winter days turn my bones to ice if I'm not careful." She pushed aside her lap blankets and accepted my proffered arm. "Enough of that, let's go through to the family dining room. I'm sure whatever Mrs. Moriotto has made today will warm me up in no time."

I waited patiently as she stood up and brushed her skirts straight again, her movements slow and careful. *Her arthritis must be acting up again today,* I thought with sympathy. Her eyes flicked over the dirt under my fingernails and water stain on my skirt, but mercifully she said nothing. *She's probably just glad I remembered to take off my dirty apron.*

Aria led the way through the other side of the sitting room, through the darkened, disused formal dining room, and into the small family dining room where we always took our meals. I could remember many large gatherings in the formal dining room when my mother was alive, but the last time we used it was for my father and stepmother's wedding breakfast, eight years ago now. I preferred the smaller room. It had several windows onto the courtyard, a fireplace that didn't let in draughts, and was always warm since it was next to the kitchens.

Aria and I settled Beatrice into her chair and then took our usual seats. Beatrice rang a silver bell, and a moment later, the elderly Mrs. Moriotto came through with our meal, a hearty vegetable soup with fresh, warm bread. After serving our portions for us, she dipped a curtsy to the table in general, flashing a wink in my direction before retreating back to the kitchen where the rest of the staff, comprised mainly of her own family, was probably eating the same meal. I shook my head slightly at the thought. If I had my way, which you might assume I would since the entire estate belonged to me, we would all eat together. When I had made the suggestion to Mrs. Moriotto and Beatrice a few years ago, they had shared a look of equal parts horror and shock before almost talking over one another to admonish me. Apparently, as Baroness Lucedimora it was paramount I maintain certain standards. I usually allowed Beatrice to run the household as she saw fit anyway, and under their combined forces I had no choice but to acquiesce. So here we were, sitting a few yards away from each other, eating the same meal, out of the same local stoneware, with probably the same manners and topics of conversation, but with a stone wall and centuries of tradition separating us. It made no sense to me, but I was outnumbered.

"Ella dear," my stepmother's voice cut through my thoughts and I scalded my throat as a spoonful of soup went down to fast. Taking a quick drink of water, I coughed discretely and peered over at her with watery eyes.

"Yes?" I choked out.

"I didn't mean to startle you!" She replied, her brow furrowed. "It's just that your mind was wandering again. We were asking how your morning went."

Aria shot me an amused look as she took a dainty sip of her own soup. I gave them an apologetic look. "Sorry about that." I cleared my throat and set my spoon down. "Well, I finished harvesting the radicchios. The workers from the village are coming up to clean and prepare them for the New Year's feast. Before that I watered the rest of the vegetables in the solarium and checked on the seedlings. Oh, and before that I finished reviewing and signing the contracts for Chance. He was the last of the horses Deerbold Academy wanted, so if you want to add anything to your letters for Alessia do it in the next few days. Giuseppe and Gino will leave on Monday to deliver the horses, so they can take as many letters as you like to Alessia."

"Oh how lovely," Beatrice said, turning to Aria. "I'll have to finish the border on that coverlet we were making her."

"Don't worry, Mother," Aria replied, giving her a reassuring look. "That's what I'm working on this afternoon. I'll have it done by dinnertime. And I finished the saddle blankets too. She'll have lots of extra Yuletide presents from us."

I laughed. "Well my presents are going to look paltry in comparison! I'm only sending that set of daggers I bought at the bazaar a few months ago, and an old book on Spindalian warfare I found in the archive. I thought she might like to read it in her spare time."

Beatrice reached over and patted my arm. "She will love both of those things, dear, don't worry. And besides, you're the only reason she's able to attend the academy. She'll never forget that."

I frowned, uncomfortable at the reference to my financial support for her tuition. My father had been the one to set aside money for her attendance, once her skills had become clear. I had only added to it and carried out everyone's wishes. As it was, I could only afford the basic tuition and room fees. Alessia worked year round at their stables to pay for her food and any extras she needed, which was why we hadn't seen her much since she left four years ago.

Beatrice and Aria's sedate conversation swirled around me as I concentrated on my food. I made sure to keep track of it, and chime in now and again to be polite, but mainly I brooded over Alessia's distance from us, and how little I could do for my loved ones.

Soon enough the midday meal was over, and I felt my spirits lift as I escorted my stepmother and stepsister back to their afternoon occupations. There was something in me that could never stay down for long. Life held too many adventures and surprises to be sad. Grabbing my cloak and mittens from their peg in the entry hall, I pulled them on and headed out to meet the workers from the village. Not exactly a grand adventure, but sometimes hard work could prepare you for a better adventure than chance could ever do.

CHAPTER TWO

Luca

I took a final glance around my room as the servants hefted the last of my trunks through the open door. All was in order, as it always was; not so much because of my own love of order, although I could never rest easy until my surroundings were immaculate, but because of the team of servants assigned to care for my rooms and person as the Crown Prince of Charmagne. I'll be missing all the help in a few days, that's for sure. Deerbold Academy was swimming with princes, and a few princesses, and all were expected to take care of themselves. After almost four years I was used to it, but it had been a shock during my first semester.

My eyes strayed to the closest of the enormous windows overlooking the formal palace gardens. Despite the cooler temperatures, groups of nobles paraded through the gravel paths, their brightly colored clothing sticking out against the dull background of dormant plants. *I certainly won't miss juggling courtiers for the next few months.*

I turned toward the door with quick step, grabbing my riding gloves off a small table and passing into the hall to begin my trek across Cintola Palace toward the stables.

"Your Highness!" a soft voice called out just as I reached the bottom of the elegant main staircase. I turned to find a liveried servant making his way toward me. Stepping to one side, I waited until he reached me.

"Your Highness, the king has requested your presence in his study." The servant bowed once more and I dismissed him with a nod, turning away from the most direct route to the stables and instead heading toward the royal study.

What could this be? I had said my goodbyes to my family at dinner the evening before, a grand occasion with most of our most powerful nobles invited. We often had such occasions the evening before I left for the Academy. Since I was the Crown Prince, most of what I did was considered of great importance for our country. *Just one more reason I love Deerbold. I can sneeze there without a single person becoming concerned for my health.* By comparison, Cintola Palace could be stifling.

As the door to my father's study came in sight, I couldn't help wondering again what business he had with me. My family didn't usually come to see me off when I set out for school. Other than my younger brothers, who, although they were almost adults, still looked like little kids and acted like puppies; the rest of my family tended to be a little distant, if not downright cold. The dynamic of most royal families had to be a little different from our subjects, but I didn't realize how dysfunctional my own was until I got to know some of the royals from other countries at the Academy. Whatever my father was calling me into his study for right now, it wasn't going to include a warm goodbye.

I nodded to one of the guards outside the door. "The King summoned me here."

The guard saluted and turned, knocking on the door and taking a half step through to announce my name and title. My father's voice rumbled in response and the guard stepped all the way through, holding the door open while I entered, and then closing it again as he passed back out.

I offered a short bow to my father, who acknowledged it with a flick of his eyes before motioning me forward. He continued reading the document in front of him while I walked over. Impatiently, I waited before him for several minutes as he finished.

My eyes strayed to the formal gardens visible through enormous windows behind his desk, searching out the enormous wall at the back, obscuring the work yard and stables. My carriage was waiting there even now. Just a few minutes with whatever business the King thought warranted his son's attention and then I could shrug off the mantle of court life again. *For a few months anyway. What will you do to escape when you graduate?* I sternly pushed that thought aside. I would have a country to assist in running. I couldn't, and wouldn't, escape that duty for as long as I lived.

Finally my father set his papers down in a neat pile, slid them into a nearby folio, and pushed them in my direction. I barely spared it a glance, waiting instead to hear what my father would say.

"That is a marriage contract your mother's office has drawn up for you," he declared, eying me steadily. I couldn't help the tightening in my jaw at the reference to my marriage. *This again. I should have known.* Not trusting my irritation over the subject to surface, I said nothing.

"You're now twenty three years old," he began again. "When I was your age I was already married to your mother, with an heir on the way, or so I thought. When your sister was born I wasn't even disappointed that she was a girl. We had many years ahead of us to try for more heirs, and of course we managed to produce three." He paused and narrowed his eyes. I could barely keep my own from rolling, knowing what he was going to ask next.

"How many heirs have you managed to produce, my boy?"

"None, as you know, Father," I replied as evenly as possible.

"That's correct. And as you aren't married, you aren't even trying to secure our line. Nor have you been openly courting or pursuing anyone to fulfill the role of consort! As Crown Prince, it is one of your primary duties to ensure our family's succession, especially now, before you have to step onto the throne yourself and rule." Father looked back down at the contract folio on his desk and leaned forward, rubbing his chin. "I've promised to allow you to choose your own wife instead of arranging a marriage as is our custom." His eyes flickered to mine for an instant and a bolt of fear went through me. *Could he be thinking of reneging on that promise?*

He must have read my thoughts because he gave a great bark of laughter and stood up. "Never fear son, I'm not going to go back on that promise." His sudden mirth dropped from his face. "I have my own reasons for not wishing that situation on you. You'll rule better if you have a partner you can trust at your side, even if she doesn't bring the largest dowry or family influence." I shifted on my feet at the reference to his own rocky relationship with my mother, the Queen. They presented a calm front to the world, but any royal insider was well versed in how little they truly got along.

My father nudged the folio toward me again, then drifted out from behind his desk, folding his hands behind his back and looking out over the gardens.

"In this instance, I happen to agree with your mother. Lady Emilia is probably your best option, both politically and personally. Her family is impeccable, their wealth is enormous, it would strengthen our influence over the largest landholder on the coast. She's obviously been groomed for the role since she was young. She seems pleasant enough, and beautiful too. It would be easiest for everyone, including you, if you accept that alliance."

Each reason he listed buzzed around my brain like an angry hornet. They were all true. She was beautiful and pleasant, the picture of a perfect consort. As my sister's best friend, I had spent a lot of time near her from a young age. She never argued or misspoke. She was graceful and intelligent, and extremely accomplished in acceptable courtly arts like dancing and singing. Her political connections made her the most sought after partner of our age group. But even so, there was something about her that made me wish she would fall madly in love with someone else and elope with them, taking the possibility of our alliance off the table forever. I drew in a deep breath and released it steadily, trying to think of a diplomatic reply to my father. *No doubt I will marry her, and maybe it's the certainty that a choice that should be mine is already made by circumstances that makes the match so unpalatable.* "She does seem to be the best candidate," I admitted.

My father shrugged. "As I said, the choice is yours. I will support whatever candidate you decide on, even in the face of your mother's and the Litorale family's wrath if you choose elsewhere. So don't say I've never done anything for you!" He sent me one of his hearty grins and I couldn't help crooking a smile in return. "As long as your wife is a good partner, can produce heirs, and can learn to be a docile queen, we can deal with the rest."

"Thank you, Father."

"However," he interrupted, his face becoming serious, "your time is up." I tensed, half wondering if he was going to make me choose right now, on the spot. "At the end of your final semester at that Academy, we are planning a ball to celebrate your promotion to Lord High Admiral of the Navy." I nodded warily, trying to follow his train of thought. "At that ball, you will be expected to announce your engagement and present the future Crown Princess."

A reprieve. I relaxed slightly. My father was known for pushing people's buttons in order to get what he wanted. He had done that to me as his son and direct heir all my life. But he had always been oddly protective of his promise to let me choose my own wife. *A result of his own marriage, and witnessing his parent's marriage, no doubt.* My grandparents' marriage had become so bad that they had never produced any other children. The pressure to secure our family line had fallen squarely on Father's shoulders, and he was eager to make sure I continued that duty. *Five months. I can make a choice in five months.*

"Thank you, Father. You and I both know that my choice is probably made for me anyway, but I will write to you from school to confirm when I've made up my mind."

He gave me a searching look, hands still clasped behind his back, then nodded and turned back toward the window. "Fare well then, son."

"And you, Father," I replied, bowing to his back before turning and making my way out past the guards and back toward the main hall of the central palace. As I passed through into the doorway, I had a clear view through to the other wings of the palace.

"Drat." I said under my breath, spotting a blur of brightly colored gowns and blonde hair. *Emilia and Marietta*. They were surrounded by a gaggle of Ladies and clearly waiting to see me off. They had done so the last few semesters of my schooling, each Lady tearfully conveying their desire for my wellbeing and safe return. It was heartwarming, if sometimes transparently a ploy to advance their marriage suit, but I was in no mood to be surrounded by potential brides right now. Marietta had claim on my time as family, and would push Emilia my way until the last moment, probably delaying my departure even more.

Trusting that my nondescript traveling clothes would obscure me from view, I turned to the other wing of the palace, slipping out the first door to the gardens that I could find.

Gravel crunched under my boots as I pulled the hood of my cape over my head and made my way through ornamental hedges and dormant flower gardens. There were several near escapes with other courtiers, forcing me to backtrack and take roundabout paths, so I found myself headed toward the gardener's door, at the far end of the wall separating the formal gardens from the work yards. Tugging halfheartedly, I smiled in relief when the door swung open. It was usually unlocked in summer, but during winter months it was locked during days they weren't working.

I passed through quickly, pulled the wooden gate firmly closed, and started down the main path through the work yards. My eyes caught sight of the summer smithy and softened. Cinderella's memory never failed to bring me a smile. I could still hear that bell like laugh sometimes, free and full of joy, just like the rest of her. *I wonder how she would respond to my current predicament.* Probably a mixture of laughter and startling insight. If only I could write to her to find out. *She probably wouldn't want to put down on paper whatever blasphemous things she truly thought. And maybe by now her parents have trained all that out of her.*

I couldn't help going over to peer inside the blacksmith's furnace, something I did any time I happened to pass through the tradesman's yard. I refrained from dirtying my riding gloves by poking around the fireplace. As usual, no glinting diamonds winked from the cold bed of ashes, only soot and slag. *Still no gems, Cinderella,* I told my memory.

She had never showed up to my coronation ball, as promised, so I had never figured out which family she belonged to. I often wondered what she was like now, whether she was as demure and accomplished as the other ladies at court, or whether she was as strange and carefree as she was all those years ago. I hoped it was the latter. It was people like her that I wanted to be a good ruler for - the quiet ones whose hard work and good will was what gave our country strength and prosperity.

My father had little time for the common man beyond feast days and tours of the country. He was focused always on politics and expanding our border with Pelerin. I was more interested in what our country already has to offer, and how we could use it to make us stronger. And the sea, of course. Always the sea. It called me in my dreams. *Another reason Emilia would make a good queen, her estate controls much of our southern coastline's defenses. It would be a natural way to convince Father to let me focus my time after graduation on strengthening the Navy and spending more time on the waves. Perhaps making inroads with the Dwarven Republic.*

I sighed, straightening up and starting back toward the stables. *And there lies a reason why that alliance wouldn't be a great fit for me "Luca", not me "the Crown Prince". The Litorale family hates the Dwarven Republic, and Father values our alliance with Snowdonia more than he should. The Litorales would give me easy access to the Sea, but would make the path toward a treaty with the Republic more difficult.* I drew another breath, releasing it with a frustrated huff - a liberty I could afford, here in the cold tradesman's yard where no one was around to notice a prince. I quickened my pace. I would be even more free at Deerbold, so the faster I got on the road, the faster I could enjoy freedom, most of all from my marriage problem.

I turned back onto the main path, heading purposefully toward the stables again.

My head bodyguard, Major Antonio Guerren, was standing outside the stable as I rounded the last workshop. I flashed him a grin, but he didn't return it, keeping his face stoically blank as usual. He was only a few years older, but he had served a tour at the Pelerine front during their war with the Beasts. That experience had made him seem decades older than me, even if he didn't look it.

"Major Guerren, are we ready to depart?" I asked, noticing my favorite gelding, Percivale, saddled and stamping the ground a few feet away.

"We are ready to leave at your command, Sire," he replied, not bothering to give me a salute or bow, but instead continuing to scan the courtyard. I had demanded he give up the usual protocol while on duty years ago, something my father would hate if he knew. *One of a thousand things he hates about how I live my life.*

"Unless you desire additional delays, Prince Luca, may I recommend mounting your horse? If we leave by the Northern Gate immediately, we would avoid the party of courtiers in riding dress currently making their way in our direction."

I cast a quick glance over my shoulder and caught sight of the colorful flock of ladies I had avoided in the palace.

"By The Lady," I cursed under my breath and turned back toward Antonio. He was standing next Percivale, holding the reins for me. I said a quick hello to my horse before pulling myself up and claiming the reins from my guard.

At Antonio's signal, the advance guards started forward and he mounted his own gelding, a sturdy bay. We fell into position next to each other, spurring our mounts into a walk. I chanced a glance back to see my sister's face twisted in exasperation. Next to her, I could see Emilia's heart shaped face drop into a crestfallen frown before my carriage rumbled out of the carriage house and blocked my view. It carried my baggage and a place for me to sit if I became tired to ride. *And now it gives me a chance to ignore my sister and Emilia without making a scene.* I laughed under my breath as we swept out of the gates, only slightly ashamed at my cowardice.

The winter air was crisp and energizing. Percivale was steady under me, and my cloak and gloves kept the chill at bay. We had a long ride ahead but I didn't mind. It gave me time to adjust from courtly 'Crown Prince Luca' to just 'Luca', the Deerbold Academy cadet.

As we passed through the city, many subjects stopped to bow toward the carriage. I didn't disabuse them of the notion that their prince was inside by waving. The hood of my cloak disguised my face enough that I could be anyone. Another bodyguard perhaps, or one of the higher orders of servants. I used the opportunity to take in the crowds at my leisure.

The streets were noisy and full of bodies going through their daily business. Those in the street jumped quickly to the sidewalks at the blast of my advance guard's trumpet. Most bowed or waved, cheering happily, but others hung back further, staring at us as we went by with open resentment. *Ignore them*, my mother's voice sounded in my head. Her motto since I was a young boy, and first started to notice that not all of our citizens loved the royal family. *Not worth our time and beneath your notice. If they don't know better than to respect their rulers, they'll deserve whatever fate they get.* Instead of ignoring them over the years, I had felt a growing desire to know *why*. Why did they dislike us so much? Especially since every move we made as a family, from the people we marry and the way we dress and act, has always been spent for our country's wellbeing. Did they not understand? Did they envy the wealth of the palace?

I refocused on the road ahead, our column slowing as we navigated a sharp turn in the road. A muffled thump sounded from behind me and I turned to look. As I watched, a rotten apple was lobbed toward my coach, just before one of my guardsman reached the thrower. I stared in shock until Antonio called my given name softly.

"Don't draw attention to yourself, we need to keep moving," he urged. I gave him a sharp nod and faced fully forward in my saddle, forcing my eyes to look at the road before my horse, not the crowd on either side.

I could control what my eyes saw, but I couldn't block out the noise. The crowd had largely fallen quiet after the thrown vegetables, so I could hear some of the offender's yells as he was being taken into custody.

"Bunch of bloodsuckers they are while we starve in our beds!" His words were muffled beyond hearing as we rounded the turn, but his accusation rang in my ears. *Starving in his bed?* Our kingdom was prosperous. There weren't any citizens starving, that I was aware of anyway.

As we left the city gates, we were able to pick up the pace so I focused on my ride, successfully pushing the incident from my mind. *Probably a madman anyway.*

We kept a quick pace throughout our trip, sticking to the well cared for highways and spending the nights in large and well appointed inns until we approached the far north of the kingdom. As the terrain became slightly mountainous, we were forced onto smaller dirt roads, winding their way through tiny villages until eventually spilling through a small valley leading directly to Spindle. The road was narrow but well maintained, used as it was for trade on a regular basis. The border towns were sparsely populated, but ancient, and the locals had regular contact with the few towns on the other side in Spindle.

The border was impossible to miss. On Charmagne's side were low, scrubby mountains, dotted with farmland and fruit and olive groves. As the mountains sloped toward Spindle, they evened out gently, and an ancient forest sprouted abruptly along the edge of the two countries. The trees loomed over the landscape, tall and leafy. Although they weren't obviously magical, they let off an aura of sentience that was unnerving even though I had become used to them over the years. The trees had stood guard for many centuries, and would do so for many more.

Whether I lived or died, ruled well or poorly, married and had children or died alone; it would all would be nothing to them, my whole life was entirely beneath their notice. A shudder passed through me, causing my shoulder blades to hitch up.

We crossed the border with little fanfare. There were no cities here, nor any guards asking us to state our business. We had been at peace with Spindle for generations. We were not allies, so we had little contact, save for the small trade of the locals. *No, the only sentinels here are the trees.* They seemed to loom over the path almost as if they were observing us.

I shook my head, brushing the fanciful thought away. *Marco and Dante would never stop teasing me if they heard I was spooked by a few trees.* Teasing was about the only thing my little brothers seemed to be good for. They would be headed to the academy in a few years as well passing through the trees in their own turn.

As it always did, Deerbold Academy appeared all of a sudden. The road wound it's way around a particularly thick grove of shaggy trees and spilled into an unexpected clearing, revealing practice yards already full of cadets, with buildings grouped around the edge and disappearing into the trees again. A large stable block stood to one side of the practice yards, and we followed the gravel drive around to it. I bit back a sigh of relief as I slid out of my saddle. Other than the one rainy day I elected to spend in the carriage, I had ridden the other four days. As much as I had loved the fresh air and sun, I was more than a little saddle sore.

One of my year mates, Alessia, stepped forward from the entrance to the stables, holding her hand out to grab the reins of my horse. As usual, she gave a little bow before I could stop her.

"Alessia, we're all cadets here. You aren't supposed to bow," I scolded her halfheartedly.

She gave me a wry grin. "Yes, Sire, as you say."

I rolled my eyes, peeling my riding gloves off and stuffing them into a pocket in my cloak. "It's not as I say, it's as the Headmistresses say. They're in charge here. You'll have time enough to bow and scrape after we've graduated." Alessia was one of only a few commonborns who had been accepted to Deerbold through a lottery. As odd as it was at first to see a woman in the role of a warrior, she had a valiant heart and could stand toe to toe with any of the rest of us in the arena. I was hoping to pull her into my personal guard once our post-graduation duty assignments were served.

She chuckled and gave my horse a pat on it's head. "It's good to have you back, Luca. Deerbold was quiet without you." She began to lead Percivale away, calling out as she did, "Raleigh is back already too. He's with Briar Rose in the tack room."

I grinned. Raleigh was a Spindalian prince, and like me and Alessia, was a cadet at Deerbold, though in a different year. I followed Alessia and Percivale through the stable doors, turning toward the tack room to say hello to my other friends.

I poked my head into the tack room; a snug, wood paneled room tucked away from the horse stalls. Raleigh was there, slightly disheveled as he cleaned mud off of a set of reins. Briar Rose was looking hardly any better, her sensible work dress smeared with mud and bits of leaves sticking out of her hair. She was muttering irritably as she inspected a saddle and casting dark looks at Raleigh every now and again.

"Nothing's changed since I left, I see," I commented, drawing their attention toward me. Raleigh smiled when he caught sight of me, wiping off his hand and shaking my outstretched one before returning meekly to his seat under the stern gaze of Briar Rose.

She watched him for a second, a flash of something like concern crossing her face before she turned her attention to me. "It's you, is it, Luca? About time you returned. Maybe you can keep this lunkhead out of trouble for five minutes of the day." I raised my eyebrows as she gestured to her dress. "We go out for one ride, 'just a quick breath of fresh air' he promised me. Of *course* we ended up in a marsh, covered in mud. The Benefactor is due this evening and will probably want to ride the bounds with us as usual. So now we're stuck cleaning our tack and will have barely enough time to make ourselves presentable!" She clucked her tongue at Raleigh as she turned back to her own task and I tried to repress a grin, especially as I noticed Raleigh beginning to perk up under her familiar rambling scolding. I rolled my eyes at the two of them. Sometimes they seemed more like old friends, other times they seemed more like lovers in a spat.

Briar Rose was a fixture at Deerbold Academy. She wasn't a cadet, or instructor, or even a servant, although she drifted around the edges of all of those roles from time to time. She was a ward of the Headmistresses, an orphan they had taken in as a baby, and raised here at the Academy. She had no noble standing, but walked among us all as an equal. She and Raleigh were almost never apart. They probably couldn't help being close because they had each grown up with the weight of making this academy a success; Raleigh as part of his duties to his family, and Briar Rose as the default heiress to the Headmistresses. They teased and fought with each other freely, and I had wondered at times whether Raleigh would try and convince her to marry him. If I had half as much trust in and attraction to a woman like he did with Briar Rose, I would snap her up in an instant.

Instead I have five months to figure out how I'll propose to Emilia. She would certainly never scold me in front of someone else like Briar Rose did with Raleigh, nor would she tease me out of a bad mood. *Emilia is beautiful... and she does vie for my attention, although she's too well bred to outright flirt. Maybe there could be attraction there if I let it?* It was hard to picture. After all the years I had known her, I still felt like I didn't know what went on under her charming exterior.

I realized with a start that I had been staring at my friends. Thankfully they hadn't noticed, and they appeared to have settled there spat from only a moment ago. She was standing before him, laughing as she rubbed a spot of dirt off of his shirtfront, while he tugged gently on a dead leaf that was snarled in one her golden ringlets, drawing out another chuckle as he complimented her fetching hair ornaments.

My heart constricted painfully. *That's what I want. That easiness and familiarity. The fights and challenges. The indefinable spark. That's the type of relationship I want with my queen.*

Slowly I pushed back at the feeling of regret and loss threatening to overtake me as I watched my two friends banter back and forth. They could be this way sometimes, so wrapped up in each other that they forgot everything else. Alessia and I had become used to it over the years, and teased them about it whenever they became too annoying. But now I just wanted to get away from them, away from what they had - or could have, if they ever figured it out.

I opened my mouth to say goodbye, then closed it again as they turned their backs to me, clustering around the mud caked saddle to work on it together. Quietly, I slipped through the open doorway and back through the stables. I didn't have time to mope around. I had five months of hard work ahead of me, and then it would be time to face my future.

CHAPTER THREE

Ella

"So I switched the care instructions for Star Chaser since he's been a little nervy. Traveling to a new home is bound to make that worse for a bit. Luckily we have Alessia there so she'll know what all my notes mean," I said, sharing a smile with my head groom, Matteo Farini. He was as scrupulously attentive to our horses as I was, which was what made him such a good employee. I knew he would point out anything I missed.

"Sounds right to me, Lady Ella. I'll go over the changes with her when I hand over the family mail. She'll see the lad right."

I nodded, stacking the papers neatly and sliding them into a carrying case while Matteo stepped aside to speak to one of the grooms. I was in Matteo's office in our stables at the foot of the mountain my castle was built upon. The flatter terrain was better for exercising the horses, though I sometimes wished it was a closer walk to home. I jumped, almost dropping my case as the door swept open and hit the wall. My best friend, Gia, burst into the room.

"Ella, I've just come from home. Papa is ill - he isn't able to get out of bed, and he's worried about the horses."

A bolt of concern darted through my heart at the strained expression on Gia's face. "Oh no! Well we can't have him worried about the horses. Come on, let's go see. Do we need to call a doctor? What happened?" I put my carrying case into Matteo's hands as we hurried out of the stables, Gia rattling off an update over his sudden cough and fatigue.

Although she was about my own age, Gia's parents were old enough to be my grandparents. Gia had arrived as a surprise long after they had given up on the idea of having children. Her father Giuseppe was my steward, and had been my father's steward before that. In a somewhat unusual move for our country of Charmagne, but not so much for our little backwater corner of it, he was training his only daughter to take over stewardship of the estate, with my blessing of course. Gia would step into the role as naturally as breathing when the time came.

We clambered into the little dogcart she had driven down from the castle, and she spurred the ponies into a quick trot, speeding us up the winding drive and through the open castle gates in only a few minutes, disturbing a handful of chickens that had somehow found their way into the courtyard. I helped her tie the ponies up to a hitching post near our smaller, residential stable in the courtyard, noting the strain and concern wrinkling her brow.

"Is he lucid at least?" I asked, my own worry mounting.

She gave me a tight look. "Yes, he's completely fine mentally, except a little agitated over the horse transfer. He doesn't want to let you down. I've told him I'm capable of doing it, but I think he needs to hear from you that you aren't disappointed."

We picked our way across the courtyard as quickly as we could. I managed to trip over one of the many uneven cobblestones but caught myself before I could fall. As we passed through the heavy wooden kitchen door, I turned to lean my weight against it, holding it in the warped doorframe while Gia pushed the bolt through again. It tended to swing open if not latched properly, and if we let a draught in that put out her mother's kitchen fire we would only add to the family's worries.

Gia led the way down the dark, narrow passage in the servant's corridor, finally entering her parent's small apartment.

Her father was laying on a couch before the fireplace, bundled up in just about every blanket they possessed, appearing drawn and tired. His wife crouched on stool in front of him, coaxing him into taking a little broth. She looked over as we bustled toward her.

"Stop right there, the pair of you," she declared, her face more lined than usual and the gray in her hair matching the pallor of her skin. "Don't come any closer, in case it's infectious."

"Mama!" Gia protested, "We know it's -"

Aida cut her off with a look, setting her spoon into the half empty bowl and putting both down on the raised hearth next to her. "I know it's probably just the pneumonia again. It's that time of year. But just in case, I don't want you two to catch anything."

I gave Aida an understanding nod, transferring my gaze toward what I could see of my steward. "Giuseppe, I understand you aren't feeling well enough to work today," I said kindly. I needed to tread carefully or he'd force himself out of bed and work until he died if he felt even the slightest hint that he was letting the estate down.

He held a clean handkerchief up to his lips, covering a few hacking coughs before giving me a feeble smile. "I'm afraid this has come on at the worse possible time, my lady. I know we have to get those horses over today to fulfill our contract, but I don't see how it will be possible." I chewed on my lip, considering the situation.

"I've already said I can do it Papa," Gia admonished him. "Matteo and one of the grooms will be there to help with the animals, and I'm sure I can handle a meeting with whichever Headmistress is accepting the transfer." Her voice wobbled at the last sentence and I shot Gia a covert look. She was three years younger than me, close in age really, but I was used to a lot more responsibility than most twenty-three year olds. Although Gia was dependable and intelligent, she probably wasn't ready to take a meeting with one of our best clients.

Giuseppe coughed again and Gia bit her lip, hovering as if she wanted to go over and help her mother rearrange his blankets. The Moriotto family were dedicated to helping me keep Lucedimora Castle running. As my Steward, Housekeeper and Cook, and Stewardess-in-training, I couldn't do anything without them. But it also meant that when one of them was sick, it affected almost my entire staff. There was no way I could ask Aida to preside over the kitchens today, nor ask Gia to run off all day delivering horses and meeting with clients.

"Gia, I'll take the meeting with the Headmistresses. It's probably time I meet with them in person anyway - they're our best clients." Gia gave me an anxious look but I snagged her hand and gave it a squeeze. "I'd rather you stay here so you can be close to your father. Right now I'd like you to run into the village and see if the doctor is available. I want his opinion just to be sure. And stop at Maria's house to see if she can come up to cook. You'll have to oversee the workers about the fence. You know the spots in the back pasture, right?"

She nodded, a determined look on her face. "I know for a fact that Leonardo has a light day today, so I'll get him to come up to help as well."

I relaxed, glad to hear that her betrothed would be available to help. He was a steady, dependable sort, and wouldn't hesitate to do whatever was needed. "If that's true, you could probably put him in charge of the work crews once you showed him the broken areas. Then you can focus on monitoring everything else while I'm gone," I instructed.

We turned at the sound of another cough from Giuseppe. Aida helped him take a sip of water before turning to give me a wan smile. "Thank you, my lady. I appreciate the help with the kitchen, and the doctor of course."

I held up my hands. "It's the least I can do! I only hope Giuseppe is well again soon! That's what matters most." She nodded, wiping a tear away discretely as she turned back to her husband.

"Alright Gia, let's get to work," I said, pulling my friend away from her family. I closed the door gently behind us and we paced back toward the courtyard. "Can you go right now to fetch the doctor and Maria? Stepmama is having one of her turns but I can put Aria in charge until you get back."

She nodded as I pushed on the kitchen door to ease the pressure off the latch until Gia could pop it back up again. The door slid outward at a ponderous speed. Gia let out a bark of exasperated laughter. "And maybe I can get Leo to look at this old thing while he's up here. If nothing else comes up that is."

I chuckled as the huge door finally opened wide enough for us to pass through, then turned to push it closed again with Gia's help. "Tell him I'll have enough to pay him extra from the horse sale today if he can do it quick."

Gia rolled her eyes at me. "You know he'll do it for free if I ask him."

"Yes, we all know that you have him wrapped around your finger," I teased her. "But we're making a little extra on this contract because of their last minute changes, so I *will* actually have room in the budget to pay him. You can think of it as an investment toward your wedding."

Gia quirked a smile but it soon faded under the worrisome day ahead. I patted her arm. "He'll be alright. It's just pneumonia again." She swallowed heavily and nodded. I pulled her into a quick hug, trying to pass along some comfort and optimism before releasing her. "Can you wait a few moments? I need to run in and give Aria an update and change into something a little nicer for my meeting." She nodded, then broke away toward the small castle stable while I turned toward the front door to the main wing.

I could hear Aria plucking away at her lute in the music room, her clear soprano telling the story of a shepherdess searching for her lost love. *She really has the most beautiful voice I've ever heard,* I thought with a smile as I hurried down the entrance hall toward it. *I wish she had more opportunities to entertain company. If I can just secure a contract in Pelerine now that their market has opened up, I just might be able to afford to take us to the Capitol every now and again.*

The door to the music room was open, revealing Aria's slim form perched on a chair in front of one of the long windows, singing and playing with her eyes closed. I hated to interrupt such a tranquil scene, but time was against me.

"Aria," I called, and she started in her seat, laughing as she turned toward me.

"Ella you scared me! I guess I was caught up in my song. I was singing for Mama earlier, but her headache only got worse so I left her alone."

I frowned sympathetically. "I hope it doesn't last all day. I wish I had time to check in on her, although I'd probably just make things worse." I grimaced. "And that's not the only problem today. I need your help."

Aria's gentle smile turned to one of concern and she laid her lute down on a nearby table. "Whatever's the matter?"

"Giuseppe has taken ill again," I declared and she gave a little gasp of distress. "Aida doesn't want us to go near him, so don't bother offering to help. You know what she's like when he's ill." Aria frowned and nodded as she stood up, her cornflower blue dress matching her eyes and her lily white sewing apron giving the impression of a sunny blue sky. *If Aida would only let her in she could probably sing Giuseppe right to sleep and calm the rest of us down too.* Aria seemed to do that wherever she went.

"How can I help," she asked gently, gliding over and taking both my hands in hers. I squeezed gratefully.

"I just need you to be in charge until Gia gets back with the doctor and kitchen help. We absolutely *must* get our horse shipment over to Deerbold today, so I'm going with Matteo to complete the contract. I'll be back by nightfall. Hopefully you won't need to really do anything, but you know how it is around here. It never rains but it pours."

Aria flashed smile, then lowered her voice even though no one was around to hear us. "Can we afford the doctor and kitchen help? I'm sure I could pitch in with whatever needs done if we can't." Worry hovered over her brow and my heart filled with compassion for her offer. "Well we need a cook and someone to oversee mending the fences, sister dear." Aria's face fell. She was a terrible cook, and certainly couldn't be trusted to know what to do with a fence. Her talents were more suited to traditionally domestic arts like music and sewing.

I patted squeezed her hands again then dropped them. "Don't worry. Once I get the horses delivered we'll get the second half of our payment, so we'll have more than enough for once. As to the rest, I have it all worked out with Gia. Your calming presence should be enough to see us through the day. Why don't you bring your lute up to the front parlor so you can still play and sing while you keep an eye on things?"

Without hesitation she ran back to pick up her abandoned instrument, grabbing an extra blanket to ward off the chill in the front parlor, and followed me into the hall. I poked my head into the chilly room, looking doubtfully toward the dormant fireplace. Aria squeezed in behind me, following the direction of my gaze.

"Off you go," she scolded me. "It looks like Gia laid out the kindling the last time this room was cleaned. I think I can manage starting a fire. I wasn't born in a castle, you know." I gave her a rueful grin and held up my hands in surrender. It's true that I was the one who had been born into a noble family, but sometimes the ancient duty I worked to uphold as a landholder made me feel more like a laborer than a lady.

"Alright, I'll be off then. Maria should be up to cook today, but you'll have to scrounge what you can from the larder for you and Stepmama until she gets here."

"We'll be fine Ella," she assured me with a smile. "You just focus on getting to and from Deerbold safe and sound, and give Alessia a kiss from me and Mama."

"I will, and a hug too," I promised, giving Aria a quick hug as well before she turned away to light the fire. I took a deep breath and made my way to the stairs. Pausing as I looked at the frayed carpet, I double checked my boots to make sure I wasn't tracking mud everywhere. Thankfully the dark leather was only dusty, not caked in mud or worse from the stables earlier.

I jogged up the stairs and down the hall, bustling into my own little bedroom in the corner. Opening my wardrobe, I pulled out my nicest wool riding habit out. Quickly, so as not to keep Gia waiting as well as to reduce the amount of contact my skin had with the frigid air in my room, I stripped down to my chemise. I stepped into my riding skirt and pulled it up to my waist, fumbling over the ties with my cold fingers. After I was positive it was secure, I pulled my arms through the scarlet jacket, adjusting it so my chemise lay properly underneath it. My fingers now chilled through and trembling, I fastened the buttons along the front and smoothed down the fabric that flared out from my waist to cover my hips. The style was faintly reminiscent of our military regiments, without the armor or chain mail over top.

Picking up the burnished hand mirror on my dresser, a precious inheritance from my mother, I examined my hair with a flicker of irritation. This deep into winter it was more copper than strawberry, which wasn't exactly fashionable. That never bothered me - actually I reveled in it because it reminded me of my mother's deep auburn hair. *Anything that keeps a bit of her with me is beautiful.* It was the wisps of hair escaping from the braids on top of my head that provoked a frown.

"Well, that won't do. But I don't have time to fix it properly." Holding my mirror out as far as my arms extended, I looked at my riding habit, considering what could be done to make myself look every inch the Baroness Lucedimora, capable of completing my own contracts and running my own estate. "And the Headmistresses are Spindalian, so they won't be judging whether I'm at the height of Charmagnian style," I reminded myself.

Putting my mirror down, I opened the top drawer on my dresser, looking through the various hair ribbons and ornaments I kept there. If I had known what the day would bring, I would have had Gia help me braid my hair more securely and weave a few ribbons through it. My eyes lit on a little black velvet flat-cap with a netted hair covering. Not as fashionable as the jeweled snoods I remembered from before Mother died, but it should keep most of my hair in place, even during a long ride. Nodding to myself, I carefully disentangled it from the surrounding hair ribbons and hastily fixed it into place on my head.

After a quick check in the mirror, I pulled on a sturdy cape and found a pair of clean riding gloves before rushing out of my room.

Hesitating at the top of the stairs, I sent a guilty glance toward my stepmother's room. *I should really check on her.*

I shook my head. If her headache was bad enough that she couldn't listen to Aria's music, which she adored, she wouldn't want a visit from me. Instead, I pulled the hem of my skirts up a few inches and ran down the stairs as quickly as I could and straight through the front door.

Gia was waiting out front with the dogcart. Hiking up my skirts, I scrambled in and settled on the board seat as she clicked the ponies into a trot. With a last glance at my castle as we swept through the gates, I took a deep breath and prepared myself for the day ahead.

CHAPTER FOUR

Luca

Kicking backwards, I pushed the door to my small but comfortable dorm room shut with my boot before crossing over to my desk and sitting down with a thump. Lunch had been plain but filling, as usual. At Cintola Palace our dining table was filled with delicious but complicated dishes, and I dreamed of plain chicken and vegetables after a few nights back. Today however, the food sat in my stomach like a rock.

Not the food. It's these letters. I threw the two missives a servant had given me on my way back to my room on the desk in front of me, bracing myself to read them. I had been back for only a few days, settling into my rooms and preparing for the semester to begin. *Classes haven't even started and my parents already writing me with orders.* It's not that I minded the duty I had toward my kingdom, but that I wished my family would write with something besides business. Raleigh received regular letters from his parents and siblings, even his grandparents, the reigning monarchs of Spindle, and half the time they didn't include even a single piece of royal business.

What is wrong with me? Irritation flared at the feelings of jealousy in my heart. I drew in a deep breath, allowing my irritation to release as I exhaled. Then I grabbed the first letter that came to hand and opened it.

My father's script jumped out at me. For once, I read through his news with a growing smile on my face. As I came to the end of the missive I tossed it back onto my desk with a whoop.

Jumping out of my chair I paced back and forth the few steps afforded to me in my private chamber, every sense thrumming with happiness. *Father has granted my request for a naval expedition!*

I had submitted a proposal almost a year ago, when we began discussing my promotion to Lord High Admiral. My desire to expand our Navy had been a source of irritation to my father from the first time I expressed an interest. *But now, at last, I have a chance to show him what our country's future could be!*

My good mood lasted until I opened the second letter. My mother's flowery handwriting scrawled across three pages, wasting no time scolding me for not saying goodbye to Lady Emilia and insisting that I make it up to her, suggesting a few peace offerings I could choose from. *Take it from me, you'll regret it in twenty years time if you allow such a wound fester. She was embarrassed in front of the entire court when you slipped away so quietly. Have you grown so like your Father in your disregard of proper chivalry?* She continued on in the same vein for at least a page, before switching to instructions regarding how and when I should propose. I could barely finish the entire letter without wanting to tear it into pieces.

Nowhere does she ask my thoughts on the matter, or even how I am. I threw my hands up in disgust. I should know better than to expect anything else.

A series of staccato raps sounded at my room door, knocking me out of my disgruntled train of thought. "Come in!" I called, glad for any distraction.

The door opened to reveal a man I didn't know, obviously a guard of some sort. A thrill of alarm swept through me and I scrambled to remember where my closest weapon was.

"Prince Raleigh to see you, Your Highness," the man said, glancing around my room with eyes that missed nothing.

I could see Raleigh over his shoulder, shaking his head in disgust. "Yes, of course, he knows he's allowed in any time," I told the guard, the sudden tension dissipating as I realized it must be Raleigh's bodyguard. *Curious,* I thought as the guard stepped out and Raleigh came inside, closing the door behind himself.

"You've never had a guard before," I said to Raleigh, a question in my tone.

He shambled over to my bed and flopped down, closing his eyes in an approximation of the frustration I had been feeling over the last few days.

"New protocol for the entire family," he said by way of explanation. "Can't say why, since we're not supposed to discuss personal security matters to foreign powers," he glanced over at me with a flicker of a smile, "which includes you old friend. Sorry."

I huffed a laugh. "It's easy to forget when we're here, isn't it? Someday I might be negotiating treaties with your older brother. Or at least our bureaucrats will be."

"Better you than me. Edwin's mind is like a maze. If he's ever gotten to the point of a conversation in his life I'll eat my hat."

I burst out laughing, the sound freeing something in me that had been locked up during the winter break. Sitting here joking with my friend was almost healing in a way. I quickly sobered as I remembered the probable reason for his new protection.

"I know you can't tell me any specifics, but can you say if you're in danger?"

He scoffed, rolling into a sitting position on the side of my bed to face face me. "Here? In the middle of my own country, surrounded by weapons instructors and powerful fairies and friends? Not likely. But it's my grandmother's orders so I can't exactly argue. It's put a bit of a damper on things this semester."

"I can imagine," I commiserated. "What does Briar Rose think of it?"

Raleigh shrugged. "She hasn't minded actually. One of the Headmistresses got permission for me to move around without him as long as I'm with one of them, the instructors, or Briar Rose. They've probably cast enough protective spells on Briar over the years that there's not a chance of anyone hurting anything within a mile of her."

"Well that's a relief. Don't want trouble in paradise, do we?" I gave him a halfhearted grin as I pushed the remains of my letters into a drawer on my desk.

Raleigh looked up sharply. "What do you mean by that?"

I turned toward him more fully, leaning back in my chair, some of the irritation I felt from Mother's letter returning. "What do I mean? I mean that if Briar Rose wasn't happy, you couldn't be happy either."

"Well of course I wouldn't be happy if my friend wasn't happy. What a ridiculous thing to say."

"Ah yes, your friend."

"Yes, she's my friend." Raleigh straightened up, anger flashing in his eyes. The sight of it stirred up anger in me. I was out of time to find my own other half, and here he was, having spent years with the woman who was obviously his soul mate, and yet he wanted to pretend that he wasn't in love with her.

"Well if you say so," I spat with barely an attempt at nonchalance. "I was simply making an observation. And I'll go ahead and make another one. If I had someone like Briar Rose in my life, I would do whatever it took to keep her there. And I certainly wouldn't be so cowardly as to not confess my feelings!"

Raleigh ripped out of his seat at those words, fists balled at his sides and nostrils flaring. "Cowardly!? How dare you! What do you know of my feelings toward Briar? It's got nothing to do with you. I ought to box your ears!"

I pushed out of my seat as well. *Someone needs to teach this stuck up hothead a lesson.* "You want to fight? Fine. Let's go to the sparring yard, right now, and settle which one of us is right!"

Without a word, Raleigh stomped out of my room, banging the door open so forcefully that it bounced off of his bodyguard. The soldier recovered quickly, realizing after a moment that it was a fit of temper and not an attack. I paused only long enough to pull off the new tunic I was wearing and replace it with a plainer, patched one that I used for sword practice. Pushing the door to my room shut behind me, I stalked toward the practice yards, grabbing a sword from a stand near the pitch on my way out.

Raleigh was already there, sword in hand and performing a series of familiar warm ups. As soon as he saw me, he broke off, calling out, "First to yield loses. Spindalian rules."

I furrowed my brow in surprise. We usually sparred with the more controlled Cadet rules. Spindalian swordsmanship was much less refined, allowing for any hits necessary to win except to the face or groin. This wouldn't be an orderly back and forth. *I must have really hit a nerve. I wonder what that's all about.*

I didn't have time to wonder because in the next instant, Raleigh let out a roar, sprinting at me with sword held out in front, barely giving me enough time to bring my own weapon up to block and sidestep. Our steel rang out against each other, a clanging scrape as we pulled apart.

All the practice weapons were spelled to make it impossible to strike anyone too deep. It allowed us to have more realistic practice sessions, but I had never thought to test it before now. *I hope the spell holds true. Raleigh certainly isn't holding back.*

My own ball of anger and frustration only grew at the thought. Why should he be so angry just because I brought up his girl? *I'm* the one with no choices in front of me. *I'm* the one with a family that doesn't care, that doesn't share my vision for our country.

With a frustrated growl I paced forward toward my opponent and brought my sword down at an angle, slicing toward his neck. He easily blocked, twisting to knock my blade away and using the momentum of the block to slide by me. We turned toward each other again, exchanging a quick flurry of strikes before parting.

Raleigh appeared more focused than when we started, no longer radiating anger. He tended to be that way - impulsive, acting before he thought and then settling into a steadier frame of mind. It was a tendency I had to work hard to curb within myself. But while our fight seemed to be calming Raleigh down,

I felt my own self control disintegrating even further. *And after all, he's the one who called Spindalian rules.*

The next time he struck out at me, I used a block we've practiced time and again in swordsmanship class, then stepped to the side and slammed the butt of my sword into the side of his jaw in a clumsy but effective strike.

Raleigh stumbled back, his eyes lighting up. "So you do have a little fire in you after all, Luca!"

I ground my teeth together, pushing him into another brief engagement, breaking apart after he was almost successful in tripping me. We were both sweating by now, the weight of our swords and the quick pace of our fight taking it's toll after almost a month of Yuletide celebrations at home. Raleigh looked positively calm, despite the way his shoulders heaved with every breath. As I stared at him, he cracked a smile, clearly having moved past whatever had gotten him riled up to begin with.

"It's nice to get a practice bout in before tomorrow," he said, almost nonchalantly. His eyes darted to our left and his smile grew even wider. Like a fool, I followed his gaze, only to see Briar Rose leaning against a post, her eyes following Raleigh. The sight poured oil on the fire of my temper.

Raleigh used my distraction to his advantage, getting the tip of his sword under my hasty defense and ripping an inch tear in my shirt. "By the Lady," I swore under my breath before getting my sword up again to defend against another volley of attacks. Before I quite knew how he did it, Raleigh slid his sword around mine in a looping maneuver, leveraging it out of my hands to go flying away from both of us. I brought up my fists, but to no avail. In a moment the tip of his sword was at my throat.

"Yield, Luca," he demanded with a smile, his chest puffed out with pride. Although he kept his eyes trained on me, I knew his awareness was on the one watching him.

"I yield." The words came out as a growl, and as he lowered his sword and gave me an easy smile, I backed away, eager to get away from my two friends.

"Luca don't be a sore loser!" Raleigh called. Part of me wanted to go back and patch things up, but I was still too angry at the world to guarantee that I wouldn't make things worse. I turned away, giving a dismissive wave. "I need some space. I'll see you at dinner," I called, jamming my practice sword back into it's stand and stomping my way toward the stables. I needed a ride if I was ever going to regain my temper.

CHAPTER FIVE

Ella

I took Matteo's proffered hand and hopped down lightly from my favorite horse, Heartfire. After giving her a grateful pat, I pulled off the saddlebag and dug out the care instructions Matteo would be communicating to the head groom here, then waved him on his way. Peering around, my eyes caught on Alessia striding through the stables and I smiled. Her jaw dropped when she noticed me, then she ran up and gave me a cracking hug.

"Ella! You didn't say you were coming! Oh, it's so good to see you!"

"And it's wonderful to see you! Giuseppe has taken ill again so I'm coming in his stead. Oh, and don't let me forget. I have letters and presents for you from home." I dug my contracts folio out of the saddlebag then handed the bag to her.

She started to peer inside then closed the top of the bag again quickly. "No, I'll wait until I have time to enjoy them," she said. "I'm due to help with the horse transfer. Will you be around for another hour or so? That's how long it usually takes to get them settled and review their notes."

I nodded. "I have to meet with one of the Headmistresses for their signature, but I'm sure there will be enough daylight afterward to catch up for a bit."

Alessia gave me a sunny smile, then nodded at something behind my back. "There's the Headmistress now." I turned to find a regally dressed, gray haired lady sweeping quietly into the stables, her eyes trained on the new horses.

"Remind me again which one she is? I've never met them, and I can't remember how Giuseppe described them," I murmured to Alessia.

"That's Headmistress Weald," she replied, "the Woodland Fairy. She's not the only woodland fairy of course, but she's the head of that department." Alessia's tone was admiring, and I looked more closely at the woman, *the fairy*, in front of me.

"I can't believe I'm seeing a real live fairy!" I whispered back to Alessia. "She looks so normal!" My stepsister gave me a strange look and I laughed. "I know, I know. You've been living here for four years, so you're used to them by now. But it's still strange to me. Nice strange. But strange."

Alessia opened her mouth in reply, then closed it again with a snap. She crooked me a smile and reached up to straighten my cap. "If you're ready, I can go introduce you to her."

"That would be perfect, thank you." Dusting off the my riding habit as discreetly as possible, I tucked my folio under my arm and followed Alessia over to where the Headmistress was conferring with one of her grooms.

"Headmistress Weald, this is my stepsister, Lady Sorella Fenice, Baroness Lucedimora. Ella, this is Headmistresses Gladiolus Weald, The Woodland Fairy."

"I'm so pleased to meet you in person," I said, realizing I didn't know the protocol for meeting a fairy, let alone a high ranking one from a foreign court. I settled for a deep head nod, and she gave me one in return.

"Likewise, Lady Fenice. I see you have brought us only the finest, yet again, and my head groom assures me that all seems to be in order. Shall we adjourn to my study to discuss business?"

I nodded and she led the way at a brisk pace, taking a direct route across the paved courtyard and through the doorway of a timber building that reminded me almost of a schoolhouse, or a small chapel. A feeling of cheerful competency hung about it.

The front door lead directly into some sort of reception area, buzzing with cadets. I followed closely on the Headmistress' heels as we wound our way through students balancing stacks of books, parents issuing streams of instructions, and a surprising amount of hound dogs.

"They're for hunting instruction," Headmistress Weald told me when she noticed my stare. "Lilac, that's the Songbird Fairy, in charge of animals you know; she says they're better left to roam at will here. Not the usual done thing with hunting dogs, I know, but it does seem to work." She paused and sent me a stern look. "Not that we would deign to do so with your horses, Lady Fenice. I hope you realize that. Lilac assures me they're better off under the care instructions you provided. Completely different animals. The dogs complain if they aren't left free. Your horses are all very well mannered."

I offered her a smile, my brain going a mile a minute. *Is this what Giuseppe has had to deal with every time he's come here? It seems a very odd place.* My steward had never mentioned the feeling of tightly controlled chaos that permeated the air, but maybe that was because the semester was just starting. Alessia had never written home about it either, but it's not the sort of thing she would notice. Her mind was filled with weaponry and fighting styles.

The fairy passed through an open doorway into a cozy study, decorated in greens and browns. She flicked her hands toward one end of the room and the fireplace sprang to life, instantly bringing the temperature of the room to a comfortable level. *I wonder if Aria ever got the fire in the drawing room going properly. Sure would be nice if we had a fairy on hand to start them by magic.*

A flush chased across my face at the blasphemous directions my mind had gone. Trading with the fairies was not prohibited, but magic in Charmagne certainly was. If I ever voiced that thought aloud in Charmagne I would be under investigation in a minute. *You're getting too used to dealing with mages,* I scolded myself.

"Do have a seat, Lady Fenice," the fairy said, indicating a leather chair in front of her desk. I focused back a the task at hand, choosing one of the seats and placing my folio on the desk as I sat down.

Our conversation moved at a brisk pace, and I had difficulty keeping up with the Headmistress' questions. In the end, I was mentally exhausted, but happy with the outcome. Although I knew the value of my horses, I was too sympathetic to other people's points of view to maintain a hard line when negotiating. That's why Giuseppe was still insisting on heading these things up for me even in his old age. Thankfully, since this was the fulfillment of a previously negotiated contract, there were only a few items that had cropped up in the meantime to settle. I had managed to bargain for an additional fee for the last minute accommodations I had made, and promised to send her a new contract for the next semester. A fine day's work.

Alessia was waiting for me in the reception room, and after bidding farewell to Headmistress Weald, she demanded I come have a look at her room. She led me through a plain but comfortable dormitory until we came to her own bedroom, which I had never actually seen. It was small, orderly and scrupulously clean. Very much reflective of Alessia. Whitewashed walls stood under a timber framed ceiling. She had a small window overlooking a garden plot, with a view of a corner of what looking to be training yards beyond. After an agonizingly short visit of unwrapping Yuletide gifts and trading the latest gossip from Lucedimora, we made our way back downstairs, heading toward the stables.

"Are you excited to graduate in a few months, or terrified?" I asked as we meandered between buildings.

Alessia scoffed. "I'm neither excited nor dreading it. I'll be placed at a military post soon, which will be fun. But if I'm posted anywhere other than a unit that will see action, I can't say I'm excited about that. I just have to take it one day at a time, and deal with what's in front of me."

"Well, whatever comes, just know you have a family that

loves you back home, and we're all so proud of you."

Alessia grinned and pulled me into a brief side hug. "I know that. I miss you all so much, but I *know* that I'm on the right path for me."

"Good," I replied, contentment over her happiness blossoming in my heart. "That's what we all want for you. And I swear, we'll try to find a way to all make it to your graduation ceremony in a few months."

We stopped in front of the stables and I signaled to Matteo to come over once he was finished his conversation with the Academy's head groom.

"So what classes will you end up taking this semester?"

Alessia grimaced. "All the usual martial arts classes of course. And you'll never believe this, but I'm actually taking Spindalian Flora and Fauna. There's a gardening portion where we have to identify plants and their uses."

I tipped my head back in a laugh that my stepmother would definitely classify as too loud for a Baroness. Alessia couldn't stand gardening or farming, so the thought of her in that class was just too funny.

"Yes, I know," she said ruefully. "I was so happy to get away from all that at Lucedimora, and yet here I am. Supposedly it will help us understand poisons and antidotes in case any of us are selected for royal guard duty."

I shook my head still grinning at her. "Well hopefully you'll learn a lot. And of course I would love to read through any notes you take so I can use that knowledge back at the castle. I think it's a great thing that you're getting outside of your comfort zone. It's so important just to take a leap of faith sometimes and trust it will all work out."

"Sure," she replied, putting her arm around my shoulders and pulling me in for a bone cracking side hug. "I can't tell you how glad I was to see you today, El. But make sure to give Giuseppe my love." She released me to peer through the stable doors. "It looks like Matteo is going to get your horse. He must be trying to look good with you here to observe him. Usually it's all Giuseppe can do to get him to leave off talking to the head groom."

I chuckled, knowing too well how hard it could be to distract Matteo from a conversation on horses once he got started. "I almost wish he would keep talking, just to make our visit longer. But I'm sure you have things to do to prepare for classes tomorrow, and we really should leave soon to make it home before dark."

Alessia crooked a sad smile at me, then stuck her head back through the stable doors to check on Matteo. A sudden prickle across my back made my shoulder blades jump, and I shrugged to dissipate the feeling - as if someone was watching me. Glancing discreetly around the bustling courtyard, I couldn't see anyone paying me anything more than a passing glance, so I rolled my eyes at my own dramatics.

CHAPTER SIX

Luca

The sweat from my sparring match was beginning to cool on my skin, leaving a ghostly itch in it's wake. The physical discomfort only added to my mental anguish, although my temper was finally starting to ease a little.

I know I have a lot to be grateful for. No one has complete freedom over their life. We all have expectations and responsibilities that force us to give up things. I would have a life free from poverty and powerlessness, but every personal choice I made would have to also serve my country. There were many court ladies who would give almost anything to become my queen, but in exchange I couldn't trust that any of them cared even a small amount about Luca, the person, not the prince.

I huffed out a breath, running a hand through my hair. Like most problems, this would pass. There was a solution here somewhere. A solution that would allow me to exist as a person while also being a good king someday. If I was patient everything would work out. I snorted. *You're being an entitled prig again.* An accusation Briar Rose had leveled at every one of us royals one time or another.

My breathing had calmed considerably as I rounded the corner of the Headquarters building. Although it was located on the edge of Deerbold Academy, it was the center of operations for the entire site. The ground floor held the Headmistreses' studies and a waiting room for anyone with appointments. On days like these, the beginning of a semester, it was sure to be packed with cadets requesting last minute changes to class schedules and living arrangements.

I flicked my eyes up to the dormant rose vine that crawled along the timber and plaster structure up to the second floor. The top of the building contained the Headmistresses' living quarters, as well as Briar Rose's chamber. The sight of the rose vine sent a stab of annoyance through me once again, but not nearly so sharp as before. Raleigh had climbed it many a time over the years to get to Briar Rose's room outside of curfew. *And yet he has the audacity to claim he's not head over heels with her.* I snapped my eyes away, focusing instead on winding my way through the stream of cadets moving in and out of the Headquarters as I walked by on my quest for the stables. Just as I stepped into the paved courtyard, laughter rang out above the murmuring voices, like sunshine bursting through fog.

My feet slowed to a stop. All around me I could hear the chattering shouts of students, the clip clop of horses on paving stone and the steady thrum of footsteps. Not even an echo of that phantom laugh. The sudden flight of hope it had stirred in my heart swooped low again.

I shook my head. *You're hearing things now. If you can't handle the stress of your final semester of school and a marriage you knew would be happen eventually, how will you handle the day to day running of your kingdom?*

My head snapped up as another peal of laughter reached me. It wasn't the tone of it that caught my ear, but the joy embedded within. The sheer unadulterated happiness that struck a chord of longing and fellow feeling. I searched in the direction of the sound. *It came from near the stables.* My eyes flowed over dozens of bodies milling around the area until it snagged on a shock of reddish hair, almost glowing against the pale stone of the stable wall. *There.*

Time stopped. For a moment, there was no noise, no movement. I existed half in the present, half in a moment a decade past, before the disappointment of growing older set in. My heart skipped a painful beat in hope.

Cinderella?

Somewhere in the back of my mind, I noticed that my feet had begun moving of their own accord. My vision had narrowed to the young woman across the courtyard, taking in every surreal detail as she laughed with Alessia. She was dressed in a bright red jacket, which clashed slightly with her hair, but added to the overall impression of a lively spark, ready to set the dull courtyard that surrounded her on fire. Just like before, her hair was pulled up, but had partially tumbled down in a little halo. My mind was blank as my feet sped a little faster. *I have to get to her before she disappears again.* I had so many questions, had thought of her often through the years, always with the certainty that I'd never see her again. But here she was. In front of me, laughing again.

Alessia turned to poke her head through the stable door and shiver seemed to pass through Cinderella. She shrugged her shoulders and quickly looked from side to side before refocusing on Alessia, who turned to say something briefly before ducking her head back inside. I weaved between bodies in the courtyard, ignoring anyone who came near. The few remaining yards seemed to take ages, and my heart beat painfully as I closed the gap. Suddenly, I was there, standing beside her as she fiddled with her riding gloves. *It's her. It's definitely her.*

"Cinderella?" I asked, incredulously. A shock seemed to go through her entire body, and she stiffened from head to toe before turning toward me, an expression of wonder on her face.

"Luca?"

I broke out into a grin so wide it hurt my face. *She remembers me too.* "Yes, it's me. And it's you! How are you here?"

She broke into a smile of her own, taking a step toward me as she answered. "I have business for my estate here, actually. But what about you?"

"I'm a cadet. It's my last year - I'll graduate in a few months."

"That's fantastic - congratulations!" Her generous smile was sincere and I drank it in.

She turned to Alessia who had wandered over from the stable door and was looking at us with a confused smile. "Wait," Alessia said slowly, "Do you two know each other?"

"Yes," Ella replied, laughing. "Or at least we met a long time ago when we were just children. Luca was very kind to me when I was in the middle of one of my madcap schemes." She turned her smile back to me. "Thank you for being so nice that day, and for remembering me all this time."

"It was my pleasure, Lady Ella," I replied in all sincerity. "I'm even more grateful that you've remembered *me* all this time."

My words ignited a splash of red against her skin that came and went like an itinerant flame. The effect lit a spark inside my chest, and the urge to make her blush again, or even better, laugh out loud was almost irresistible.

Alessia shifted on her feet. "Ella, how could you have never mentioned that you've met -"

I cut her off just in time. "Alessia, why do you think she would know that a lowly knight like me was attending this Academy?"

Alessia scoffed. "Luca, everyone knows - " but I cut her off again. "We never exchanged family names all those years ago," I explained, "so we had no way of knowing who the other person was." Ella nodded, then jumped as a groom tapped her shoulder. She turned to speak with him for a moment, and I seized the opportunity to give Alessia a look.

"Just be quiet for now. Don't blow my cover. I'll explain it all later," I hissed at her, half commanding, half pleading.

She pursed her lips for a moment, considering, then gave me a tight nod. I dropped my shoulders in relief, taking a quick breath and praying my thanks to the White King above under my breath.

Ella turned back as the groom walked over to a pair of two magnificent horses. She looked back and forth between Alessia and me. "You two must know each other since you're in the same year."

Alessia nodded. "We're year mates. I'm sure I've written home to you about him, although maybe you didn't realize who it was at the time."

Ella gave a shy laugh, "If only I had known, I would have come in Giuseppe's stead long before now just to meet you again." To my increasing interest, that blush stole across her face again, leaving splotches of red that lasted only a few seconds. She gave a nervous laugh and gestured behind her. "If you had seen me earlier we could have had time to catch up. But now I have to head home if I want to get there before dark."

I glanced over her shoulder to where the groom sat, already mounted on his horse and was holding the reins of the other one.

"It seems we must be destined to meet only when I'm rushing off somewhere else," Cinderella continued with a crooked smile.

My heart panicked for a moment at the thought that she would escape me again, but quickly took hope as I remembered my original aim for coming to the stables. "Could you stay a few moments? I came to exercise my horse just now, so if you wait, I will escort you home. If that's agreeable to you that is," I added hastily.

A wide, sincere smile broke out across her face. "Well I wouldn't want to put you to any trouble. It's a two hour ride. But if you still want to come, or come part of the way, that would be lovely."

My smile stretched so wide it almost hurt. "Just give me a few minutes my lady, and I'll be back with my own horse." She dipped her head in a deep nod and I executed a shallow bow as she turned toward her horse, using a mounting block to pull herself neatly into the saddle. "Alessia, why don't you help me get Percivale ready," I said as I grabbed her upper arm and half dragged her into the stables with me.

As soon as we were out of sight I let up the pressure on her arm and she ripped it out of my grasp. "What *was* that?" she demanded in a low voice as we crossed the threshold of the tack room and stopped in front of my locker.

"How do you know her?" I demanded, throwing a blanket over my shoulder and hefting my saddle off of it's stand.

Alessia squared her jaw before grabbing my bridle and reigns from their hooks and answering. "She's my sister. So again, I want to know what all that was about back there."

My jaw dropped. *Her sister? All these years I've been friends with Cinderella's sister and never new it?"* I shook my head dumbly. Alessia pressed her lips into a line and then stepped around me to lead the way out of the tack room and down to Percivale's stall. I trailed in her wake, mind racing.

"Wait," I demanded when I caught up to her. She ignored me, opening the stall door and putting a hand up to Percivales nose as he whinnied a greeting to her. I followed her in, patting my horse's nose as well before setting the saddle and blanket to the side. As Alessia turned to close the stall door I leaned around Percivale to get some answers.

"She told me she was a Lady, but you aren't of the nobility. How can she be your sister?" Alessia stiffened, pausing for a heartbeat before pushing the stall door closed and latching it. She turned, offering me a brush she had snagged from the bin, her face a mask. "She *is* a Lady. A Baroness actually. I'm only her stepsister, so no, not a member of the nobility."

I breathed a sigh of relief and turned back to Percivale, starting to brush him down with quick strokes. Alessia stared at me for a moment before moving to join me with a brush of her own.

"I though you always said that rank doesn't matter to you when choosing your friends," she muttered, a hint of accusation in her voice.

"It doesn't!" I protested, looking at her in surprise. "Of course it doesn't. You've heard me talk about what court is like. I'd prefer friends of common birth compared to that lot. It's not that. Only I didn't like the idea that she had lied to me about something like that."

Alessia nodded, focusing on the task in front of her instead of looking at me. "Ella is honest to a fault. She wouldn't lie about even the smallest thing, let alone try impersonating something she's not."

A small smile played at the corner of my lips, a feeling of triumph welling up in my heart as I refocused on brushing as quickly as possible without making Percivale nervous. *I don't know why that feels so important, her honesty.* My thoughts and feelings were a jumbled mess so I ignored them in favor of speeding my work along.

"Why did you stop me from saying who you are out there?" Alessia asked. I hesitated, choosing my words carefully as we moved around to the other side of the horse.

"I mentioned that we didn't exchange names when we met originally. She still doesn't know who I am. For now, I just want to be that person she met ten years ago, while I have the chance." My hands stilled as a new thought occurred to me, and I rounded on Alessia, my tone harsh. "Don't tell any of our friends about this, I'm begging you." Alessia's frown deepened and she opened her mouth to respond but I cut her off. "Just this once, do me this favor. I'll explain everything when we have more time, I promise."

She stared at me, obviously disapproving, and took a step closer. "If you're trying to trick or take advantage of my sister, I don't care if you're my crown prince - you'll pay for it."

I had to smile at my friend's protectiveness, even if I was a little annoyed by the slight on my honor. "Have I ever made you think I would do that to someone?" I asked, but Alessia's fierceness didn't lessen. I held up my hands, "I promise, I'm not trying to trick her. I just want a chance to be known as only Luca for bit, before all my responsibilities come down on him. Even here, where we all treat each other as equals, everyone knows who everyone else is. You just mentioned my title in your threat to me, after all. Even if you feel comfortable enough to threaten me, it still hangs between us, friends though we are."

Alessia looked stricken, then turned back to Percivale, crouching down to clean his forelegs with quick strokes. I finished his flank and then grabbed his blanket and saddle, placing them on his back and pushing the cinch strap toward Alessia as she held her hand under his girth, offering to secure it. We both moved to the front of the horse as we worked together to fit his bridle and reins. Percivale stood docilely, only stamping his foot every now and again in eagerness for the impeding exercise. As we finished adjusting the last piece, Alessia stood back and looked at me.

"Fine. I'll keep your secret - for now. But you *will* tell me what's going on when you get back, and you *won't* break her heart."

My own heart stuttered for a moment at her words and I whipped around to face her. "Why do you say that? Do you think she might like me?" A thought flashed through my mind. "Has she mentioned me before?" I asked, searching Alessia's face.

She turned to stroke Percivale instead of looking at me. "No, she's never mentioned you before. Or that ridiculous name you called her." I could see her roll her eyes as I watched her profile. "But I've never seen her blush like that with a man." She took a deep breath and released it. "She's been too busy running the estate and trying to take care of the rest of us to have time for suitors, so you need to be careful not to lead her on. She and I have had our differences over the years, but she is my sister, and she deserves your respect. She needs… she needs looking after in her own way sometimes, for all that she does what's best for everyone else."

I nodded, looking her in the eye when she turned to and held her hand out for my brush. "I promise I won't hurt her. You can trust me."

"I do," she said simply, snagging my brush and heading out of the stall without another word. I leaned my forehead against Percivale's nose for a moment, collecting my stuttering heartbeats until they were a little more calm.

"C'mon Percivale, let's go see Cinderella."

CHAPTER SEVEN

Ella

I settled into my saddle thinking about the man who had just dashed into the stables. Luca? After all this time? I had thought about the boy from the palace grounds now and again through the years, wondering if he had gotten in trouble that day like I did for being late, or if he had risen through the ranks in the stables over the years to become head groom. One of my recent goals was to secure a contract with the palace stables, and I had half hoped that he would be the person I negotiated with for that contract, if only to see what had become of him.

"Well he's obviously gotten further than head groom if he's a cadet here," I muttered to myself.

"What's that my lady? Ready to go?" Matteo asked.

"It was nothing. Actually, we need to delay our departure for a few moments. One of the cadets will be escorting us home. He's an old acquaintance of mine, so we thought we might... catch up during the ride." *Is this really a good idea?* I didn't know the man Luca had become after all. Making conversation for two hours with someone I didn't know well suddenly seemed impossible. *He was so fun to talk to all those years ago. Unless he's horribly changed, we can manage.* The thought of leaving without him seemed worse than a long ride with stilted conversation.

"Yes my lady," Matteo replied in a doubtful tone, but kept his thoughts to himself.

I sat quietly, curiosity over Luca's circumstances growing the longer we waited. *I thought Alessia was the only common born in her year. So could he possibly be the son of a nobleman? Why would he have passed himself off as a stable boy all those years ago? Surely I would have heard if a commoner was conferred a title over the last few years. It hasn't happened in generations.* I chewed on my lip, going over every snippet of our conversation when we were children. With a start I realized something. "He never said he was a stable boy. I just assumed!" I hissed under my breath as I felt the color drain from my face. I couldn't help feeling how I must have appeared to him then, talking a mile a minute and assuming he was a servant. *Now I <u>really</u> don't think a two hour ride to catch up will be very fun.*

Alessia appeared at the entrance of the stable, followed closely by Luca who was leading a striking dappled gelding that I was surprised to recognize as one of the first sales I made after my father's death.

"Percivale!" I exclaimed, smiling at how well he looked. I caught Luca's surprised laugh and felt a flush ignite over my face. I groaned internally. *He is so disgustingly handsome, it's not fair. And between my red hair, red coat, and red face, I probably look like a beetroot. Wonderful.* I couldn't help but laugh at my sudden insecurity. *After all, even a beetroot deserves to enjoy being a beetroot!*

Alessia came over and squeezed my ankle as Luca mounted up. "Take care," she said earnestly.

I looked down with a frazzled smile. "You know I will." Then I leaned down to whisper, "But quick, you said you're friends - is he nice? Only, I think I made a bit of an idiot of myself when we first met, and I'm afraid he'll be laughing at me this whole ride."

Alessia's grip tightened on my ankle for a fraction of a second before releasing completely. "He's good. And don't worry, he doesn't think you're an idiot." She brushed her hands off and muttered almost to herself, "Quite the contrary it seems."

That last comment gave new life to my blush and I opened my mouth to question her further, but she stepped away to make room for Luca and Percivale.

"Are we ready, my lady?" Matteo asked from my other side.

"Yes, Matteo. This is Luca. He'll be joining us for the ride. Luca, this is my head groom, Matteo."

"M'Lud," Matteo greeted him with a brief nod. After Luca returned a nod of his own, the groom urged his horse into a walk and led the way out of the courtyard.

I turned to wave at my stepsister just before we passed through the gate. She stared after us with her hands on her hips, her expression a grim line before quirking up and answering my wave with her own.

We proceeded single file for a time, winding our way through the narrow streets of Deerbold's campus and navigating the traffic of students, parents, and staff that milled about seemingly at random. As the road approached the forest again, Matteo pulled a little way ahead, putting a discreet distance between us while still being close enough to call.

Percivale's hoof beats sounded a little quicker, and I could sense him and Luca coming closer. My heart jumped in my throat as I tried to think of something to say before he was within speaking distance.

He pulled alongside, and we stole a glance at each other. I couldn't help returning his smile. His gaze held nothing but friendliness, and maybe a touch of the same shock that I was feeling. As if all the intervening years between our last meeting and now had faded; their pains and hardships too. Now we were two young teenagers meeting again, unburdened with cares and responsibilities.

"I reared the horse you're riding," I said finally, nodding toward Percivale. "That's what my business at the academy is - we have a contract to provide mounts for new cadets."

"It's an impeccable horse," he replied quickly. "One of my favorites." I smiled but somehow couldn't think of anything else to say. *You're usually a chatterbox! Think, Ella, think!*

Luca let out a disbelieving chuckle. "All these years I've thought of you as far away. Not only have you been close by, but

I'm friends with your sister, *and* you raised my favorite mount."

My mouth pulled into a crooked grin. "I didn't raise him, really. That would have been my father and the grooms mostly. But I did complete his contract. I remember because he was always so well behaved, and he was one of the first I sold after ..." I hesitated, biting my lip as some of the sorrow from the intervening years crept in. "After my father died," I continued lamely. Luca's eyebrows plunged in sympathy.

"I'm sorry to hear that. Although I knew that Alessia's stepfather had died, so I should have realized that was your father. It must be hard without his guidance."

I nodded, stealing another glance at Percivale before looking back at Heartfire. Both had been reared by my father, and both were exceptional mounts. I felt confident that I had managed to combine the love of horses that both my parents felt, as well as their skill, into my own methods. But I would never forget the feeling of drowning I had felt for the first several years after my father's death; let alone the devastation of my mother's death. I shied away from that thought, and turned back toward Luca with a rueful smile.

"So I realized while I was waiting for you that you must be the son of a nobleman. And I had mistaken you for a stable boy that day! I'm so embarrassed. I do hope you'll forgive me!"

Luca's face took on a slightly pink glow under his tan and he shrugged his shoulders. "I never corrected you. And if I remember correctly I was in my old riding clothes. So it was a natural assumption. And to be honest, I was hoping to surprise you at the ball the next evening. But you never came! Or at least, I never saw you there."

I couldn't help a surprised laugh from escaping. "Well I can forgive you for not correcting me, that would have been a great laugh to have seen you all dressed up at the ball. We could have danced together and sneaked out to look for gemstones."

"Exactly!" He exclaimed, then looked at me as if to scold. "But you never came. I don't mind telling you it ruined my entire evening. My parents were highly disappointed in me."

I shot him a sympathetic look. "I'm sorry it ruined your evening." I hesitated a moment before continuing. "The truth is, we had word that morning about a disaster at our estate. There was an equine flu that killed off almost half our stock. Our steward begged my parents to come back home. They were both heavily involved in that side of things."

Luca sucked a breath in through his teeth and gave whistle. "That's devastating."

"Yes I suppose it was," I replied, giving my head a little shake. "Except my mother was trampled by one of the sick horses when she went to check on them, and she died just a few days later. Next to losing her, the pain of the rest of it seems insignificant."

We rode in silence for a few minutes after that, and once I collected myself from the memories of that day, I worried I had put too much of a damper on things. Just as I opened my mouth to move the conversation forward, Luca chimed in again.

"I'm so sorry. To think that I was annoyed with you for not showing up, and mad that my parents had yelled at me in the days following the ball, but you were dealing with all of that..." he shook his head. "What a good reminder to get out of my own self absorption every now and again."

"Oh no, that's not at all what I was saying!" I protested.

"I know, I'm just talking to myself. I tend to get wrapped up in problems that feel so big to me. And it's not that my problems aren't real, it's just that I can build them up to be so much worse than they are. There's always a silver lining somewhere, isn't there?"

"Yes," I nodded firmly. "I completely agree with that. Even the worst of situations can lead to some good. I wish desperately that my mother had never died. But since she did, I've also gained my stepmother and two stepsisters, and I love them to bits."

Luca gave me a soft smile and I looked away, fighting an insipid glow at the approval in his eyes. After a moment I regained my composure and straightened in my saddle. "Enough about my family, what of yours? Do your parents regularly scold you, or was it just a one time thing at the ball?"

Luca huffed a laugh. "Yes, unfortunately, I do seem to be on the receiving end of scolding from both of them more frequently than not. But they have high expectations of me, and I like to go my own way, so it's probably inevitable."

"Ah, the age old disagreement of how to run the estate. I was lucky to have never run into that with my own parents, and my stepmother is happy to let me run things as I see fit without interfering. Where is your estate, may I ask?"

Luca hesitated a moment, then threw me an embarrassed smile. "We have properties scattered around several parts of the kingdom," he said with a shrug. "I have two younger brothers, so they will inherit as well, but my favorite is the Barony of Lontariva. It's a small town really, on the Royal Isle. Have you heard of it?"

Properties scattered all over? His family must be an ancient one, although if they've kept control of all of those estates over the years, they probably married into new money, which would explain his shyness. There was a bit of a horror in some circles about noblemen who married into rich commoner families. This far from the capitol, there wasn't much room for that sort of attitude, as evidenced by my father's marriage to my commoner mother, and their popularity with the local gentry. But if he came from the notoriously rigid south, or even more likely by his accent, had been raised in the capitol, he probably carried at least a modicum of shame over it.

"I haven't heard of it," I replied finally, with an apologetic look. "I must confess that my geographical skills are mostly focused on estate business. Since you probably don't have much need for horses on the Royal Isle, it's not somewhere I've ever looked into. That sounds very mercenary of me, doesn't it?"

Luca grinned. "No indeed, merely efficient."

"Almost as bad, at least to some of our class. You could never be seen with me in public." I chuckled self consciously, then couldn't suppress a truer laugh at the though of me, with my country fashion, too loud laugh, and penchant for 'efficiency' moving among the nobles I remembered from the capitol.

"What is it?" Luca inquired with a curious smile.

"Oh, nothing. I was just imagining me attempting to move among the elites in the capitol. I haven't been back since I saw you actually. If I went now, everyone would probably faint dead away at my rustic ways."

Luca frowned. "Not at all. Or if they did, they wouldn't be worth your time. I would be proud to have you on my arm at the capitol."

His words brought up a picture of us promenading through the ornamental gardens of the palace. *I'm sure I could withstand fainting nobles and scandalous looks if I was on **his** arm.* I blushed at the thought and focused on the trail ahead of us, avoiding his gaze entirely. "Well, you're very kind to say so, although I'm sure your parents have definite plans for your marriage, so you'll be scolded yet again for escorting me around in public." I turned a grin toward him and noted with curiosity a stricken look that passed across his face, replaced in almost an instant with a conspiratorial grin.

"Well, it's a good thing I've built up such a thick skin over the years then, isn't it? If a scold is what I have to pay to get you on my arm in front of the beau-monde, then so be it. I'll wager we'll take our stroll together before the year is out, so prepare yourself now!"

I tried and failed to suppress a laugh, finally just tilting my head back and letting it fly. *Stepmother would be so embarrassed right now. He's flirting outrageously and instead of demurely accepting his attention I'm laughing like a hyena.*

But when I looked back at Luca, instead of looking offended or disgusted by my lack of manners, he was laughing too. A flash of fellow feeling tugged at my heart, and I found myself wanting to make him laugh even more.

"I shall certainly be honored to perform in such a spectacle. May I suggest that we finish our promenade in the tradesman's yard where we first met? We might demonstrate my efficiency by completing our original task together, searching for diamonds in the blacksmith's furnace. That way, we can offend the court by our outlandish behavior, and at the same time continue working on our theory."

We both burst into laughter, and I had to wipe at a few tears leaking out of my eyes. Matteo glanced back at us with a perplexed look, but turned back around without comment. Luca corrected Percivale's gait as he had been a little spooked by our outburst, but then grinned over at me again.

"That is certainly a date. Although we'd better keep our excursions to ourselves. If I remember correctly, the original theory was proposed by a heretic. We wouldn't want to flirt with too much disaster on our first outing. We should save at least a little for our next one!"

I laughed again, my heart soaring at finding the open minded boy from my memory still existed in the man he had grown into.

We spent the rest of the ride oscillating between lighthearted banter and more serious conversation about our families, duties, and plans for the future. I hadn't spent such a glorious afternoon in years. So immersed was I in our conversation, I jumped in my saddle when we left the tree line of the great forest.

"Oh." I said in surprise, slowing Heartfire as Luca did the same with his horse. I called to Matteo, who was still a little way ahead, to wait for a few moments. I looked back over to Luca.

"Well, we're technically on my estate's land right now, so you've seen me home." I pointed toward where the last ochre rays of the sun reflected off the sandstone walls of Lucedimora Castle, standing proudly on it's motte in the distance. "That's my home, Lucedimora Castle. Not that we weren't safe in the forest, but you can be sure I'll be safe in my own small territory." I smiled as Luca glanced at Lucedimora, then back at me with a slightly lost air. *It looks like he enjoyed our time as much as I did*, I thought with relief.

"We... we're given a free day on Saturdays." He swallowed heavily and my heart thumped painfully in my chest as I tried not to read too much into what he was saying. "I know it's a bit of an imposition, since you have an entire estate to run," he continued, "but I've enjoyed our ride together so much I can't help asking if you want to do it again."

I opened my mouth, my mind racing to make sure I was understanding what he was saying over my sudden nerves and the rushing in my ears.

"Not this whole ride!" He exclaimed suddenly, a flush stealing across his cheeks. "I thought maybe we could meet halfway. Do you remember the old ruins we passed, by the spring?" I nodded. "We could meet there for lunch. I'll bring a basket from the kitchens. We could compare notes on our findings about Vallens' theory over the years. I've been checking blacksmith's forges whenever I could you know."

He suddenly seemed a bit vulnerable, and that, combined with his memory from our first meeting made my heart wobble. "Elfkinde's theory," I corrected him, shyly.

"What?" He asked, his brow furrowed.

"It's actually Maestro Elfkinde's theory. Vallens was the one I had been reading, but he thought Elfkinde's theory was all bunk." I licked my lips, my nerves frayed as we hovered on the edge of committing to our next meeting. *Stepmama would never approve of me going to meet a man alone in the middle of the woods... but Alessia knows him, and says he's good.* I made a quick decision, and tried to cover up how nervous I felt by attempting to earn a laugh. "I can see I'll have to correct your sorely lacking education on Elfkinde's theories, so I suppose we must! Can't allow the Baron of Lontariva to go about the rest of his life improperly attributing heretical theories to the wrong dusty scholar!"

My impishness earned a bark of laughter from Luca and I smiled in return. "So does that mean it's a date?" He asked, his expression suddenly earnest.

I swallowed hard and nodded. "Yes, next Saturday, for lunch. I'll be looking forward to it."

His eyes searched mine and then crinkled in a wide smile. He put a hand on his chest and nodded deeply in the approximation of a bow. "As will I, my lady." He glanced toward where Matteo was waiting, and I followed his gaze, noticing the sky's swift descent toward night.

"You must go too!" I exclaimed. "You'll be riding in the pitch dark soon!"

"Never fear," he reassured me, dropping his voice to a whisper. "I have a light charm. All the cadets do, so I won't be in any danger."

My jaw dropped at the casual mention of magic, and he winked at me, pulling a smile and shake of my head in response. "Still," I said, my voice low as well. "Take care. And I'll see you on Saturday."

Reluctantly I nudged my horse into motion, quickly catching up with Matteo. The two of us sped off toward Lucedimora in an attempt to beat nightfall. I felt Luca's eyes on me the entire time, my shoulder blades itching in anticipation. *Saturday.*

The ride from the edge of the forest to the castle gates took no time at all. It was dark by the time I came out of our small personal stable.

"Ella?" Gia's voice called across the dim courtyard. Her shape was outlined against the kitchen door, and in a guilty flash I remembered her father, my sickly steward.

"Yes, it's me!" I called, picking up the hem of my skirts and rushing toward her. The lights in the main part of the castle were dim except for my stepmother's room. *I'll have to check on her before I go to sleep.* I hurried into the warm kitchen, turning to help Gia close the door against the winter chill.

"How did it go?" she asked as she slid the bolt home.

"Fine, fine! But how is your father?"

Aida's voice drifted from across the room. "Pneumonia again, the doctor says," I turned in surprise to find her sitting at the rough hewn kitchen table, a bowl of stew before her. "He prescribed the usual medicine, so Giuseppe is sleeping quietly now. It will be a rough couple of days, but at least we know what we're dealing with."

I nodded in sympathy, throwing a glance at Gia. She crooked a smile and shooed me toward the table before walking over to the stew pot.

"Mama, Ella looks done in, so if you can't stand the sight of her sitting with us common folk, you'd better get yourself down the passage to your room because I'm going to serve her some stew," Gia told her mother matter of factly.

Madame Moriotto pressed a hand to her chest and lifted her eyes skyward. "This once I think I can pretend that my vision isn't what it used to be, I supposed," she replied, eliciting a grin from me and Gia. "I hope your journey wasn't too difficult my lady?"

Now that the concern over my friends was settled, I felt able to smile again. "No, it wasn't difficult at all. I feel guilty saying it, but I had a wonderful time."

Madame Moriotto smiled kindly, "You're not to worry my lady. We had it all under control in your absence, and the doctor has fixed up Giuseppe right as rain. I'm glad you had a chance to get it out. There's a bit of color on your face that I don't often see, and if it isn't overstepping my place, I'm glad of it."

I blushed harder, resisting the urge to press my hands to my cheeks. There was a churning in my heart that hardly felt like happiness, so mixed as it was with tiredness and from the exertion of the day and wonder at the turn of events in seeing Luca, not to mention bashfulness at the thought of our next meeting. I focused instead on wolfing down my stew, the sound of Aida and Gia's conversation flowing over me like a comforting blanket. As soon as I finished I took my leave, passing through the dark dining room and into the dim hall of the main residence. I poked my head through the door of the sitting room we used in the evening but it was dark so I continued on upstairs.

Entering my room, I smiled to see a fire burning cheerfully in the grate, warming the entire space. Although I longed for a bath, I contented myself with washing at my basin and ewer before changing into a nightgown and robe. Pushing my feet into a pair of worn slippers, I slipped out of my room and walked over to my stepmother's room, tapping on her door and waiting for her invitation before passing through.

She still inhabited the master bedroom, as I had no desire to remove her from it when my father had died, even though she had tried to get me to agree. I was content with my smaller childhood room, and as I approached where she lay on the four poster bed, I had to admit that my stepmother graced the master suite with more poise than I could usually muster, sick though she was.

Aria sat on the side of the bed, dressed in her own nightgown and robe, a frillier version of my own. Beyond her, my stepmother sat propped against her headboard, holding a cold compress against her forehead and offering me a wan smile.

"Come in, Ella dear. Aria tells me that you rode all the way to Deerbold today as Giuseppe was indisposed. You must be so tired!" Her voice was tight with pain, but she beckoned me forward. I walked around the opposite side of the bed as Aria and took a seat as well.

"Yes, I made the trip in his stead today. And although I am tired, I found it rather energizing as well. The contract was concluded neatly, and I was able to visit with Alessia for a time. She sends her love of course." I hesitated, a desire to keep my meeting with Luca to myself warring with a desire to maintain the openness I had always shared with my family. The old familiar patterns won out and words tumbled from my mouth before I could stop them. "And I met an old acquaintance there as well. He accompanied me home and I ... well actually I've arranged to see him again next week." I could feel my skin heating with each word and I couldn't help fidgeting in my seat a little under my stepmother and stepsister's surprised glances.

"An old acquaintance?" my stepmother asked after a moment, setting her compress down on the counterpane to focus better on my face. "Where do you know him from, my dear?"

"Oh, from years ago, when we were children. I met him at the palace, the day before the prince's coronation ball. I had mistaken him for a groom actually, but it turns out he's the son of a nobleman!" My stepmother's eyebrows raised and I blushed at her look. "Alessia knows him well," I rushed to assure her, "she was there when we met again in the courtyard today. And he didn't tease me at all for mistaking him for a servant all those years ago. He was wonderful about it really." My words came out in a tumble, eliciting a slightly exasperated smile from my stepmother. I paused, drawing in a breath to steady my jumbled nerves from the day.

Aria closed her book and placed it gently on the night stand, leaning forward with a smile. "This sounds like something from my book of fairytales, Ella. You say he escorted you home? Quite the knight in shining armor!"

I laughed, eliciting a wince from my stepmother, who pressed her cold compress back to her forehead.

"Sorry Stepmama," I said in more hushed tones. She waved my apology away.

"Never mind that Ella. Tell us more about this Luca. You say you've arranged to meet him again?"

"Yes - I know it's a bit forward of me, but he asked to see me again on their day off and I ... well I suppose it's just one meeting. I'd like to get to know him better. That is, if you think it's appropriate."

My heart sunk at the thought that my stepmother might object to meeting someone she hadn't vetted previously. She was never in great health through the winter months and wouldn't be able to accompany on our rides. And Aria wouldn't be considered an appropriate chaperone. As Baroness, I technically could do as I liked, but I always valued my stepmother's discernment.

She looked at me steadily for a moment before giving a gentle smile. "If you have already agreed to meet him, and you truly wish to do so, I won't stand in your way." Aria and I looked at her in surprise and she gave a quiet laugh. "Oh I know, it's a bit scandalous of me to agree, but you're old enough and wise enough to behave as you should. And don't for a minute think I won't be writing to Alessia to make sure he is who he says he is! But as long as she approves of him and knows his connections, I'll be satisfied."

My heart soared at her approval and I leaned forward to squeeze her hand again. "Oh thank you Stepmama! I know it's silly, but I truly am looking forward to making a new friend. He makes me laugh so much - it's rare to meet someone like that."

She squeezed my hand back before settling further down on her bed. "Yes my dear, that is quite rare, and not something to be passed up lightly. I'll be wanting to hear more about him in the morning, but for now I think I had better have some peace and quiet. Good night my girls."

Aria and I bid her goodnight quietly and stole out of the room. The second we closed the door my stepsister rounded on me with a huge smile. "A suitor! Is he handsome? Oh he must be to have turned your head so much!" I shushed her, grabbing her arm and dragging her down the hallway. We stopped outside my bedroom door and I drew a breath as I considered what to say.

"He's *not* a suitor, Aria, just a friend. Although I must admit that he *is* handsome…" Aria burst into giggles and I put my hands over her mouth, stifling the noise so it wouldn't disturb Stepmama. "Oh do be quiet! I can't help the fact that he's handsome, but it has nothing to do with me wanting to get to know him better. He's even more wonderful in who he is, you know, on the inside. Kind, and interesting, and witty… there's just something about him that's so intriguing!"

"Oh I see," Aria said in a mock serious tone. "You're saying he's handsome from the inside out!"

I rolled my eyes as she stifled another round of giggles. "Aria you are a menace right now - anyone would think you're a moon-eyed teenager!"

She rolled her eyes back at me. "None of us stop being moon-eyed teenagers, no matter how old we grow. Just think of Mama when she talks about my Papa or your father. She gets this look…" Aria shot a sly glance at me, "why, it's almost like the look you had when you were telling us about Luca!"

I threw my hands up in the air. "I don't know what you've

done with my sister, but this teasing harpy in front of me is not her! *Aria* can usually hold a conversation without bursting into a fit of giggles."

My sister gave me a placating look. "Fine, fine. It's just that we don't often get opportunities to tease you about men, so I have to take what I can get. I'm glad you've met someone... how did you describe him? Interesting?"

I rolled my eyes again, grabbing her shoulders and spinning her in the direction of her own bedroom before giving her a little push. "Off you go, little sister. You're obviously overtired from the stress of the day and need rest."

She started down the hall, spinning in the approximation of a waltz turn to give me one final cheeky grin as she replied, "Yes indeed, I'm happy to leave you to dream of your prince charming, sister dearest!"

I couldn't help laughing at her as I walked into my own room. My smile grew wider as I thought of the day, and there was a flutter in my chest as I thought of Luca. *A nobleman. Someone of my own rank, who can understand the importance of running an estate, and the duty involved in it.* I tried, and failed, to push down the sudden hopes dancing across my heart and brain. My eyes landed on my little writing desk and I hurried over to it. "If Stepmama is writing to Alessia, then so shall I - I want to know more about him before next week!" Biting my lip, I scratched down the first of my jumbled questions.

CHAPTER EIGHT

Luca

The first few days of classes flew by, and although we were all too busy for much fraternizing, I couldn't escape Alessia's pointed looks. Finally, she caught me alone in the library and cornered me near the understandably empty "history of taxation" section.

"You promised you would explain what's going on, Luca. I promised I wouldn't blow your cover, and even though I received letters asking about you from Ella and my mother, I've conveniently left out several key details so as not to break my promise. So I'm asking, what are your intentions with my stepsister?"

My heart stuttered into a new rhythm at the thought that Ella had been asking about me, but I refrained from asking further like a gushing schoolboy. Instead I laid a hand on Alessia's muscled shoulder.

"I've already told you, I just want to get to know her better. I promise that's all this is. And you have no idea how liberating it is to be known as just Luca."

Alessia gave me a sour look. "You know what's not liberating? Lying to your own family. My mother isn't a fool. She'll look into your lineage and family until she's sure you're an acceptable person for Ella to be around. And if she figures out that you're the *Crown Prince* and I haven't told her, how do you think that will look?!"

I grimaced. "I'm not asking you to lie - I'd never ask you to besmirch your knightly honor that way. Just keep back a few things as long as you're able, that's all."

"You have to *promise* that you'll tell Ella who you really are, and soon," she insisted.

"I certainly wouldn't want her finding out from anyone else," I reassured my friend, dropping my hand from her shoulder and gesturing toward the bookshelf. "Now, how about helping me find the volumes I need for my Statecraft Class?"

She wrinkled her nose at me, "No thanks - I'm still annoyed at you for drawing me into a web of deception. You can find your tax books on your own."

I huffed a laugh as she spun around and disappeared behind the next row of books. Our conversation reminded me that I only had one more day to get through before I could see Cinderella again, and that thought pushed me to get my work done even faster than normal.

❧ ❧ ❧

Percivale whinnied as I finished securing him to a tree near the spring. I patted his nose, then began pulling off the picnic I had packed in my saddlebags.

I spread a blanket on a patch of grass near the ruins - what was left of an old watchtower, probably from the wars of succession over a thousand years ago now. It's rough hewn stones lay scattered about, but much of the walls still stood proudly. Although winter's chill hung in the air, it was warm enough in the canopy of the trees that I didn't think we would need a fire.

My ears strained, and I couldn't help listening for Cinderella's approach above the burbling water from the spring, the rustling of the leaves, and the creaking of the enormous tree trunks. I had rearranged the food and plates ten different ways before the sound of hoof beats reached my ears, making my heart jump to my throat. Heart in my throat, I shot to my feet and a moment later Cinderella flashed into view, dressed in the same riding habit as before and perched atop her horse, Heartfire. My mouth went dry at the sight of her, a wave of doubt that I would be able to keep her interest long enough to even finish our meal sweeping over me.

She broke into a radiant smile and my nerves dissipated instantly. *This is why she won't leave my mind - she wears joy like a cape.* Still grinning, I moved forward to help her down, her compact frame light under my hands as I supported her to the ground. She didn't meet my eyes for a moment, busying herself with securing her mount, but my insides warmed as I caught sight of a flush around her neck. *She's just as affected as I am by our nearness,* I thought with equal parts wonder and triumph.

When she finally turned back to me, I offered her my arm and a courtly bow. "May I escort the Lady to her forestly feast?"

She accepted with a laugh, and I tucked her hand under my elbow greedily.

"I don't believe I've ever had a forestly feast before so I'm interested to see what's included. I'm half expecting a selection of tree bark and pond water."

I grinned. "I hate to disappoint, but it's mainly meat pasties and a crock of fresh fruit I was able to beg off one of the cooks at the Academy kitchens. The only forestly thing about it is the setting."

She smiled up at me as I helped her settle onto the blanket and I froze, blinking into seafoam green eyes, and absently noting a spray of freckles across her nose and cheeks. *Each one looks like a kiss from the sun.*

I dropped her hand gently, hoping she hadn't been able to read my wayward thoughts and turned to take my own seat.

"Thank you anyway," she said, arranging her cloak to fall around her shoulders without getting in the way while we ate. I handed her a plate filled with food and we each tucked in with gusto, exchanging pleasantries as we ate. As we finished, our conversation turned toward the ruins beside us.

"I never knew these were here," Ella admitted. "The first time I ever stepped foot in the forest was when I came to deliver the horses last week." She turned to smile at me mischievously. "Perhaps that's a good thing. If I had known about some tumble-down castle ruins as a girl I would have sneaked away as often as possible to explore them!"

I laughed. "Let's make up for lost time and explore them now. I've passed them every year for the last four years and never stopped to have a look." Pushing up off the ground I offered my hand again. She put her plate aside, pulled her riding gloves back over her fingers, and placed hers in mine. The thin leather of her gloves was soft against my skin, but I couldn't help wishing she hadn't put them back on at all. With a gentle tug from me, she sprang up lightly, smiling her thanks before turning toward the tumbledown wall closest to us, hiking up her skirt so she could hop over it. Her eagerness was infectious and I followed quickly, half expecting the latent magic of the Spindalian forest to spring to life under the effects of her pure heart.

Blasphemy now? Mother and Father will regret sending me to Deerbold Academy no matter how much our relations with Spindle are strengthened if you let these thoughts out. I followed the swish of Ella's skirts around the corner of another wall, letting my bare fingers trail along the rough stone of the wall to my right. *I wonder what Ella would think of such things - would she be flattered that I associate growth magic with her, or disgusted by the taint of such a thing, as most pious Charmagnians would do?* Deep in my thoughts I almost ran into her as I rounded yet another wall.

"Oh excuse me!" She exclaimed as I caught her by her arms. She smiled up into my eyes. "I was just coming to make sure you were with me - look what I found!" She turned away and I reluctantly let her go, my eyes following where her hand pointed.

A shock of white hellebore flowers grew under and around a crumbling window frame, which overlooked a perfectly maintained drinking well with a picturesque wooden roof. It made a lovely scene.

"I'm can't believe these are blooming in the winter," Ella said, bending to snap off one of the blossoms. "They're beautiful." She spun around and tucked the flower into a buttonhole on my dark blue overcoat, taking me by surprise. "There, now you look like the hero in one of those romantic novels popular in the capitol," she said with a laugh. I looked down at the white flower, stark against my dark coat.

"Do you read many romantic novels?" I asked, curious.

She made a face. "Not as many as I'd like, I never seem to have the time! But my friend Gia does. She's getting married in the summer so she says they're good inspiration." Ella laughed again. "As much fun as those stories can be, I always have trouble seeing myself in them. They don't write many novels where the Prince swoops in to sweep the maiden off her feet while she's mending fences or pulling weeds. Usually the maiden is doing something maidenly and virtuous like sewing or singing." She paused. "Come to think of it, that sounds exactly like my stepsister Aria. She's beautiful enough to be the fair maiden in a love story."

My eyebrows shot up as I looked at the beautiful woman in front of me. *What about Ella? Her pale green eyes - they could hypnotize even the most hard hearted of villains in a fairtyale, let alone the hero.*

"You can't believe that you're not - " I stuttered out but she cut me off, holding up her hands and giving me a wry look.

"I'm not fishing for compliments, don't worry! I'm quite happy with how I look." Her expression turned sly. "But tell me the truth, have you read many romantic novels?"

I opened my mouth to respond, a lie on my lips, but the truth dropped out before I could stop myself. "Yes actually, I've borrowed several from Briar Rose. They're quite good," I replied with a sheepish grin.

"Yes they are, aren't they?!" She agreed with a smile. "But think back to all the ones you've read. What do the heroines look like?"

I thought back to the novels I had read. "Well, it depends. Most of the Charmagnian ones have blonde hair and blue eyes, but the Spindalian ones usually have dark hair and eyes."

"Exactly, not a red haired heroine among them." She shrugged and turned away to look at the flowers again. "We're too busy running the world to be bothered waiting around for a prince to save us from hard work."

A laugh burst out at her joke, not just because I adored her no nonsense attitude, but the ridiculousness of our situation. *You should tell her who you are - she'd probably laugh even more.* My smile swept off my face and I squashed the thought down. *Not yet, I want to enjoy being just Luca for a little while longer.* I looked down at the flower in my buttonhole, wondering if she would have dared treated me so familiarly if she knew who I was. Ella's skirts swished in the corner of my vision and I followed as she turned another corner in the ruins. Before I knew it, she had disappeared through a doorway, shrouded in shadows. When she didn't pop her head out again right away, I stepped through the door as well, finding myself alone in a dank spiral stone staircase. Ella was no where in sight.

"Ella? Are you alright?" I called, stepping to peer around the bottom of the stairs in case she went to look in the dark space beyond.

"Yes, fine!" Her voice floated from above, muffled slightly by the stone.

"Did you go up these stairs?" I called back in disbelief.

Her laugh sounded like a bell. "Yes - come up and look!"

I shook my head and turned toward the wide, crumbling steps, muttering a prayer to the White King as I put my weight on the first one.

Somehow I made it to the top, stepping out onto a reasonably sturdy landing, which opened into a small room, one wall of which had crumbled almost completely away, although the other walls still seemed fine. Ella knelt in the middle, poking the ashes contained in a makeshift fire pit. *That looks as though it has seen frequent use.* She turned back to me with a grin.

"Can you guess what I'm doing?" she asked, and I moved to join her.

"It's not a forge so it won't have ever gotten hot enough to prove our theory," I replied, pulling a stick from a nearby stack of firewood and pushing the ash around as well. A puff of cinders shot into the air as our two sticks collided, some of which landed on our sleeves.

"My name seems to suit you," I teased, setting down my stick and reaching out to brush the soot from her red jacket.

She rolled her eyes and held still as I swept the last of it off her. She snagged my arm and helped clean my sleeves as well. "If I'm Cinderella than you must be Cinderluca," she teased back.

"Only when I'm with you," I accused, "I'm usually quite civilized otherwise!"

Her hand stilled on my arm and I could feel the weight of her touch through the layers of clothes. "I find it hard to believe that the only time you pursue your curiosity or get dirty has been the few times you've been in my presence. I'm sure your parents aren't spending all that money sending you to Deerbold without you having the chance to break out of the stuffy rules of the capitol every now and again!"

She continued brushing at my sleeve, a slight frown marking her brown. The urge to smooth it away loosened my lips.

"My time at Deerbold has been some of the best years of my life, actually. Mainly because of what you said - I can get dirty and and pursue my interests without having to worry about the pressures of … of my family duty." I admitted.

Ella glanced up, sympathy filling her eyes and marking her forehead even stronger. "I know exactly what you mean - about the pressures of family duty. It can be a burden at times, and difficult to carry alone. I hope you have family and friends that support you like I do. And I suppose I should be grateful that I don't have to worry about fulfilling the expectations of convention at Lucedimora. No one there even raises an eyebrow when I turn up dusty and dirty from whatever job needs doing."

The corner of my mouth turned up into a smirk. "Surely your prince charming will raise an eyebrow or two to find you in such a state whenever he comes along!"

Ella scoffed, "He's welcome to raise as many eyebrows as he likes whenever he chooses to dignify me with his presence - so long as he gets off his high horse to help mend the fences."

We both burst out laughing, my face hurt from smiling so much. As we got to our feet, Ella looked around the room.

"It looks like someone has been coming here to use this fire recently. I wonder why they've come up here? Surely it would be warmer downstairs, where it's more enclosed?"

I followed her gaze, puzzling over the location of the fire pit. It's true that it would be warmer near the base of the staircase. In this room, not only was there a downdraft from the staircase that seemed to extend at least one more level up, but the wall that had crumbled away was facing northeast, ensuring that the room would receive prevailing winter winds at full blast.

"It is curious," I agreed, and shrugged my shoulders. "My only guess would be that some of the traders that use this route between Spindle and Charmagne use these ruins as a waypoint in their travels. Maybe the Charmagnian ones that don't quite feel comfortable enough to sleep a night under the auspices of the headmistresses. Their guards probably put them up in this room to make it easier to manage their security during the night."

Ella looked thoughtful. "They must fear magic very much to not risk being tainted while staying at such a comfortable place as Deerbold. Alessia says the headmistresses often host travelers, and hold hospitality as a cardinal virtue."

I nodded. "It's one of the tenets of the code of chivalry all of us knights are encouraged to live by. And I happen to agree with it wholeheartedly."

A shiver shook Ella's frame and she wrapped her cloak around her shoulders tightly. "I would much rather spend the night at Deerbold rather than in the middle of these trees. They seem a little too sentient for their own good, if that makes any sense."

I leaned in closer, the scent of dusty stone and wood ash mixing with linen starch from her clothes. "I would advise not voicing your displeasure so loudly, if that's how you feel. They might hear you, you know."

A bark of laughter escaped her lips and her hand snaked out from under her cloak to smack my arm. Sparks skittered in my chest in response to her touch and I caught her hand, tucking it under my arm quickly. She stepped closer to my side, shaking her head as she smiled up at me.

We passed out of the old room together and onto the first of the spiral stairs, her warmth at my side thoroughly distracting. "Well my lady, since you've been impressed by the sentient trees and the tumbledown tower, may I interest you in the overgrown courtyard next?" Her chuckle echoed in the stairwell, throwing audible sunshine into the shadowy places and warming me from the inside out.

We spent the next hour going over the rest of the ruins, discovering unexpected corners and making each other laugh. Her warmth drew my soul out to rest, and I couldn't help finding ways to touch her whenever I could: holding her hand as she climbed over old wall foundations, tucking her arm in mine as we crept through narrow hallways, offering assistance in wiping off cobwebs and dust once we were out in the open again. She was so alive and magnetic and sure of who she was that I couldn't help wanting to be close to her.

When the sun began sinking into the tree line, I suggested that I escort her home again.

"There's no need," she protested, bending over to help clean up the remains of our earlier picnic. I finished loading the crockery into my saddlebag and attached it to Percivale, then turned to help her fold the blanket.

"I'm perfectly capable of riding home on my own. It's less than an hour ride." She paused as we brought the corners of the blanket together, her eyes distant for a moment before handing over her corners to me and bending to pick up the ones hanging down. "Now that I think about it, I wonder who lived at this castle, back when it was functional. My family must have fought them during the border wars." She gave me a prim look as we finished the last fold. "The Fenice family used to be very important hundreds of years ago you know. We defended the only valley through the Alpesian Mountains. It's down to us that our borders aren't smaller - at least on this side of the country. I bet we defeated whoever lived here so badly they surrendered and left their castle for ruin!"

I smiled and lowered my voice. "Again, maybe you don't want to say that so loudly - some of these trees might be old enough to remember, and I doubt they're Charmagnian sympathizers."

She chuckled and turned toward her horse. "Fair point, Luca. And now I think I *will* take you up on your offer of an escort - at least until the edge of the forest. I don't want the trees getting any ideas."

I hustled to stuff the blanket into my other saddlebag, then jogged over to Heartfire and offered my hands as a mounting block for Ella. She smiled her thanks and stepped into my joined hands, steadying herself on my shoulder as she stepped up and over the saddle. Heartfire hardly shifted at all under her slight frame, and I turned toward my own horse.

After seeing her off at the tree line once again, I pushed Percivale into a gallop, letting him stretch his legs on the relatively smooth path back to Deerbold. My heart felt light enough to float away after such an afternoon. *And she agreed to see me again next Saturday.* I only hoped I could concentrate on my lessons in the meantime.

CHAPTER NINE

Ella

I held still as Aria tucked the ends of my braided crown in and secured them with a few well anchored hairpins. My stepsister had appointed herself my lady's maid on Saturdays whenever Luca and I were meeting - which was most Saturdays in the last few months. Other than one weekend when he was scheduled to do field exercises with his martial arts class, and one where I simply couldn't get away from overseeing the plowing; we had continued to meet in the forest. Often we kept to the ruins, eating a picnic lunch and exploring at our leisure, or just sitting and chatting on the blanket. More recently we had explored along the forest a little more - our last such outing having revealed a beautiful sunny spot on the bank of a creek.

"I'm thinking of taking Giuseppe's fishing tackle," I announced to Aria, who craned her head around mine to meet my eyes in the mirror. "Why would you do a thing like that? He loves fishing!"

I let out a peal of laughter. "Not like that! I meant I'm thinking of borrowing it. I could take it to my next... my meeting with Luca next week. Today we're going on an outing in Spindalian village, but next week we're having lunch by a little creek and there's a prime spot for fishing there."

Aria chuckled as she re-focused on my hair. "That sounds

more like you. But why do you want to lug fishing gear all the way into the forest? Does Luca like fishing?"

"I guess I'll find out," I replied, fighting a grin. "Most gentlemen do, don't they? Or at least they pretend to when they're at their country houses." Aria's tinkling laugh sounded softly from behind my head.

"You're thinking of Lord Ricarlo's son," she accused, referencing one of the few noblemen who spent time at the country seats near our house. He was a few years older than us, and had attempted to court Aria off and on through the years, to no avail. He often talked about how much he enjoyed various "gentlemanly" sports, although we had never heard of him participating in any of them yet. "From the sounds of things Luca is a very different sort of man."

"Yes, I think I can say he's quite different. But he can be… not stuffy, but sort of conventional. Not in himself, but just in the way he lives his life. He's doing everything that's expected of a nobleman, and quite right since he'll have to take care of his own estates, but sometimes I like to shock him with my wayward ideas. A woman fishing should do the trick, don't you think?"

Aria squeezed my shoulder and stepped away to pick up my riding hat. "I think you have a very peculiar way of flirting," she replied as she began fixing my hat over my hair at a fetching angle. My eyes jumped to her reflection but she studiously focused on her task, failing to hide her smile. I watched an inevitable blush steal across my face in the mirror.

"If fishing is flirting, I have a lot of questions about those sporting trips the other gentry arrange during the summer," I quipped, earning another laugh from Aria.

"There now, you look perfectly elegant for whatever you choose to do," she replied, "flirting, fishing, or otherwise."

I pulled her into a quick hug. "Thank you for your help. My hair always ends up falling halfway out by the time I return anyway, but at least I look presentable for the first hour or so!"

Aria hugged me back then turned away. "I'll go make sure Mama is up so you can say goodbye before you leave."

I followed her out of the room. "I just have to run up and feed the doves. I'll stop by her room on the way down." Aria turned off the main upstairs passageway to knock on her mother's door while I continued down the passage and into the ancient square tower in the corner of our keep. I left the door propped open to allow through what meager light felt bold enough to venture in behind me - hardly enough to see by. I knew my way by feel, so I managed not to bump into the odd tables and chairs placed along the walls as I passed by doors to the old chapel, the library, and our disused guest chamber, before making it to the spiral stone staircase that thread it's way from top to bottom of the ancient tower. Light filtered into the staircase through arrow slits, and I was reminded of the crumbling tower Luca and I explored on our first meeting in the forest.

Our explorations had sparked my curiosity about the ruins, and I had spent many spare hours combing through the dusty archives that comprised at least three quarters of our library. At last I had found mention of the castle across the border - Weacombe. It belonged to someone referred to as the Duchy of the North in Spindle, which I had read about in other treatises squirreled away in our archives. Although we didn't have any surviving records from the time, several of our family histories recount stories of the Fenice family having fought directly with the evil Duchess of the North during those wars, of besieging Weacombe and having held the line quite spectacularly. *So strange to think of that crumbling tower as a thriving bastion of war, beset against my own castle stronghold. Now Weacombe is in ruins and Lucedimora is a dusty provincial outpost, hardly remembered by those in power.*

I mounted the last step to the third floor of the tower and stepped into a long sitting room full of light. When Lucedimora was a place of war, I doubted that there had been so many windows, but sometime in the intervening centuries, one of my ancestors had installed a large number of floor to ceiling windows at intervals on three of the room's walls. According to a floor plan I had found, this room used to be the family's solar, although now it was a combination of sitting area, storage room, and sleeping area when the days were too hot to sleep downstairs. When I was younger I used to come up here to read and nap in the sun on winter days, but for the last few years there had been precious little time for that. I hurried by the frayed divan and stacks of boxes and into the old fashioned dovecote.

The dovecote occupied a corner of the top of the tower and had been abandoned for several generations before I took a fancy to keeping doves when I was a teenager. Father had helped me clean and repair the roosts and establish a little family of doves, and I had kept them ever since. After Alessia went to to Deerbold it had become our only way of regular communication, since we couldn't often find someone willing to carry mail into Spindle. Our messages had to be quite short to accommodate the doves' small carrying cases, but it was nice to know we could say hello.

I swept into the dovecote, holding my skirts up so that they wouldn't brush any of the inevitable mess on the floor. Carefully shutting the door behind me, I quickly set about refilling the food troughs while fending off the friendly birds as they flew down to greet me.

"Off you go Graywing," I scolded one bird. "I'm in a rush today," I added more gently as I pulled him off of my shoulder and set him down by the food trough. A few others landed in front of me and I couldn't help saying hello to each of them.

"I'm going to see Luca again," I confided in my feathered friends. "So I can't stay and chat." I shooed the last of them toward the food and picked my way back out, dashing through the door and shutting it firmly behind me.

Making my way back down the tower and into the family wing, I tread softly to my stepmother's bedroom, entering quietly after Aria responded to my knock.

She and my stepmother were seated in two chairs before a roaring fire, and I was surprised to see my stepmother turn to me with a smile.

"Ella darling, I hear you're going out to meet with that young Master Luca," she said, stretching her hand out to me. I paced forward and took it, squeezing it for a moment and giving her a warm smile.

"I'm glad to see you out of bed Stepmama!" She squeezed my hand back before letting go and picking up the embroidery she was working on.

"Yes, I'm feeling much better today, although still a little weak." She glanced up at me with a look of mock censure, "If I continue healing at this rate you can expect a chaperone on your next outing with your young man!"

I laughed, ignoring her comment about my "young man". "You would be welcome to come any time, of course."

She waved me away with a tired smile. "I wouldn't interrupt your one opportunity for a little flirting my dear, don't worry. Now off you go. I'll want to hear all about it when you get back."

"Then I'd better get going so I'm home to amuse you with my tales before you miss me." With a wave I practically skipped out the door to her room, happy to see her feeling better and full of excitement for the day ahead.

❈ ❈ ❈

My ride to our meeting place sped by in a flash, the sun warm on my face and the air around me full of promise. Luca was already there, as usual, but this time we had company. Alessia, Briar Rose, and Raleigh were standing near their horses. They had obviously been talking but were now looking in my direction, welcoming smiles on their faces.

"Hello!" I called, giving my sister an extra warm smile and trying to not to let my eyes slide over to Luca.

"No, don't bother dimsounting," she called back to me as I moved to get down from my horse. "The village isn't far. Let's ride over now and get some lunch first thing!"

I grinned as she mounted up and walked her horse over next to mine. "Luca said you all go to the Vernal Equinox Festival in this village every year. I confess I'm a little nervous at the amount of magic it sounds like they perform openly."

Alessia gave me a repressive look. "Oh Ella, just relax. They're good people. We've been going there for years. They know some of us are foreigners so they don't bother us."

I shrugged. "I know that! It will just be very odd, that's all." I nodded toward Briar Rose who was mounting up behind Raleigh. "Doesn't she have her own horse? I thought she was the ward of the Headmistresses. I'm sure they bought one for her."

Alessia glanced over and shrugged. "Briar Rose isn't much of a one for riding actually. She has one of the best mares in the stabl. Truesight, her name is. One of the first ones your father sold the headmistresses I believe. But Briar Rose took her out yesterday to ride the bounds with the Benefactor so she didn't want to strain her even more today. She's getting old."

I gave Alessia a puzzled look. "Weren't there any other mounts available?"

She rolled her eyes, lowering her voice as Luca mounted and the others came toward us. "Yes, but she doesn't like riding any other horses - she only likes Truesight. And to be honest, she and Raleigh are two peas in a pod. They like doing everything together. It's so annoying sometimes - especially when they're bickering like today."

I laughed and looked back over at our companions. Sure enough, as they came into earshot, I could hear Raleigh complaining to the young woman seated behind him. "You know Carrots adores you and would never act up. I offered to let you have him today but you insisted on riding double so I'm not that interested in complaints over how I'm holding the reins."

"I'm not *complaining* about how you're holding the reins, I'm *correcting* how you're holding the reins. If you just move your elbows a little more - " she nudged his elbows slightly, although I couldn't see any change in posture on Raleigh's end, "There. Isn't that better?"

"No!" He replied with a shake of his head. "It's exactly the same as before."

Briar Rose rolled her eyes behind his back. "Nuance is lost

on you. It's better for me, anyway, and Carrots too I'm sure." The horse snorted in seeming agreement, earning a glare from Raleigh.

Luca cut in before the bickering could continue. "Allright children. Now that our guest is here, let's behave." He flashed a mischievous grin my way as Briar Rose and Raleigh began a series of protests. Luca motioned to me and Alessia before turning his horse back down the forest path. "Sorry children, I can't hear you - do try and keep up!" He called back as he urged his horse into a trot. Alessia and I shared a grin and made to follow him.

After a short ride through the forest, we came upon a clearing dotted with timber framed cottages, one small timber chapel at one end, and a dearth of colorful tents covering every open space right up to the tree lined edges. Campfires smoked next to some stalls selling food. Fiddles and flutes filled the air with cheerful melodies, and to one side of the village couples danced in a line.

Luca came over immediately to help me dismount. Although I was perfectly capable of doing so on my own, I had to admit that I looked forward to his assistance every week when we met. His shoulders were strong under my hands - his hands on my waist sent flutters through my stomach. As he lifted me down, I felt as light as a feather, catching the ghost of scent mingling with his skin - bergamot and sandalwood.

"Hello Cinderella." He grinned down at me, his wide smile almost too charming to be real.

"Hello," I echoed, slightly dazed and fresh out of any witty responses. A second later I realized I still had my hands on his shoulders even though my feet were firmly planted on the ground, and his hands were still on my waist. Snatching them away as if I were on fire, I attempted to disguise my lapse in thinking ability by turning to grab Heartfire's reins. Luca's hands dropped away too, and I attempted to quell the butterflies in my stomach as we all secured our horses in a nearby temporary stable.

"So, where do you usually go first?" I asked the group once our horses had been settled.

"I'm starving for venison skewers from the Huntsman's stall," Alessia announced. "I've been dreaming of them since the last festival." Luca nodded as Alessia looked at me. "He usually has a bunch of different kinds of skewers but the spicy ones are my favorite - you have to try them!"

"Sounds delicious!" I said in agreement. Luca held out his arm and I took it, feeling my face heat to be so close to him. After a moment, he offered his other arm to Alessia, who stared at it and then laughed oddly.

"I'm no Lady, Luca. I think we all know that." She turned away and started toward the Huntsman's stall.

Luca paused to look back at Raleigh and Briar Rose. "Are you two coming?"

They shared a glance. "I'm not really that hungry. Would you rather go see the wares at the tinker's stall right now?" Briar Rose asked Raleigh.

"That suits me, prickly Briar, or is it it sweet Rose now?" he answered in a teasing tone and offered his arm.

"You're incorrigible," she replied as she took his arm with a familiar ease and gave us a smile. "We'll catch up with you in a little while." They turned away and ambled into the crowd, Raleigh's head bent toward Briar Rose as they conversed steadily.

I looked up at Luca. "They seem very hot and cold together," I said, nodding toward the retreating pair.

He crooked a smile, "*Very* hot and cold. And everything in between. Not the sort of relationship I would thrive in, but I couldn't imagine one without the other."

"Are they betrothed?" I asked, furrowing my brow. I thought Alessia would have written with such news, and worried that I had missed a chance to offer congratulations. *I hope they don't think I'm rude.*

"No, no. And don't mention such a thing near them. I committed such a folly at the beginning of the semester and ended up being thrashed in a bout on the fighting green by Raleigh for my impudence." He grinned down at me, seeming oddly happy about losing a fight.

"Surely not! What a terrible thing to do to a friend!" I protested.

He tipped back his head to laugh, his muscles jumping under my hands. "Not at all," he replied, still grinning. "It's the most fun way to settle an argument between friends that I can think of. Besides, I was so mad at being beaten, I stomped my way over the stables to run my horse, and what do you think I found instead?"

I wrinkled my nose. "Briar Rose, ready to thrash you again for attempting to thrash Raleigh?"

Luca let out another laugh, and I couldn't help joining in, glad that I was able to make him smile. "Not exactly, although I would have loved to see her try. No, I found something much better." He grabbed my free hand with his and brought my fingers up to his lips. "After years of searching, I found my Cinderella," he said, pressing a gentle kiss to my knuckles. I swallowed heavily as he settled my hand on top of his arm, keeping it there with his own. *Oh **why** didn't I take off my riding gloves,* I berated myself. *What would Stepmama say if she knew what you were thinking?!*

I cleared my throat as delicately as I could. "Well, next time you lose me, I hope you try thrashing Raleigh as a restorative rather faster. Ten years seemed a long time you know."

Luca laughed again and tugged me forward. Alessia was no where in sight, but the village wasn't large so we caught up to her at the Huntsman's stall in a few minutes.

A pretty young woman with pale skin and dark hair was handing her a packet of skewers, her cheeks apple red from the heat of the cookfire. Behind her stood a man with sandy hair and a face as hardened as hers was open.

"I'm guessing he's the huntsman," I whispered to Luca, who snorted next to me.

"I'd wager that Snow hasn't hunted a day in her life," he replied, nodding at the woman. "But the huntsman would never sell anything if he operated the stall on his own. He's not exactly welcoming, as you've already noticed."

I glanced his way again, a chill going down my spine as I noticed his hard eyes on me. I offered a tight smile. *I wouldn't like to know what happened to make him that way. Although...* I glanced back at Snow, who was nodding at something Alessia was saying. *Whatever brought them together would be a a story I **would** like to hear.* I watched them as Alessia and Snow chatted while Snow continued selling food. Although she and huntsman never spoke a word, they seemed to move with one accord, as if their focus was on each other, not the tasks they were doing.

Alessia finally noticed us as we stepped up to take our turn. "Finally," she said, craning her neck to look behind us. "Where are Raleigh and Briar Rose?"

"They wanted to go to the tinker's stall instead," Luca said, then smiled at Snow and waved to the huntsman who nodded back.

"I got you a spicy venison one, but if you're hungry you should try the vegetable ones too," Alessia said, gesturing toward the cooked skewers resting on the side of the cookfire.

"I always recommend the vegetable ones, milady," Snow said, smiling sweetly at me. "It seems most people prefer the meat, but I promise you'll love it if you try it!"

"We'll have two venison ones and two vegetable ones," Luca told her. She turned to wrap up our order as Luca bent his head closer to mine. "We can come back if you want more, but there are so many other stalls here that you'll want to try, just wait!"

We ate our skewers as we walked. They were amazing, but so was all the other food we tried. Now and again we would run into other cadets enjoying their day off at the festival. We always seemed to just miss Raleigh and Briar Rose, finally spotting them among the whirling couples on the dancing green.

"They look like they're having fun," I observed, watching with a smile on my face as the pair slowed to a stop and clapped for the musicians with the others.

"Would you like to dance?" Luca asked, making my heart jump into my throat. I glanced at Alessia, who crooked up the corner of her mouth.

"Don't mind me, I'd prefer to sit instead. Off you go."

I set my bag down next to her and turned back to Luca and nodded nervously. He lead me toward a corner of the green just as the music started again for a new dance.

"Thankfully this one is simple, nodding toward some of the dancers who had already started up again.

"Well it sounds like - yes it is," I exclaimed, watching the others in relief. "It's just like a country dance I've seen at our own village. Similar music too."

We grinned at each other as we traced the movements together a time or two. I had to adjust two step changes, which were the opposite of the dance I was familiar with, but our occasional fumbling missteps just made us laugh all the more. The sun began to set in earnest as we progressed around the green, and by the time the dance was over, twinkling lamps lit up all at once, mirroring the stars beginning to appear in the sky above.

"How beautiful!" I gasped, staring around in wonder.

"I know," Luca replied softly, but I could feel that his eyes weren't on the lanterns. A flush swept across my face and every nerve tingled. I turned to meet his eyes, my mouth suddenly dry at the serious look on his face.

"There you are!" Raleigh's voice boomed across the floor, causing Luca and me to both take a step back as his missing friends came into view. "We haven't seen you all day!"

"It's getting late," interjected Briar Rose at his side, looking with concern at me. I smiled back, trying to meet her blue, *or are they green?*, eyes, but her distractingly perfect golden hair drew my gaze instead. *How can her hair stay so perfect all day?* I lifted a hand to my own hair surreptitiously. As expected it was half tumbled down, and I tried to tuck a few wisps back into my braid.

"I'll escort her home," Alessia said, walking up behind Raleigh and Briar Rose, both our bags on her shoulder. I reached out to take mine as Luca protested that we could all escort me home.

"No it's fine. The stablemaster said I could take tomorrow off to go home, so I'll ride back tomorrow afternoon. I wasn't able to visit over winter soltice so it would be nice to see my mother and sister.

"Allright," Luca said, sounding a little crestfallen. I felt the same. As happy as I was to have Alessia coming home for a day, my mind raced to find a reason to extend my time with Luca. There wasn't one of course. *Be grateful for extra time with your family. This isn't a romance novel - and you and Luca aren't ... well anything more than friends at this point.*

I glanced up as Luca took my bag from me, slinging it over one shoulder. *If we hadn't been interrupted maybe ... oh I don't know, maybe **something** would have happened!*

I tamped down the breathless mixture of frustration and happiness I felt as we walked back to our horses. Our group was quiet except for the ever chattering Briar Rose and Raleigh. After a long day their constant noise grated on my ears.

All too soon Luca was helping me mount Heartfire. We ambled down the forest path until it split, waving goodbyes as we went our separate ways: the cadets back to Deerbold, Alessia and myself back to Lucedimora. For the first time ever, I wished that maybe I wasn't going back to Lucedimora that night after all.

CHAPTER TEN

Luca

The thump of my boots on wooden stairs rang loudly in the quiet of my dorm. If I'm not quick I'm going to be late for our last drill before finals. I practically flew down the long hallway on the first floor, my footsteps slapping heavily against the stone floor while I mentally checked that I had all my gear again. I wasn't nervous about passing our martial arts final. I'd been training for military service since I was young, after all. But I wanted to get the best score possible, not only for my own satisfaction, but to do my country proud as well.

Ella's face flashed across my mind and I smiled. Even though I knew she wouldn't be there to watch our finals, I wanted to impress her too. She's usually the one who impressed me with her strength and ingenuity. *Both characteristics that would make her a perfect queen.* My throat felt dry at the thought. Not the thought of her as my queen, but the obstacles my family would present, and the tiny, niggling sense of doubt that she wouldn't want to *be* my queen after all. And the darker corner of my mind, whispering that she would be all to happy to be queen once she found out who I was... if she didn't know already and was playing a long game like all the other courtiers.

I pressed my lips together and stamped that thought out of my mind. Ella wasn't like that. If anything, from the half heretical things she said, I would have my hands full convincing her to actually join the royal family. She loved *me*, not my position. That though brought a smile to my lips and a little more bounce to my step. *I have to make her mine, and soon.*

I pushed the door open a little too forcefully as I rushed outside, lunging and just barely catching it before it smacked Alessia in the face.

"Sorry!" I gasped with a shocked laugh. She glared at me and shook her head, waiting as I closed the door more gently behind me.

"We aren't at drill practice yet, Luca. Knocking me out with a door isn't going to get you any points."

I laughed again as she cracked a smile too. We fell into a quick step together, heading toward the practice yards. I hadn't seen her almost all week. All of us cadets were busy with last minute assignments, extra practice sessions, and preparations for leaving. Those of us who were graduating had even more things to take care of as we got ready to move into the "real" world. None of it left much time for socializing.

Alessia glanced over at me, her face serious again. "I've been meaning to ask you…" she trailed off, looking uncomfortable.

"What is it?" I prompted, steeling myself for an uncomfortable conversation. I thought I knew what she was going to ask.

"Since I haven't received a message from Ella demanding to know why I didn't tell her you're the Crown Prince, I'm assuming you haven't told her." She looked sideways at me, but I kept my eyes on the gravel path in front of us.

"No, I haven't told her yet. But I will. Soon."

"You said that months ago, Luca. We're running out of time. She deserves to know before you leave for good."

I pressed my lips together again, then grabbed her arm and pulled her to a stop. "I'll tell her this Saturday. I was planning to anyway. I can't exactly ask her to - " I stopped myself just in time and hastened to cover up my almost confession. Alessia opened her mouth to ask me a question I didn't want to answer right now. Not when I didn't know what Ella's answer would be yet.

"I'll tell her. But right now we need to get to practice."

She took a breath to say something else but I started jogging toward the practice yards. We really were going to be late if we didn't hustle.

"You had better stick to your word, Princeling, or we are going to have problems!" she called after me. I ignored her as best I could. It was a little difficult since my heart agreed with her unspoken assessment of me - *coward.*

The crunch of boots sounded on gravel and I turned my head, expecting to see Alessia catching up to me, but she was standing where I left her, staring after me with a suspicious expression on her face. Instead, it was Raleigh who jogged up beside me, a questioning look on his expression.

"What was that all about?" He asked with a laugh. "You may want to spend an extra year at the academy preparing if you're inspiring more threats than devotion from your countrymen."

I huffed a laugh as we slowed down, heading towards the lockers on one side of the practice yards. "That's a complicated situation. Most of my countrymen aren't related to the woman I ... love." I fumbled over the words, my heart constricting as I spoke them out loud for the first time ever.

Raleigh wolf whistled. "Love is it? You did seem starry eyed when we went to the Spring Solstice. And maybe again at the May Day fair, but Briar Rose made me dance so much I didn't notice what you were up to." He grinned at me and I rolled my eyes at him.

If anyone could understand, he can. Taking a quick glance around to make sure no one was close enough to overhear, I lowered my voice to confide in him.

"You know I didn't tell Ella who I was at the beginning. Me being a prince, I mean."

Raleigh nodded. "I remember you warning us when we went to meet her at the Spring Fair. How did it go when you finally told her?"

"That's the thing... I haven't," I admitted with a grimace. His eyebrows shot up to his hairline.

"You haven't told her?" His voice carried a little and punched his shoulder as I shushed him.

"No! And keep your voice down. It's just… it's never seemed like the right time. When we're together, it feels like nothing else matters except the two of us… it's as close to magic as I'll ever come," I quirked a grin at him.

Raleigh rubbed the shoulder where I punched him thoughtfully. "I can relate to that. And being a prince can intrude on things in the most unlikely ways." He stared across the courtyard as he continued more seriously, and I glanced over to see Briar Rose passing across from the Headmistress' headquarters to the stables with quick strides.

"It's rare to find someone who sees beyond what the world thinks is important about you, and even rarer if that person loves you for what they see. You have to do anything to keep that person close."

"That's the problem," I grumbled. "I don't think Ella is going to be over the moon about becoming a princess. It's part of the reason I keep putting it off. I like just being me, and I just want to be sure that she'll love me enough to stand with me at court before I tell her…"

Raleigh re-focused on me with a laugh as Briar Rose disappeared into the stables. "She doesn't want to be a princess? No wonder Briar Rose likes her so much." He shook his head. "It's always the ones that are hard to get that won't leave your mind, huh." I nodded in heartfelt agreement as he continued. "But when are you going to tell her? She deserves to know before you ask her anything… permanent."

I sighed, strapping on my sword. "I know. I'm telling her this weekend. I can't exactly ask her to marry me without admitting what she'd be getting herself into, could I?"

Raleigh grinned at me while he finished strapping on his own sword. "Precisely. Now let me go beat your head in to get the message through, you romantic old fool."

I awoke to a pounding on my door that sounded in time to

the throbbing of my head. I groaned as I sat up, watching a letter slide under my door as I rubbed my temples. My body hurt all over from sparring with Raleigh and Alessia, the later of which seemed out for blood anytime we stepped onto the practice green for a match.

I perked up as my memory caught up with me. *Post means it's Saturday. Saturday means I'll be seeing Ella later.* I pushed myself heavily off the bed, downing a cup of water I always kept on my dresser at night in one swallow before trudging over to pick up my post. I groaned again as I looked at it.

One was very obviously correspondence from the palace, and the flourishes in the address looked like the handwriting of my mother's private secretary. I flipped it over to check the seal. It was my mother's. I sighed internally and broke open the bulky envelope. *She must have written a book.* Another envelope tumbled out from between the pages of my mother's letter, this one slim and ... I held it to my nose. *Rose scented?* I turned it over. The Litorale family seal was impressed on the wax holding it closed. My eyebrows shot up. *What is this doing in my mother's correspondence?* I set it down on my desk and turned my attention to my mother's letter, settling into my chair for what promised to be a long read.

Ten minutes later I threw the pages onto my desk in disgust. Besides some logistical instructions for the upcoming ball, she had spent the rest of the letter complaining about how inconsiderate I was for not officially proposing to Emilia before the ball, and then singing praises for the lady in question as well as her whole family. Not once had she expressed concern for me, or indicated that she missed me, or even congratulated me on graduating from the academy like a dutiful young prince. Instead her entire focus seemed to be on making sure I secured Emilia's hand as soon as possible since she was in such high demand among suitors at court. She added in a postscript that poor Emilia had been so eager to congratulate me on my graduation, and so concerned that she wasn't able to attend the occasion in person since it was in a dangerous mage country that she had encouraged Emilia to write me a note.

I turned toward the other envelope with something like dread in my chest. It was against courtly conduct for an unmarried lady to be writing to an unmarried man, so the fact that my mother had facilitated it didn't bode well.

Picking up the letter, I slid my hand under the seal, breaking it with a pop, and unfolding the note. It was thankfully short.

Dear Prince Luca,

*I hope I am not too forward in writing you, although your dear Mother, The Queen, assures me that our long acquaintance, and the ties our families have, would never make it unseemly. I took advantage of her offer as a means to offer you my heartfelt congratulations on your graduation from the academy. Our country will be overflowing with joy to have you home again, safe. My only regret right now is that our family could not come to the commencement ceremony in person. My wise Papa has declared it to be too dangerous for the likes of us ladies, being hosted in a country of magic-users. For my part, I would brave any fear I have for such a place and would bear with however many prayers of repentance our priest would find necessary to assign me in consequence. But I shall obey my dear Papa, as my duty as an unmarried daughter, though it keeps me from offering my support in person to those dearest to my heart. Once I am officially betrothed that duty would transfer to my intended, of course. Indeed, may I confess that I **do** have a few fears of that strange country you are in even now, as you read my letter? I shudder to think of crossing paths with magic users on a regular basis, and give thanks that our royal family has rid our borders of such people over the years. One would feel constantly on guard against them, never able to trust whether the person beside you had a true heart, or one filled with twisted magic. Your sister laughs at me, saying she wouldn't give a fig for any magic users that crossed her path, but I can only be honest about my own need for a hero to protect me. I admire the courage you must have after attending their school for four years - your sacrifice is for the betterment of your country. You have always borne your duty with such grace and strength, ever since we were* *children. May I be bold and say I speak for all our people, and those of my own duchy especially, that we are looking forward to celebrating your return in the majesty and splendor you deserve, and look forward to a golden future ahead of us?*

With all affection,
Lady Emilia Litorale

I threw the paper aside and it drifted down to sit atop my mother's letter as well. Her comments about magic users, the slight over the honor of the Headmistresses, the Benefactor, Prince Raleigh and his family - it was disgusting. *And not the words of a diplomatic Queen.* The future was increasingly dependent on good relationships with countries that permitted magic. The Litorale family had always been stringently vocal against such people. No doubt Emilia subscribed to one of the beliefs popular at court about marriage, that a wife would adopt only those beliefs that her husband chose to espouse, although how that view was reconciled with the Queen's own conduct, which was often in opposition to my father's, I could never fathom. And I couldn't quite imagine Emilia saying what Ella and I had often discussed - that although we still felt some degree of discomfort with magic, we couldn't judge magic-users as any inherently more evil than anyone else. If I married Emilia, even if she brought herself to say something similar in public, or at least not contradict me, I would know she fundamentally disagreed, and her judgment irked me. And her tone... she never said anything outright, but ever sentence seemed pointed to her expectation that we would be married, though I had never spoken to her about such a thing.

*It doesn't matter. You're not going to marry her. Ella will choose you, in spite of the duty that will place on her. She **will**.*

I turned to shove both letters into the fire, but stopped short. It was warm enough that we didn't need fires in our rooms, so the hearth was cold. Instead I shoved them into the bottom drawer of my desk, and set about preparing for the day, anticipation at my discussion with Ella beating irregularly in my chest.

Ella rode up only a few minutes after I finished setting up our usual picnic lunch. This time I had brought extra candles, setting them around the grotto near the old well, and spreading our blanket out nearby and putting the champagne in a shady corner to settle before we opened it. *Assuming all goes well. It **is** going to go well!*

I helped her down from her horse, my stomach twisting oddly as I tried not to stare. Her seafoam green riding habit made her light green eyes almost glow, and made the strands of gold in her reddish-blonde hair gleam brightly. I let go of her trim form as if she burned me, and she turned her eyes on me in concern.

"Luca, what is it? Has something happened?" she asked, brow wrinkled in sympathy as she stepped forward to take my hands. I swallowed heavily.

"Nothing's happened, at least not yet. I'm just a bit... nervous, that's all."

I watched her throat bob up and down and she squeezed my hands. "About leaving the academy? It will be a big change. If I'm honest, knowing it will take you away... it's not a change I'm welcoming, no matter that I'm supposed to be congratulating you right now." She offered an apologetic smile and I couldn't help answering it with one of my own. Hearing her say that she didn't want me to leave warmed my chest, soothing the nerves that plucked at my courage. *Now's the time. Tell her who you are.*

I tucked one of her hands under my arm and began leading her toward the picnic area I had set up. "Have you received your invitation to the royal ball?" I asked. *I can tell her that I'm the one hosting it.*

"Yes," she replied, smiling up at me, her face open and ingenuous. "I've confirmed my attendance. If I'm honest, I was hoping I would have a chance to see you there." She smiled wider and gestured to the formal military uniform I was wearing today. "Especially now that I see how nice you look in your uniform. It would be a treat to see you outshining the splendor of the court."

She paused and looked back up at me anxiously. "You are going, aren't you?"

My smile slid off my face as my nerves took over again. *What if she doesn't want to brave living life at court for you? Or worse, what if she changes once she realizes what she could have as the crown princess?*

She could obviously read my nerves on my face, because as I hesitated, she squeezed my arm in compassion. "You're so serious today. Is there something you need to tell me about? Or maybe..." she swallowed nervously, "maybe some*one*?"

I looked down at her in surprise, then understanding, pulling us both to stop before we rounded the corner to our picnic. "No, no!" I assured her with a laugh. "Although, I suppose you could say yes, in a way." Ella furrowed her brow but stood patiently, waiting for my explanation.

"My parents have been expecting me to marry someone for awhile now, but I'm under no obligation to marry her, and I've never led her to believe that I was interested... although," I hesitated, but my conscious forced me to honesty, "Emilia probably expects me to marry her too. Our families have discussed the expectation for so long, she's probably thinking it's inevitable. I was too, if it came to that, before..." I hesitated, my head and heart full of the woman in front of me.

She stood still, her lips parted slightly, eyes searching mine. "Before what?" she asked, her voice almost too quiet to hear.

"Before you," I answered, lifting my free hand up to trace a finger down her cheek. She closed her eyes at my touch, breathing in deeply. I let go of the hand I had tucked under my arm, framing her face gently with both of mine as I bent toward her. She tilted to meet me, eyes still closed. Our lips met gently, the moment of our first kiss stretching out infinitely as every fiber of my being seemed to align in the sweet rightness of the touch.

The bones of her face felt delicate under my fingers, her skin perfectly smooth and soft under the rasp of my callouses. My heart thrilled as her hands slid up my arms, resting gently on both my wrists before reaching across to frame my face, her bare hands smooth against the rasp of my stubble. I broke away after pressing several soft kisses to her lips, pulling her against my chest and pressing my cheek down on the top of her head.

"So this is what this feels like," I observed in wonderment.

"What?" She asked, pulling back slightly to look up at me, her eyes dazed.

"Love," I replied, feeling my face heat at my admission.

Her own skin flushed red and she smiled, her eyes full of hope.

I glanced over her shoulder toward where the picnic was set up, just out of view around the corner, then back down at Ella. "I want to ask you something, but first..." I swallowed, my thoughts scattered to the corners of the earth, the feeling that I was going to mess things up squeezing my breath as I focused on one goal - I had to make her mine.

"Oh don't do that," she protested, bouncing on her feet for a moment. "Don't make me wait. What do you have to ask me? Just ask!"

I smiled down at her eagerness, and forgetting my plans, gave in to her request, sinking down to one knee in front of her and capturing one of her hands. My breath caught in my throat and my nerves thrilled in excitement. "Ella, would you be my wife? I can't promise that we'll have smooth sailing all of our days, but I can promise that I'll love you with every breath I have left. I know I can't live without you by my side, and I promise to try and be worthy of being by your side."

Her eyes widened as a wide smile bloomed on her face. "Yes, of course!" she cried, before pressing a few more kisses to my lips, each as light as a butterfly. Her joy was dazzling, and she pulled me into a tight hug, forcing me off balance enough that I had to catch myself with one hand, while holding Ella steady with the other. She tipped her head back, letting out one of her carefree laughs, the sound of it drawing my soul out.

"Come on," I said as I got to my feet, tugging her forward toward our picnic. "Let's eat. Then we can ride to Lucedimora to get your stepmother's blessing - *if* I can get it." She smiled and danced a step ahead of me, twining her fingers in mine.

You didn't tell her, you idiot. I pushed that thought away. *It wasn't the right time. And let's just enjoy this happiness for now. You can deal with the rest after you get her stepmother's blessing.*

CHAPTER ELEVEN

Ella

The massive gate to the castle stood open wide as it usually did in the daytime. I grinned over at Luca, riding beside me as we approached my home. We slowed our horses in tandem, Heartfire tossing her mane in pride as she edged a little ahead of Luca and Percivale. I caught sight of Beatrice and Aria sitting on a bench in the shady little garden to the side of the living quarters, and I raised a hand in greeting as I lead the way to the stable. My stepmother and stepsister had been oddly solicitous of me in the last few days, not wanting to leave me on my own and constantly asking me how I was feeling. Maybe they could tell that something big was coming, just based off of my own feelings. I did try not to read too much into Luca's feelings, but I couldn't help falling in love anyway. As it turned out, I wasn't reading anything into his feelings, he loved me too. My grin stretched even wider at the thought.

Luca and I stole looks at each other as we stabled our horses, catching each other's eyes every once in awhile and grinning. He offered his arm and my nerves fluttered as I took it.

"Are you ready to face my stepmama and stepsister?" I asked, biting my lip as we started towards them.

"As ready as I'll ever be. But I *am* a little nervous," he replied, and I laughed. As we reached the garden, Beatrice and Aria stood to greet us with warm smiles. Aria tried to hide the curious glances she was shooting Luca's way, but Beatrice kept her eyes trained on me.

"Ella, darling, it's nice to see you back so early. And may I ask who we have the pleasure of meeting today?"

Luca opened his mouth but I couldn't help bursting out, "This is Luca, Stepmama, my fiance."

Beatrice's eyebrows lifted even as a small smile grew on her lips, as Aria put her hands to her chest and gasped. Luca looked down at me with an accusing smile and I couldn't help laughing.

"Sorry! I was too excited." I turned back to my family. "Stepmama, this is Lord Luca, Baron Lontarive. He's the man I've told you about." I turned to Luca again, gesturing to my stepmother and sister as they curtsied. "Luca, this is my stepmother, Lady Beatrice Fenice, Dowager Baroness Lucedimora, and her daughter, my stepsister Miss Aria Dunaelfen."

Luca bowed to them and offered one of his too charming to be real smiles. "I'm pleased to meet you. Ella has told me so much about you."

"Indeed," my stepmother replied, folding her hands in front of her. "Ella has spoken about you quite often too, and you may be sure I have questioned my other daughter about your character well before now." Luca flashed another grin at her, and my stepmother seemed to relax under his charm. She held her hand out to me, and I took it with my free hand, clinging to Luca with the other.

"Is it true you have become betrothed to my stepdaughter?" she asked Luca, squeezing my hand.

"Yes, madam," he replied, giving her another short bow. "I accompanied her home today to ask your blessing."

She smiled at him and squeezed my hand once more before dropping it. "That you do not need, but you may have it freely. If Ella has chosen you, than I will support her in whatever way I am able."

Luca bowed yet again, and I suppressed a laugh at the slightly ridiculous formality of it all. Aria rushed up and I dropped his hand to catch her graceful hug.

"I'm so happy for you Ella!" She said in my ear, then stepped back to curtsy to Luca. "And I'm very pleased to meet you, Lord Luca," she said.

"Just Luca will be fine, please. If I'm to be one of the family we may as well be brother and sister right away."

Aria laughed her tinkling laugh and stepped back to Stepmama's side. Beatrice smiled at her before turning her attention back to us.

"Would you both excuse me for a few minutes? I must instruct our cook to make an extra plate for dinner. If you mean to be my stepson, Luca, let's start right now as I insist you stay for dinner."

"Of course, Lady Beatrice," he replied with a bow. Stepmama nodded and drifted away as Aria looked expectantly toward me.

"Shall we give him a tour? I'm sure you're bursting to show him our beloved Lucedimora."

I laughed and nodded, and we proceeded to spend the remainder of the afternoon poking into all the corners of the castle, as well as the larger stables down the mountain. Dinner that evening was a minor miracle. Mrs. Moriotto managed to provide a delicious roast venison and vegetables, fresh strawberries, and cheese for dessert. Simple, compared to what Luca might eat when in the capitol with his family, but judging by how much he ate, he loved it too.

All too soon I was standing at the gate with him as he prepared to leave for Deerbold. Beatrice and Aria had bid him farewell already, standing just out of earshot.

"I loved seeing Lucedimora and meeting your family," Luca said, looking around fondly. "I can see why you love it here."

I grinned at him. "We can talk about logistics later, but I do hope we can stay here at least most of the year once we're married."

He crooked a smile back at me. "I would love to spend most of our time here. And we probably can, although after my father dies we will have to be at the capitol most of the time. Hopefully that won't be for a long time."

"Agreed! May your father live a long and happy life!" Luca grinned at me as I continued. "We'll figure it out when we have to. I'm sure I can set things up by then to be run by my steward as long as I can run back and forth as needed."

He took a half step toward me, then flicked a glance at my family and stopped short. He took my hand instead and pressed a kiss to it. "The next time I'll see you will be at the ball. You'll meet my family then, and we can announce our engagement." He pressed a kiss to my knuckles which thrilled me straight to my heart. "Until then let's keep everything a secret. I need to finish my exams and go home to prepare everything. We'll tell the world at the ball."

I laughed, pushing down the desire to press a kiss to his lips under the watchful eye of my stepmama. "If we aren't careful, we may upstage the prince!"

Luca froze and I laughed again. "I'm kidding!" I exclaimed, squeezing his hand. "No one will pay any attention to us, so don't worry about incurring royal disfavor. Only - promise me a dance before we announce anything? We can count on my family's support that night, but you said your family has different expectations for you. I'd like at least one worry free dance with you before we have to disappoint them with your choice of wife." I grinned, but I also couldn't help a niggle of worry worming it's way through my stomach.

Luca's hand tightened on mine. "If my family isn't immediately enchanted by you, they're not worth our time." He sighed. "But you're right, they're probably not going to be as encouraging as your family was today." He pressed another kiss to my knuckles. "You have my first dance - I promise."

In a flash he was mounted on his horse and leaving through the gate, Gia and her father closing the huge wooden door behind him. The quiet of the courtyard was deafening as I strained to hear the hoof beats taking my heart away from me.

Ella - glad you found your charming prince. Love - Alessia. The note was brief, but surprisingly sentimental. I rolled it up back up and dropped it into my pocket, fully unhooking the carrying case from the dove that brought the message. As soon as it was free, the dove hopped over to the fresh food I had laid out, cooing softly. A shaft of afternoon sunlight filtered through the roost, filling it with a warm glow that matched how I felt inside.

After one more look around to make sure my doves were all happy, I made a careful exit, latching the door firmly as I backed into the top floor of the tower. Although it had lovely views, it was more of a junk room than anything else. It was difficult to heat in the winter and could be irritatingly hot in the summer. The only reason I came up here on a regular basis was to tend to my doves. To my surprise, Beatrice and Aria swept into the disused sitting room of the tower, whispering to each other in urgent tones.

We all stared at each other for a brief moment until my stepmother cracked a smile. "How are your birds, my dear?" she inquired softly.

"Fine, Stepmama. I just had a message from Alessia. She congratulated me on my betrothal. Luca must have told her." My face flushed red at the mention of my new fiance, and Beatrice and Aria glanced at each other. I noticed that my stepmother's face looked a little pale and stepped forward.

"Stepmama, are you feeling alright? You look a little pale - did you come up here to find me? Is something wrong on the estate?"

Beatrice waved me away with a tired smile. "No dear, all is well. Aria and I just came up for some fabric for the ball. Now that we know it will be the announcement of your engagement we want your dress to be perfect. I have some Snowdonian fabric stored up here somewhere that will suit your hair and eyes to perfection. It's from before I married your father, and now I know why I saved it all these years."

My face broke out into a smile at her words. *Always thoughtful and kind, even when she isn't feeling well.*

"I don't want you tiring yourself out on my account. I was

planning on making over one of my mother's old court gowns anyway. I found one of the later ones could be made to look modern with just a few changes."

Beatrice smiled fondly at me. "Dear girl. As lovely as it would be to see you where your poor Mama's old gowns, I think she would agree that you deserve something new for a new chapter in your life. It won't be any trouble at all, you'll see. You remember I was the best dressmaker and weaver in the village before I married your father. Aria and I shall have you fitted out like a queen, you'll see."

I laughed, putting my hands on my hips. "If you can turn me into a queen I'll be much obliged to you. But tell me where the fabric is, I'll carry it down."

Aria stepped forward before Beatrice could reply. "Oh Ella leave it with us. I'll carry it down for Mama of course, but we want to make it as a surprise for you. Run along and let us work for once!"

I pulled first Beatrice and then Aria into quick hugs. "You two are treasures. With all you have going on with Alessia graduating you're still thinking of me."

Aria laughed and shooed me toward the stairs again. I looked back as my foot hovered over the first step down. A shaft of afternoon sunlight flashed through the open door to the old guardroom next to the dovecote, illuminating dusty swirls in a bath of gold. I could see makeshift shelves and old trunks stacked beyond the door as it swung shut again. I turned back to the spiral stairs, concentrating on the worn in steps - picking the same way down as hundreds and thousands of others had done before me, wearing down the stone a little at a time, until all of us combined created a groove for the foot to find.

As I got to the bottom of the staircase I sighed. It was nice to think of all the others who had lived in Lucedimora and given it life before - and nice to think that they left their mark here; but I should probably add repairing those stairs to the list of things to do sooner rather than later. *You could lose a shoe on those things.*

Moving through the first floor of the castle, I passed out of the front door and crossed the courtyard over to the solarium. The oppressive scent of green growing things mingled with dirt and stone as I walked through the rows of lettuce and greens. The citrus trees growing by the walls were heavy laden with fruit. *Maybe I'll divert one or two laborers from the hay fields to pick lemons and oranges in here.* I sighed. I was happy that our first hay harvest was upon us - on a horse farm, growing quality hay was of paramount importance to feed our stock. But the timing couldn't be worse. By all signs, this week would be the best to harvest, but it meant that I couldn't leave Lucedimora to attend Alessia and Luca's commencement ceremonies. *At least Aria and Beatrice can go. They deserve to see her graduate.*

My eyes caught sight of an open letter on my desk as I passed through the door to my study. The other reason I couldn't go to the graduation ceremony. I sat down on my wooden chair, pulling the letter toward me to read it again in the failing afternoon light.

As it had earlier this morning, the letter produced mixed feelings. A bit of triumph, certainly, and a feeling of excitement that comes when a new opportunity arises, but I couldn't help admitting that I felt just a touch of resentment. When the courier came to deliver this letter, I had been in the middle of determining whether Giuseppe and Gia could oversee the harvest for me so I could go to Deerbold with my family. I had to put those plans away immediately and instead go find them to let them know we needed to prepare the guest rooms immediately.

I had been corresponding with a Monsieur Thomas Marchand, of the increasingly famous Enterprise Marchand in Pelerin. They were traders of international renown, and had recently become known as the favorites of the Asilean Court, only newly opened for trade to the outside world. By all accounts, the Marchand family were the ones that could win me contracts with the nobility of both Pelerin and Asilea - if I could convince them that my horses were good enough.

"I'll finally get the chance to do that, but it means missing the ceremony." I shrugged, setting the letter down gently into one of my side drawers of my desk. *If I can broker a good deal quickly, maybe my new in-laws will be a little happier that their new daughter-in-law isn't just an obscure country noblewoman. I won't be rich anytime soon, but at least I'll have a growing business!*

I winced. A growing business run by a woman. Probably just as difficult of a sell to my in-laws as being a poor country noblewoman. "Well that's too bad for them. Luca and I have made up our minds. We'll find a way together. And besides, we're the same rank, so they can't complain too much." Smiling, I turned back to my desk, pulling out a blank piece of paper to compose a confirmation letter to the Marchand family.

CHAPTER TWELVE

Luca

"Luca!"

I waved one last goodbye to Raleigh and Briar Rose before turning in Alessia's direction. She stepped under the eaves of the stables, dripping from the rain shower outside.

"Are your mother and sister still here?" I asked as she wrung out her blonde hair.

"No," she laughed, nodding toward the sky outside. "Thankfully they left last night, not too long after the ceremony. They wanted to get home to help Ella with the guests. Lucky too or else they wouldn't have gotten far in this weather."

They must have ridden here on horseback. I forget how little they actually have for a noble family.

"I wanted to catch you before you left - " Alessia hesitated and I froze, certain she was going to question me about Ella. Instead she broke into a smile. "I got my orders this morning - the royal guard! I know I have you to thank for that. Otherwise they never would have requested someone like me."

I grinned. "They would be idiots not to. And Antonio put in a word for you too. He may be a bodyguard, but he has a lot of clout with the royal guard. Besides, if you think about it, it just makes sense to have a female guard for the Queen and Princess Royal, you know?" Alessia broke out into a grin and I pulled her into a side hug.

"Although once you're my official sister-in-law, you'll technically be related to the royals, so will it be weird guarding your own family?"

She pulled away and rolled her eyes at me. "The whole reason I got into this gig was to serve the royal family... annnd so I could learn skills to protect Ella's investments once I served my terms. The life of traders can be pretty dangerous depending on where your shipments go."

I smiled. "Well, Lucedimora's interests are soon going to be my best interests too. We'll both guard Ella's business in our own ways."

Her face turned serious. "Speaking of Ella, how did telling her —"

"Sire," Antonio's gravelly voice broke in on Alessia's. Although his tone was quiet, it held an air of competence that made anyone within hearing stop and listen. "Your carriage is ready. The rain is beginning to clear so we must attempt the first leg of the journey immediately. This way." He bowed to Alessia then turned and held his hand out toward the royal carriage waiting in the courtyard. The rain really had turned down to a drizzle in the last few minutes.

I waved to Alessia. "I'll check in on you once you're settled at the palace. See you then!" She waved too and I tried to ignore her eyes on me as I climbed into my silk lined carriage. Settling back into the cushy seat, I let out a breath. *Time to look toward the future.*

* * *

The road home was messy and took longer than usual. By the last day the weather had cleared up enough that I rode Percivale instead of letting myself be confined to the carriage. We arrived in the city as most people were inside eating dinner, and the usual crush of crowds was lighter. Those who were out didn't bother cheering as we sped by, just stood the side of the road quietly, trying not to be splashed by the carriage as it rumbled through puddles on the cobblestone streets.

The lateness of the hour meant I was able to get away with a quiet meal in my apartments instead of being paraded in front of whoever was the at the royal table tonight. Even so, my apartments seemed cavernous and cold in comparison to my cramped dorm room at Deerbold, and even the cozy dilapidated castle at Lucedimora. I sighed. "With the right people, we could make this palace feel different. Just a few days longer," I muttered to myself as I made ready for bed, pulling back the heavy coverlet and sliding in between luxurious sheets. Ella had given me the address of the apartment she and her family would be staying in for the ball. *She'll be here in two days.* I would make sure I was there to greet her. I rolled over in the dark. *And I'll tell her then. Before the ball and everything else, so we have time to talk it over. She'll be upset, but I know she'll stand with me.*

❊ ❊ ❊

I stared at the harried looking woman in front of me. "She's not here?" I repeated back to her.

"No, sir, as I said - they haven't shown up yet." She fidgeted with the edge of her faded but respectable blue apron. "Delayed on the road probably. They paid half in advance so I'll hold the rooms another day, but they're not here now." She shut the door in my face as a pair of children called her name from deeper inside the apartment building.

I looked over at Antonio, but he was scanning the streets instead of looking at me. I glanced at the flowers in my hand, wondering what I should do with them. *I can't bring them back to the palace. The maids would talk and my mother would be questioning me within five minutes.* I took another look at the stone face of the row house in front of me, but there was no counsel to be had there. Turning instead, I jogged down the front steps and into the street, Antonio my silent shadow.

As I meandered slowly back in the general direction of the palace, I spotted a pair of smartly dressed young ladies walking together on the sidewalk just ahead. *I can give them the flowers to enjoy. I'll get new ones when I come back later.* I moved toward them and was only a few steps away when my eyes caught sight of a girl and her mother, sitting on the front steps of their cramped row house, shelling peas for their supper. Their clothing was clean but patched and frayed in places, and although they seemed contented enough in their work, I wondered with a start whether they ever had much time for anything *but* work. My feet slowed as I watched them, echoes of conversations between my parents and their friends, sermons by the archbishop, even soulfully earnest speeches from leaders of charitable organizations ran through my mind. All my life I had been taught my duty toward the lamentably backward poor. How they clung to drink and sinful pursuits instead of trying to raise themselves up. But these two raggedy persons in front of me didn't seem full of vice. And I wondered how often they had a break from work to admire the beauty in this city, away from the cramped street they lived on. *Could they even leave the city to experience the rest of our country? Has that little girl ever seen the ocean?* I could give them a bit of beauty right now instead of wasting it on the two other ladies who probably had fresh cut flowers every day of their lives.

The two fashionable ladies I had originally been heading toward smiled and giggled as the passed me by, and I could see them making eyes at Antonio, hiding smiles behind their fans as he gave them a curt bow. I stepped back so they could pass, then altered my steps toward the crooked little rowhouse.

"Excuse me, madam." The woman didn't look up from her work but her daughter did, observing me with wide, curious eyes that held a touch of distrust. She tugged on her mama's skirt as Antonio stepped closer to me.

"What are you doing, milord?" he asked in a low voice. I

ignored him, focusing on the mother as she finally noticed my presence. She stood up quickly, putting her basked of peas down on the step beside her and tugging her daughter around slightly so she was half hidden behind her skirts.

"Excuse me for intruding, madam," I repeated myself with a slight bow, "but the friend that I had bought these flowers for has been delayed on the road. Instead of letting them go to waste I was wondering if you would like to have them."

The woman's entire body seemed to tighten, and her face went from wariness to full on anxiety. She glanced from the flowers, to my face, to Antonio's face and then back again. I hesitated, not sure how to overcome her shyness at the offering of a gift. And it seemed like there was something a bit more to shyness in her reaction, though I couldn't understand what it might be.

Antonio pushed forward, tipping his hat toward the woman. "He means nothing by it, truly. He's trying to be kind."

I shot a look at him, vaguely offended. "What else would I mean?" I hissed at him, still holding the flowers toward the ladies.

Antonio looked at me and I got the sense that he was refraining from rolling his eyes.

"My mister wouldn't like it, sir," the woman finally said, bobbing a short curtsy and directing her words at Antonio. I glanced back over at her, understanding dawning. *She doesn't want her husband to think she's accepting someone's attentions.*

"For your daughter, then?" I asked, smiling at the curious set of eyes gazing at me from behind her mother's skirt. The mother tightened her hold and nodded down the street.

"There's a shrine to the White Queen down that way. We don't see flowers of that quality laid out for 'er often, if it doesn't offend his lordship." I glanced down the street as Antonio tipped his hat again.

"Thank you, I'm sure my master will have no qualms in leaving an offering for the Queen. And we won't be passing this way again, so please don't worry." I frowned at Antonio again, but nodded at the anxious woman again as he began to steer me towards the supposed shrine.

"What was that all about?" I asked my bodyguard once he let go of my arm.

"That's not how people interact here," he replied, somewhat cryptically. "Giving flowers like that, it carries more meaning than it does in the upper classes. That woman would have been looked on with suspicion by her husband and her neighbors. Just stopping to talk to us could be enough to set her neighbors tongues wagging. The upper class usually don't mean well when they come to neighborhoods like these."

I furrowed my brow, startled. "What about charitable organizations and the like?"

Antonio breathed out a rare laugh. "They would be up to no good in such a neighborhood too, no doubt. They usually stick to the slums. It looks better all around if they're helping the worst off."

"That's a bit cynical Antonio. Surely anyone desperate would be glad of whatever help they could get!"

Every line on my bodyguard's form when silent even as we continued walking. "Yes, surely they would, milord," he answered after a moment. I had the impression he meant exactly the opposite, as nonsensical as that would be.

Antonio slowed and I followed his gaze to a little alcove in the moss covered wall across the street. In it stood a small statue of the White Queen as she was usually depicted, veiled and crowned, her head bowed and face hardly discernible. In my mind she always emanated a feeling of humility laced with sadness.

With a quick step, I crossed the cobblestone street, surprisingly clean in this quiet section of road, and laid my bouquet of flowers on the ledge jutting out just in front of the statue. It was strewn with several flowering weeds and one other tiny bouquet of violets, wilted and half dried from what little sunlight ever reached this alcove. There was nothing so grand as my own offering. *We haven't forgotten you, Lady,* I told the statue, feeling

I should at least say something, even if only in my head. *Your example of sacrifice and humility is still honored here.* The words rang slightly false in my head as I thought of the gold gilt altar in the royal cathedral. The altar was for the Creator of course, but the decorations venerated the White King well above all the other Shepherds, and certainly above his own wife. It's not that we didn't honor her, but that, as the Archbishop put it, we honored her through honoring her husband.

I stepped back from the shaded altar, the sandstone weathered and crumbling under moss. Here, in the lower parts of the city and among the common folk, I knew she was venerated more often.

I tore my eyes away from the quiet, hidden face and motioned to Antonio. I had things to do today beyond musing over semi-mythical Shepherds.

❈ ❈ ❈

We arrived back at the palace well before lunchtime, and in an effort to continue evading the notice of my family and any other inconvenient nobles, I decided to check in on Alessia. We skirted the royal halls and wound our way toward the guard headquarters, mercifully not crossing paths with anyone inconvenient. *Probably half of them are at home getting ready for tomorrow, and the other half are attempting to get a peek at the arriving royals.* I would be called into the welcoming party during lunch in an hour or so, and although I never looked forward to such things, I had to admit to being a little curious. We would be welcoming the usual ambassadorial delegation from Snowdonia, and a minor prince and ambassador from Pelerin; but for the first time in living memory we were welcoming delegations from Asileboix and Sherwood as well. I guessed my father was hoping my learned ease with magic users would smooth any tension for the Asileans and Sherwoodians. I knew he was seriously interested in maintaining the balance of power now that Asileboix had a

Pelerine princess. Asileboix and Sherwood had long been allies, but as they were tentatively opening their borders with Pelerin, my father would be quick to get his hooks into them as well. As always, he wanted every advantage over our so called ally to the north. *It's the way of kings. I'll have to think of such things as well some day.*

Antonio jogged a few steps ahead of me to open the door to the palace military headquarters. I stepped through, startling the guard on duty when he finally recognized me despite my nondescript clothing.

"Your Royal Highness!" He exclaimed, jumping up from his desk and bowing deeply. "How may we serve you?"

"At ease, soldier, I've only come to check on an old friend. Where has the female guard been stationed? Is she on duty now?"

The guard eased his stance slightly but seemed even more anxious at my words. "She is not on duty currently, Sire," he admitted, hesitating.

"Well, where is she then? At the mess? Practice yard?"

"I believe she's at her quarters, Sire." The soldier swallowed nervously.

"At this time of day?!" I exclaimed as Antonio went quiet and still behind me. "Is she ill?"

"No, Sire," the guard replied, his eyes darting toward the offices just beyond his desk. "Perhaps if you would like to speak to the Captain? He's in his office just now and he would be able to give you more details about her …" he trailed off, swallowing heavily again.

I stared at him, considering. *If she's not ill, then something here is amiss. They accepted her application. Why isn't she on duty?* I nodded to the young guard who stepped over to the Captain's office door, knocking and slipping inside to announce me before scrambling to get out of the way. The Captain was on his feet and bowing as I entered the room.

"Captain Strazza, I've come to inquire about a former classmate of mine, Alessia Dunaelfen. The guardsman outside said she's in her quarters right now. Why is she not on duty or working?"

Captain Strazza's eyes flicked toward Antonio before meeting mine again. "Prince Luca, welcome." He cleared his throat but continued confidently. "To be blunt, the Queen and Princess Royal have refused to be guarded by her, and I haven't yet found a unit that she will... fit in with."

Be accepted more likely, I grumbled to myself. Out loud I asked, "On what grounds have my mother and sister rejected her? Was her training found lacking? I know from experience that it isn't." Antonio stirred beside me.

"No, Sire, not at all. She has... I admit to my surprise, she's been found to have more than adequate training for a guardsman... guardswoman, of her age. I believe it was the appropriateness of her gender for the role that they objected to."

I huffed out a sigh. "And my father?"

"I didn't see fit to bother him with such a problem yet. Our focus is on the upcoming events and the security of our visitors."

I frowned. His answer was quite right, in general, but it was wrong for my friend. "Why not assign her to one of the details guarding the Asileans or Sherwoodians?"

"Sire!" he exclaimed, unable to keep the shock from his voice. He coughed slightly, knowing his duty called him to never betray an emotion toward a royal. "Sire, I'm sure you are more than aware that we are under orders from the King to ensure that the royal representatives from all our guests, but most especially the ones from the ones we have no formal treaty with, are to be kept from being offended at all costs. I could not in good conscience assign them a guard which has so offended our own royal family. Surely they would be angry to find that we valued their security so little that we assigned them a woman!"

My jaw dropped. Antonio moved forward slightly but I put my hand up to stop him, not even bothering to look at the anger I knew would be on his face. "Have you done not even a *moment* of research into the culture of our new guests?!" I demanded. "If you had bothered to ask anyone who knows, which includes myself, and Major Guerran here, then you would have realized that the militaries of both Asileboix and Sherwood are routinely staffed with and run by women. In fact, if I recall correctly, the female delegate from Sherwood is a renowned warrior in her own country, and is celebrated for turning the tide in their civil war! Far from being offended by being assigned a female guard, it would be a gesture of tolerance and welcome." I cut my tirade short, flexing my hand to release the tension that had balled my fists up as I talked.

"Sire, I must assure you - "

I cut the Captain's protests off with a sharp gesture. Slowly drawing a breath in through my nose, I released it in a controlled exhale and re-centered my anger, releasing it along with my breath. *I can't expect traditions to change in a day, or even my lifetime. Patience.*

"Order Lieutenant Dunaelfen to her new duty station with one of the foreign delegations immediately. I will accompany her there, just to ensure she is settled properly.

The Captain ground his teeth together but saluted, calling his aide into his office and issuing a series of commands. I paced the room as I waited, movement the only antidote to the frustration threatening to spill over. Antonio remained still and seemed to be having intermittent silent conversations with Captain Strazza. They knew each other well, and I knew that Antonio served with him for years before becoming my bodyguard.

Finally Alessia appeared, saluting her captain before bowing to me. She didn't betray any recognition or curiosity to my presence, simply stood to attention as Captain Strazza gave her the new orders. The aide turned to lead the way out into the hall, and I swept out behind him and Alessia.

As we turned a corner on the servants stairs leading up to the lavish royal guest suites I caught up to my friend.

"I hope my interfering doesn't cause too much trouble for you. I heard what happened with my family and I'll work on it. But I didn't want you sitting on your hands in the meantime," I whispered.

She grinned back at me. "I suppose I'll be having trouble for my entire career, regardless of your interference. I'd rather have a Prince on my side than not." I laughed quietly. "Thanks, though," she continued, before looking forward once more. I fell back a step or two, and then a few more as we reached the landing for the royal suites.

We approached the first set of suites, which had a Charmagnian guard on one side, and a guard with a foreign livery on the other side. The aide spoke to the Charmagnian guard, who took the new orders stoically, as the foreign guard fiddled with a brooch around his neck.

Just as the aide was completing his orders, the door to the suite opened and a tall, dark haired woman stepped out, dressed in a long tunic over dark leggings, with a shocking number of tattoos and scars scattered over her face. She looked directly at Alessia, who I was proud to see didn't betray even a shred of nervousness as she bowed in the lady's direction, even though the woman fairly oozed danger. The aide swallowed heavily as the foreign guard spoke to the woman, gesturing at Alessia as he did so. She nodded once, eying my friend before looking over directly at me.

Her eyes were gray and hard as granite. She seemed to size up my every strength and weakness in an instant. With a suddenness of movement, she strode over to me, dipping her head in an approximation of a bow as she approached. "Am I right in thinking you are Prince Luca?" she asked, her voice low and rich.

As shocked as I was, I managed to keep my voice. "Indeed Lady, although I confess I do not know your name. If we had met before I'm sure I would remember it."

She laughed, the sound brief and gravelly, as if she wasn't used to doing so. She looked younger for a moment, almost my age. A man in dark leathers stepped into the door frame, distracting her for a moment with his presence, but she turned back to me again, the ghost of a smile dropping from lips. "I am the delegate from Sherwood. Lady Hood of Barnesdale, The Red Rider. I knew you because you have the feel of a prince hanging around you, if not the look, at least at this moment.

It was my turn to laugh, and I looked at my plain clothes ruefully. "I hope I can take that as a compliment, that I look Princely even when dressed plainly. I hope you don't take offense at my attire. I simply came to ensure that your new guardswoman was installed properly. I can vouch for her skill myself, as she was a classmate of mine until recently. We wish to honor your customs with her presence here."

Lady Hood looked at me with a trace of approval and a hint of interest. "I am sure her service during our stay will do you proud. I look forward to speaking with you further, Prince Luca." She tipped her head again and stepped back, stopping to shake hands with Alessia before turning toward the forbidding looking man in black leathers and walking back into her suite.

Relaxing slightly, I shared the briefest of looks with Alessia before heading back toward my own rooms. Time to prepare for lunch, which promised to be much more interesting than the usual welcoming party.

* * *

"Still not here?!" I exclaimed, more to myself than the woman in front of me. The streets around me and Antonio were swiftly settling toward darkness, and I needed to get back to the palace for the feast. Threads of panic twined around my heart, whispering to me, *she won't show up again. You'll miss your chance with her. She's discovered who you are and rejected you.* I shoved those doubts down ruthlessly but the echoes remained in my mind. The woman shrugged and went to close the door but I put my foot out to stop her. "Please, would you put these flowers in their chambers? And allow me to write a short note? I had expected her.. Them by now." The woman raised her eyebrows at me and I sensed her disapproval. *Young men shouldn't be writing to women who aren't their wives*, her folded arms seemed to say.

"She's my fiance," I protested to her silent criticism.

She huffed out a breath and rolled her eyes. "So they all say. I don't have pen and paper."

"I have my own," I told her. "Just give me a moment." She nodded and turned to pull a stub of pencil and packet of notepaper from my pocket. I carried both on me as a force of habit from being a student so long.

I hesitated over the words. I had meant to confess who I was before the ball, so she knew what she was walking into, but I couldn't do that through a note. The blank page stared at me until I finally thought of something to say.

Ella, I hope you didn't meet with trouble on the road. I'll come back to check on you tomorrow morning if I can, but if not, I'll see you at the ball. You haven't come to your senses and thrown me over have you? I wouldn't blame you if you did, but it would take the light right out of my life. I trust you, I trust I'll see you soon.
With love,
Luca

I cringed slightly at the vulnerability of my words as I re-read it, but the impatient foot tapping of the landlady reminded me that I didn't have time to craft a perfect message. I turned to the stone balustrade beside me, setting my new bouquet of flowers down on it and using it as a desk to fold my message into a letter-locked square, before handing the message and flowers to the landlady. She took them and turned with a flounce, slamming the door behind her.

Antonio made no comment as we marched back toward the palace, and I was busy silencing the growing echo of doubts in my mind.

CHAPTER THIRTEEN

Ella

My toe caught the threshold of the doorway as I leaned back through to grab the latch, almost sending me into a heap on the floor. Thankfully I caught myself on the edge of the door, standing in a precarious wobble for a second before huffing out a laugh and pulling the door shut carefully behind me.

I took a minute to re-center myself, inhaling a deep breath through my nose and stretching my neck back and forth as I exhaled, releasing the tension in my shoulders. The evening sun filtered across my skin, still strong enough to warm but not strong enough to burn. After suffering under it's strength all day while working on last minute chores, I could still appreciate the life it gave to everything it touched.

Bending slightly, I caught the rough braid of rope serving as a handle on the bucket of peas I was transporting to the kitchen. It wasn't heavy, just cumbersome, but I took my time across the uneven pavers in my castle's courtyard. *I hope Gia was able to get most of our packing done. If not, we'll be up most of the night at this point.*

My eyes flicked to the row of upstairs windows of my stepmother's bedroom. She and Aria had been sewing our gowns for the ball over the last week, rising at dawn and working long into the night. Other than a quick round of measurements for a new white cotton under-dress, they hadn't allowed me to see any of their work.

"Leave it to us, my dear," Beatrice had said, giving me a peck on the forehead before shooing me from her workroom. "This is the sort of thing a former seamstress lives for!"

So I hadn't interfered, especially as my expected absence meant I needed to make sure every part of the estate was in proper working order. I didn't want Giuseppe and his helpers to worry while I was gone. Lucedimora never seemed to prosper when the Fenice family wasn't home, according to legend. *As the last member of the Fenice bloodline, it might just have a meltdown while I'm gone!* I grinned at my silliness and tore my eyes away from my stepmother's windows. Hopefully they had finished their work this morning and spent the rest of the day resting before our travels. Although Aria would be hearty enough, Beatrice had been looking pale again over the last few days, and even at her best, the long journey ahead of us would be tiring.

"I hope we've left enough time to recover from the road," I muttered to myself as I stepped through the open door to the kitchens.

"What's that milady?" Aida turned toward me as I placed my bucket on the kitchen workbench.

I offered her a tired smile. "Oh nothing really. Just that I hope we've left enough rest time in our travel plans for Lady Beatrice. I would hate for her to not enjoy the ball because she's been working too hard."

"Well you won't have to worry about that," Gia said grimly, sailing in through the door that lead to the main wing of the castle. "Your stepmother won't be going anywhere at this point," she announced bluntly, dropping a tray of half eaten toast and tea by the washing up pile.

"What do you mean?!" I demanded, following her movements with my eyes as she dumped the food remains into the slop pail and stacked the dirty dishes with the others. Gia turned around and shot a glance at her mother before giving me a sympathetic look.

"I just came from her room. She has a splitting headache and could hardly eat or drink anything today."

"Oh no!" I cried, reaching behind my back to untie my work apron. Gia paced over to help me as my fingers fumbled with the knot.

"I told her to just make over one of my mother's dresses!" I said as Gia hung my apron on it's peg. "This is just what I was afraid of - she pushed herself too hard. But surely if she rests tonight she will be well enough to go?"

Gia shrugged. "She wouldn't let me pack for them today, saying she wouldn't need it. Aria is still with her - go see them now. If you can talk her into it, we can start packing before the light fades. I finished ours earlier."

I rushed through the door to the main wing, trying to smooth the furrows between my brow. My feet stumbled on the stairs again, but I managed to catch myself on the railing, my heart pounding at yet another near miss. I slowed to a halt outside my stepmother's room, waiting until my breathing slowed before pushing through the door.

Beatrice lay on her bed, her eyes closed as Aria sat beside her, dabbing her face with a cool washcloth and singing quietly. Beatrice's hand rested on an elegantly painted wooden box, nestled protectively against her side.

"Stepmama," I whispered, approaching the bed with soft steps. Her eyes flicked open and she gave me a small smile threaded with pain.

"Ella, dear," she whispered, beckoning me forward, and Aria shifted to make room for me to sit.

"Gia said that you wouldn't let her pack for you. Surely you'll be well enough to travel by morning!" I meant to say it as a statement, but my voice wobbled and it came out as more of a question. A futile question really. When Beatrice's migraines were as bad as this, she was invariable bedridden for days or weeks. There would be no traveling for her.

My stepmother just closed her eyes. Aria too my hand in hers and I turned toward my stepsister. She looked tired as well, and sadness pulled at the edges of her mouth. "You know Mama won't be able to go, I'll stay to tend her. You and Gia must go alone." I opened my mouth to protest, but Beatrice's tight voice cut me off. "This isn't what I wanted, leaving you to meet your future family on your own, but you *must* go. I'll be fine in a few days, and this is a moment of your life that you cannot miss."

My vision blurred in the darkened room as tears welled and spilled freely on my cheeks. Aria's hand tightened on mine.

"At least we'll be sending you in style," Beatrice continued, managing another small smile. "Gia has already packed your gown away, but I have a gift for you here, a loan really." She patted the box next to here, and Aria pulled her hand free to pick it up. The colors of the designs painted on the lid and sides seemed to glow even in the shadowy room: swirls of blue and green, with specks of yellow that seemed almost like stars. I stared at them as Aria carefully removed the lid. It must have been the tears in my eyes because for a moment, it seemed the stars really twinkled with lights of their own. I blinked rapidly and when I looked again, all I could see was paint.

Aria pushed the open box toward me as Beatrice continued. "These are an old family heirloom, passed down for generations and kept close over the years. Every bride has worn them for their betrothal in my family, as far back as memory serves. I would be honored if you would take part in that tradition, Ella. Though you aren't my blood, you must know that I love you as if you were my own." My tears started flowing again freely at that declaration, and I wiped them away before gently lifting my stepmother's hand to my lips and pressing a gentle kiss there.

"You must promise me that you will wear them to the ball - no other shoes!" She continued, her tone surprisingly fierce. My eyes flicked to Aria, but she was staring at the box with a solemn expression. I followed her gaze, curiosity growing as I could trace the outline of a pair of slippers laying under the sturdy protective cloth.

"I'm honored Stepmama, but if they've been in your family

for so long, well... what if they don't fit me?"

Aria snorted as Beatrice breathed out a pained laugh, lifting both her hands to press against her temples. I shot a puzzled glance at both of them. I wasn't mad that they were laughing, just confused. They knew just as well as I did how small and dainty my feet were. Beatrice always claimed that they were the mark of a gentlewoman, but mainly they were the mark of clumsiness; their small size making it harder for me to balance, especially on days like today when I was so tired.

"Go ahead and take a look - you may be surprised," Beatrice said, and Aria nudged me with her shoulder. I stretched my hand out toward the box, pulling the layer of fabric to the side and gasping.

Nestled in a nest of beige cloth sparkled the most beautiful shoes I had ever seen. "Are they - is that -" they looked as if they were made from glass, although the thought was so absurd I couldn't make myself voice it.

"Yes, they're made of glass," Aria whispered, her voice as awed as I felt.

"As you can see, they're small enough that I think they'll do nicely," Beatrice murmured and it was true. The glass slippers were so dainty they were sure to fit my tiny feet. I glanced back over to my stepmother.

"But I thought you said that every woman in your family has worn them..." she gave another tight laugh.

"Never mind about that dear, it's not important. I know they will fit you fine, and although they may not look it, are the most comfortable shoes you'll ever wear. Even if you dance all night your feet will not ache."

I looked back at the shoes doubtfully, hesitating for a moment before daring to run my finger along the smooth side of one of them. They were of a high heeled design, though not so high as the heels that were currently popular in court. The glass was clear, tinted a just barely pale blue color, like the sky on a winters day. Threads of silver and gold shot through the glass in barely discernible whirling patterns, glittering subtly. I couldn't imagine these delicate works of art bearing my weight, let alone holding up under the strain of a night of dancing.

"They're quite sturdy, Ella, don't fear," Beatrice said, reading the doubt in my face. I smiled at her, but her expression remained solemn. "When you put them on, you'll feel how strong they are. But I must have two promises from you. First, that you'll wait to put them on until just before you leave for the ball. Second, that you *will* wear them for your dance with Luca."

I nodded solemnly, warming at the concern for me in my stepmother's eyes. "I wouldn't want to tempt fate by putting them on before the ball anyway. With my luck I'd trip and shatter them."

Beatrice laughed again and patted my hand. "There's no danger of that. You wouldn't be able to break them if you tried! But you spoke true - there's no reason to tempt fate." She closed her eyes again and I hurried to cover the shoes back up. Aria plucked the lid to the box off the bed, sliding it gently into place as I picked up the precious gift.

"I'll be back in a few minutes Mama," Aria said, but Beatrice didn't even acknowledge her. We passed out into the hallway quietly, shutting the door behind us. I trailed behind as Aria led the way to my room, contemplating the change in our plans.

"Are you sure you can't come? I hate to think of you here, missing your chance to shine," I said, already knowing her answer.

She shook her head, placing the glass slippers in my trunk and closing the lid before turning to look at me fully. "Someone needs to stay with Mama. This will be an opportunity for Gia to buy things at the Capitol for her wedding that she otherwise wouldn't get. She'll be by your side at the ball. And Alessia will be nearby too..." Her voice trailed off, almost as if she was convincing herself that *I* would be okay.

"But you'll be missing out!" I exclaimed, coming over to take her hands.

She blinked at me for a moment, before offering a soft smile. "I am content, sister dear, except that I can't stand beside you when you meet Luca's parents. But you'll be okay. You're strong."

She squeezed my hands and then passed out of my room, heading back to tend to her mother. I sighed and put my hands on my hips, my stomach grumbling loudly to remind me of the time. "I *am* strong," I told myself, "but even the mighty Charmagnian army marches on it's stomach." With one last glance at the trunk holding my borrowed slippers, I headed back to the kitchen.

* * *

I held my breath as Gia cinched the last of the ties for my sleeves closed. She stepped back to to open the box on the nearby end table, taking a moment to admire the heirloom glass slippers before bending to help slip them on my feet. I wobbled a second as she stepped back and gave me an appraising look, but true to Beatrice's word, the dancing slippers were incredibly comfortable. To distract myself from the nerves leaping in my stomach, I gave a little twirl, forcing my skirts to billow out around me in a blue cloud shot through with silver and gold. "Do I pass muster?" I asked, as I came to a stop, quirking a smile at Gia.

She gave a quiet chuckle. "You'll do, Ella, you'll do. I'll wager anything you like that your Luca will be giving you a kiss tonight!"

I laughed again, stepping forward to accept the light cape she put around my shoulders before turning to help her put her's on. She was wearing Aria's gown tonight instead of the plainer dress she had originally planned on using. The spring green color contrasted nicely with her dark hair and brought out the amber flecks in her eyes. Since she was shorter than Aria by several inches we had been forced to adjust the skirt at the last minute, but Gia had managed to create a few flounces that added a touch of luxury, and I had managed to not mess up the sewing.

We made our way carefully down the narrow stairs leading from our second story rented apartment. The landlady poked her head through from her parlor as we came down, one of her small children asleep in her arms. Her lined face broke into a soft smile as she caught sight of us.

"You ladies are a vision, if you don't mind me saying so," she said in whispered tones over the baby's head. "Your young man will be beside himself, milady," she offered a cheeky smile at me and I couldn't help a blush in response.

"It's his parents that I'm worried about," I confided impulsively. "I'll be meeting them tonight. I hope I give a good impression."

The landlady chuckled again. "I wouldn't worry either way, milady. Your in-laws will be a trial to you no matter what."

"I heard that Gloria!" a voice laced with humor called through the door. I peeked over the landlady's shoulder to see her elderly mother-in-law seated on a sofa with the other two children, a book open on her laugh. The two women exchanged a laugh that sent a twinge of longing through my heart. *Maybe I could have a relationship like that with my mother-in-law someday, once we get to know each other. She could never replace Mama, or even Stepmama, of course… but it would be nice to have a relationship like that.*

The landlady turned back toward me as Gia poked her head out the front door to check on our carriage. "We're only teasing Lady Fenice. Your beauty will win them over at first sight tonight, never fear. Enjoy yourselves."

I gave her smile and a nod as she turned back into her parlor. Gia rushed back over to me, reaching up to help me pull the thin hood of my cape up over my hair. Our capes were more to keep our gowns and hair in place during the ride to the palace than to keep us warm. The carriage was too stuffy in summer to travel without the windows down, and we didn't want dust, dirt, or wind to ruin the looks we had spent hours creating this afternoon.

"Is the carriage ready?" I hadn't seen our footman in the entryway, and assumed he must already be waiting.

Gia cleared her throat. "In a manner of speaking, yes."

I raised an eyebrow. "Do I dare ask what that means?"

She pressed her lips together, obviously suppressing a smile. "Come outside and see. It seems that Luca sent a present for you." She pulled open the front door an I stepped through and stopped short at the sight in front of me.

An elegant carriage sat waiting at the bottom of our steps. The wooden frame was made from a slightly orange tinted cherry wood, and the gilding around the windows and runners glinted gold in the fading evening sunlight. I looked over at Gia in consternation and she let out a nervous giggle, shrugging her shoulders. I turned back to the carriage, noticing that it was manned by no less than four footman, one of whom was our own Piero, looking slightly out of place next to the impressive uniforms of the others.

I stepped toward him and he bowed. "Milady, this carriage was sent to you by Lord Luca. I thought you may prefer it to our own." His eyes were wide, and through his nervousness I could sense excitement to be a part of such an impressive operation.

"Thank you, Piero. It will certainly be an adventure. There's room for you to ride along, correct? I'd feel more comfortable if you accompany us."

He bowed again. "Yes, milady, of course."

I nodded and one of the other footman stepped forward to open the carriage door, bending his head in a bow as Piero assisted me through the door, Gia on my heels. We sunk down onto the sunset colored velvet cushions, staring at each other with wide eyes.

"Either this is an overblown apology for not being able to accompany me to the palace himself, or Luca hasn't been forthcoming with how much wealth his family owns," I whispered to Gia.

She waggled her eyebrows at me as she leaned back on the seat across from me. "Probably both!"

We both startled slightly as the carriage began moving forward in a smooth motion. I couldn't help leaning toward the window to watch the city go by outside.

As we approached the palace, our progress slowed down to a snail's pace, while my nerves quickened. *I hope he isn't wondering where we are. That's a silly thought - of course he is. I just hope his parent's aren't upset by the delay.* There was nothing to be done about it.

Finally, well after sundown, we arrived. The footmen guided us to the still lengthy entrance line and we took our place at the back, waiting to be announced. Every now and again, the sound of string instruments in the ballroom reached our ears, and my feet fairly itched to be dancing. I forced myself to be calm, gazing about instead with Gia at the luxury of the entrance hall.

"I can't imagine what it would be like to live here," she whispered, and I nodded in agreement. The walls were filled with murals painted by the best artists in the country. The lofty roof was held up by enormous columns, banners strung up between them and lit up by enormous chandeliers. Everywhere we looked there was expensive art work and ornate furniture - the type you wouldn't dare sit down on for fear of damaging.

An enormous clock dominated the space where the marble staircase split in two, ticking off every minute as we finally started edging up one set of the stairs. It seemed we were among the last to arrive as no other attendees fell into line behind us. Every time the bells rang the quarter hour, my anxiety tightened a little more.

My hand went to the silver star-burst necklace hanging at my throat, one of the few heirlooms I had left from my mother's jewelry collection. I touched each tip of the star in turn, twisting it on it's chain. I hadn't seen Luca since we arrived. No doubt he was inside the ball, dancing with the lady his parents expected him to marry, wondering where I might be. *Just hold on a few more minutes.*

Finally, a little after the clock struck a quarter to midnight, we arrived at the top of the staircase. I handed my card to the footman, who handed it to the majordomo, who examined it with a sour look before motioning us forward.

The music ended just as he opened his mouth, and his booming voice seemed to ring out in the pause, "Lady Sorella Fenice, Baroness of Lucedimora, and Miss Giuseppa Moriotto."

The violins started again as I took my first steps down the interior staircase, Gia trailing somewhere behind. I looked up at the sound and nearly stumbled as I caught sight of Luca on a dais almost directly across the room, surrounded by courtiers. Our eyes locked and for a moment everything stilled, a motionless beat of silence while my entire being locked into place.

Then his mouth curved, and my heart restarted. My feet began moving of their own accord, pacing smoothly and confidently down the stairs, Luca's gait matching my own as he stepped onto the floor, the crowd parting around him seamlessly.

We met at the same time at the bottom of the stairs. He held out his hand as he approached and I took it in a smooth motion, marveling at how harmonious our motions were.

The first notes of a waltz floated into the air, and we stepped into it without a word, communicating only by smiles. My heart felt as though it had floated away, out of my chest to hover somewhere over Luca. I didn't care to catch it again, not with the way he was looking at me, eyes overflowing with love and joy, hands strong on my back as he lead us through the other couples.

The world around blurred into a rainbow of colors and movements that couldn't touch us, had nothing to do with us. We floated through it, in it, but not of it. Our eyes were only for each other, our love the only thing that mattered. All of our movements seemed fated before we even stepped into them.

Though I'm not an expert dancer by any means, I didn't stumble even once. My feet followed my partner's lead without hesitation and all my former anxiety about conducting myself well melted away. As we progressed around the floor, the certainty of our future grew in my heart. As the music came to a close, Luca led me through one last turn, slowing with the last notes of the waltz. We stood facing each other, breathless and inches apart as the other dancers applauded the orchestra.

"You're here, my love," he whispered, smiling down at me in

wonder.

"Yes, always," I answered back simply, breathlessly. His other hand slid to my back, and I found mine sliding to his chest as he pulled me even closer. There was nothing else but the two of us, his heartbeat thrumming under my fingers, my own answering it's song. He bent his head down as I stood on tiptoes, our lips meeting in a soft promise with the full weight of our devotion behind it.

A shock of warmth swept over me, from head to toe, almost physical in the way it touched every fiber of my being. *What in the world?* We pulled apart slightly at the same time.

"What was that?" Luca gasped, his brow furrowed. I shook my head, a flush tracing the path that the warmth had traced only a moment before as I realized we were in the exact center of the ballroom. There was no one else nearby, an empty circle surrounding us as the other dancers looked on. *How could I have forgotten myself so much that I just <u>kissed</u> Luca in front of an entire ballroom. It's going to be the scandal of the season!*

I looked back at Luca, seeking refuge in his eyes. He was watching me, his brow furrowed. A desire to leave the dance floor and declare our intentions before his parents could start protesting was overwhelming.

"Let's go speak with my parents," Luca said, his voice low. He tucked my arm under his and began leading me toward the edge of the dance floor. My feet fell into step willingly beside him, unconsciously matching the rhythm of the chimes as the enormous clock began striking midnight. My brain felt scattered by the warmth of his arm on mine and the noise of the clock and the weight of the colors and candlelight of a court ball.

We arrived in front of a magnificently dressed couple near the royal dais just as the clock finished striking. "Father, Mother..." he turned, spinning me around to face the ballroom as well, his voice deepening into a baritone that carried across the room, "Good people of Charmagne, let me introduce my future wife, and your future queen, Lady Ella of Lucedimora."

My feet, which had been tingling since the end of our dance, snapped together, sending a shock up my body, through my arm and into Luca.

"Ow!" we said at the same time, and looked at each other in alarm. The shock of the charge seemed to put my brain back into gear because everything fell into place in a moment.

"Your parents are... the king and queen?!" I demanded in a hoarse whisper. Before Luca could respond, a number of guards stepped forward, drawing our attention back to his parents. His father listened as one whispered in his ear. The queen stood as still as death at his side, her face frozen in a calm expression but her eyes staring daggers at us. My eyes flicked to two richly dressed young ladies standing just over her shoulder.

One wore a dark gray gown edged with gold filigree and dark gemstones, a splendid golden diadem on her intricate hairstyle. Her face was pinched in barely concealed rage as she stared at Luca, the spitting image of the queen. *That must be Princess Marietta - his sister!* The other had the face of an angel, her eyes wide as she stared at me with an expression I couldn't read. Her gold and white dress was elegant and simple compared with her companion's, her hair half held back by a braided crown before flowing elegantly down her back. She had on very few jewels, but their extravagance left her power and wealth in no doubt. Her beauty and poise made me feel small of a sudden, though I instantly squashed that instinct down as a nuisance.

My eyes flicked back to the king as he opened his mouth to speak to the assembly.

"We have much to discuss with our son on this happy occasion. Enjoy the celebrations tonight in true Charmagnian style!"

His eyes swept over the pair of us as he turned, assessing and stern, but he lead the way out of the ballroom without a word. The Queen turned to say something to the two women at her side before following her husband. Luca and I trailed after them, the guards sweeping in around us on all sides.

My thoughts tumbled over each other as we strode down the hall, my steps becoming less sure the further we went. *Why did I kiss him in front of an entire room?! And my future in-laws...* "Why didn't you tell me that you were *Prince* Luca?!" I demanded in a whisper. Luca looked down at me with a tight expression.

"*That's* what you're focused on right now?! What exactly *was* that back there?!" he demanded back. I frowned at him, struggling to recall what he was talking about. *He kissed me just as much as I kissed him, so why is he blaming me? After all, he's the one who deceived* **me** *about who he is - and he hasn't said sorry!* A wave of disappointment swept over me, tasting of sour grapes in my mouth. I opened my mouth to demand answers, but was distracted as we swept into a sumptuous receiving room. The doors slammed shut behind us as guards took up their position.

CHAPTER FOURTEEN

Luca

I looked around the Blue Reception Room, the soothing shades of ocean blue it was decorated in doing nothing to calm my nerves. Captain Strazza appeared amongst the other royal guards and whispered into my father's ear again.

"You foolish, foolish boy!" My mother's strident voice cut across the room. She paced back and forth in front of my father, just inside the rough circle the guards were forming around our family. "I know you to be selfish, but you must add stupid as well?! Announcing a joke like *that*," she waved a bejeweled hand at Ella's direction, not bothering to look at her, "as your future consort in front of the entire court? Leaving us to clean up -"

Indignation at her insult to Ella cut through the confusion I felt at the events of the last few moments. I took a breath, preparing to put a stop to her insults when my father's voice cut through the room like a knife.

"Enough." He didn't even need to shout. The decades of command he had wielded as king gave him an unquestionable authority that rarely made raising his voice necessary. My mother, ever the outwardly dutiful queen, snapped her lips closed immediately, but her eyes spewed poison at me. My father turned his attention to Ella, who was hovering by my side.

"You will submit yourself to a magic examination immediately," he announced. I felt her stiffen beside me as two Holy Examiners wearing the black robes of the Cleansing Order stepped into view.

"Father, you can't be serious! Just because she isn't from a high ranking -"

He cut me off with a sharp motion. "A magical artifact was detected and believed to be on her person."

I went completely still, remembering the surge of sparks that had passed through me from Ella earlier; first when we kissed, then when I announced our betrothal. Even at the time it had tasted almost like magic, something I was used to at the academy, but not here at the palace. *Could a rebel faction have invaded the ball and placed a spell on us, attempting to ruin the royal family's future? We need to find whoever did it, not humiliate Ella just because she's not Emilia.*

"Even so!" I replied, grabbing a hold of Ella's hand in reassurance. "We shouldn't waste time -" this time Ella interrupted me, squeezing my hand as she dipped a curtsy to my father.

"I will gladly submit to an examination if it will put your minds at rest and help catch whatever mage is here tonight."

I looked down at her with pride and exasperation. Of course she would approach the situation using common sense instead of angling for a position of power. She wasn't trained to view every interaction at the palace as a gain or loss of control. Even moments like these. *Especially moments like these. She can't start a pattern of giving in to every power play my father makes, even if he is the king. They'll crush her soul in no time.*

As if she could read my thoughts, Ella looked up at me with a small, reassuring smile, patting my hand before dropping it to step forward. I rocked forward on my toes to pull her back, the desire to keep her safe by my side almost overwhelming, but stopped myself at the last minute. The faster my father was satisfied she was of no harm, the faster the examiners could move on to catch the real culprit. *If she's willing to do this, I need to let her make her own decisions. We can talk later about surviving court politics.*

The examiners stepped forward on either side of her, their deep hoods hiding their faces. The only sign of their humanity was their blindingly pale hands, stark against coarse black robes. The brothers of the Cleansing Order took vows renouncing the light so that they can focus solely on cleansing our country of the darkness of magic. There were always several assigned to the palace to prevent rebel mages from attacking the royal family. If there was one here tonight, they would discover them.

Each examiner pulled out a small, round hand mirror. The ornate working of the silver frames looked heavy and tarnished, and as I watched them sweep the mirrors over Ella in tandem, I could see candlelight reflecting off of runes worked into the twisting designs.

Ella held still as the examiners moved around her in perfect unison, reflecting light off of their hand mirrors across every inch of her skin and dress. I let out a breath I didn't know I was holding as they finished their search. I had seen them perform such searches often enough to know that if there was an artifact, or if Ella were a secret mage the reflected light from the mirrors would leave a glowing trail across her skin, illuminating the magic within. As expected, there was nothing to see.

Suddenly the examiners lowered their mirrors and stepped back in unison. "Reveal your shoes," they commanded Ella, their voices so similar it could have been one person speaking.

A frown appeared on her forehead, but she reached down and pulled the hem of her ball gown up a few inches to reveal them.

A glow spilled out onto the floor, causing those of us standing near to stumble backward. All eyes were riveted to the pair of beautiful - *was that glass?* - dancing slippers on Ella's feet. They were clear, shot through with patterns of gold and silver that seemed to swirl and dance as they revealed a pattern of magic threaded throughout the shoes. My eyes shot to her face, confusion and suspicion warring in my chest. She stared down at the magic objects in apparent shock, her mouth hanging open.

"Can you disable them? What is their object?" Captain Strazza's voice cut through the tension in the room. The holy brothers kept their mirrors directed at Ella's feet steadily. The longer they did, the more magic was revealed. It seemed to crawl around Ella, tracing pathways toward her heart.

In another sudden movement, they turned the mirrors toward me. I took an involuntary step backward, then froze as a vise gripped my heart. Threads of golden, glowing magic were illuminated, twining together and writhing as they reached out. My eyes traced the line of magic as it made a path through the air; a path that ended on my chest, right over my heart.

Thoughts and questions flashed through my mind rapidly as voices broke out across the room. *A love spell? It can't be anything other than a love spell. Has she fooled me this entire time? Her plan all along to bind me to her and gain the throne?* I shook my head. None of my feelings for her felt fake. We had fallen in love quickly, yes, but quite naturally. We both valued the same things. We sparked each other's curiosity and desire to learn new things. We both felt a deep sense of duty to our responsibilities - felt called to serve as well as lead. *She hadn't changed so much since she was a child. Surely this couldn't have been a long laid plan? Surely my feelings for her are real.*

My eyes snapped to her and I found her staring back at me, desperation and fear in her eyes. *Was that fear that she was discovered?* Part of me wanted to reassure her, protect her, but I couldn't make my feet move. It was as though I could feel the sensation of magic squeezing my heart, binding it, and I didn't want to move closer to the source of that entrapment.

"It's a binding magic," the examiners said, their voices deep and ominous, "drawing their hearts together."

"Was this your plan all along?" I found myself asking, giving voice to the kernel of doubt in my heart and desperate for reassurance.

A dart of pain flashed across Ella's face that I almost felt in my own heart. The question had wounded her. As quickly as I saw it, it disappeared. Her mouth snapped shut and she turned toward me fully, releasing the fabric of her dress and folding her arms across her chest.

"Frankly, Luca, if you believe that, than you're an idiot and you don't know me at all."

The remark stung, and I took a step toward her, folding my own across my chest and unconsciously mirroring her pose. "Oh really, is that such a stupid question to ask when you've brought a magical artifact in here that's somehow binding the two of us together?! What am I supposed to think?!"

Across the room behind Ella's back, my mother opened her mouth, her face contorted with rage. I waited for her strident tones to lash out, but my father held up a hand to stop her, his eyes darting between me and Ella.

Ella hadn't noticed any of this. She shifted her hands to her hips, her skin mottled red with anger, stark against the silvery blue of her gown.

"Even if I was trying to bind you, which *obviously* I wasn't, what would be the point? You already proposed, and I already accepted. There is no legal reason standing between two people of the same rank who want to get married. And up until a few minutes ago, *you* let me believe that we *were* of the same rank! The trivial detail of you being a royal *somehow* conveniently slipping your mind all this time. Binding us together would have been a little overkill, don't you think?!"

The subtle accusation over my deception rankled, but the desire to retreat from admitting guilt in the midst of all my swirling emotions won out. I adopted my coldest court manner.

"Please don't allow yourself to equate the use of illicit magic in forcing someone into love with the fact that yes, I allowed you to believe that my highest title was that of Baron. It's not as if I actually lied to you. And what about your deception with those shoes?! How do you explain that?!"

"If you believe that I used magic to force you to - " Ella bit her words off, drawing herself up and taking a deep breath. "If that's what you believe about our relationship than you obviously never trusted me at all. I'm having a hard time trusting you after discovering you're a *liar.*"

My temper surged at the accusation and I felt heat on my face, disrupting the icy demeanor I was attempting to project.

"I won't object if you want to break off the engagement," she continued. "Perhaps it will be best for everyone." Her words broke over me in a shock, and although her expression was still full of anger, there was despair there too, and tears slipped free from her sea green eyes. *She thinks that I - well I guess I was being a little unfair.* Regret at expressing my doubts before thinking about them logically trickled through my heart.

"*Were* you trying to trap Prince Luca into marriage?" My father's commanding voice startled Ella, who turned toward him, her skirt swirling around her as she surreptitiously wiped tears from her eyes and squared her shoulders.

"No sire, I was not attempting to trap him into anything," she replied, dipping into a regal curtsy. When she stood back up she looked him directly in the eye, respectfully, but not a hint of the awe that kept most courtiers looking slightly off to one side.

"Too used to being queen of her own little domain," I muttered ruefully, hoping my father didn't react unfavorably to her directness. I saw Ella's hands clench and wondered if she had heard me. I opened my mouth to assure her that I hadn't meant it as an insult, but my father interrupted again.

"How then, do you explain the shoes?"

Ella's posture wilted a fraction at that question. Her hands unclenched at her side, and she smoothed the sides of her skirt nervously.

"I was... I was given them, Your Majesty."

"By whom?"

I could read indecisiveness in every line in Ella's back. After another second of hesitation, she clasped her hands together in front of her stomach and drew in a deep breath.

"By my stepmother, Sire, but she can't have known what they were!"

By her stepmother?! I shook my head, trying to follow the implication. *If her stepmother is a mage, that would mean her stepsisters -*

The doors behind us burst open and we all whirled as one to

face the intruders. A pair of guards stepped through, their hands gripping the upper arms of another soldier whose hands were bound before her.

"Alessia!" Ella cried, taking a few faltering steps forward until she was level with me. The guards pulled up short, forcing Alessia to stop as well.

"What is the meaning of this intrusion?" my father asked, his voice stern.

"Sire," one of the guards spoke up, his voice tight with controlled urgency, "we found her performing magic from her post near the ballroom. We've disabled her with the cuffs and brought her to you right away."

A wave of cold shock swept over me as I looked to my friend. She didn't even glance my way, somehow managing to stand to attention, even held between her fellow soldiers with her arms bound.

She's a mage? All these years and I never saw her using magic, or being taught magic. And she never thought to tell me? Secrets were coming to light faster than I could see tonight.

"No that can't be right!" Ella exclaimed, drawing the barest flicker of a glance from Alessia.

"Bring her to the examiners," my father commanded, motioning to the black clad figures still standing in the center of the room. "They'll soon find out what sort of spells she cast."

"There's no need, Your Highness, I'll confess freely," Alessia announced, her voice strong and laced with note of resignation.

Ella drew in a shaky breath next to me and almost stumbled. I reached out to steady her but she shook me off, her eyes fixed on Alessia as the guards dragged her toward the examiners.

"Explain yourself, then," my father ordered as the examiners stepped to her side and pulled out their mirrors.

Alessia drew in a deep breath and released it, scattering the sparkles of magic already being revealed around her in the reflected light of the mirrors. "I made a simple working, nothing dangerous. I haven't violated my oath to protect and serve, except in the matter of performing magic. It was a spelled message to alert my mother and sister that they were compromised."

Beside me Ella put her hands up to cover her mouth, her eyes trained on her stepsister.

Alessia didn't notice, standing as if she were giving a report at the end of her shift. "I could feel the magic of the glass slippers as they were activated, and then the working of the examiners a few minutes later. I knew it wouldn't be long before they would be traced to my family. By the time you get to Lucedimora, they'll be gone."

Ella seemed to crumple slightly next to me, her usual steady vitality appearing fragile when I glanced over at her. *She looks as shocked as I feel. Could her stepfamily really have hid their magic from her all these years, just as Alessia did from me at the academy?*

After a moment of indecision, my need to comfort her won out over my doubts. I took a step in her direction, but stopped and turned around once more as the doors opened yet again.

"Prince Andrus and Princess Rosebelle of Asileboix have requested an immediate audience, Sire," a guard's voice rang out.

I glanced back at my parents. My mother looked as if she was going to burst if she couldn't give vent to her shock, but strangely enough, my father looked more amused than anything.

"Let them enter," he ordered, folding his arms across his chest as my mother lost control so far as to hiss in frustration. "Perhaps they'll provide a little clarity to this mess of an evening." Puzzled at his attitude, I turned back toward the open doors as the guard stepped back to allow the royals through.

CHAPTER FIFTEEN

Ella

A long with everyone else I turned as the newcomers entered the room; the exotic rulers of mysterious Asileboix. They swept through the doors in a swirl of expensive matching dark blue brocade. *Stepmama would love to see such craftsmanship!* I thought, before banishing all thoughts of my stepfamily and their lies from my head. Instead, I distracted myself from the roiling emotions in my chest as the foreign prince led his princess through through the maze of sofas and overstuffed chairs until they came to a stop in front of the king.

The princess is almost as tall as the King, I noticed somewhere in the back of my mind. *The prince even more so.* Although Prince Andrus was dressed in the first cut of fashion, it was understated, and did nothing to hide the air of a barely tamed wildness that hung around him. His wife was beautiful in an unapproachable sort of way. The bodice of her dark blue dress was covered in a trail of red applique silk roses, a nod to her name as well as to the Asilean royal colors, and a sheer blue cape flowed to the floor from her shoulders. *She looks like a fae queen just stepped out of the night sky.* Of the four royals gathered in a little knot, she looked the most in control of any of them. My own king seemed to be torn between a sense of amusement at the absurdity of the evening and an increasing level of frustration at each event, and

Queen Narcissa had the look of an exquisite china teapot that was about to boil over.

The royals of both countries exchanged regal nods, and the king motioned Luca to step forward. As he joined them, I felt a tug in my heart. *If I marry him, I would be the one receiving royal guests like Prince Andrus and Princess Rosebelle.* I looked back at the ethereal Princess; tall, beautiful, and commanding where I was short, certainly not classically beautiful, and tended more toward bossiness than an air of command. *Not to mention scatterbrained. I can't imagine Princess Rosebelle being scatterbrained for a minute.*

I pushed the thoughts of my inadequacies aside. *I'm marrying Luca, not the crown, so if he wants me to stand beside him, then that's all that matters.* My glance strayed toward Queen Narcissa. Maybe Charmagne wouldn't expect their queen to be the picture of graciousness anyway.

Still, I felt small in a room full of royals and guards. *I wish Luca was still by my side. Or at least Gia was somewhere nearby.* With a start I realized I had forgotten all about my best friend. She must be somewhere in the ballroom still. *Hopefully she's escaping notice for now.* A sense of loneliness swept over me. I was in a room full of powerful people, had been caught using a magical artifact, and probably had very little say about much of my future. My heart gave an extra squeeze as my sense of self tilted slightly. I wasn't used to not being in charge. At Lucedimora, my word was as good as law. Here at the palace, I was no one.

Well Creator, I prayed, a tinge of desperation coloring my thoughts, *or White King, or White Queen… or anyone who's listening for that matter. I guess I'm just trusting there's a plan here somewhere. If you wouldn't mind making it a little more apparent, I would be eternally grateful.*

"I beg your pardon for the interruption, King Cirro, but we heard reports of magic being used during the ball." Princess Rosebelle's voice was conciliatory, but firm. "We wanted to assure you that our party had nothing to do with it, and offer our services in investigating the incident."

"The, occurrence, as you call it, seems to be an internal Charmagnian affair, Princess Rosebelle. It appears that spell was placed on our crown prince, binding him to his chosen bride without his consent. Although we are still attempting to understand what happened, we harbor no suspicions that your party has violated the terms of your visit."

"If that is the case," Prince Andrus rumbled, "we would be happy to examine the object and determine a way to break the spell as a show of good faith."

My heart throbbed at the idea, violently protesting being broken apart from Luca, even though I had suggested such a thing not long ago in response to his doubts about my love. *Everything is happening too fast. I need a moment alone to process all these revelations.*

"That would be useful in the extreme," King Cirro replied to Prince Andrus, shooting a speculative look my way. The Queen also turned her poisonous blue eyes on me and opened her mouth to spew some of that venom in my direction, but she was interrupted once again by the King.

"Narcissa, go back to the ballroom and entertain our guests. Make no excuses and do not dare give off any indication that all is not going according to plan. Discuss nothing with Marietta, or anyone else."

The queen gave him a tight nod. "I'll expect a full report once you've managed to break the spell on Luca," she told him, then swept around the room and out the door, not sparing even a glance at anyone else.

"Have you confirmed that she is of no threat to us?" King Cirro called to the examiners and he motioned to my stepsister. Alessia stood tall and proud, every inch the royal guard she had fought so hard to become. *Now she'll never be allowed to serve. She'll be lucky to have a decent jail cell as a mage.* My heart turned over again and I tried to catch her eye. She ignored my completely, her jaw set in stubborn anger as she looked at a point on the wall opposite of her.

"The bonds hold her tightly," the examiners responded in

unison. I glanced down at the iron worked cuffs holding her hands tight together. *They must be preventing her from accessing her magic.*

"Then take her to a cell, and do not dare remove those cuffs," the King ordered to the guards still standing on either side of her. "And you go with her. I require you to stay near her cell overnight, in case there is need of you," he ordered to the examiners. They bowed and followed Alessia and her guards out of the room.

With a trickle of dread, I felt the King's attention focus back on me. "What will you need in order to break the spell on my son?" He asked Prince Andrus, his eyes still on me.

"Have you an apothecary, or an alchemist's laboratory nearby?"

King Cirro shifted his attention to the Prince. "We do not deal in alchemy here," he replied stiffly, "but we can certainly retire to the royal apothecary's apartments."

"They should have any ingredients I may require."

"Then follow me," King Cirro commanded, leading the way out of the room. Luca headed straight toward me as the party began moving toward the door.

"Come on," he said, grabbing my hand and tucking my arm under his unceremoniously. I allowed him to lead me through the door but said nothing, my head too full to be able to organize a coherent sentence. Prince Andrus and Princess Rosebelle had stopped just outside the door in the hallway and were conferring with two fierce looking foreigners in low voices. King Cirro was giving orders to his head guard a few paces away, so Luca and I stopped to wait, Luca leaning forward to hear what his father was saying.

"Red, I'll probably need your help, so Eddie, would you escort Belle back up to our apartments and stay with her and the baby until we return?"

"Are you expecting any problems?" the other man asked in a low voice. His accent marked him as a Pelerine, but the tattoos snaking down his throat declared him as one touched by magic.

Pelerin was a country that until recently had outright banned magic and magic users.

"No, but I'd rather have someone I can trust with my wife and child while there's a little uncertainty going on here. You know how delicate our mission is."

"And don't worry," Princess Rosebelle said in a chiding tone, "Hazel's here to help me with the baby so I won't be asking you to change any diapers."

The woman next to Eddie snorted a laugh and he rolled his eyes at her before offering his arm to Princess Rosebelle. The Princess stood on tiptoe to give a kiss to her husband before making their way down the hallway to the main palace.

Prince Andrus and the remaining woman, Red, turned to follow King Cirro, and Luca and I fell in behind them. None of us spoke as we walked down successive hallways, leading us from the more impressive public rooms of the palace to what were clearly rooms of a more bureaucratic nature.

Finally we entered a room that could only be the apothecary, attached as it was to an infirmary ward. After a quick consultation, Luca led me to a chair at one end of the room where Red and Prince Andrus where examining various ingredients in glass jars and pulling pieces of odd looking equipment from cupboards. I watched with a numb disinterest as they mixed several ingredients together in a bowl and heated the mixture in the fire. Red wandered over and crouched in front of me, forcing my gaze to switch to her. I looked at her fully for the first time since I saw her in the hall.

My eyes widened before I could help it and the corner of her mouth quirked up in amusement, telling me she had noticed my shock. I blushed, but couldn't fault myself for the reaction. She was the single most untamed woman I had ever seen. I had noticed vaguely as we walked that she was almost as tall as Prince Andrus, but up close I could see the trail of dark tattoos on her face, matching some of the ones I had seen on the other man from the hall, and stark against her pale skin. Not only that, but she had several scars across her upper lip and almost too many to count on the knuckles of her hands that she rested against her knees. Her dress was a rich crimson - a simple design that allowed the quality of the fabric to speak louder than any embellishments. A flash of silver caught my eye from the sleeve at her wrist. *Is that - that's a knife handle isn't it?* Startled, I looked back up to the woman's pale gray eyes, but there was no threat there, just understanding and brisk competence. *If Princess Belle was a Fae Queen of old, Red is one of the Red Queen's fabled Shield Warriors.* My mind seemed to be full of fairytales this evening.

Red glanced up at Luca, who was hovering somewhere behind me. "We are about to perform several tests, some of which involve spells. Please inform your father so that he isn't caught unaware."

I felt, rather than saw, Luca perform a stiff bow and saw him make his was over to King Cirro out of the corner of my eye. The King nodded and crossed his arms, seeming to ask several more questions of Luca. My eyes strayed to the array of guards flanking the two royals. I hadn't noticed their entrance and was startled to realize they were probably present because of *me*. My eyes flicked back toward Luca, then bounced away at the dark robed shadow behind the King. One of the examiners had entered the room, to make sure my *magic* shoes didn't hurt anyone. I snorted quietly, a thread of hysteria in the sound that I couldn't pretend wasn't there. "The only person in danger of being hurt would be *me* if these glass slippers break under my weight and stab me," I mumbled to myself.

"Not necessarily," a deep voice rumbled from my right. I turned to find Prince Andrus much closer than I had anticipated. He had rolled up his shirtsleeves and was holding a bowl of steaming liquid in one hand. The wildness of him seemed to only increase upon close inspection.

I swallowed heavily. Although in some ways Prince Andrus seemed more polished than the fierce woman crouching in front of me, there was something about the way he carried himself that made my spine stiffen. Not because he seemed bad, but because he was intimidating. There was something in me that reacted immediately to any attempts to intimidate me. Perhaps it came from working with horses since I was a child. Even if an animal, or person, is bigger and stronger than me, I've always known that I'm in charge of my own self. And when I feel like someone is attempting to control me, my instinct is to dig down to that bedrock of self knowledge existed.

"How could a pair of shoes hurt anyone except the wearer?" I asked, directing the question more at Red than Prince Andrus. "Unless I take them off and throw them at someone I suppose."

Red's mouth quirked up in amusement. "I'm sure if you're thinking of doing so then your man would probably deserve it," she replied, her eyes darting toward Prince Andrus as she lowered her voice. "In my experience, a pampered prince needs a partner with a firm hand. You can just ask my cousin there about that."

My eyes widened in shock and I couldn't help darting a glance over at Prince Andrus. He rolled his eyes at his cousin and huffed an irritated breath.

"Red, I might remind you that I'm here as part of *your* diplomatic mission, so if you'd like my help to play nice with the Charmagnian royals, you might consider skipping the teasing during a serious investigation."

I looked back to Red and blinked as she shrugged her shoulders. "I told Robin I'm no good at this sort of thing." She lowered her voice to a whisper only I could hear. "And if you ask me, that prince over there could use a person who isn't afraid to throw her shoes at him for being an idiot from time to time."

Despite the fear and disappointment flooding my heart, I couldn't help crack an answering smile at the scarred woman in front of me. "I could never do that!" I protested as my eyes slid his way for a moment. "I'm not saying he doesn't need it, just that I couldn't throw glass slippers at him. Maybe a pair of sandals," I admitted with a shaky grin.

"That's the spirit, milady. Now, if we chat any more Prince Andrus will positively start growling at the pair of us, so down to business. I'm afraid we're going to need a drop of your blood.

Do you faint at the sight of blood?" Her tone was curious as she pulled the small knife I had seen hidden up her sleeve a few minutes ago out into the open.

I stared at it, then swallowed heavily. "No, I never have before. Although if I'm being honest, I'm feeling a tiny bit faint at all the events of the evening, so I can't make any promises. Are you *quite* sure this is necessary?"

"Yes milady, it's necessary. You can be sure your King will want to get to the bottom of everything tonight, and our methods are much nicer, and more efficient, than those of your 'examiners'."

"They're not *my* examiners," I said primly as I held my hand out. Red chuckled quietly as she turned my palm upwards, nicking a small cut on the pad of my ring finger. Prince Andrus bent swiftly to place the steaming bowl under my hand, and Red squeezed a few drops into it, then onto a small creamware plate before murmuring a few words. I gasped as I watched the cut heal almost instantly. *Magic.*

"Sorry," she said in a quiet tone, "I should have asked before doing that. It's just a reflex, but I know you don't use magic to heal in your land."

"You do in *your* land?!" I exclaimed, forgetting to keep my voice down for a moment. Taking care to speak more normally, I examined my hand a little closer. There was no sign of the cut.

"Yes, of course. There's no reason to let something like that get infected. Now, let's have a better look at your shoes if you don't mind."

Blinking at the change in topics, I reached down to pull up my skirts a few inches and stick my feet out as Red settled down on her knees in front of me, her crimson gown pooling around her like a stain.

She reached out gently, holding my feet still as she examined the swirls of silver and gold in the glass. Little motes of magic still swirled around them, but were quickly disappearing. *Maybe the effects of the examiner's revealing mirrors lasts longer on objects? The magic trail between me and Luca isn't visible anymore.*

I looked a little closer and gasped, drawing Red's eyes to me. "There's cracks!" I said, dropping one side of my skirt and pointing to several hairline cracks radiating around the shoes. I made to kick off the shoes, fear that my earlier joke about the shoes breaking was coming true, but stopped myself just in time. I didn't want to hit Red in the face, and I had a strange reluctance to hurt the shoes as well.

"They weren't there before?" Red asked. I shook my head and she frowned back down at the shoes, then closed her eyes and breathed a few words over them. The room was quiet for many minutes as she seemed to concentrate on whatever spell I assumed she had just cast. I watched her face anxiously, looking for any sign that would tell me what was going on. Finally she opened her eyes, and stared down at the shoes, raising her eyebrows.

"Well?" Prince Andrus' voice rumbled from near my elbow again. I barely kept myself from jumping in my chair. Red looked up at him thoughtfully.

"It appears to be a love spell," she replied, and I drew in a sharp breath as the King's voice cut in over the conversation.

"So she *has* bewitched my son?!" he thundered.

"No, no, not at all, Sire," Red reassured him calmly. "It's just a classification. This one seems to *test* the wearer's love for her intended partner, and his for her. If it's found true, the binding spell is released." She turned back to Prince Andrus. "For all intents and purposes, it's as if they're already married, according to the gypsy custom," she gave him a significant look and he looked thoughtful.

I'm sure I looked panicked. "What do you mean we're already married like gypsies? Why would my stepmother give me such shoes!? She's not a gypsy!"

Red looked back at me. "You would have to ask her that of course, I have no idea. If she's not a gypsy, maybe her ancestors were. I *can* tell that it's a true family heirloom. They've been used many times, and presided over many happy marriages." She traced several of the glowing golding lines swirling inside the glass of the shoes. "These golden lines seem to represent marriages of true love." She pointed to one of the glowing silver threads, which were less common than the golden ones. "These seem to represent relationships that were tested and found lacking."

"And the cracks?" I asked, in a whisper.

She looked at me with knowing eyes. "My sister-in-law is better at divining the true meaning of spellwork, but I know enough to tell you this: the cracks in your shoes will not splinter and hurt your feet, but they will splinter and hurt both your heart, and that of your beloved, if they aren't fixed. The nature of this spell has bound your hearts and souls together at the moment your bond was tested and approved." My mind drifted back to the shock I had felt when Luca and I kissed at the end of our dance, and then again when our engagement was announced. Red continued, her tone matter of fact. "If you cannot repair the distrust between you, the consequences will be painful, and potentially deadly."

"Deadly?" The King's voice boomed across the room. He was staring at my shoes with a mixture of anger and irritation. "Remove the spell, immediately, and I will consider almost any terms to an alliance with your countries."

Red shot a startled look toward Prince Andrus, whose eyebrows shot up. She shook her head in response and turned back toward the King, standing to face him fully. "I'm sorry King Cirro, I cannot undo the bond. There is no one among us who could."

"What do you mean!?" The King demanded, taking a half step toward us before stopping and glancing back toward my shoes. I stifled the urge to hide them behind my skirts again. *Don't give in to urge to hide, Ella. Stand your ground. You're innocent in all of this and have no reason to feel shame.* The thought that my stepmother *must* have known what she was giving me hovered around the outside of my mind, but I batted it away. I couldn't to examine that truth right now.

"The magic in these shoes is old - centuries old. Every time they were successfully used, the magic was only strengthened. There *are* ways to undo a heart bond, although they're never easy. But in this case, since an enchanted object was used to create the bond, it's a different matter. We would need a master in several fields at least: fairy engineering, heart bonds, layered spells, and probably several other types of magic I haven't even thought of in order to understand the complexity of this spell."

The King and Red stared at each other for a charged moment before Luca took a step forward to stand next to his father.

"You mentioned that the cracks in the shoes could harm Ella and me," he said, gesturing toward the shoes. "How? And how can we prevent that from happening?" We locked eyes for a moment but I couldn't read his feelings. His distance, across the room, standing by his father instead of standing by me, spoke loudly enough. My eyes jerked back to Red as she turned to lok me.

"The cracks in the shoes are just a physical representation of what's between the two of you. They represent the distrust that's sprung up between you. As to how to repair them..." she shook her head and looked me directly in the eye. "Do you have any ideas?"

My mouth dropped open before I could stop it. "Me?!" I squeaked. My heart raced and I suddenly remembered the last time I had felt like this, when my father's stable master had been quizzing me on riding technique before allowing me to mount up and participate in the local hunt for the first time. He had asked a question about the actual hunting part of the Hunt, which I had never studied before in my life. I hadn't been able to even guess at the answers.

"Yes," Red repeated, gesturing toward the shoes. "Surely you have some sort of feel for the magic in the shoes. What is your specialty?"

"My specialty?" I asked dumbly, glancing from the shoes to Red again. "What specialty? You mean what type of horse breeds do I specialize in?"

It was Red's turn to look confused. "Horse breeds? What do

they have to do with anything?"

Luca took several steps forward, not quite coming to my side, but enough to be properly included in the conversation. "She runs a highly respected horse stables. But... you mean her magic specialty don't you?" My eyes flew to his face, which was as white as a sheet as he stared at Red and then Prince Andrus. I followed his gaze and found Prince Andrus' eyes on me. He looked solemn as he nodded, then lifted the plate still held in his hand. "The test I performed confirmed it. You have very strong mage properties in your blood. You must have felt your magic long before now?"

I stared at the plate that held several drops of my blood. *Mage properties? Felt my magic? What would magic even feel like?* I thought back on my life, thumbing through memories like pages of a book. *Surely feeling magic would be obvious. But no, there's been nothing...* I stared back at Prince Andrus, tipping my chin up confidently. "No, I've never felt magic before, you must be mistaken."

He shook his head and I looked over at Red. Her expression was firm, although not unkind. "There's something within you, I can feel it." She glanced over at Prince Andrus and a questioning tone entered her voice. "More so now than when we first encountered her, wouldn't you say?"

He nodded and gestured toward the blasted shoes again, "If she's telling the truth, maybe her inborn magic has been suppressed all these years, and has only now been unlocked from the strength of that spell."

Panic struck my heart and I rocked in forward in my seat, an instinct to dart out of my seat and race for the door overtaking me. I wanted out, to get away from the words these two foreigners were saying, sealing a doom over me as nonchalantly as I imagined the academics at the royal academy debated an interesting find in their collection. I gripped the arms of my chair, dropping my skirt so that it covered the cursed shoes that started this mess and focused on calming my choppy breathing. My eyes darted toward around the room, seeking safety somewhere, and landed on Luca.

There was no welcome in his expression, only horror. My heart cracked in a great heave, and I surged to my feet, all thoughts of the shoes breaking gone from my mind in a reaction to the judgment I read on his face. Addressing myself to the king, I dipped into a shallow curtsy.

"I swear I had no knowledge of any magic within me before this moment, Your Majesty. I am willing to swear it under pain of death, or a truth spell, if it will make you believe me." My eyes slid to Luca's as I said so, but I snapped them back to the King. If I were to read disgust in someone's expression, I would rather it be from King Cirro than the one who held my heart in his hands. Unexpectedly, King Cirro didn't appear disgusted at all. If anything, he looked impatient.

"Yes, yes. A truth spell will be sufficient. Would you perform one for her Prince Andrus?"

"Yes, if the lady truly wishes it," he replied and I nodded.

King Cirro motioned toward me in a few testy swishes of his hand. "Then go ahead. But before you do, you haven't said yet - what can be done to remove the spell and stop the broken glass from hurting my son and Lady Fenice?"

Red folded her arms. "From what I could tell, they'll have to heal the distrust between them, and also speak the wedding bonds of your culture. It should be enough to heal the cracks between them, but to be sure, I'd want to ask the owner of the shoes."

The King raised his eyebrows. "I'll be taking those shoes to get a second opinion. But if that's what it takes, we seem to have no choice. No one responded to him, so after a thoughtful moment, he gave a swift nod, motioning for Red and Prince Andrus to proceed with the truth spell.

The spell itself was odd. I clasped hands with Andrus, mine small in his larger ones. I felt a compulsion to speak true to his questions, but it wasn't intrusive, more gentle and persuasive, coaxing me to speak more than I would have anyway. It mattered little to me. I had no secrets, and I answered everything readily, my thoughts racing over what would become of the people on my estate once it became known I was a mage. Would they disinherit me? It hadn't been done in generations, but that was because most magic users in our country had long ago been rooted out. In the past, even supporting a mage could be grounds for disinheritance. *What noble would invest in Lucedimora, situated so far from the capitol and too close to Spindle? They would let it languish, caring nothing for the people or it's history?*

I was recalled to myself as Prince Andrus ended the truth spell, the gentle warmth of the incantation retreating and leaving me very cold indeed.

"If you had orchestrated this situation yourselves I couldn't applaud your statesmanship more." The king's words filtered through my foggy thoughts as he spoke to Prince Andrus and Red. "I find myself in a situation of utmost importance to both my family and my kingdom, and only the the two of you seem able to help me." My eyes moved dully to Prince Andrus' face to see how he reacted to such a direct statement, but he merely looked amused.

"I regret that I really must insist we know nothing about it, although we certainly won't refuse any opportunity to grow a closer relationship between our countries. Both Sherwood and Asileboix are run by mages, so if your future queen is a mage, it would bind our interests to yours even closer."

King Cirro looked thoughtful at his words, which surprised me. Although my family had always been ambiguous in our attitude toward magic, the royals had a fearsome reputation for anti-magical purity. But the King seemed more contemplative than disgusted. *Unlike some.* I very studiously ignored Luca. It was safer to ignore than to receive more of *his* judgment.

"The shoes, Lady Fenice," the King said, startling me from my thoughts. I stared at him in shock, wobbling on my feet a bit, and he gestured toward Red. "Please release the glass slippers into their custody this evening. Then you will be shown to a guest room where you can rest." His tone was commanding, but not cruel. *Just used to being king in his own domain,* I thought ruefully, remembering Luca's words from earlier.

Hesitating a moment, I stepped out of the shoes that had wrought so much change to my life in the last few hours. Part of me hated them, but another part of me was reluctant to be parted from them. *The spell no doubt,* I thought bitterly as I bent to pick them up. Red bent at the same moment and we almost knocked heads.

"Sorry," I whispered, my voice wobbling as I discovered I was almost out of control.

"My apologies as well, Lady Fenice," she replied, her own voice strong and sure, lending me a little strength.

Luca appeared beside me, but didn't offer his arm. Possibly because both of mine were now employed in holding me skirts up so I couldn't trip, but I remembered his look of disgust from earlier, and didn't bother checking to see if he still wore it. If he was disciplined enough to stand this close to the secret mage, he was disciplined enough to hide his true feelings. I wanted even less to look upon a mask.

The walk to my guest room proved to be extremely short - only a few flights of stairs and a corridor over. As a guard fiddled with the door to the room, I unconsciously took in the utilitarian nature of the halls, and the thin but steady trickle of guards passing through the corridors. It didn't hit me until I walked through to the darkened interior and a few candles were lit and placed in plain brass holders - I was in the guards' barracks.

A pair of guards did a quick check around the comfortable but hardly extravagant room. I watched them unseeing, my grasp over my composure holding by a hairs breath. As they walked back toward the door, giving me a wide berth, Luca spoke to me for the first time since we had discovered the magic.

"I'm sorry this room isn't ... but we weren't expecting you to stay and it would hardly be fit to put you in the ..." he drew in a deep breath behind me. "You'll be safe here. I'm sure my mother will arrange for clothes and the like."

"Thank you," I managed to grind out, frustration and sadness warring to betray themselves in my voice. I wanted to speak with him, but not right now. Not with guards present, and the pain of his reaction to me still fresh. Not to mention the discovery of a part of myself I knew nothing about, and part of my stepfamily that felt like a betrayal.

"Then I'll bid you good night," he replied after a moment, and I felt him leave, the soldiers filing out behind him before pulling the door shut, a gust of air blowing out one of the candles as it did.

I took a few faltering steps and sank to the floor in front of the spartan bed on one side of the room. The light from the sole candle by the door hardly reached so far into the room, but I didn't care.

I pressed my head forward against my arms, leaning against the bed to prop myself up as great wracking sobs shook my body. My entire world had changed this evening, but not in the way I had planned. Instead of conquering the hearts of my beloved's parents, and taking our first step toward the rest of the golden future we had planned together, I was facing a future that was vaster, darker, and more dangerous than I had ever imagined. There was a chasm between the Ella of this moment, and the Ella of only hours before. Magic barred the way back to the girl I had been, and it exposed everything I thought had been true for a lie.

How can I see a way forward when everything I've believed in has been ripped away? I asked the Creator, my heart cracking as surely as the glass slippers had earlier. *Are you even listening? If you're supposed to be a champion of creating and growing, why have you let everything I've built from the ashes of my childhood be broken to pieces in one fell swoop? Couldn't you have let it be done gently instead of ripping it to shreds in one evening?*

I heaved another sob before stopping my anguish cold. There was no use wallowing in sorrow tonight. Tomorrow would bring my cares out all over again, and not only mine, but those I was responsible for: Alessia, Gia, Beatrice and Aria, all those who worked and lived on my estate, and of course my horses and business. As sad as I was at Luca's deception, and all that had been revealed, I was weary too.

I didn't bother waiting up for the queen to send a servant to me. I stripped off my ballgown and accessories until I was in my shift, hardly able to look at the silvery blue and gold gown that matched those cursed shoes so well as I laid it out on the floor. Bringing the lone candle closer to my bed, I blew it out before slipping under the covers of my bed. There was a little moonlight that illuminated the edges of my room, but despite my despair, I didn't stay awake long enough for my eyes to adjust.

CHAPTER SIXTEEN

Luca

Breakfast was a strained affair. On one side of the table were my mother and sister, seated in offended dignity; on the other, Princess Rosebelle cradled her baby with effortless grace. I spent half the meal tensing for the baby's inevitable cries, which somehow never came, and the other half watching the Asilean royals warm interactions with curiosity. Of course most of my real attention was rooted on Ella, seated on the other side of the long breakfast table from me, looking far too at ease as she helped entertain the baby. *I'm glad she's not having a bad time, but couldn't she at least be as mixed up as I am?!*

My mother's disapproval of Ella's easy interactions with a baby, as well as her kindness toward the foreign royals was uncomfortably apparent, at least to me. My father looked more bemused by it that anything else, when he wasn't involved in a deep discussion with Red and her counterpart, Captain Eddie Marchand. I had expected frosty silence and heavy glares to be served all around with the eggs and toast, but instead there was the ghost of Ella's sunny laughter sprinkled with soft words. *If only they were directed at me.* We were too far away to interact with each other this morning.

After breakfast, one of Princess Rosebelle's attendants came to take the baby, and everyone except my mother and sister retired to my father's study to discuss the situation. It all felt like a strange dream - I finally had what I desired, Ella as my betrothed, but instead of exultation and building our dreams, our path was snared with magic.

I frowned as we took our seats in my father's study. Somehow Ella had ended up on a sofa with the delegates from Sherwood, forcing me to sit in a nearby chair instead of directly next to her. Despite the revelations of the last day, I wanted to face this conversation next to her. Now she was flanked by Captain Hood, the most famous warrior of the Mage Realms, and Captain March-and, the infamous Shadow.

"I have two issues I require your counsel on this morning, but my first thought may dispose of both of them neatly. If I recall your description of the shoes' spell correctly, my son and Lady Fenice must marry before it can be broken. If they were to marry quickly, I'm sure I could have the church grant an annulment, considering Lady Fenice's newly discovered magic, and the spell would be broken - correct?"

I glanced over at Ella, my agitation over her magic roiling in my chest and clashing with anger at my father's casual discussion of divorce. Her face was white but her jaw was set. Her eyes flicked to mine, but I couldn't read what emotion was in them before she looked away.

Next to her, Lady Hood leaned forward with her hands on her knees. "That's not how the spell works. It's centered around the couple's love. If anyone attempts to break their bond, a curse will be released. They must marry, and remain married unless they reject their bond from their heart."

I felt my father's eyes on me, but I didn't waiver from Ella's face. "That's easy then," he said, his tone almost casual, "it seems both my son *and* Lady Fenice lost trust in each other last night. Perhaps their bond is already broken."

Ella's eyes flew toward me, startled, and the fear in them gave me hope. *She's afraid I don't love her anymore, that I don't trust her. That must mean she still loves and trusts me!*

I couldn't help the smile that curved my lips up, even as I

desperately hoped she wouldn't misinterpret it. On the contrary, every line of her body seemed to relax as she let out a quiet breath, and one corner of her mouth quirked up in response.

"We would know if that had happened, King Cirro. The curse would have already been released and from what I could tell, the effects on Luca and Ella would be apparent."

My father stood, leaning his fists on his desk. "How then can we avoid this curse? I don't take kindly to being forced to marry my son against his will to a mage under threat of a curse. This is the sort of thing my ancestors worked so hard to prevent."

Out of the corner of my eye I could see Princess Rosebelle sit fractionally straighter in her chair as her husband spoke beside her. "Are they being married against their will? I thought the entire reason they're in this situation is because they wanted to get married in the first place."

"No," I interjected, the words drawn from deep within my chest, "no, our union would not be against my will, at least."

I was rewarded for my speech by watching a flush of red sweep across Ella's face as she glanced my way again. "Nor mine," she replied, her gaze serious. *I do wish they'd leave us alone for five minutes. I can only guess at what she's thinking right now and I want to talk all this through and make sure she's alright.* As much as I needed a few minutes alone with her, I also knew that we needed to work through a way forward in such a complex situation with my father's guidance. Just the fact that Ella seemed to have magic would be a problem for a future Charmagnian Queen. Getting the public to accept her, let alone the church, could be insurmountable. I pushed that thought aside. Ella would be a perfect queen. *Surely there's a way forward.*

My father stood up straight and folded his arms across his chest. *He's still trying to find a way out of this - even after he promised that my bride would be my choice!*

"Then perhaps there could be a long engagement - I could extend Luca's naval engagement for a much longer period of time. Long enough for both of them to get over this nonsense."

"With spells of this nature," Lady Hood continued, "the

longer the couple waits, the more distracted they'll become until they won't be able to focus on anything except their bond."

My father snorted with distemper, and I balled my fists in my lap. Before I could say anything, Prince Andrus spoke up.

"I know that Charmagne is not a haven for magic users, but by all accounts, Lady Fenice was not aware that she had magic, so she's hardly at fault."

"Besides," Princess Rosebelle said smoothly next to her husband, "as we've discussed in our meetings since our arrival, we all desire stronger ties between our countries. I'm sure even Spindle would look with great interest on Charmagne if the crown prince were to marry a known mage. Perhaps you allow the wedding to go forward, and for the couple's wedding tour you could send them on an international tour in the Mage countries. It would be a reflection of how their marriage would surely strengthen the ties between us."

I watched my father blink several times at Princess Rosebelle's words, a sure sign that he could see the merit in what she was saying. "Would a month be too long for the glass slippers' spell to prepare a wedding?" he barked out suddenly to Lady Hood.

She looked over at Prince Andrus for confirmation then turned back to my father. "That seems reasonable to me. There's no way for me to read that level of detail in the spell, but if you start to see ill effects on Prince Luca or Lady Fenice, you could always move the wedding up."

My father gave a sharp nod. "Then we shall prepare a ceremony as soon as Luca is finished with his first mission command. That will give us enough time to prepare the wedding tour with each of the countries you mentioned."

"If that is the case, I would like to extend an invitation to the newlyweds to attend our wedding in Sherwood at the end of their tour. We would be honored by your presence," Captain Hood said, and Captain Marchand nodded as well.

"We accept," my father said before Ella or I could answer, and although he outwardly displayed his usual slightly cranky but commanding demeanor, I could tell by the way he was tapping his fingers on his leg that he was full of glee at the potential gains he could make for Charmagne through blossoming relationships with Spindle, Asileboix, and Sherwood.

"Well, I suppose we will have many details to iron out over the next few days before we leave to go back to our own countries, but for now, I'd like to take the opportunity to get to know your future daughter in law a little better. Could I steal her away for the day?"

My father acceded to Princess Rosebelle's request, and before I knew it, the ladies had swept her from the room, the others trailing behind, leaving my father and myself alone.

* * *

"I suppose I should have dealt with you last night, but I was simply too busy," my father said, anger readily apparent in his voice. "I spent half the night consulting with the examiners about the safety of having a mage in my palace. All I could get out of them in the end was that we probably weren't in any danger, but that the evil of her existence would eat through every brick in the palace before we could blink. They were very upset that I didn't send her to the cathedral with them to be cleansed immediately."

Anger surged at the thought, and I rose out of my chair, my fists balled at my side.

"Relax!" My father said with a frown. "I wouldn't send the poor girl with them even if I *did* think she was a danger. She's proving much too useful as a bridge to a better treaty with Sherwood and Asileboix, and she's brought with her the glimmer, yes an unlooked-for glimmer, of a treaty with Spindle. That's something no Charmagnian King has managed in centuries! Centuries my boy!" His frown turned into a grin as he rubbed his hands together.

Disgust at his mercenary ways warred with satisfaction that he was more at ease with the situation than I first would have guessed.

"I'm glad you're satisfied, father," I said, walking closer to his desk and crossing my arms over my chest.

"Oh I wouldn't say I'm satisfied. If you had just contracted with Emilia and been done with it like I said, things would be much easier for all of us, including that poor girl you've dragged into the middle of things. She's obviously not used to court politics. If she truly did have suppressed magic, she could have gone her whole life without knowing it, if not for you. Despite the sudden possibilities in terms of foreign relations, it's the domestic ones I'm concerned with." He sighed heavily. "Snowdonia will *not* be happy when they hear of her abilities, not to mention the Archbishop. Our people will be distracted enough by wedding festivities that I doubt they'll care whether she's a magician or not. Still, we have a mountain of work ahead of us that could have easily been avoided."

I bridled at his words, even though I had been thinking through each of those problems over my sleepless night. "Obviously I had no idea she had magic, or that she would be wearing magic slippers - I never would have approached her as a potential partner if I had known! I'm not so blind that I wouldn't have been able to for see the problems you listed. But she is the right partner for me, and is intelligent enough that she can learn how to operate in court to become the queen Charmagne needs in time!"

"All right, all right! You have to admit it's a big mess. But even so, I will admit to your ears only that I've admired the pluck she showed last night when she upbraided you for not revealing you're the crown prince. If you did such a thing, you deserved every bit of the public trouncing she gave you. Although it was a bit unladylike, I could forgive that under the circumstances."

Shame at my deception heated my face, but it warred with the warmth in my heart at my father's unexpected compliment to Ella.

"Besides, she did show remarkable tact this morning by not interrupting while I negotiated with the Asileans and Sherwoodians. Yes, she may have what it takes, with training of course."

She was probably just still in shock this morning - if she was on form she would have probably given Father a heart attack with some of her opinions on the royal family's attitude toward magic or the common people. Although, it's probably not the best time to bring up those items right now, especially if he's is feeling favorably toward her.

"I'm glad you can see some of her better qualities, Father," I said instead. "She'll surprise us all, I think."

"Yes well," he grunted back, sitting down in his desk chair. "I still think you should take the time during your naval mission to work on falling out of love with her somehow. It will be easy enough to do once you're married, believe me, so you may as well get it done beforehand so we can break the spell and get out of all the difficult bits of this alliance without losing the goodwill of the Mage Countries."

I barely kept from rolling my eyes. "I don't think that's how love works, Father."

He waved his hand at me, focusing on the papers in front of him. "You're dismissed. You'll still be leaving in a few days for your assignment. There's no time for you to be mooning on about true love and all that."

After a short bow, I took my leave, relieved at how positively the king had taken the events of the last day. *Now if only my mother could be convinced to see past the issue of magic.*

* * *

Antonio fell into step a few paces behind me as I exited my father's study. As much as I enjoyed his company, I had become used to not requiring a shadow everywhere I went during my time at Deerbold Academy. *I shouldn't need a bodyguard in my own palace. There must be a reason our people are so restless as to present a danger to us even though we sacrifice every aspect of our lives for them.* Images from our ride out to Deerbold in the winter flashed through my mind, as well as people I had met during incognito trips into town. Although times were good, there was still poverty in plenty of places, and mistrust between strangers.

"*There* you are, Luca," a screeching voice interrupted my thoughts. I cursed silently, realizing that my distraction had caused me to head towards the main staircase of the royal wing. It was a shorter route to my room, but was often filled with courtiers hanging around, not to mention my own family.

My sister rushed over with mincing steps, her elaborate taffeta day dress rustling as she approached. Over her shoulder, I could see Emilia and my heart sank even more. Her eyes were clearly red, and although she was dressed and made up as perfectly as ever, she didn't give off her usual air of sparkling solicitude. I stepped off to the side of the hallway as they came closer, partially obscuring us from view behind a huge potted plant.

"Marietta, I didn't realize you were looking for me," I replied in a low voice, noticing how Antonio took a position slightly further away from us for privacy's sake.

"Not *looking* for you?! After last night's madness?! Of *course* I would be looking for an explanation. And we both know that you owe one to Emilia." Marietta lowered her screeching to a whisper. "She's devastated of course, although she isn't making a fool of herself in front of everyone. *I* know how hurt she is inside."

I drew in a quick breath and spoke through gritted teeth. "I'm sorry to hear that of course, but do you think *here* is the appropriate place to discuss it. I'm quite sure Emilia wouldn't want you yelling about her broken heart through the all the palace halls."

Marietta threw up her perfectly manicured hands in exasperation. "And now you have the temerity to accuse me of being unfeeling toward my dearest friend, when you haven't even apologized for *your* unfeeling treatment of her in front of the *entire* court. You *will* do so, and you will do so right *now.* Only then can you both plan on how to get out of this mess."

I huffed out an irritated breath. "Marietta, there is *no* way to get out of - "

"Not that with that attitude there isn't. Now, I'll give you two a few minutes alone, so use it wisely." She flounced off in a rustle of maroon and blue, leaving Emilia and I staring after her.

I suppose I do owe Emilia an apology, if she was hurt by my actions. I probably didn't handle that the best. And she's a good person, even if she's not for me.

I turned toward her, and frowned when I noticed how hard she was trying to keep herself from crying. I had never in my life seen so much emotion from her. *She must truly be hurting to allow such feeling to come to the surface, where anyone passing could see.* My eyes darted around until they found a nearby alcove seat, embedded in the wall behind the stairwell. It wasn't exactly private, but it was close and out of sight of most of the foot traffic.

I held out my hand. "Come," I commanded her gently. With one hand holding a handkerchief up to her face, she placed the other other in mine. She wore no gloves, which was unusual for her, and another mark denoting her distress. Her skin was smooth and cool, the bones of her hand remarkably small. *If you squeeze to hard you're going to crush her.*

I led her over to the alcove and we took a seat, facing each other. She retained a surprisingly strong grip on my hand, and I let her. She certainly wasn't hurting me, and she seemed to need the comfort right now.

"Lady Emilia, my sister says that I've hurt you by my choice last night. I suppose I can't pretend that there may have been expectations created by others, although I hope I never created any myself. If that's true, I am sorry. I care for you very much as a friend, and of course my sister's friend. But really, you'll see that it will all work out for the best."

Emilia's glance darted anywhere but mine for a minute while she dabbed at her eyes, but after a moment she visibly pulled herself together and looked at me with vulnerability. "I agree, Prince Luca, I believe the Creator *will* work it out for the best.

You know that I, along with the entire court, prays continually for your future, and I trust that the White King is guiding you to the path you should be on, even if it's taken a strange turn for the time being." I blinked at her words. I hadn't expected those sentiments when Marietta left me alone with her. *Maybe she hadn't been led to believe that she would be my queen as much as I thought? Either way, she obviously has a good heart.*

"I must confess that for now, since you alluded to our circumstances earlier, I am bitterly hurt and disappointed, but I trust in your honor and dignity of course. And I'll do my best not to embarrass you in front of the court while I tend my heart. I hope you can allow me permission to admit such a thing."

Another tear slid down her cheek and the sight struck my heart. *I had no idea that she felt so strongly.* She had always kept her emotions so tightly lidded under a gracious exterior; something I had admired in contrast to my sister's loud transparency. *And my treatment of her probably wounded her more deeply than I know. I'll have to be sensitive to that moving forward.* In remorse, I raised her hand to my lips, pressing a light kiss of gratitude there.

"Of course, Lady Emilia, take your time with whatever you need. You have the heart of a saint in your patience with me. Please believe that I sincerely never meant to hurt you."

"I do," she whispered, looking timidly down at her hands.

"Luca," a voice said, and I turned in my seat to find Ella standing over my shoulder. I was happy to also see her friend and servant, Gia, standing a few steps behind. I had dispatched a servant to find her first thing in the morning so that Ella would have a friendly face in the palace, not to mention all her clothes and personal items. They must have come from the hallway behind me, which led to a series of lavish guest rooms, currently housing the foreign royals. Lady Emilia's grip on my hand tightened reflexively before she dropped it, allowing me to turn fully toward Ella.

"Ella?" I asked, torn between a desire to get Ella alone now that I had the chance, but to also make sure that the heartbroken woman behind me was taken care of.

Ella drew in a breath through her nose, looking oddly irritated. *Maybe she didn't get along with Princess Rosebelle as well as she thought.*

"I certainly wouldn't want to interrupt your day," she said in a strained voice, "but I would like to speak to you privately right now, while we're both free."

I opened my mouth to say yes, but was reminded of Lady Emilia as she shifted in her seat, her skirt falling over my right leg. I glanced back at her, and my heart tugged. She was still clearly a mess, and as well as I knew her, I was sure she wouldn't want to be seen in this state by the rest of the court.

I turned back to Ella. "I'm not free right now Ella, but how about about in thirty minutes? I just need to escort Lady Emilia to my sister's chambers, and have someone find my sister."

Ella opened her mouth and then shut it again, and I could just hear her foot tapping from under her dress. "Very solicitous of you, I'm sure. Unfortunately I only have a few minutes to change before I go on an outing with Princess Rosebelle. Couldn't you step away right now?"

Ella didn't look in distress, although she was obviously annoyed by something. We certainly had much to discuss after the events of the last day. *Too much for just a few minutes.* Lady Emilia's delicate sniff behind me reminded me of my duty to the lady.

"It will be better to wait until this evening when we're both free. I'll find you when you come back from your outing if I can."

Ella pressed her lips together and nodded, not even sparing a glance for Lady Emilia behind me, although that could have been out of delicacy for her obvious distress. I watched her walk toward the staircase for a moment, Gia at her side. Although her dress wasn't as ostentatious as the courtiers chattering in little groups around her, she cut a striking figure with her strawberry hair and swift stride.

Lady Emilia distracted me from my admiration as she set about putting herself in order. "Come along," I said, offering my arm. "I'll escort you to my sister's rooms and send a servant to find her so you have a friend nearby."

A grateful smile graced her wan face as she took my arm, leaning more heavily than was usual as we stood. *She's more delicate than I imagined. I know that's fashionable these days, but I hope a little heartbreak isn't going to make her ill. I'll never hear the end of it if that happens.*

It only took a few minutes to deposit her in my sister's rooms and dispatch a servant, and I was debating whether to find where Ella had been moved to today so I could speak to her before she left after all, when the sound of pounding feet and unbridled laughter alerted me to the presence of my two younger brothers.

At seventeen and sixteen years old, Marco and Dante could almost be twins. They were basically the same height and build, both with my father's strong nose and chin, and both with wavy blonde hair. The only difference between them was that Dante had inherited our mother's blue eyes instead of father's brown ones.

"Luca!" Dante panted as they skidded to a stop in front of me. "We were just coming to look for you!"

"Come on," Marcus grinned at me, grabbing my arm and dragging me toward my set of rooms. "You've got to get changed." I checked over my shoulder to see Antonio keeping up as my brothers dragged me into my rooms, scattering servants as we went.

"What's all this about?" I asked, laughing at their antics as the door shut behind us.

"Get changed!" Marcus urged as he dropped my arm and turned toward our other brother. Dante pulled several sets of of unobtrusive clothes that could belong to any commoner. They were even patched and a little frayed around the edges.

I shook my head and accepted my set from Dante. "What do you have in mind boys? Since my betrothed is busy right now, I *suppose* I could join you in one of your madcap schemes."

"It's not a scheme!" Dante protested.

"Not *much* of a scheme anyway," Marcus corrected. "We haven't sneaked out together in a long time, but today's the day to do it. You have to see what's going on!"

I paused in the act of pulling on the rough brown work shirt over my head, giving them both a suspicious look before pulling it on fully. "What exactly is going on? Will we need guards?"

"No, no! Don't be such a downer," Dante protested. "You'll be pleasantly surprised, don't worry."

"Speaking of guards," Marcus mumbled as he finished tightening the ties on his shirtsleeves. Cracking my door open, he beckoned to Antonio, who slipped through the door silently.

"I know we could never shake you on our adventures so we have a change of clothes for you too Antonio," he said, beckoning toward Dante.

Antonio raised an eyebrow at me and I nodded. He stepped over to Dante who handed him another outfit excitedly. "It's great fun Antonio, you'll see!"

It took even more stealth than usual to sneak from the palace at this time of day, but by using some of the many cramped servants passages, we managed to blend into the crowd near the kitchens and make our escape through the service entrance.

As usual it took a little to make the adjustment from palace walls to walking down the street, but I soon reveled in the freedom it afforded me. Freedom from fawning courtiers and political pitfalls, but not from noisy street vendors and rude pedestrians. As far as they were concerned, we were a band of potentially troublesome youths, so no one took the time to get out of our way, let alone bow and scrape.

Today however, the mood on the street was one of celebration. Houses and businesses had strung up little swags of fabric to decorate their houses. Here and there pockets of people danced to whatever music was available: a fiddle, clapping hands, or even just singing the tunes of popular ballads so that the dancers had a rhythm to move to. Nearly everyone had a drink in their hand, and the noise was deafening. People we passed shook our hands and called out blessings. Caught up in the spirit, we did the same, grinning from ear to ear to see such genuine happiness.

"What's it all for?!" I asked Marcus, hoping I already knew the answer but not sure I could trust that hope.

"For Lady Ella - and you of course!" he replied, grinning.

I shook my head, not daring to trust in the crowd's jubilation. They probably only rejoiced in the pomp and circumstance of a wedding, not in the lady herself. *And they certainly won't rejoice once they know she's a mage.*

"Oh don't spoil it," Dante said, dragging me toward a nearby tavern that was bursting with customers. "Come one, let's get a drink and something to eat."

"No drinks for you, young masters, unless you'll have cider," Antonio warned in his gravelly voice. Dante made a face at him and Marcus just laughed, holding the door open for the rest of us as we pressed inside.

There was a crush all the way to the bar. We somehow managed to grab our drinks, having to re-order Dante's when he tried to make off with a beer, but somehow found a booth just as the prior occupants were leaving. A barman brought over a loaf of bread and cheese, tossing them onto the table with a grunt before diving back into the crowd.

My stomach growled as I tore into the bread. It was thick and grainy, not anything like the fine bread of the palace, or even the hearty bread I was used to finding in taverns like these when Antonio and I snuck into the city. I flashed a look at him as I chewed, but he focused on his food, eating as methodically as he usually did.

"This stuff's hardly worth eating," Dante grumbled as he stuffed another piece into his mouth.

"Probably out of supplies with all the celebration going on. Be glad of a meal you stuck up sot." Marcus shot back, and Dante rolled his eyes. I looked around the room at the other patrons, noticing that most had crusts of similar bread, and there was very little meat.

A voice from the booth next to ours caught my ear, and a

strained to listen.

"I have a cousin that works in the palace there, in the kitchens, sure," it said, ponderous and self important. "He says that there's word that she even has-" he cleared his throat in an attempt to lower his voice, but he still had to shout to be heard by his companions over the nose, so it didn't really work, "...magic!"

There was a moment of silence from the table before someone else burst out. "Surely not! That family?! Allowing the Prince to marry a girl with magic. Preposterous."

"No, no," another voice chimed in, this one reedy and nervous. "I've heard the same. My Betty's brother was working during the ball. He said it's true! And what's more, she's not been locked up, or anything."

There was another moment of silence, and I shushed Dante and Marcus when they tried to get my attention as I strained to hear what they would say next to such a scandalous accusation.

"Well, I'll believe it when I see it. But if they're finally seeing sense about... all that, maybe there's hope for us yet," the second voice said thoughtfully. I let out a breath I had been holding, although I didn't relax. One group of commoners didn't hold the opinions of all. And I knew that the church preached as loudly as ever against magic. *But maybe our fight won't be as big as I've been thinking.*

We spent another hour wandering the city, partaking in festivities as we found them, and listening to the gossip about the beautiful Lady betrothed to the prince. The tales of the ball had been twisted in the telling, with people claiming the Lady had tried to run from the prince, but left her shoe on the stairs, giving him a clue to find her again, and old ladies sobbed as they recounted how her evil stepmother and stepsisters had mistreated her all her life, only to abandon her once they found out that the royals were taking her in. I shook my head and smiled, wondering how such embellishments occurred.

As evening threatened to come around, we headed back to the palace, our ears ringing with joy and our feet tired from dancing and dodging carriages in the street. We slipped back through the noisy servant's entrance and into the quieter and more stilted royal wing of the palace. I would have rather stayed in the joyful celebrations on the street.

CHAPTER SEVENTEEN

Ella

My veins ran hot and cold in alternating currents. I forced myself to hold my head high and not look back as I left Luca sitting so cozily with Lady Emilia. She's clearly angling for him, and believes she can catch him. Ignoring the looks of the perfectly coiffed courtiers all around me, I silently remonstrated with myself. She was upset. Maybe she truly was in love with him, and she's heartbroken. Have a little compassion Ella! Besides, she can try all she wants. If Luca has as much integrity as you believe he does, it won't matter.

I stumbled as I started up the staircase, refraining from cursing at the tittering laughs I heard from behind bejeweled fingers. Instead, I raised the hem of my skirt a little higher and lifted my chin.

"I'm not sure what's so funny about almost falling," Gia muttered at my side as we neared the top of the stairs.

"If we had nothing better to do than stand around and stare at each other all day, I'm sure we would find any change in scenery, even a country mouse nearly falling on the stairs, a pleasant diversion," I told her primly. She snorted a laugh as we turned the corner of the hallway, startling a servant.

Gia's presence soothed my nerves a little, although I couldn't fully let go of my insecurity at my newly discovered mage status, nor the creeping suspicion that an old flame might be luring Luca away from me before my very eyes. *She's obviously a court darling. And comes with less baggage than I apparently do. Maybe it's fate…* I shut that thought down before it complete itself. *What matters now is that we chose each other. Either our love will stand up under the test to our characters, or it wont, and we'll deal with the consequences either way.*

We strode into my room and Gia pushed the door shut behind us with a grateful sigh. "I'm glad to have a minute away from everyone's stares," she said, coming over to where I had already started taking off my nicest day dress. "But I can't believe they haven't moved you to a nicer room. You're practically in the dungeons!"

A laugh bubbled up at the thought. "They probably want me close to the soldiers in case my magic goes on a rampage or something. Little do they know, I'm more comfortable in a room like this than I would be in a cavernous suite filled with expensive breakables."

Gia shook her head with a smile as she helped me pull on my traveling suit. Although it wasn't very fancy, it was a better choice for a carriage ride into the city than any of the prettier dresses that my stepfamily had made for me. A pang hit my chest at the thought of them. *Have they really betrayed me?* **Why did they give me those shoes?!**

"You'll have to get used to that soon Ella," Gia said, pulling me from the depressing gravity of my thoughts. "Once you're the crown princess, you'll be living in the very best of the rooms here, with dresses that cost more than Lucedimora makes in a year!"

I shivered, the weight of all of that wealth like cold water down my back. There was so much excess at the palace that it made me uncomfortable. *Maybe I can sell some of the furnishings in my new room to pay for upgrades to Lucedimora's kitchen. Gia's mother would love that!*

The ghost of shame filtered through my thought and even though I brushed it away I couldn't deny it's whisper. Here I was thinking of selling things I didn't truly own and had never worked for, all to benefit my own estate.

Don't be so hard on yourself. Every waking moment for the last five years had been spent building and planning and rebuilding to keep Lucedimora from crumbling. Even though I was in a stable spot now, I knew how quickly the costs of running the estate could pile up and drown us. The instinct to get ahead would probably never leave me.

If you're going to sell priceless art you could at least use the funds to help those who are actually desperate. Even though running my estate was far from a cushy life, I knew it was also a trove of resources that others could never access. If I was truly kind hearted, I would think of helping those people first before I would truly help myself. "I suppose the Archbishop would say I should leave it to the White King to help those of the poor that are deserving, and leave the rest to their fates... but somehow that just doesn't sound like it makes sense," I muttered absent-mindedly.

A tug of the laces tying my sleeves to my bodice jerked me back to the present.

"And *do* keep some of those blasphemous thoughts to *yourself* Ella," Gia instructed sternly, clucking her tongue.

I grinned. "Yes Gia. Although if I'm going to slip up and let them out, I suppose doing so in front of the foreigners would be better than in front of our own King and Queen."

She laughed and shook her head, and I turned toward the only mirror in the room - a shaving mirror that sat on a plain dresser in the corner. I stood on tiptoes to take a slightly better look at my skirt, and then bent down to get a view of my collar and hair. The mirror was much to small to see anything other than little glimpses of my appearance. *Gia would never let me go out in an embarrassing state. But it's always nice to see for yourself that you're well turned out.* I rolled my eyes at my vanity and chuckled, turning back to my friend.

Her expression was serious as she handed me my gloves. "Ella, about Prince Luca in the hallway... I know it didn't look good, but I think he was just trying to help a lady in distress. Some men can't see through a woman's machinations like that. Remember David in the village? He nearly broke up his family for trying to help the baker's sister. We all thought he was sweet on her and his wife kicked him out. He didn't realize that the woman he was trying to help had been spreading rumors that they were in love, and that's why he was gifting her food and clothes and such."

I opened my mouth but she cut me off before I could say anything. "They're all the same Ella. People are people whether they're poor villagers or princes of the realm. And you can be intelligent in some ways and extremely stupid in others all at once. And some men feel they need to fix every crying woman's problems no matter the cost. Your Luca looks like one of those. Maybe he can't help it, the way he was raised."

I pursed my lips. "We'll see. I agree with you, at least to an extent, Gia. How he behaves when I talk to him about it will tell me everything I need to know. Honestly, I'm madder about the fact that he hid his rank from me than anything else right now." I sighed. "Although even the day I've spent at the palace around courtiers whispering over everything is enough to show me that maybe I could understand feeling the need to hide such a thing, especially if your heart was involved."

I shrugged, trying to shake off the cloak of emotions that weighed heavily on me right now. I needed to focus on figuring out my standing right now, and if I had read the King's words and actions correctly, cementing my security here at court was dependent on how instrumental I could be in creating a strong bond with the Mage countries. For whatever reason, the King seemed very interested in turning them his allies.

"I wish you could come with me on the carriage ride," I said to Gia. You've stood by me even though -" my chin trembled but I steeled my resolve. "You've stood by me even though it turns out I have magic. I don't think I've said how much I appreciate that, truly."

My friend rushed over and pulled me into a bone crushing hug. "You said it loud and clear with all the crying you did this morning, never fear." I laughed and she let me go, turning to lead the way toward the door. "Even if there was space for me I'm too busy. I have a second cousin that works as a seamstress here. I have a feeling that she might make a good lady's maid for you, or at least know someone trustworthy that would do a good job. I wish I could stay here with you myself but -" she stopped just before she pulled the door fully open and turned to look at me with an anguished face.

"I know," I rushed to reassure her. "Your Leonardo needs you, and *I* need you back at Lucedimora with your father. Only knowing that you two are there, running things probably even better than I can, will keep me going here." I paused, drawing in a steadying breath. "If I'm honest, I want to run back home as soon as possible. To make sure all is well, to question my stepmother and stepsister about... but I need to face the mess in front of me first. If all goes well here, all will go well at Lucedimora too." I punctuated the thought with a brisk nod, and Gia gave me a soft smile.

"We'll take care of everything just as you'd want us to, don't worry. Besides, I wouldn't I wouldn't be much help at a palace. I can see enough to have a little compassion for the way these spoiled rich people were raised, but I also have such a strong desire to drag each one out to the fields for a full day of work that I'm sure I would give in to the urge before the week is out."

A laugh burst out of my chest, too loud and bouncing off the walls of my sparsely furnished room, but the picture Gia had put in my mind couldn't be denied.

"I'm glad I'm not the only one," I gasped between peals of laughter. Gia's shoulder's shook as she laughed with me, and a some of the tension tied up between my shoulder blades loosened.

We took a moment to pull ourselves together before stepping into the corridor. I flicked a glance to the guards stationed on either side of the door. One looked straight forward as usual, not even looking in my direction. The other seemed like he had just flicked his eyes away from us, and was clearly fighting a smile. *He must have heard what we said - and agreed!* I don't know why the thought surprised me. I had been thinking of the guards here only in terms of a potential threat to me, or a power being used to contain the threat of my magic. But they were simply people too, and if they had been raised away from the lavish lifestyle the court exuded, they had surely thought that a good day of hard labor might clear up some of the nonsense at the palace pretty quickly.

My steps were lighter than they had been since before the ball as we followed the attendant that had been waiting to escort me back to Princess Rosebelle.

※ ※ ※

The carriage jolted forward, hitting a bump in the cobblestones a second later that jostled Princess Rosebelle, her friend Hazel, Lady Red, and myself a second time.

"And that's why they always start the royal carriages moving under the portico and away from the adoring eyes of the public," Hazel quipped. "They wouldn't be so adoring if they saw that you royals get jostled around just like the rest of us." She turned a sarcastic grin toward Princess Rosebelle who let out a very unladylike snort and leaned forward in her seat.

"Seeing that I'm royal only by marriage, hopefully the adoring public would forgive me any lapse in grace I have from a moving carriage."

"I have royal blood flowing through my veins on both sides of my family tree, and I'm probably the least graceful out of everyone in this carriage, so let the public adore something else," Red replied, her deep voice threaded with sarcasm. The others chuckled, and although I couldn't help cracking a smile, I didn't dare laugh at the warrior woman beside me.

"I'm excited to have a chance to see the city," Rosebelle said as we pulled out of the palace gates and turning toward me, "and I'm especially happy you agreed to come with us, Lady Fenice."

"Ella is fine, Princess Rosebelle," I replied, offering a smile. "And I'm honored that you invited me."

"You may call me Belle, if you like," she replied with a sincere smile. "We don't have any cities of this size in Asileboix or Sherwood, so coming to Charmagne is such a treat. I remember going to the capitol of Pelerin as a child, but I haven't been back since then. And Charmagne is so different!" She turned toward the side of the open carriage as we pulled into the city proper, and we all followed suit.

The carriage wound it's way through cobbled streets lined with sandstone buildings, sticking to the main thoroughfares where the palace guard cleared the way ahead of us. On either side, masses of ordinary people stopped to cheer, the sound following us down the street like an undulating wave. At first the noise overwhelmed me, and I tried to emulate what I observed of Princess Rosebelle's behavior out of the corner of my eye - graceful waves and a calm smile. In contrast, Lady Red generally ignored the cheers, her eyes scanning the crowd in the same way that our guards did, looking for potential threats. Beside Belle, Hazel beamed in honest enjoyment, waving at children and babies and eliciting smiles. Soon, I found myself becoming, not exactly comfortable with the attention, but comfortable in my own skin at least, and I began waving and laughing as well, startling myself and those in the crowd when I called back responses to those cheeky enough to call out a silly rhyme. More people pressed in, respectful of the invisible barrier our guards maintained, but getting close enough to throw flowers and call out blessings and jokes. The atmosphere felt almost like a solstice fair, and my heart lifted.

Still, around the edges of the boisterous crowd, I could see people who weren't cheering. Some wore scowls, dressed in rags and clearly malnourished. *The sight of four finely dressed ladies in a gold gilt carriage probably feels like a slap in the face for them,* I realized with a jolt of guilt. Still others, much better dressed and clearly not missing any meals, made signs of protection against evil as we passed. They ignored the ones in rags on the edges of the streets, focused as they were in their ire toward us. *How can I win such people over, who hate me because of something I was apparently born with? We've been taught to do so since birth.* My joy somewhat diminished, I still tried my best to enjoy our ride and explain what details I knew of the capitol to Belle and the others. Soon the carriage pulled into the countryside, away from the crush of the city, and we stopped at the top of a small hill.

A structure had been built there with views all the way to the great Charmagne Lake, which was really more of an inland sea. The pavilion had been set up with a table and chairs, and a luxurious picnic lunch was laid out on the table. As we ate, we relaxed into lively conversation that slowly turned more thoughtful as we discussed our countries of origin, and their differences.

"We grew up much as you did in that regard," Belle said, gesturing to herself and Hazel as our conversation turned toward magic. "I spent much of my youth alternating between studying what we *thought* was the arcane history of magic with my father, and then covering our tracks when he seemed to go too far in procuring books or magical artifacts. There was a part of me that sort of wanted to believe it was all true, but the prevailing attitude in Pelerin has been that magic is either an evil art, or wasn't real."

"That's started to change," Hazel added, popping a grape into her mouth. "With the Battle of Asileboix ripping apart all illusion as to what the Mage countries are like, more and more people are becoming open to the idea of magic. Especially since the Pelerine royal family has been seeking a treaty with Spindle. Oops, I probably wasn't supposed to say that."

Red laughed. "I don't think that's a state secret. They haven't been very discreet in their machinations. Besides, you're Asilean now."

I popped a grape into my mouth as well, biting down and reveling in the cool sweetness as it spread across my tongue.

The air was warm, coaxing me into a relaxed stupor as insects buzzed in the long grass covering the hillside. In the distance, cattle lowed, the sound carried by a soft breeze that brushed our skin just enough to keep the sweat away, but not enough to chill.

"I would like to visit Pelerin," I reflected, twirling another grape between my fingers. "If I could see a place that once rejected magic, but is beginning to embrace it, I might feel better about my own situation. As it is, I can't help think that once my magic becomes common knowledge, the court will turn on me, and our people too."

Hazel sat up poker straight in her seat as Belle and Red turned thoughtful eyes in my direction. I avoided their gaze, still too uncomfortable with this new part of myself to be able to defend it from any judgment I read there.

Belle responded in an understanding tone. "Although I can't pretend to know what it's like to discover that you've had magic all along, I do know the feeling of what you thought was your reality being stretched by too many truths at once." Startled, I met her gaze, hope blossoming in my chest.

"Yes," she said with a little laugh. "Luckily I had Hazel by my side when I moved to Asileboix, and we knew we would have to become comfortable with magic in some ways. But discovering the extent of the magic - the shift that my husband and the others go through. That was startling to say the least."

A part of the hope in my chest fizzled. Princess Rosebelle was in the exact position that Luca was in right now. She had fallen in love with a Prince who was secretly a shifter. But Prince Andrus had complete command of his magic, and lived in a society where it was not only accepted, but needed. I was out of my element in so many ways. I had only the barest notion of how to behave in the court etiquette, and without a doubt I had *no* talent for navigating politics. Usually my strength came from knowing what was most important to me, and what my strengths and weaknesses were; but now there was a newly discovered magic inside me that I knew nothing about. I couldn't even trust myself these days.

"How... how did you move beyond that?" I asked her, my voice low and faltering. Luca and I had fallen in love fast, but it was true. I wanted what was best for him, but I also wanted him for myself. *If what's best for him isn't me, I must bring myself to find a way to sever our tie - without hurting him.*

"I didn't really," Belle said, sharing another look with Hazel. "It was alarming at first, but mainly it just made all the pieces of the puzzle that was my husband come together. It didn't change who he was, just made him more... him. And I'm only interested in supporting him to be the best version of himself that he can be. His magic makes him strong. If I were to deny that part of him, I wouldn't truly love him."

Her words cracked something in my heart. *Could Luca ever come to feel the same for me? To love me enough to encourage my magic, not just tolerate it? He hasn't even made an effort to come talk to me about the ball.*

"In some ways it was harder for me, but in other it was easier," Hazel added. I turned toward her, curious. "The only reason I was in Asileboix was to support my friend in a country that seemed strange at every turn. The important thing for me was to try and see everyone and every thing with an open mind and an open heart." She chuckled. "Besides, magic can save us servants a lot of time and effort in everyday tasks, and I won't say no to that!"

I laughed with the others, her point sticking in my mind. *If we truly do put this wedding tour together, I simply must look into some of the labor saving spells that they use in the mage countries. If we could improve the lives of the working class here, it would be such an improvement.*

"If you like, I could arrange time for you to speak with Captain Marchand," Red spoke up, looking at me thoughtfully. "He grew up with Belle and Hazel, and found out he had magic only within the last year. He's still walking his own path toward accepting and understanding this new part of himself, but I am sure he wouldn't mind sharing his experience."

A genuine smile grew on my face, matching the warmth in

my heart. "I didn't realize he - that makes me much less alone, thank you." I shut my mouth before my voice could wobble, emotions threatening to overwhelm me. *I'm not alone in this.* There were others like me, discovering magic when they hadn't wanted it. And they had learned to live with it, even benefit from it. I could too; if I could figure out how to access it.

"How did he learn of it? I have no sense of my own magic at all. I only know about it because you and Prince Andrus discovered it."

"That may not be uncommon for your situation. Eddie didn't realize he was using magic his entire life because his isn't very apparent." She flashed a grin at Belle, who rolled her eyes, before continuing. I watched the exchange between the princess and the warrior with interest. "His magic has gifted him with the affinity of command. He can use it in other ways of course too, now that he's aware of his magic. But his natural tendency is boss every one around for their own good. It serves him well in the military."

"It's irritating beyond belief in regular life," Belle said, making the other two laugh.

"That's because *you* like bossing people around too much to appreciate someone else doing it with more power," Hazel accused, making Belle roll her eyes again while Red laughed. I couldn't help chuckling quietly as well. Being in the presence of three good friends was comforting in it's own way. *I hope I can establish such friendships in my new life.*

Red turned back toward me. "Eddie grew into his magic slowly, without much notice because it expressed itself in a very natural way for someone in his position. Your magic seems as though it was suppressed in some way. I'm surprised you're not feeling the after affects of the suppression spell being released. I wouldn't blame you for alternating between screaming from the rooftops and crying on the floor."

I shot her a startled look. "Well, I have felt like doing that when I'm not being shepherded around to different events, but I just thought it was a response to all the changes I've had to adjust to over the last day."

Red nodded. "I'm sure that's part of it, but I'm willing to bet that some of your internal turmoil is from the spell beginning to unwind. It may become more volatile as the days progress." She turned toward Belle. "I sent a message to Eileen last night. She's sending a suppression charm for Ella. If you can manage to get permission from King Cirro to allow the use of a charmed object, Ella can wear it until we find an appropriate teacher for her." Rosebelle nodded and Red turned back to me. "We use such charms to ease the magic of our youths with more volatile magic. As long as you wear it, your magic should unwind in a more controlled manner, long enough for you to test it's boundaries and discover your talents. Is there anything you've always had an unnatural talent for in the past?"

I frowned, thinking over my life in the past few years and shook my head. "I'm good with horses, although my stable master is even better. I'm good at running my estate, but I was taught to do that from as long as I can remember, so I had *better* be good at it by now. I do tend to tell people what to do, but that's only natural since I've primarily been either running my estate, or branching out in my business... and things don't always go my way, that's for sure," I scratched the back of my hand ruefully, remembering my mental exhaustion while negotiating with the Marchand family representative a week ago.

The Marchand family?! The connection suddenly snapped into place and I glanced at Red. "Is... is Captain Marchand related to a trading family from Pelerin by any chance?"

She lifted her eyebrows. "Yes, he's the oldest son, although his younger brother has taken over the position of heir. I believe he's been opening some negotiations with several businesses here in Charmagne. He stopped at a few on his way into the capitol before the ball."

I huffed a laugh. "Yes, Thomas. He stopped at Lucedimora on his way into the capitol. I didn't make the connection before now." I had been trying to secure a connection with the Marchand Trading House for at least a year now, and although my visit had gone well, I hadn't been sure whether I would be able to stand out to him among a tour of other businesses. Now I was having lunch with his soon to be sister-in-law. *There must be a fairy godmother watching out for me somewhere. Or maybe my magic just brings me good luck?* My parents faces flashed through my mind and I shook my head. *Not good enough luck.* I repressed a sigh. Like anything else, I would need time and persistence to work out my magic and my place in this new life I was in. I sneaked a glance at the women around the table, now engaged in a discussion about Thomas' enthusiasm for his business trips around Charmagne. *The first thing I need to do is start building a family of friends around me in the palace. If I had women like these at my back, I would feel much more secure as I start to figure my new life out.*

※ ※ ※

I stilled my urge to bounce on my heels as the guard who had escorted me to the dungeons spoke with another guard about my request. The waiting area we were in had no windows, as it was underground, but was lit with bright candles along the walls. The unscented candle wax did little to cover the tang of rough sandstone and dusty corners that tickled my nose. *At least it doesn't smell worse.* I always imagined dungeons as places of filth and decay, with moaning prisoners begging for mercy. From what I had seen so far, it could pass as a spruced up version of the cellar in my own castle. Dark because of it's location, but clean enough and certainly not full of dangers beyond a stray mouse.

After my outing with the foreign royals yesterday, I had arrived back just in time to dress for dinner. I spent an evening as the plainest person in a room of sparkling wealth. I wasn't exactly a country mouse, dressed as I was in my ball-gown of gold and silver shot blue, but I had only the one dress fine enough for a royal dinner, and now it reminded me of the disastrous ball the evening before. Not to mention, the shoes that matched the dress were in royal custody now, so I had to be content with my best walking day shoes; and they weren't nearly fine enough to match such a dress. I felt awkward and out of place, worried that my lack would be mocked by the others, and irritated with myself for caring about such a thing.

Luca had been seated at the opposite end of the table from me again, and other than a few looks in my direction, was absorbed with his seating companions, Lady Emilia and Lady Red. As Lady Red wasn't much of a conversationalist, that meant Lady Emilia had engaged most of his time.

After dinner the men and women has separated for evening entertainment, and I soon left for my room, tired from the day and unable to pretend to be interested in the card games the women were playing. I wanted to meet with Luca and regain some even footing with him; to find out what he was thinking and how he felt about my magic, and to develop a plan for how we would move forward, or how I would begin to create a life for myself here at court if I couldn't go back to Lucedimora. I hated inaction, and card games were not a big enough distraction from the truth that I was standing still.

This morning, Gia managed to track down a page to help her find Luca's rooms. When they arrived however, Luca was already gone, apparently meeting with some naval officers about last minute preparations for his upcoming mission. Since my latest attempt to connect with Luca had failed, I decided to try and gain clarity on another piece of my fractured life: my stepfamily. This time I asked one of the guards stationed outside of my door for help, while Gia left to check back in on the potential lady's maid for me.

A door clanged and my guard beckoned to me, the same one I had caught smiling the day before. Apparently I was going to be allowed to visit my stepsister, who was even now sitting in jail for a crime we apparently had both committed - having magic.

I followed my guard through a massive iron door into a dark hallway, lined with cells. Another guard closed the door behind us, then lead us onward. Our shoes scraped on the stone floor, sending up whispery echoes to bounce against the walls. A few faces appeared at the small grills in some of the cell doors, but none of the occupants spoke, simply watched our progress down the hall. I shivered as we reached the other end, fighting my imagination as I wondered what each prisoner had done to end up here. Had they committed terrible crimes? Or were they here for something outside their control, like Alessia?

The second door led to a cramped staircase that wound even further down into the earth. When we got to the lower level, the prison guard lifted an iron portcullis, allowing me and my guard to pass into a shorter hallway, but not following us through.

"I'll remain here to lift the portcullis when you're through," he said as he dropped the barrier between him and us. "It's warded for protection, so I'll not raise it if she uses her magic against you." The guard at my side shifted, then nodded at the other before turning and indicating the door on the right hand side of the nearly dark hall. "The prisoner is in this cell. I'll remain here if you… if you need aid."

I swallowed nervously and drew a breath. "Thank you, sir, for the offer. She is my sister, though; she would never harm me. Or any of her fellow guards."

The guard blinked at me for a moment, before offering a bow. "Sergeant Madrigal, madam, at your service."

I blinked back, unsure of what he was trying to convey by offering his name at this moment, in the dungeons of the palace. *Is he offering his support because he's seen the situation I'm in, or is he just tired of having me call him 'sir' or 'you there'?*

"Thank you Sergeant Madrigal," I said after a brief pause, and he lifted out of his bow. Stepping toward the cell door, he peered through the small grill in the door and then slid the bolts free, unlocking the door from the outside and holding it open while I walked through.

The cell was about half the size of my room, but not overly cramped. A single bed lined one wall, and a chamberpot sat against the other. Alessia stood to attention in front of her bed pallet, although she relaxed when she saw me. We stared at each other for a charged moment, neither one of us knowing how to break the silence.

"Are you well?" I asked finally. Her cell seemed clean and adequate, but that didn't mean she wasn't being treated badly.

"Well enough," she replied, pressing her lips into a thin line.

"You're not... they aren't..." I trailed off, waving my arms vaguely toward her, "because of your magic?"

"If you're asking whether I'm being tortured because of my magic, then no."

My shoulders sank in relief and I let out a breath. "Since they've mostly left me alone I had hoped they would do the same to you, but I'm glad to hear it from you. I've been worried."

I wrapped my arms around my waist, hugging myself instead of my stepsister. She gave off a prickly air of hostility or impatience. She used to do that right after our parents had married, and I had thought it was because of the changes to her life. I hadn't seen it in awhile though, and was confused.

"What do you mean they've left you alone? You thought they would harm you because of my magic? Didn't you tell them I'm only your stepsister?"

"No, I'm sure they know our relationship, especially since Luca is your friend." Alessia snorted and my heart hurt for her for a moment. If Luca hadn't made an effort to visit with me, he surely hadn't made an effort to visit Alessia. *Probably. Or maybe he had, and it's just me that's not the priority.*

I took a breath, refocusing on my stepsister. "I meant because of your magic. They haven't put many restrictions on me because of my magic, so I had hoped they wouldn't do so to you either."

"Because of *your* magic?!" Alessia demanded, shocked.

I stared at hear, realization dawning. "They didn't tell you! Yes, I have magic apparently. It was sealed somehow. I never knew of course or else I-" I broke off, realizing that Alessia *had* known she had magic but had never told me.

A bitter laugh broke from her lips and she flopped down to

sit on the bed behind her, putting her head in her hands as her laugh petered out.

"Alessia, why didn't you tell me about your magic? Or about Luca being the prince? I don't understand why you kept those things from me?"

My stepsister laughed, lifting her face to look at me sardonically. "I didn't tell you about Luca because he asked me not to. He promised he would tell you in due time. And I trusted him." She took a breath, shaking her head. "And I didn't tell you about my magic because I didn't trust *you*. We don't trust anyone with our magic that doesn't need to know. And you didn't."

Her words felt like a slap to the face, and I wavered on my feet. After I got over the first sting, I could grudgingly acknowledge what she meant, even if my heart screamed that she *could* have trusted me. *If my magic hadn't been discovered so publicly, I doubt I would would want to tell anyone either.*

"I'm sorry you felt you couldn't trust me, but I can understand keeping such a thing secret." I wanted to ask more about her magic, but her bitterness stopped the words in my throat. She didn't seem to be in the mood for sharing. "Why did your mother give me those shoes then, if your magic was so secret?"

An angry expression passed over her face and she balled her hands into fists before forcing them to relax. "I didn't know she would do that, or I would have stopped her. I suppose she thought of you as family, and wanted to test Luca's love. She shouldn't have done so without explaining everything first, so she must have been *very* confident that he loved you truly." Her voice twisted and underneath the anger I heard deep pain that puzzled me. *Was she in love with someone at the academy and been betrayed?* She certainly wouldn't open up to me about it now.

"I'm sorry that you were dragged into this mess and... and the career you've worked so hard for is in jeopardy. I've always wanted what's best for you." I said, hoping to infuse some of the concern I felt into my words.

Alessia laughed again, turning angry eyes my way. "Don't concern yourself, none of it is your fault. You didn't force Luca to love you, nor did you ask for the glass slippers, nor did you make me warn my family of their danger, nor did you ask for whatever magic you've discovered within yourself. You've made your choices, and I've made mine, and we'll both deal with the consequences, no matter how unequal they are. I know you want the best for me, I've never doubted it. Let those words ease your conscience and go. I want to be alone."

I took a step back at the almost physical feeling of anger rolling off her and turned, tears pricking at my eyes as I pulled open her cell door.

Sergeant Madrigal closed it behind me, sliding the locks home as I dried my eyes and took a few deep breaths. He stayed quiet the entire walk back to my rooms, and step by step I pulled myself together.By the time I made it back to my empty room, some of my old self confidence was returning.

Alessia was right. I hadn't asked for any of the situation I found myself in, but I was in it. It was time to move forward. If Luca wasn't available, I could work on another part of my responsibilities. Pulling some paper from my carrying case that Gia had moved along with the rest of my belongings from our lodging, I started on the first of several letters home; letters to my stepmother, to Aria, and to Giuseppe. I wanted answers, and Lucedimora wouldn't suffer in my absence if I could help it.

❋ ❋ ❋

Another sumptuous dinner surrounded by sparkling courtiers, while I sat in the same ball gown and endured pointed looks. I ignored them all, speaking politely when spoken to, but otherwise focusing solely on my food.

Gia had returned to dress me, dragging her cousin Jacquetta along in her wake. Jacqui, as she preferred to be called, proved to be a wonder, and their friendly banter had been a balm to my soul. Jacqui had suggested a few adjustments to my dress and accessories which, although they couldn't disguise the fact that it was the same dress, made me feel as though I was at least trying, which was something.

Luca had been seated far from me yet again, and had been so late to dinner that he hadn't even escorted me in. At least this time he was on the same side of the table as I was, so I didn't have to see him chatting away to Lady Emilia for a second night in a row.

A silver bell rung out above the chattering courtiers at the long table, and everyone fell silent as King Cirro stood at one end.

"We have arranged for a fireworks display over the city skyline to mark the occasion of my son's betrothal. You may adjourn to the upper ballroom or the front gardens to view them if you will. My family will be appearing on the royal balcony, along with my son's intended, to allow the people to celebrate with us."

The king turned away, ignoring his wife and the rest of his family and starting toward where the royal balcony must be. A servant appeared to pull the chair out as I stood, and I maneuvered around the person seated next to me, who was chattering animatedly with the woman on his other side. Before I could take a step to follow the King, Luca appeared at my side, seizing my arm and tucking it under his.

Shock at his presence and being suddenly anchored on his arm stole my words for a few minutes, but as we broke free of the crowd around the table I tugged on his arm to get him to stop.

"Luca, are you sure we should be doing this?"

"Doing what?" he asked, confused. "You heard my father. This is the way to the balcony." He smiled. "I didn't want anyone else to escort you so I seized my chance."

Irritation flamed at his easy smile after almost two days of ignoring me. "Who cares who escorts me to the balcony? There's no need to pretend to me that you don't wish you were escorting someone else."

Luca froze, a frown forming between his brows. "Who else would I wish to be escorting?" he asked cautiously.

My face flushed as my temper flashed. "You pretend that you

don't wish it were Lady Emilia on your arm right now? That's rich. Especially since you already acknowledged before this whole mess started that she was the one who was intended for you. And now I can see why! She's everything I'm not! How could you not give your heart to her?!"

Luca flinched at my words, and I blinked back tears, a little embarrassed by how much my emotions had gotten out of control. I didn't regret speaking what was on my heart, but I wished it had been in a calm manner.

Luca glanced behind us to the dinner party that was still breaking up, then tugged me forward into the corridor that the King had entered. I followed, still attempting to get my wobbling heart under control. Once we were out of sight, he pulled us to a stop and turned to face me, still keeping my arm tucked in his.

"I would *never* give my heart to Emilia. Even if you didn't have it so completely, she would never have it. Why would you say such a thing?"

His words caught me off guard. "Are you saying… are you saying that *I* still have your heart?"

He blew out a breath of annoyance. "Obviously. Didn't Lady Red say that the slippers would break and we would face deadly consequences if our bond was broken? We're standing here arguing like any other pair of lovers, so I think it's safe to say that our bond is intact."

Exhilaration at his oddly professed love warred with irritation at his execution. "Well… fine. That's… but how was I supposed to know?! The few times I've seen you over the last few days you've had Emilia fawning all over you. You haven't exactly pushed her away."

Luca ground his teeth together. "Are you implying that I've been less than honorable in my dealings toward her? I was just trying to make sure she felt honored and seen. She was led to believe she would marry me, and doesn't have many friends at court!"

"Doesn't have many friends!?" I whispered harshly, gesturing to myself. "And what about me?! I don't know anyone here! I'm under suspicion because of *magic* that I didn't even know that I had. And you haven't bothered to even check on me!"

Luca's jaw dropped and he took my other arm in his hand, pulling me close. "Ella, I didn't - I thought that you were busy with Princess Rosebelle and all the other things ladies do to set up their households at court. And I've had to prepare for my mission, I'm so sorry if I -"

At that moment Luca's mother and sister turned around the corner and he released me, throwing a look their way before towing me forward. "I'm an idiot. I tried to find you once or twice, but just thought you were busy," he whispered in my ear, his breath eliciting a shiver as I tried to concentrate on my words and not tripping as we hurried down the hall. "If my actions are making you doubt me, I'll never forgive myself."

I turned, leaning on him to steady myself as we continued forward. "I didn't doubt you, not really, I just didn't know what you thought after everything that had happened and I - I needed support."

Luca squeezed my hand as we slowed to a more sedate pace as the balcony came into view. "I'll find time for us to talk before I leave for my mission, I swear it." His gaze was fierce as he willed his sincerity in his eyes, and my heart felt lighter than it had since the ball. Before we could speak anymore, we were whisked out onto the royal balcony, the fireworks starting as we stepped outside. A roar went up from the crowd as Luca and I stepped up to the railing, eyes trained on the beautiful display in the sky. The noise was overwhelming, but Luca was like an anchor at my side. Unwinding our arms, he put his around my waist, pulling me close. I let myself lean against him, ignoring everything except our connection and the sparkling sky.

As the final boom reverberated through the air, a trail of fire tracing it's dying path back down to earth before fizzling out, I turned to see if we were heading back inside. Luca turned at the same moment and I laughed, steadying myself against him so I didn't fall. Our eyes locked, and before I knew what was happening, he dipped his head down to mine and captured my lips in a searing kiss; gentle, slow, and full of assurance of his love. I was dizzy with it by the time he pulled away, leaning his forehead against mine briefly. Then he laughed and tipped his head toward the crowd. Suddenly I realized that the roar I had heard wasn't my blood rushing in my ears from the kiss. It was a thousand Charmagnian subjects cheering our highly immodest display. My eyes flew back to Luca and he grinned at me apologetically before lifting his free hand to waive. I couldn't help grinning, sure that my cheeks were as red as my hair, and waving as well.

As we finally turned to go inside I caught sight of the King and Queen standing to the other side of the balcony, a study in contrasts. The Queen's mouth was pinched in disgust, and her eyes were narrowed in judgment. She stared at each of us in turn before sweeping into the palace, not deigning to share space with us for a moment more. The King gestured for us to follow the Queen, one eyebrow raised and barely suppressing a grin. I blinked at the tacit approval, wondering if we had fully won him over or not. *No reason to let your guard down. His approval probably has more to do with the cheering crowds than his son's happiness.* I squeezed Luca's arm tight as we crossed the threshold of the door. *I'll never let Luca have to guess as to whether my love for him is conditional on political maneuvering or not. That's one thing I can give him, that he might not be able to find elsewhere.*

CHAPTER EIGHTEEN

Luca

"You're here," I breathed, the tingling of anticipation I had been feeling all morning clicked into place under my ribcage as I caught sight of Ella. She was dressed in a pretty sea green gown that brought out the color of her eyes. A picture of the two of us, sailing on an ocean that matched her dress and eyes flashed through my mind. *Let that be a vision,* I begged the White King. He wasn't known for visions, but legend said he wrote the future in the stars, so maybe it could be true.

Ella raised her eyebrow and quirked a smile as I came toward her and brought her hand to my lips. "Your note told me where to be and when. Did you think I would ignore such a chance?"

I grinned, basking in the warmth of her assurance and wishing I didn't have to leave so soon. *If only she could come with me, safely somehow.* I grinned wider and she gave me a mock scowl.

"I was only wondering how I could make a sailor out of you in the next day, so I could take you along on my first command."

A chuckle broke free from Ella, warming my heart. "I'd make a terrible sailor. I tried boating once on a creek near our house and fell in and nearly drowned. And I can swim! Something about the water makes my head get turned around. I'll stick to the land and my horses, thank you. I could run a horse along the beach while you go sailing, how about that?"

I still had a hold on her hand so I brought it up to my lips again, brushing a kiss to the back of it again lightly, and reveling in the way her eyes softened.

"Yes, it may be better that way. I imagine you'd have taken command of my ship in the first day if I let you on board with me, and worse, have it running better than I would by week's end. My pride couldn't stand the bruising that would be."

Ella tipped her head back and let out an unfettered laugh. As always, my heart lifted with the sound, and I felt lighter than I had a few minutes ago.

"I know as much about sailing as you know about running Lucedimora. Less probably," she added, tilting her head thoughtfully. "After all, you were raised on how to run a country, and from what I've seen of Cintola Palace so far, the working of it is a bit like running Lucedimora, just more. More staff, more work to get done, and much, *much* more drama."

"That was one of the things I adored about going to Deerbold Academy - escaping the drama of the palace. Speaking of which, if I know anything about these gardens, they're full of courtiers ready to pounce on unsuspecting royalty. Let's get moving before someone finds us." I tucked her hand under my arm and looked around. "Where is your guard?" I asked urgently, a tendril of fear uncurling in my heart. "You should have a guard with you at all times, Ella. Now that you're linked with me - you need to be safe!" I whispered urgently, my sudden anxiety over her vulnerability making my tone harsh. Somehow she seemed beloved by the commoners already, but that would probably just paint an even bigger target on her back for the shifting factions of court. Although my father ran a generally peaceful kingdom, there were those who would do anything for gold. Including murder.

"Luca, it's all right," Ella replied in a low tone. She squeezed my arm and jerked her head over my shoulder. One of the palace guards stood behind a nearby hedge, and beyond him stood my personal guard Antonio. I frowned. "That's a palace guard. You should have one of the royal guards. I'll have that changed right away."

"Don't," Ella said urgently, drawing my attention. "I like him. He's been surprisingly kind and doesn't seem to fear me despite the magic I carry." Her hand went up to her necklace, a carved gray stone rock that seemed at odds with the pretty dress she was wearing. She followed my gaze and let go. "It's a suppression charm. Lady Red gave it to me, with your father's permission. It's supposed to suppress my magic to a tolerable level, until a teacher can be arranged for me." Her smile turned rueful. "I'd wager I don't even need a guard because of my magic. Most of the others either shun me for it or are afraid of me." She nodded toward the palace guard. "Sergeant Madrigal is one of the few that doesn't seem to fear me or look down on me. I'd rather keep him."

I nodded and we started forward down the gravel path. The sun was high above, it's light glinting off of the gold and copper in Ella's hair. Being close to her, touching her, just felt right. It eased the ache in my chest that had been a constant companion the last few days while I had been focusing on preparing for my mission. I didn't like to think of what it would be like to spend a month away from her. A flash of inspiration hit me and I changed course at the next intersection.

"Are you ... is it hard for you, knowing that I have magic?" Ella asked tentatively as we came to a gate in the enormous back wall of the formal guards. I lead her through, then stopped on the other side to face her fully.

Her face was lined with tension, her fear at my answer obvious. I thought over my words carefully, wanting to be honest but above all, wanting to make sure she felt loved.

"It's a little uncomfortable, if I'm truly honest." Ella flinched, and almost as a reflex I put my hands on either side of her waist and pulled her closer. She met my eyes, her expression confused.

"It's a little uncomfortable, but only because it's new and unexpected. And I worry for how it might make life difficult for you. But I'm not uncomfortable with *you* Ella, just all the ways I need to grow as a person and as a prince." I sighed. "Ever since

I was sent to Deerbold, I've been slowly learning that our attitudes about magic in Charmagne are outdated. I couldn't see a way forward on changing our laws and public opinion, and I just gave up on seeing real change during my father's and my rule. Now change is upon us. It has to be, because the woman I love has magic, and there is *no one else* I'll have by my side. No one," I practically growled the last words, surprising myself at the intensity of my feeling. *Is that the heart bond between us that makes me feel so strongly? It doesn't seem like it. I felt that way before the ball.* Having her here felt like a dream come true, and if it took a heart bond to keep her here, then so be it.

She stood before me, tears gathering in her eyes and I was struck again by her words from the night before. "If I'm feeling uncomfortable, you must feel like a ship tossed around in stormy seas," I said, daring to press a furtive kiss to her forehead and hoping no one was around to see. *As future King and Queen we're supposed to be the models of decorum. But it's all I can do not to whisk her away somewhere all to myself...*

"Yes," she said, her tone soft and a little wry. "All of these changes are making me dizzy. I'm here at the palace contemplating becoming Queen someday! And I have *magic!* And my family - " her breath hitched and she took a breath before continuing on. "I've already lost my mother and father. It seems as though my stepmother and Aria have fled the country, and Alessia is in jail." She tipped her chin up to look me in the eyes. "I can't loose them, Luca. I need - I need to talk to them, to understand what they were thinking. But whatever it was, I'm sure it was well intentioned. I love them, and I know they love me. But I'm afraid they're gone forever, and I can hardly dare think of what Alessia's fate will be. There's a part of me that is desperate to run back to Lucedimora and hide while you're gone, but I can't go back leaving Alessia in jail here, only to return to an empty home. But I don't know how to fix it."

I pulled her toward me fully then, wrapping my arms around her in an attempt to cover her from all her concerns. She took a deep shuddering breath, releasing it in a sharp blast before stepping back slightly. I let her go reluctantly, tucking her hand under my arm again and leading her forward on the path.

"I've been thinking about what to do with Alessia," I said, glancing over at Ella. "It's just possible that I could persuade my father to release her into my custody, to allow her to prove herself as my personal guard on my mission. She and Antonio know each other well, and would work well as a team for me I think. If she proved her loyalty in that way, perhaps my father could bestow a lesser judgment on her, or maybe remand judgment to my discretion. I can't get around the fact that she performed magic so publicly, and that's illegal, but I could make sure the punishment fit the crime more than it might otherwise. And hopefully my father will see sense and start repealing some of the magic laws."

I looked over at Ella to see what she was thinking, and was struck by her beauty all over again. Her eyes were shining, full of hope and soft with some emotion that I greedily hoped was all for me.

"Do you really think you could make all that happen?" she asked quietly. I nodded, pride that I could serve my fiance and her family in such a meaningful way filling my chest. *I only ever want to make her feel this way, feel loved and cared for. Take some of her burdens from her.* A tinge of guilt tugged at my conscience.

"Ella, I'm sorry - truly sorry - that I didn't tell you I was a prince. I really meant to do so much earlier. Before I proposed, definitely. Somehow or another it never seemed like the right time... I was scared, if I'm honest. Scared that acknowledging it would either make you want me for the wrong reasons, or push you away because you wouldn't want the challenge of being with me. But I let that fear take away making that decision for yourself, and I can see now that it took away a little of your trust in me. I'm sorry."

Ella's eyes stayed soft but she pressed her lips together. A sliver of fear slipped through my heart. *Will she condemn me for my cowardice? She should.*

Instead she sighed. "You shouldn't have done it. I detest deception, and yours made me doubt your heart for a little while too. It helped nothing." I felt my shoulders tense at her words, but forced myself to hear them patiently. She was right, after all.

"But the truth is, I can see why you might do it. After being in the palace for only a few days, I can't imagine what it would have been like to grow up here. Everything seems to be a play for power over someone else." She shuddered, and I loved her for it. "I won't play you for power, Luca, I promise that. Don't lie to me again, because I don't deserve that, and neither do you. And I'm not someone you have to protect yourself from."

I slowed to a stop again, opening my mouth to respond but couldn't form anything to say. She had seen right through me into the darkest corner of my heart and spoken the words to bring light and warmth there.

Her eyes searched mine for a moment, and as if she knew my struggle, she lifted her hand to mine, pressing a gentle kiss to my knuckles, as gentle as mine had been to hers earlier. Her soft lips pressed an ocean of love into my skin, leaving a tingle of promise behind of what we could have if we faced our struggles together in the years ahead.

Stones skittered on a path just ahead of ours, announcing the presence of a someone on a nearby path. I pulled Ella forward, towing her somewhat ungraciously around the work yards until we had almost reached the destination I had in mind. The crunching of footsteps sounded again so I pulled her around the nearest shed, hiding us from prying eyes. She looked at me with wide eyes, clearly startled, and I put a finger over her lips, ears listening as the scrape of gravel grew louder. *Please don't let our guards be seen. I don't want them interrupting my last minutes with Ella.* The crunching slowed for a moment before speeding up.

I breathed a sigh of relief as I realized that the sound was heading off in another direction. I looked back over to Ella, my eyes catching on the finger I still had pressed to her thin, pink lips. Hesitating, I lightly traced the curve of her top lip, then curled my finger so that my knuckle braised her skin as I traced the rest of the way down to her chin, reveling in the slight intake of breath my actions provoked. I leaned closer. There was nothing as important as her right now, and us, together. I paused, my lips a few inches from hers, desperate to kiss her but needing assurance that it was what she wanted too.

"May I?" I asked, hanging on to the last shred of gallantry that had been drilled into me at the Academy, and praying that she wanted my kiss as much as I wanted hers.

"Please," she breathed, her lips parting as she spoke and giving me all the invitation I needed. They were soft as they met mine, soft like the look in her eyes, like her touch on my arm, like her forgiveness of my flaws. I wanted more of it, more of her. A corner of my mind beckoned, urging me to shake off every responsibility and duty I had and lose myself in her and us. But I knew that wasn't what either of us wanted. With every shred of willpower I had, I kept my lips soft too, allowing the sweetness of the moment to spread across my heart until the memory of her kiss was the anchor of my heart. Then I broke away, surprised as she pressed one, two, three more quick kisses to my lips before pulling back as well.

"Maybe it's good you're going away before the wedding," she said breathlessly and my heart thrilled. "I don't know if it's this bond between us, or if all couples feel this way, but when we kiss I feel like forgetting everything and just…" a flush swept across her cheeks and she shook her head, trying to hide a shy smile.

"I don't know about you, but I felt this way before the ball," I replied, lifting her hand and pressing another kiss to her knuckles.

"I did too," she said breathlessly, eyes on my lips, "but it's becoming more and more distracting every day!"

I laughed, pressing one more firm kiss to her hand before drawing her up. "You've never spoken a truer word. But our time is short. Let's go see my father about Alessia. He's usually reviewing paperwork around this time in his study, and I think the two of us together will make more headway than myself alone. But first, I thought we'd check on something."

Ella tilted her head curiously and I couldn't control a wide grin as I pulled her around the side of the shed, and into the empty blacksmith's yard."

"Care to test out a theory?" I asked.

"Always!" she laughed, and my heart tripped over itself.

❊ ❊ ❊

Trumpets rang out with a bright sunny trill, the signal for my unit to begin moving out. Alessia was already mounted next to my horse, which was being held steady by Antonio.

I turned to my father, who stood a step above me on the front staircase of Cintola Palace. I bowed and he nodded as I straightened up. "Be bold and run a tight ship. This is your first big international test, Luca."

My first test was surviving and thriving at Deerbold, I corrected him in my head. I moved down the line to my mother, who looked at me with her usual cold expression. "Farewell, Prince Luca," was all she managed to say, and I bowed before moving down the line to my sister. She sniffed, offering her hand, which I bowed over.

"Come home with more sense between those ears than you have now." I glanced up and she jerked her head behind her to where Lady Emilia stood, looking stoic and pale. I repressed the urge to frown and straightened up. "As usual, no guarantees, sister dearest," I said, drawing snickers from where Dante and Marco stood beside her. I moved down the line to them, shaking both of their hands and wishing I could scoop them into a hug. It was against protocol however and I didn't want to leave them at the mercy of my mother's lectures for the next day and half.

"Do come home with more sense between those ears, dear brother," Dante mimicked in a quiet falsetto just barely audible to our sister. She sniffed and sent him a glare which he ignored. "Don't forget to write," he added in a more normal tone of voice. "I'm still hoping father will let me go on the next mission, so I'll need to be prepared."

I grinned at my brother, who was nearly as mad for the sea as I was. "You can prepare best by getting convincing him to let you train with the navy at the seaports next year. I'll help you put together a proposal when I get back." He grinned widely and I turned my attention to Marcus.

"Yes, make sure you come back," my other brother said to me. "I like my position as 'spare' very much thank you, so I need your sorry hide to stand between me and running this country." I laughed and resisted the urge to ruffle his head before turning to Ella.

"Just come back to me," she whispered as I bent over her hand. Her words twined around my ears, full of sorrow at our parting and anticipation for our marriage upon our return. I pressed a long kiss to her knuckles again, remembering our stolen moments in the garden earlier that day.

"I'd search the whole kingdom for you if I had too when I get back, so take it easy on me and just wait," I whispered, eliciting a smile. My own expression turned serious. "I'll write, but I can't put anything serious in my letters in case they're opened and read. You do the same. But promise to write. I'll be dying to hear from you."

"Of course I will," she whispered back, her hand tightening in mine. I pressed one more kiss to her knuckles and forced myself to step back and turn away. Like ripping a bandage off I just needed to go.

In a few minutes I was mounted on Percivale, Antonio beside me as our unit moved forward down the road. Just before I went through the main gate into the city, I couldn't resist glancing back. The rest of my family had gone inside, leaving only Ella standing on the steps, staring after me. My heart turned at the sight, but I forced myself forward. On towards duty, and away from love.

CHAPTER NINETEEN

Ella

Slowly I forced my feet to turn and head back into the palace. The last of Luca's unit had thundered through the gates a moment ago, and the dust was already settling. Turning away felt like a betrayal, as if I was turning my back on him as he went to danger. With a start I realized I was the only one left outside.

I moved slowly into the entryway, passing through over-sized wooden doors decorated with scroll-work and held open by two servants whose only job was to open and close the doors when people came through. *I wonder what they do to amuse themselves between visitors.*

My eyebrow lifted as I noticed Queen Narcissa standing near a side table with an enormous display of flowers. She was picking at the blooms, throwing ones she didn't like in a pile on the floor next to the table. I pressed my lips over my teeth in an effort to not comment on the mess. A servant would come by to clean it up as soon as she left, no doubt. But what was the point of throwing them on the floor? I took a swift breath through my nose. *Not a good time to tackle that mystery.*

"Lady Fenice," the queen said, staring at me with the same cold look she had given Luca during his goodbyes; the same cold look she gave everyone when she wasn't pouring vitriol from her eyes.

I walked over to her reluctantly, dipping a curtsy and waiting for her to spit out whatever was on her mind. *Be kind, you don't actually know her that well. Maybe it's not her fault she looks like she always swallowed something sour. Maybe you'll look the same after being queen for two decades.* I shivered at the thought, and caught a gleam of triumph pass across Queen Narcissa's face. *She think's I'm afraid of her,* I realized. *I'm just afraid of **becoming** her.*

"I think it's best if I set a few expectations immediately, Lady Fenice. Luca had sent a messenger requesting an update on when the Crown Princess Suite would be available for your use. I didn't have a chance to inform him that installing you in such rooms, before you are actually the crown princess, would be improper considering your unmarried status. They are to remain empty until Luca's marriage. It is only at that point that his wife, whomever she may be, will occupy those room. Have I made myself clear?"

I blinked, trying to understand the subtext she was conveying with her words. *Whomever Luca's wife would be? She thinks she still has a chance to get him to marry Emilia.* With effort I prevented myself from rolling my eyes. *In time she'll realize that you're Luca's choice and he is mine. Maybe not until the wedding day, but still.*

"Perfectly clear, Your Highness, thank you," I replied in the most cheerful voice I could muster. The Queen pursed her lips and picked at the flower bouquet with even more ferocity.

"In fact, I must tell you that all of our guest suites are currently occupied from attendees at the ball. Any that aren't are undergoing a cleaning process." She paused, shooting a pointed look at me. "Our staff seems to be a little behind for some reason, so I'm afraid I don't have any servants available to transfer to you. At this point, you'll need to stay in your rooms for the foreseeable future. I hope you won't feel slighted since they're so much smaller and less grand than the other rooms." She paused and then spoke again just as I opened my mouth to answer. "Of course, I didn't think," she uttered a tiny utterly false laugh, "perhaps you'll be more comfortable in them. They remind you of home, I expect. And closer to the stables. I understand you're more at ease in a stables."

My eyes widened at her rudeness, but she didn't wait for a response. Throwing down one more sprig of flowers, she turned and floated away, her steps graceful but rushed, as if she couldn't stand being near me for another moment. I gazed after her, then turned toward the poor flower display. It was a bit of a nightmare by now, large gaps from where she had picked out flowers, allowing others to fall into mixed up clumps as they leaned against one another.

Bending down, I began sorting through the pile on the floor, the scent of roses and lilies washing over me. Most of the flowers were still fresh, and there didn't seem to be a pattern for why she pulled them out. Picking the nice ones up, I began slipping them into the vase, rounding out the arrangement as best I could.

"My dear! I hadn't heard you had a talent for flower arranging!"

I turned at the unfamiliar voice and was met by a middle aged courtier, dressed all in shades of iridescent lavender. *Beatrice would love to get her hands on that fabric.* The thought of my stepmother reminded me that I hadn't heard back from her, opening an ache in my heart I wanted to forget.

I pasted a smile on my face, eying the woman in front of me and steeling myself for another difficult interaction. She looked like every other courtier I had seen; large blue eyes, blonde hair, petite, almost waifish figure, and styled to the height of fashion. I guessed she was in her late forties, although she didn't have nearly the number of wrinkles on her face that I would suggest.

"Do excuse me, but have we been introduced?" I asked, running through the few people I had met since arriving at the palace. Most of those were servants and guards. I would have remembered this woman.

"Oh! I didn't think that you wouldn't remember me. For shame! But of course, I haven't exactly been a very good godmother, have I?"

My brow wrinkled. "Haven't you?" I asked, wondering why she was telling me this and wishing she would let me go back to arranging the flowers.

"Yes, I must not be doing a good job if you don't even remember me. I suppose I haven't seen you since… since your mother's…." She trailed off, a look of genuine grief passing over her face before disappearing in favor of a wide smile.

"I am your godmother, Ella. My name is Lady Zelmira Fatana, Duchess of Simona. Your mother and I were great friends growing up. Seconds cousins once removed on our fathers' side, so we kept each other amused during family functions as children."

My jaw dropped and she stepped closer, taking a few of the flowers from my hand. "Close your mouth my dear, you don't want to catch any flies." My mouth snapped shut as she continued her stream of words in a lower tone of voice while slipping blooms into the bouquet.

"I hadn't realized how much time had passed since the last time I checked in on you. We live so far apart, and of course you didn't need me when you were little. I was going to make an effort after your dear mother died, seeing as how you would need a mother figure of some sort, but your father remarried so quickly I didn't even have a chance! And from all accounts your stepmother was doing fine, although perhaps if I'm hearing the rumors correctly I should have checked in on you beforehand. And of course when your Papa left us you were fully grown and I didn't think you'd want a courtier sticking her nose into how you were running things in charming Lucedimora. I'm starting to realize that I should have made some attempt. Didn't you get my gifts at least?"

Memories came to the surface as she spoke. I *had* seen her before, over a decade ago at my mother's funeral. She had been as beautiful in her grief than as she was standing before me now with sunny smiles.

"Yes I, I suppose I did get your gifts," I replied, remembering the sporadic packages that had arrived on my birthday a few times as a child. Most of them had seemed completely random.

Once she sent me a crate of bonbons that had been completely spoiled by the time they arrived. Another time it was a single pearl, with just a note reminding me to brush my teeth so that they stayed pearly white forever. I had sold the pearl after my father died, but had always remembered to brush my teeth.

"Thank you," I added lamely as she finished with the bouquet. "And I do remember you now."

She looked over at me with a saccharine smile and nodded once. "As I said, when I think about it now, I haven't done a very good job as godmother have I? Your poor Mama would be shaking her head at me."

She looped her arm with mine and started dragging me deeper into the palace. "Now, having discovered that the mystery girl is my very own Ella, I'm determined to right my wrongs as a godparent. I'll teach you everything you need to know to put the right foot forward here in the palace. Starting with your wardrobe." She glanced down at my pretty, but relatively plain dress. "Not that your dress doesn't look quite well on you, but it's better suited for the country, wouldn't you agree? Where are your rooms exactly?"

Questioning the wisdom of allowing Lady Zelmira to barge into my rooms and re-do my wardrobe, I still found myself leading her there. "But darling, aren't we heading toward the barracks? I thought the Crown Princess' Suite is on the upper levels of the - oh no, don't tell me this is..." she trailed off as we stopped in front of my door.

"Home sweet home, for now at least," I said as I pushed my bedroom door open. Jacqui sat on my bed, sewing, but she jumped up when she caught sight of the pair of us.

I waved her back down. "It's alright Jacqui. This is Lady Zelmira Fatana. She's my godmother."

"Just Zelmira dear, we're practically family after all," she instructed in a dismayed voice as she looked around my room. I shut the door firmly behind us. "Where do you keep your clothes?" She asked, noticing the distinct lack of a wardrobe. I pointed to a few pegs on side of the room. Her eyes widened and

I couldn't help a laugh escaping at her expression.

"It's not much compared to what most of the court has, I'm sure, but it's not the end of the world," I said, tamping down on my mirth. Lady Zelmira pursed her lips at me.

"It certainly *looks* like the end of the world. I count three - no four dresses total! That's hardly enough for one day, let alone a *month* while you wait for the Prince!"

"Five," I said, pointing to the dress Jacqui was working on." Zelmira patted her hairdo in a gesture of frustration. "Yes well, I'm sorry to say that simply won't do." She wandered over to Jacqui. "You seem like you know your business at least - Jacqui was it?"

My new lady's maid nodded and moved to dip a curtsy. "No never mind all that dear, you continue on with your work." I watched with amusement as Zelmira drifted over to my clothes pegs, muttering under her breath.

"...has her in a closet smaller than... not even a fabric swatch from the royal seamstress... CLEARLY angling to make things harder..."

"Lady Fatana... Zelmira, that is," I called, drawing a kind but slightly vapid smile from my godmother. "I do plan on expanding my wardrobe, but I simply don't have the funds to dress as the courtiers do, and I don't have the desire. I appreciate that you want to help me, especially as I don't have many friends here," I swallowed a lump, thinking back to the tearful goodbye I had with Gia earlier this morning, followed by another goodbye with Luca that wrenched my heart even harder. Really Jacqui was my only friend, and I had just met her. "The thing is, I can't be something that I'm not." My hand drifted up to the stone charm necklace hanging against the dip between my collarbones. I didn't exactly know *what* I was right now... a Lady away from her castle, a mage without access to her magic, a fiance parted from her lover. I felt like a stack of contradictions, and I was fiercely resistant to changing into something the court wanted, just to make *them* feel more comfortable while I tried to figure out who I was.

Zelmira closed her eyes a drew a short breath through her nose. "Quite right, my dear, quite right. I certainly wouldn't want to turn you into a *courtier*. You're something else entirely, and we'll help you find your footing, won't we Jacqui?" She turned a vapid but kind smile on the maid, who returned a more hesitant one.

"I'll send my seamstress along with some fabrics to assist Jacqui tomorrow. I'll help you choose the designs and colors," she lifted dainty hands up to forestall my protests. "Consider it in lieu of all the gifts I missed over the years. I shall make up for those with interest. And consider too, that the clothes you wear at court are a sort of armor," she pressed her lips together and the slightly simple look she had worn since I bumped into her in the entry hall slipped into something more serious. "How you present yourself tells a story, and convinces your audience of who you are without needing to defend yourself. I'll help you craft a story that will present your strengths, and hide what you want to keep secret."

Silence swept over the room for a beat at the gravity of her words. Zelmira broke it with a quick clap of her hands. "Now, it seems that what your stepmother left out in terms of educating you on magical artifacts and the shocking strain of magic in her own family, she filled by rounding out your education on courtly manners and graces. I'm surprised she knew them so well, considering that you've all spent your lives in the back of beyond," she said with a cheeky smile. "Still, let's review a few things that will help with dinner this evening." She motioned me forward and I came willingly, interested in learning anything that could make the next month go easier. *Maybe I'm not as alone here as I thought.*

❋ ❋ ❋

Lavender scented tea wafted through the door of the parlor, and I took a fortifying breath before stepping into the room. The

Queen, Princess Marietta, and Lady Emilia were all seated and barely spared a glance my way. A few other ladies of the court were present, all with steaming cups of tea in front of them, including Zelmira.

I dipped a curtsy to the royals then walked toward an empty seat, repressing the urge to sigh. I had arrived fifteen minutes before I had been told that the Queen's afternoon tea would begin. It appeared that they had started several minutes ago, and I suspected I had been given the wrong time on purpose to make me look bad. As it was, I could probably still claim to be fashionably late at this point rather than rudely late.

Give them time. They're all still disappointed that you're not her. You would be disappointed too if Papa had given Lucedimora away to some distant cousin, or willed the stables out from under you. Perhaps they'll warm up once they realize I'm not incompetent.

Although, based off of the sermon we had all heard at the cathedral that morning, perhaps not. The bishop had preached on the dangers of magic, and magic users. It was clearly directed at me, and I could feel the stares of every perfectly composed courtier in the room. Queen Narcissa sat a row ahead of me, and I couldn't help seeing her slight nod every time the bishop brought up another danger of magic.

The king wasn't present, and I wondered what he would have thought of such a sermon. He seemed very keen on creating alliances with the mage countries. I didn't imagine he would be happy that the church was preaching against such a thing, even if it was indirectly.

I'm not happy they're preaching against it either, especially since there's nothing in the Book of Creation prohibiting magic. There seems to be many accounts of magic in the book if you ask me... which no one is at this point. Maybe they will once I'm crown princess?

I accepted a cup of tea from a servant with a murmured thank you, and lifted the brew to my mouth. I took a sip, enjoying the heat as the lavender flavored liquid slipped down my throat, fortifying my spirits as well as giving me courage to face the next hour or so of verbal sparring that seemed to be required in every court event.

I lifted my cup to take another sip, when something jostled my elbow, splashing tea onto the skirt of my seafoam green day dress, instantly staining the fabric from waist to hem.

"Oh Lady Fenice! Didn't you see me standing here?" Princess Marietta's voice set my teeth on edge and I twitched in my seat, hardly able to contain the urge to snap back at her.

"No, Princess Marietta, I did *not* see you standing there." *Why I would see her standing behind me, when she had been sitting over there only a moment ago, makes no sense.*

"How clumsy! Here, let the servant take your tea things so you can go change. You can't sit around with tea all over your quaint little gown."

I allowed the servant to come collect my things and stood up, dipping a curtsy to the Queen and Princess. "I'll come with you, dear Ella," Zelmira said, fluttering over to my side in a dress of sunshine yellow and white. "I did mention that she's my goddaughter didn't I?" she said to the group at large. She dipped a curtsy to the royals as well, then linked arms and drew me toward the door.

Murmurs started behind our backs as we walked. "...always so eccentric!" A shocked voice said. The Queen's cold tones cut through the others. "Lady Zelmira can be as eccentric as she likes. Her reading calms my headaches like nothing else. Surely she didn't realize what sort of goddaughter she would be saddled with when the child was a baby."

Her frosty words cut like ice in my heart. Her intent was to belittle me of course, which was nonsensical. But it still hurt to think that I was being talked about by a room full of women.

"Chin up my dear," Zelmira whispered as we passed through into the hallway. "They're a bunch of twittering birds, nothing more. It's a shame about your dress, but it only gives me an excuse to order you another new one!"

Zelmira's cheerfulness warmed my heart, and I couldn't help but be glad that she had decided to help me. *I hope she doesn't tire of me like she did when I was a child.* Even if she did, I would take whatever friendship and help she could offer for now. It seemed that winning the respect of my new family was going to take a lot more than holding my head high.

CHAPTER TWENTY

Luca

I put a hand out to steady myself as the ship climbed a higher swell than normal. The wooden planks of the wall next to me were smooth, covered in plaster and wallpaper here in the stern of the ship. The officers required nicer accommodations than the rank and file sailors that slept in the gun decks. I could admit that I preferred my own nicely appointed cabin on the bottom floor of this section to sleeping in a row of hammocks bedded down between cannons. But right now, that luxury was making it hard to find purchase as we crested this wave. I leaned back against the steep staircase I was descending, grabbing at the edge of a step with one hand, and scrabbling along the smooth wall with the other until I hit a bit of molding that stuck out more than the other scroll-work, and clung to it. I felt the ship crest over the wave and drop back down, bracing myself as gravity pulled me toward the staircase, then away again as the ship began to level out. As soon as I felt the floor even out for a beat, I scrambled the rest of the way down the stairs. Don't want to be caught there when the next one comes.

We were about a day's sailing out from the shores of southern Charmagne and beginning to hit rougher seas than were usual for our coastline patrol. As I had reviewed with the Captain, who, although he had more naval experience than years I had been alive so far, had listened to the review of my mission plan respectfully; we wanted to stay out of sight of the Dwarven Republic for our first sweep around the large peninsula that made up the bulk of their lands. Our treaty with Snowdonia required us to provide intelligence as to any movements along the Republic's southern coastline, as Snowdonia had no real navy, and so was largely incapable of monitoring their disputed territory's condition.

I had to admit, I was exceedingly curious about the coastline of the heretical republic. I had seen a glimpses of the country from across the mouth of the straight that divided my holdings on the Isle of Lontariva, but those had been hazy, and supposedly comprised of long sandy beach marshes with no settlements or ports. The main portion of seafaring activity in the Dwarven Republic took place deeper in the straight that ran up between our two countries, and could be a hotbed of smuggling.

Our navy already was working to combat the smuggling, so I had argued, and somehow swayed my father and the Chief Admiral into allowing, that we explore any seafaring activity on the other side of the Republic before running the usual periodic show of force up the main strait. *I don't know if I want to find anything or not.* I had to admit to myself that I felt a serious curiosity for the secretive mage colony, and dreamed that we could build a treaty with them someday. *That's another worry I'm not exactly equipped to handle yet. We've been allies with Snowdonia for so long, but an alliance with the Dwarven Republic would mean war with Snowdonia.* I shook my head as I reached the door to my private cabin. *There's enough to focus on with getting my marriage to Ella completed and facing the stigma and laws against magic and mages in my own country. Let's not add another country to that list.*

"Speaking of Ella," I said to myself as I entered my room and kicked the door shut behind me, "I'll write to her again and send the letter at our next port." I had already written a letter and posted it just before we left yesterday, and had secretly hoped she had sent a letter by courier to reach me before I left, but had no such luck. *It was foolish to even let yourself want that, Luca.*

She wouldn't have time to write to you just a day after you left! Her letter will be waiting for you next week when we stop in to refuel. And you'll be married within a month. "You won't be running a mission or a country very well if you can't stop mooning over your fiance," I muttered as I pulled out a pen and paper. But as I started writing an update of all we had done and how much I missed her, a nagging doubt entered the back of my mind. *As much as I hope she's interested in what I can tell her about what I'm doing, and about my wish that she was with me, she'll be probably more worried that Alessia and I are friends again, and that her stepsister is being treated right by the crew.*

I sighed and laid down my pen. I had been avoiding talking seriously to Alessia since her transfer was approved. But it was time to clear the air.

※ ※ ※

I found her in the small cabin down the hall from mine, which she and Anthonio shared. They worked opposite shifts, and since I didn't require a constant shadow while on-board, they were either at my side during meetings or volunteering to assist in whatever work needed done with the sailors.

Since she wasn't on duty, she should have been sleeping. Instead she was sitting on the small bed, polishing her boots. She stood to attention when she saw I was at the door but I waved her at ease. She relaxed slightly, but not completely - not with the easy familiarity I had come to expect over the last few years.

"May I come in?" I asked, motioning into the cabin. She looked over her shoulder dubiously, but made room by crossing back over to the bed and taking a seat. I shut the door behind me, and edged over to a small chest that was bolted to the floor, which probably held most of Alessia and Anthonio's belongings. Gingerly, I sat on the lid, which seemed more than sturdy enough to hold my weight.

I shifted in my seat, then sighed, not knowing what to say,

or even what I *wanted* to say to her. Our friendship had changed suddenly, and as much as I wanted the old days back, I knew we probably couldn't go back. But we could definitely move forward.

Folding my arms, I leaned back against the cabin wall and looked at her with a tense smile. "I came to check in with you. Or maybe really to clear the air between us."

Alessia looked at me in stony silence, her expression cool and professional. I sighed again.

"Well okay, the reason I came is because I was writing a letter to Ella and I knew she'd want an update on how you're doing, and would be wondering if you and I were okay. I didn't know the answers to either of those questions, so here I am."

Alessia snorted a humorless laugh. "And you thought I would know?" She slid her boots under the bed and put the lid on the jar of polish before storing it in a drawer in the dresser. "My life is not my own now that my secret is out. I'm grateful to you for getting me out of jail, and assigning me as your guard. I honestly never thought I'd breathe free air again, so thank you."

"So your answer on how you're doing is that you're grateful to breathe free air again?"

"And grateful for the part I'm sure you played in that, Your Highness," she replied.

I closed my eyes for a second, then looked at her again. "Alessia, come on. This isn't like you. I'm Luca. We've been friends for years. Don't call me 'Your Highness' in private, and don't pretend that the only thing you feel is grateful."

A twisted expression passed across my friend's face, but it was gone in a moment. "Grateful is all I've ever felt, Luca," she almost spat my name. "Grateful that my stepsister paid my school fees, grateful that I had a chance to serve as a warrior, grateful I was sent to a school where I could be tutored in my magic in secret," my eyes widened in shock, which didn't escape her notice. "Oh yes, you didn't think I spent four years at Deerbold and passed up the opportunity to learn. And I was grateful for it! Grateful too that I had a few friends, grateful that one of them was the prince of my own country, and grateful that my secret wasn't out. And now, I'm grateful that I'm not in jail."

I frowned at her, but didn't know how to penetrate the veil of sarcasm she had spread over the conversation, so I tried a different tack. "Then what about us? We've been friends for years, and you never once told me. Never even tried to tell me! I've thought back, thinking over every conversation, and there was never a time that I can remember that felt like you were trying to tell me something. How can that be?"

"Oh I don't know, I would have thought you could completely understand what it's like given your reticence in revealing a big secret about your true nature to Ella after you *told* me that you would talk to her about it! I trusted you!"

She bit off the last few words before they could really become a yell, and balled her hands into fists in her lap, tightly controlled frustration almost vibrating off of her.

Defensiveness ripped through me as she touched the old wound - always wanting to be known for myself instead of as the crown prince. *She couldn't understand! If she knew* - I opened my mouth to tell her but a sudden thought struck me. *Doesn't she though?* Now that her secret was out, she would be forever known as the mage soldier. Even I was thinking of her in those terms. Not with judgment, like many others may be, but just as a main part of who she was. And maybe she didn't want to be thought of like that, known for something that she hadn't asked for, no matter how she felt about the magic itself. *Maybe she does understand, and maybe I could learn a thing or two from her instead of always reverting back to the pain of being unseen behind my crown.*

"You're right," I said simply. Her eyebrows shot up in response. I shrugged my shoulders and offered her a half smile. "I should have told her early on. It was a cowardly thing to do. I've apologized, sincerely, and she's forgiven me. I'm starting to think I've been a world class idiot. I concealed something that in the end brings me power and prestige. You concealed your magic because you knew it would bring prison, or worse. I can't compare our situations, or feel frustrated that you didn't trust me with such a dangerous secret."

Alessia stared at the floor for a minute, then shrugged her shoulders, looking up at me with a more relaxed expression. "I'm not trying to compare burdens. And to be honest? I'm more upset with my family for sending those glass slippers. If I had known I could have prevented all of this!"

The thought made me blink. *Prevented all of this?* Even a few days ago I might have agreed wholeheartedly, but since I knew that the rumor of Ella's magic was already out, and the people hadn't outright rebelled against it, I was beginning to see glimmers of hope that our whole country's attitude toward magic could be changed. And I don't think we would be in a position to make that happen otherwise.

"Well I don't know," I replied with a grin. "We wouldn't be here now, discussing magic as we sail toward the Dwarven Republic. So maybe there's a perk to all this being out in the open after all? I would think that you would be interested in seeing the Republic, given your magic."

Alessia grimaced. "Not really. I don't know enough about them to know whether they're good people or not. I suppose I'm a little sympathetic to them because they're being persecuted for magic, which I can relate too. At the same time, they've lived freely in the peninsula for several generations now, so they can at least be themselves while they remain in their boundaries." She sighed and shot a glance my way. "I suppose I shouldn't be saying things like that to the crown prince of Charmagne, should I?"

I laughed. "You're only saying what I've thought. You know Raleigh was my best friend at Deerbold, and he's an accomplished mage. I'm sure I still have prejudices to root out, but by now you should know that I don't distrust magic on it's own. Although," I paused, folding my arms and giving my friend a teasing look, "if you do beat me in sparring next time we cross blades, I'm not above blaming it on your magic."

"Oh no," she groaned, rolling her eyes. "If you trot that out every time I beat you for the rest of our lives I'll lose my mind."

I stood up and turned toward the door of the cabin. "I'll make sure to prepare a room for you at the royal sanatorium. That will be one perk of being related to royalty. I might drive you crazy, but for your sister's sake, I'll put you up in the nicest hospital available afterward."

She chuckled and as I twisted the doorknob I couldn't help asking one more serious question.

"Are we going to be okay?"

She stared at me, her mouth pressed into a thin line, then nodded. "We'll be okay. Not the same, probably. We're both changing, and the world is too. But I'll be a good friend to you, and I expect you'll be a good friend too."

I gave her a nod then stepped into the cramped hallway. *Now I can write to Ella with at least one problem solved.*

CHAPTER TWENTY-ONE

Ella

I stormed down a hall in the palace, not even sure where I was. Well, I'm somewhere in the servant's wing, but I'm not near my rooms at the guard headquarters.

I stopped to get my bearings, drawing in a few deep breaths and releasing them, one after another, in an attempt to soothe my temper. Glancing around furtively, I was relieved to see that there was no one in the corridor with me, witnessing my un-crown-princess-like behavior. My shoulders slumped and I wandered over toward a window, hoping to orient myself by whatever was outside.

It looked into a small gray courtyard with a well and a few scrubby vines growing up the walls. Laundry hung like pennents, criss-crossing the small space going up several levels. *Well that's probably the laundry then. Not that it helps really, since I don't know where the laundry is located. But there are only two courtyards in the servant's wing, so I'm either a couple floors above the barracks, or I'm on the opposite side of where I need to be.*

I rubbed my head, the logic problem that was my location compounding the headache I had developed during the mental fencing at my wedding planning meeting with Queen Narcissa and Marietta. They had spent the entire time in mildly cutting remarks about my magic, or the strength of my relationship with Luca, or the fate of the country if our marriage came to pass. Nothing so direct of course. Each barb was wrapped in an ounce of righteous sounding concern. Instead of just telling me that they thought my magic made me evil, they engaged everyone in a lively discussion about the latest sermon at the cathedral on Sunday. The one where the priest had read through the church's theological stance on mages and sin, expounding on the horrors of the past. As the only mage in the room, surely they knew I would be uncomfortable discussing such a topic. Especially as I had only found out about my magic recently.

I gritted my teeth. *And that wasn't the only time!* Emilia had spent a different meeting where we looked at flower arrangements regaling everyone with a school lesson her younger brother had just the other day. He had been studying the mage rebellions, specifically one of the ones that had started with a mage marrying into the royal family and supposedly trying to take over the throne. I had actually opened my mouth to confront her about why she was telling that story when I was standing right there, but decided not to say anything at the last minute. I would only look like a jealous fiance in confronting her. And I didn't have any allies in that room, not even Zelmira.

*Besides, all those hurtful words probably stem from a fear of magic that's been ingrained in us since birth. Maybe I should judge them less. They grew up in the capitol. I grew up on the edge of a mage country with a father who was tolerant and a stepmother who turned out to **be** a mage.* With a shock I realized that either my father or mother probably had been a mage as well, since magic usually ran in families. I pressed my fingers along my temple again, pushing that thought away for another time. *There's probably no way to know who it was now.* And at this point, I had bigger puzzles to solve.

Looking around again, I realized that no one had come into this hallway since I arrived. Usually every inch of Cintola Palace seemed busy, with servants or courtiers, or tradesmen and visitors, or at least Sergent Madrigal trailing behind.

With a start I realized that my guard wasn't with me. He hadn't even been at his post when I finally left the Queen's salon under the pretext of having a headache. *Not a pretext, the headache was real.* The Queen had sent him to assist in fetching some sort of family heirloom that was used in the royal weddings.

Did she do that on purpose, knowing that I was almost at my breaking point? Did she plan for me to rush out into the palace unprotected? I shuddered. If she did, was it because she had decided to take care of the problem I presented in a less savory way? Surely she wouldn't - I stopped myself from going down that chain of thought too. *There's no use speculating right now. Just find your way back to your room, and there will be guards a plenty when you reach it.*

Still, the sharp slap of boots on the tile floor made me jump, and I turned with real fear to see who came around the corner.

"Sergeant Madrigal!" He stopped to bow briefly before coming the rest of the way toward me. "Excuse me Lady Fenice, but when I arrived back at the salon they said you had gone back to your room. But when I got back there, Sergeant Brine said he hadn't seen you. I've been looking for you ever since. I would highly advise that you don't leave without one of us guards again."

I huffed out a breath. "Don't worry, I was fine." He pressed his lips together in annoyance and I almost laughed. "But advice noted. If for no other reason than the fact that I'm liable to become completely lost without someone shepherding my movements."

He offered me a tight smile and a bow and I felt bad, hoping I hadn't made him think I only valued him as someone to serve me.

"Be patient with me Madrigal. I'm used to coming and going as I pleased on my own estate. I forget that there are forces at work in the palace that I know nothing about."

He bowed again, but when he rose he had a mollified look on his face, and began to lead me back to my room.

Jacqui looked up from my bed and gave me a sympathetic smile as I walked through the doors to my bedroom. "Tough meeting?" she asked. "You look like you're fighting a headache."

I laughed, massaging the side of my temple. "You're right there. I think I need some water and a quick lie down."

I made my way over to my water basin and ewer and quickly downed a cup. "Any letters?" I asked Jacqui, as casually as I could. She shook her head, and my heart plummeted. It had been a week since Luca left, and I thought at least by now I'd have a letter. I had sent him three so far. *I'll be looking like a silly lovesick fool to him.* I flopped into a chair near the writing desk and looked back over at Jacqui. "I never knew planning a wedding would require so much energy. I'd almost rather have it at the chapel in Lucedimora, with just family and a few friends rather than all this. Talking about ribbons and flowers gave me a headache today."

She gave me a pointed look. "I don't think it was the decorations that gave you a headache. I've helped make dresses for almost all of those ladies since I started working at the palace, so I have an inkling of what you've been through today."

I sighed. "I think they mean well, and even if they don't, I think it's coming from a place of fear."

"I doubt it. They don't fear you, they're just mad their plans didn't come to life with Luca. If you pardon my saying so."

"Of course not, Jacqui!" I shot her the best smile I could muster under the strength of a headache. "I value your insight. But I really hope I'm right and they'll eventually warm up to me."

Jacqui shook her head and refocused on her sewing before shooting her head up to look at me again. "Oh I forgot! There's a letter over there on the dresser!"

With a tingle of anticipation I shot out of my chair and navigated around the increasingly tall piles of fabric and dresses that dotted my room. Zelmira seemed to come over every few days, and she and Jacqui would fall into deep consultation over the creations they would make for me to wear. I was happy to leave my image in their more capable hands. I usually had dirt under my fingernails and an apron on that I had forgotten about. Not exactly the usual look for a princess.

As I picked up the letter I felt a swoop of disappointment. It wasn't from Luca, but from Gia. I frowned at myself, frustrated that my first reaction to a letter from my best friend was disappointment. I opened it and scanned the contents. Mostly information about the harvest and the barns. Toward the end she included a short couple of lines about my family. They had fled, leaving before Gia even returned home. Where they went, no one knew, although everyone seemed to think it was over the border into Spindle. *The place that started all my troubles.* I suppose Deerbold Academy hadn't given me my ingrown magic. But it did lead me to Luca. And **he** led me straight into trouble. I smiled, thinking about my fiance. *Maybe I was ready to walk into a little trouble, and besides, I've probably brought more trouble into his life than he has mine.*

A knock sounded on the door, and Sergeant Madrigal popped his head in.

"You've been summoned to the King's study, milady," he said before popping his head back out. I put my best friend's letter inside my writing desk and looked over to Jacqui. "I suppose I'd better find out what's going on. I'll be back soon."

Jacqui just nodded and continued on with her work. I wished I could stay with her and maybe take a nap. Instead, I steeled my spine and swept into the hallway, checking to makes sure Madrigal was following me before I turned toward the main part of the palace. *I wonder what the King could possibly want right now?* I hoped it wasn't a lecture about the suitability of my being the crown princess or something. *I think I've had my limit of that talk for the day.*

❊ ❊ ❊

I was shown into the King's study with a flurry of bowing and announcing and a curtsy or two on my part. *I think I got the curtsy right.* There were at least ten different types of curtsies for different situations and although I had been taught them at some point in my life, I never thought to review the etiquette until I was in a moment of needing to use one of them, and hoped my instincts would carry me through.

King Cirro looked as hale and hearty as ever, although there were circles under his eyes that I hadn't noticed before. Even so, he scrutinized me openly for a long moment after we had been left alone, with the confidence only found in people who were born into power. I knew, because I had been born into power on a lesser scale on my own estate. As Luca had muttered under his breath after the ballroom debacle, I was used to being a queen in my own domain, so I felt more than able to take the opportunity and scrutinize him right back.

He was tall and strong, with golden hair and skin and the same brown eyes as Luca. But the lines of his face told a story of decades of impatience and autocratic behavior. *Perhaps that's to be expected in a King.* Suddenly a picture of Luca with those same lines on his face popped into my mind. *No way. I will **not** let him behave like that long enough to get anger lines on his face. Not that he would do that...* If I didn't expect that behavior as Luca, then why would I excuse it in our current king?

Right now his face wore one of the slightly predatory smiles he often sported. *It's predatory because his teeth are so white and perhaps slightly too large for his mouth.* I wondered if he knew that he looked that way and used it as a technique to make others nervous.

Despite the story that his face told, and the overall impression you had that he was a man who could command a room or start a military campaign at any given moment, there was something in his posture that made me wonder if he felt weak right now. His shoulders were slightly rounded, and he held his hands clasped tightly in front of him.

"So, Lady Fenice. You're to be our next Queen in Charmagne, is that it?"

I pressed my lips together. "If that's the penance I pay for marrying the love of my life, I do it for his sake."

King Ciro barked a laugh before he could help himself and leaned back in his chair, resting his hands on the armrests in a more relaxed stance. "A penance? I've never heard anyone describe it that way. But perhaps it is. You'd have to ask my own Queen."

I pressed my lips together again, repressing whatever retort about his Queen wanted to escape my mouth. *You really need to work on your attitude today, Ella.*

"Well anyway, your story seems to check out, so I suppose I'll have to take you on your word that you don't view the role of Queen as a prize."

I frowned and took a step forward, almost stumbling over the new pair of leather shoes I was wearing, but King Ciro continued speaking before I could ask any of the questions that had sprung to mind.

"Oh yes, I had investigators check up on your account the very night we met, Lady Ella. You didn't think I would take you at your word, did you? I'm surprised your retainers haven't written to you about it by now. The reports said they were quite loyal to you, despite your newfound magic."

"My 'newfound' magic hasn't changed who I am as a person, King Ciro. I'm no less of a provider for my estate, or concerned about the people who depend on me because I'm a mage." I cringed at the bitterness betrayed in my voice. I had been struggling with that very idea for the last week, and was feeling small at the realization that I *had* expected them to take me at my word. I've always been known as a trustworthy person, and the fact that my word is law on my estate meant that literally everyone I knew took me at my word. *Of course they wouldn't do that here.*

"Well. That's not what my bishops would have me believe," he replied matter of factly. "They're all refusing to marry the two of you based on the principle that your inborn evil will slowly eat away at the foundation of our society, warping my son and any children you might have for generations."

The shock of such a bald accusation was like a slap in the face, and a warmth of anger swept through my body. I clutched my charm necklace in an attempt to temper my response.

"I could have guessed at their attitude based on the sermon I listened to on Sunday. Although I must confess, I was surprised that the Bishop was teaching based off a historical account instead of the Book of Creation. I found it to be a very stale interpretation, nothing I hadn't heard before. But of course, I have a new perspective on all things magical, don't I?"

King Ciro smiled his predatory smile with perhaps a hint of more genuine warmth than before. "I heard about that sermon. I also heard that it seemed to wash off you like water off a duck's back."

I considered that for a moment. "That sounds more like something Princess Marietta would say, rather than Queen Narcissa."

The King barked another laugh and crossed his arms over his chest. "I can't help finding that I like you, Lady Ella, although perhaps that reflects poorly on my character." He became a little more serious and leaned forward. "You've entered the stage at a most opportune time. I've been laying the groundwork to develop treaties with the mage countries for years, although I didn't think we would see fruition on that goal until Luca was an old man. The outcome of the Battle of Asileboix has opened up an opportunity this last year that I never foresaw, and your mage status may be just the bargaining chip I need to get in those country's good graces. It's enough that I'm willing to fight my own church to get you married to my son, but I am going to be clear about my own expectations for you. Get me those treaties. Be valuable enough to me to make this worth my while. I let you make nice with Princess Rosebelle and Captain Red, because it suited my purposes, and you seem like the type of person who makes nice with everyone. But do not forget, that your main objective is making yourself useful here."

The heat of the injustice of the situation he was placing me in made me feel almost light on my feet. I forgot for a moment that it was my own King that I was talking to, a person who could order my death with very little repercussion if he truly wanted it.

"Thank you for the hint, but I would like to be clear as well. *My main objective here in court will always be conducting myself as a good partner to my soon to be husband. It just so happens that assisting in securing those treaties aligns with my own objective, because they'll make the kingdom that Luca inherits more stable, and more fair to all of it's citizens. But don't think for one second that I've forgotten what my main objective is, even if you have forgotten yours as a father. I'll work for the good of the Kingdom, because it's for the good of us all, not because you'll only be kind to me if I'm useful."

The King's expression changed not in the least, except that there was a hardness in his eyes that I couldn't interpret. Fear snaked through my heart as the potential consequences of my speech, but I couldn't regret speaking the truth. I clutched my charm necklace all the harder.

With a sudden gust of movement, the King slapped his hands on the desk in front of him lightly. "Well, if our goals are aligned, that's all I can ask of an ally, isn't it? You play your part, for whichever reason suits you best, and I'll play mine. We're in a moment to seize, and I plan on getting the most out of it for Charmagne that I can."

He dismissed me with a wave of his hand, and I dipped another curtsy, belated realizing that it was a curtsy for afternoon calls rather than one suited for a King. He wasn't looking so it probably didn't matter. *Not that performing the right curtsy at the right time **really** matters in the grand scheme of anything.* As Madrigal fell in a few steps behind me, I clutched my necklace again, trying to calm the swirling feelings inside me. *When Luca gets back, we'll face all this together. As long as we're a team, we'll find a way.*

CHAPTER TWENTY-TWO

Luca

Antonio's boots clipped a harsh staccato in front of me as we ran up the stairs to the upper deck of the ship, Alessia following. Sailors rushed passed us to a lower deck, hurrying to assist as cannons were made ready to fire. Messages were relayed on silver whistles, still audible above the shouts and scrapes as the entire ship prepared for an attack.

We had finished our route to the eastern side of the Dwarven Republic and had come into sight of the Charmagnian Strait just after sunset. By some luck we had caught a Dwarven smuggling vessel heading back to it's home country. After ignoring our request to stop and be boarded, the Captain had ordered a boarding party, as was standard protocol in such conditions. Almost as soon as he had given the order, the vessel had opened fire on us, striking the rigging of our sails. I had rushed to assist in securing them and had somehow collected Anthonio and Alessia on my way back to the quarterdeck.

"You may want to get below, Your Highness," the Captain growled as I came back to his side. "Can't afford to lose you, and there's no real danger that we'll loose them."

"I can't afford not to be up here," I replied grimly, not wanting to go into a discussion about perceived cowardice and leadership. The Captain merely glanced at my two bodyguards and turned his attention back to the skirmish. He shouted to his first officer who blew a cadence on his whistle. There was a beat, and then the first of the cannons roared to life, followed by one, two, three more. Then another beat, and at the Captains signal, the first officer blew a different cadence. The entire ship seemed to relax and as the smoke from the cannon cleared, I could see why.

The Dwarven boat was in shambles. The hulk of it was still there, but much of the decking was in pieces, floating with bits of detritus in the waves. Two figures were visible on what used to be the deck. Already a pair of rowboats were being lowered into the water, their intent to capture the remaining sailors from the other boat and bring them aboard.

"That was smart work, Captain," I commented, and he flashed a grin at me, his teeth startlingly white against his deeply tanned face.

"That it was, highness, that it was. My men know their business. I see to it. But your support of my cannon retrofit proposal helped a bit, didn't it? Must be nice to see that all the effort was worth it." He winked and turned to watch the progress of the rowboats with a spyglass.

I couldn't help grinning at his comment. It was true - seeing those cannons in action had been a bit of fun, and certainly gratifying to know that the trouble I went to in convincing Father to approve retrofitting our major ships with a more reliable set of cannons was worth it. It's not that I wanted us to use them solely for grinding the Dwarven Republic down when they didn't respond to our commands, but I wanted to be prepared for anything. In the back of my mind, I could never let go of the idea of sailing the oceans and looking for new worlds to explore; of finding the lost islands of legend, the places where fae and fairies had fled after the wars of succession. If we were ever to seek out the truths of those legends, or to discover all that could be seen in our world, it would be by ship. And if by ship, we would need a fleet that was ready for any demand.

I turned my attention with interest to the scene being played out on the water down below. The rowboats had reached the broken vessel, and without any visible struggle, had captured the two survivors, brought them aboard, bound their hands, and were even now heading back.

"Will you question them?" I asked with interest.

The captain grunted. "My second officer will try. He's good at that sort of thing. Doubt we'll get anything off of 'em though. None of those Dwarves ever talk when they're captured. But they're usually only smuggling goods or refugees over to Spindle. Not great, but not a threat either."

"Protocol under our current treaty dictates they're to be returned to Snowdonia, but I'm assuming we won't do so in our ship." Alessia shifted behind me and the Captain shot her a shrewd glance before answering.

"No, not our ship. We'll drop them off with a barracks in our next port. They'll get 'em where they need to go."

The Captain turned back to his business and I watched the men row the prisoners in. *Returned to a country where they're considered outlaws for even existing.* I couldn't remember what punishments Snowdonia meted out for magic, although I knew they were much steeper than ours. We either deported or imprisoned our mages. The Examiners had artifacts that could neutralize some magic, so those convicted of unlawful practice would be shut up for life in their cloister. *What would that be like? I wonder why I've never gone there to see them. And what does Alessia think of our orders?* If her loyalty was ever going to be tested, it was now. Would she defy our laws and try to free her fellow mages?

As the prisoners were hauled aboard, I leaned over the upper deck railing to get a better look. They were rough looking, but not uncouth. They carried themselves with an air of self contained competence, as if their current predicament was only mildly interesting. There was none of the wild panic I would have expected from those about to be sent to their worst enemies. A stab of something like pity went through my heart. *And what do we gain from doing this?* Snowdonia had a number of important mining operations, but the same terrain carried into the Dwarven Republic. We knew they had mines for precious metals and gemstones too. Was it only our prejudice that kept us from doing business with them?

"How do we know they won't use their magic against us?" Alessia asked. The first officer answered this time, gesturing to the manacles around their hands. "Those are from the Examiners. Every ship in these parts carries them. They're spelled to negate a mage's access to magic. We'll have no trouble from them."

His tone was cultured but just pointed enough to give the sense that he was asking if we would have trouble from her. Irritated at his doubt, even though I had effectively been wondering the same thing only a moment before, I started back to my cabin. I would finish up my latest letter to Ella since we would be in port tomorrow. There wasn't much for a Lord High Admiral to do on ship in this type of situation. I was starting to wonder if my father approved this promotion only because it was basically a desk job.

* * *

Later as I raised to rap my knuckles against my bodyguard's door, I stopped, voices carrying under the warped space between the door and the frame.

"They brought it on themselves, choosing to go out on the high seas like this. They know we don't touch them if they're in fishing shallows. Whatever they were doing they thought was worth the risk." Anthonio's voice was low, but audible.

Alessia replied in a louder, angrier tone. "You know as well as I that they were probably smuggling mages to Spindle."

"Or iron ore, or gemstones. That doesn't concern us. Our job is to protect the prince."

"Sending them to Snowdonia is *not* protecting the prince! They have nothing to do with him!"

A frission of fear trickled down my spine. *Is this it then? Will she choose freeing them over her service to the crown?* I didn't want my friend to face the consequences of that choice, and I didn't want that betrayal from her after I stood up for her. *But is she wrong? Are those mages a threat to me?*

"You're thinking like a novice. We don't know that. Maybe they're assassins, sent to infiltrate our ship and kill the prince in his sleep." Alessia snorted and Antonio continued in a calmer tone. "I know it's unlikely, but our job is to prevent even the unlikely. But we aren't judges, and the law is the law. The prisoners aren't our business."

Alessia sighed. "I hear you. But really, if they were assassins you would have sensed their intent by now. Unless those suppression charms on them interfere with your magic?"

I stumbled a step back and froze, hoping they hadn't heard me. *Antonio has magic?* My heart raced at the thought, but I strained to hear his response.

"Do not speak of it out loud," he replied in a forbidding tone. "It is not dampened. They pose no threat. But that doesn't mean we should interfere. If you want to help other mages, then protect the prince. He's the best chance we have for changing things for people like us."

Swallowing reflexively, I tiptoed back to my room, clutching the letter for Ella that I had been bringing to Antonio to take on shore tomorrow. I had drawn a shift as one of the officers to remain on board during this port, but Antonio was going ashore.

My fingers itched to open my letter and add another page about my recent discovery, but I refrained. I had already sealed it, and I wouldn't want that information falling into the wrong hands. *Was everyone around me a secret mage?* It seemed magic had been more ingrained in my life than I had thought.

CHAPTER TWENTY-THREE

Ella

The toe of my sturdy new walking shoes caught an errant cobblestone and I lurched forward, yanking my equally sturdy brown skirt up and catching myself with a few fumbling steps before I lost my balance completely. I could feel my face go beet red, and didn't look as I responded to Madrigal's gentle inquiry.

"Yes I'm fine Madrigal, thank you. Just a bit clumsy."

The guard in front of me hadn't even turned around, whether that was because he didn't care if I face-planted in my own clumsiness, or whether he was too focused on clearing the street in front of me, I didn't know. I had a whole retinue of guards today; four to be precise. *Or perhaps that's not precise. I wouldn't be surprised if Madrigal had a few blending in with the commoners in the crowd.* As proof to my instincts, Madrigal had turned out to be an excellent and devoted guard. Though why he thought I needed more guards than just him for a walk through the city escaped me. My clothes were plain enough that I looked more like some tradesman's daughter than a princess to be. Only my personal guard unit marked me as anything special. *And because my guards are drawing attention, I have even more of an audience to witness my inevitable clumsiness on these streets. The roads near Lucedimora are better than these!*

As I passed through an intersection I noticed a nearby cart had gotten stuck in a huge pothole, and the owner was attempting to push it out with the help of a few passersby. I slowed to watch their latest attempt, tensing as they braced and counted to three, and a brief thrill of victory coursing through me as they finally got it free. I had been in situations like that plenty of times at my Lucedimora. The helpers all clapped each other on the back, congratulating their efforts and I focused back on my path. I was separate from such things now, hidden behind a retinue of guards. Which made the work I had done this morning all the more important.

I had awoken before the birds this morning, dressing simply and meeting my guards at the appointed hour. From there we had made our way to the first of a number of charities that Luca apparently supported. They were various in type and specialization, and while talking to the proprietors I realized that Luca hadn't exactly been hands-on in his support, although even his patronage had helped the people immensely. BMy aim was to interact more fully. If I had to live in the theater of court, at least I could use my income and talents to help those in the real world. *And even the queen couldn't object to such a benign activity. Although I expect she'll try.*

I tried to get the queen out of my mind as we trudged back up to the palace. I was tired, but it had been my idea to walk, a misguided effort to really experience the capitol like anyone else. Now I had sore feet and my calves were burning. Not to mention I stuck out like a sore thumb in the middle of my guards. *Would I get to do anything like this once I'm queen?* I shivered at the thought. I didn't feel equipped, and not just in training. Surely being queen required some inner character traits that I didn't have. *Then again, I've been stepping into responsibilities beyond my capability since my mother died. This is just one more. And hopefully I'll be having many, many years to prepare.*

And certainly I already had some advantages over our current queen; kindness, for example. Just this morning, on our way out of the palace, I had noticed another in what was turning out to be a long line of snubs from her. During one of the interminable wedding planning meetings that I had been invited to, she had asked me to pick between sweet pea flowers and lilies for the wedding flowers. I had chosen sweet peas, knowing full well that lilies were usually reserved for funerals. However, as we had exited the palace grounds that morning, we passed the flower carts bringing fresh blooms for my wedding in a couple days time: lilies, of course.

It doesn't matter. The type of flower doesn't matter, her treatment of me doesn't matter, all that matters is Luca and I chose each other, and we will choose a better way forward together.

We took a few side streets to get us closer to the service entrance instead of the front gates, but I could see a steady stream of elegant carriages pulling around - guests for my wedding. I didn't know the vast majority of them. And those that I did know would be judging me the entire time.

After a tortuous route through the palace, I waved farewell to Madrigal as he took up his post outside my door and pushed my way inside.

"Jacqui, I was wondering if you -" I paused in shock, the door swinging shut behind me in a slow creak. I pushed back open a half a second later, as Madrigal stepped inside.

"Do you need assistance?" he asked, eying the occupants of my room.

"No, no. I don't think they'll - they won't hurt me. I was just surprised, that's all."

He gave a curt nod and stepped back outside, shutting the door firmly behind him. In front of me, unbelievably, stood my stepmother, stepsister Aria, Lady Zelmira, and Jacqui. Lady Zelmira was eying my family with a suspicious frown, and Jacqui was wringing her hands anxiously. I couldn't take my eyes from Beatrice and Aria.

"What - what are you doing here?!" I gasped, torn between concern for their wellbeing and quelling a swell of anger at what had happened since we last saw each other.

"We're here for your wedding," Aria said softly, "at the King's invitation. He - he extended clemency toward us, especially as The Woodland Fairy requested it."

I blinked, trying to understand what they were saying. *The Woodland Fairy? From Deerbold. They must have fled there after Alessia's message. I should have realized.*

"That's... that's good." I replied lamely. My heart was pounding in my chest as I tried to filter my thoughts and feelings.

"Do you want them here, Ella? I shall have them removed if you prefer." Lady Zelmira's voice was the haughtiest I had heard yet, the sound almost chilling coming from the perfectly coiffed and impeccably dressed courtier.

I shot her a startled look, which she interpreted correctly. "Just to their guest room, dear, not out of the palace." I stifled a laugh and turned back to my family, all mirth leaving my heart.

"Why?" I asked simply, struggling to put to words the complicated knot of feelings I had. "Why give me the shoes? Why not tell me what they were? Why not tell me what *you* were? Why not tell me about the prince? Why leave me to go to the palace alone when you *knew* that I could be arrested for using a magical artifact?!"

Tears were streaming down Aria's face and Beatrice looked as white as a ghost. Even as angry as I was, part of me broke to see them like this.

Aria shook her head, hugging herself tightly around her waist. Beatrice took a step toward me, her hand held out, but she stopped short, putting her hand over her heart instead.

"Believe me, we never meant to hurt you, Ella. It was to keep you safe all those years. If you didn't know, you couldn't be arrested if we were caught. And the shoes shouldn't have reacted like that! The only tell should have been a brief flare of light as the heart connection was established or denied, and that would have been hidden by your skirts, or at least dismissed as a trick of the light! I had no idea you had magic, let alone that it would react to the spell in such a way -" she choked back a sob, clearing her throat in a most unladylike manner that was completely unlike her.

"You don't know what it's like - how difficult it is to *always* keep such a secret. To always wear a suppression charm to dull your magic. That's why I have headaches, did you know? Because my magic is strong, and obvious when I use it. Only my charm keeps my secret. So when I do allow myself to use it, it takes so much effort…"

As angry as I still was with her, I couldn't help my curiosity. "What is it? What is your magic?"

She drew a long shaky breath. "Weaving. I can weave straw into gold." Jacqui and Zelmira gasped, and I stared at her uncomprehendingly.

"Not much at a time. It takes a lot of effort. But I can do it, and weave it into my fabrics. That's why I always had a bolt or two of 'forgotten' fabric in the attic when times were tough. I worked at transforming a bit of thread every week, storing it up so I could produce a whole bolt of gold shot cloth every now and again. Just enough to make ends meet when we needed it." I blinked, memories opening up before my eyes of how when times were dire she would disappear to the attic, claiming to go searching through her jumble of old fabric boxes, and *always* managed to find a scrap of cloth worth enough to get us through whatever crisis we had been confronting. Not so much in recent years, once I had gotten the estate back on stable ground. There hadn't been a need, I suppose.

"We *never* would have given you the slippers if we had know what would happen, Ella, you *have* to believe us," Aria pleaded. The truth of her statement shone out of her tear filled eyes, but I shook my head.

"Why didn't you tell me about Luca, then? You must have known."

Beatrice sighed. "We did know, but only a short time before the ball. It's true - we could have told you, but… if I'm honest, I didn't want to meddle in your relationship - no, no that's not true completely. I was hoping he wouldn't tell you. I was hoping that the slippers would test your love before his job became and issue between you, and they would bind you together in the knowledge of true love. Because then... then we would have had a queen on *our* side. A queen that we knew would be kind to mages, and maybe later we could have shared our secret with you. And I knew you would take pity on us, and influence Luca so that maybe you two could start the path toward accepting mages in this country."

The open admission of her mercenary manipulation cut me to the core.

"Out," I demanded, pacing forward to one of my small windows, without looking at them. "Get out."

I heard Jacqui's quick step as she rushed to the door and stuck her head out to murmur to Madrigal.

"Ella, please!" Aria cried, but I didn't turn around, couldn't. I knew if I looked at them, and saw their suffering, I would relent. But I didn't want to right now. I couldn't face their pain and years of love behind it, sitting right next to my stepmother's open admission to manipulating me at one of the most critical moments of my life. I was hurt deeply, and I had a right to feel that pain before I let it go in forgiveness.

When all was quiet, I turned to find the room empty except for Jacqui. She looked at me with quiet concern and shrugged. "I had planned on showing you the dress I had made for Luca's return tomorrow night, but I'm guessing we should save that for the morning?"

I tried to smile at her but it felt more like a grimace, especially at the reminder of Luca's return, after a month of not one of my letters being answered when he had made me promise to write. There was too much to sift through, and not enough time. "How about a cup of tea for now?"

Jacqui flitted out the door to the kitchens, leaving me alone with my thoughts.

❉ ❉ ❉

"What do you think?" I asked Jacqui, performing a little twirl in front of the shaving mirror on my dresser. I still didn't have a full size mirror for some reason, but I knew I could rely on my maid to make sure everything was perfect.

"You look every inch a princess," she gushed, her smile wide with pride at her handiwork. She had worked hard over the last few weeks to create this gown herself, using a deep pink silk that was the height of fashion this year. Somehow the vibrant pink didn't clash with my pale copper hair, and a part of me had to admit that I couldn't wait to see the look in Luca's eyes when we saw each other.

I crouched down to check my hair in the mirror, giving it a self conscious pat to check that the ribbons threaded through my braided crown were firmly in place. A crown of braids was all I could afford at this point. Although Lucedimora's coffers were steady, they weren't full enough to afford frivolous purchases. *At least ones **not** connected with the stables.* I never could resist the latest technology or luxury for my business. And I certainly didn't need a crown to know how to hold my head high. I stood straight and smoothed the waistline of my dress, shimmery gold accents catching my eye. My stepmother had left several lengths of gold lace in my room last night, and after a sleepless night, I didn't have the heart to refuse the peace offering. Part of me wanted to represent my family, and magic users, even if I was still angry about how everything played out. I huffed an irritated breath but couldn't help admiring how the pale gold looked against the more vibrant pink. Jacqui and I had decided on using some of the lace as sleeve ties along my arms, creating an almost quilted effect instead of a billowy open sleeve like I was more used to. Somehow Jacqui had rustled up a few of her friends in between their own duties for my approaching wedding day, and they had all worked on sewing bands of the lace onto my stomacher, and in a trim around the edge of the overdress, which consisted of several cleverly arranged panels that opened to show off my soft white muslin under dress. Other than my ballgown, it was the most beautiful creation I had ever worn.

My hand crept up to my charm necklace, a gesture that had become a habit over the last weeks. The rough stone was incongruous among the rest of my outfit, but Jacqui had found a solution for that too. She had taken a scrap of gold lace left over from the trim and wrapped it around the stone, securing it with a few knots of thread behind. Now the gray stone provided a beautiful contrast to the gold lace, matching my outfit to perfection.

"Jacqui, you've outdone yourself," I said, beaming at her. A rapping sounded on the door and she jumped.

"That must be your escort!" She scurried over and ushered in Sergeant Madrigal, who was affected not at all by my beauty and instead sported a grim look. Lady Zelmira trailed in his wake, for once not looking quite as put together as was her wont.

"The Prince's cavalcade is almost here, Lady Fenice. We must leave immediately if we are to make it to the entrance in time."

My eyes widened in alarm and I gathered up my skirt and hurried after Lady Zelmira as Madrigal held the door for us. "But why did no one send for me?!" I gasped as we began running down the hall.

"There must have been a mistake," she replied, reaching out to steady me as I tripped over the hem of my dress. I thought I felt a slight tear and groaned, not daring to look. A grand public welcome ceremony on the Palace's front steps had been planned for Luca's return, and I certainly didn't want him to think I hadn't missed him. *Although maybe Queen Narcissa...* I shook my head. Even if she had been so petty as to tell me the incorrect time, it didn't matter now. I had to make it in before he arrived! We slowed to fast walk as we entered the more public corridors, Madrigal taking the lead and Lady Zelmira tucking my arm under hers as if we were on a relaxing, if fast paced, stroll. A trickle of sweat traced it's way along my hairline and I struggled to keep my breathing to an even level. I knew my skin was probably closer to the hue of my dress than I would have liked, and titters from various courtiers hanging about followed me down the hall. *It doesn't matter. Just get up there for Luca!*

Finally we reached the upper foyer of the main entrance, where Queen Narcissa, Princess Marietta, and for some reason Lady Emilia, were arrayed in splendor before the closed front doors. Princess Marietta shot me a murderous glare, while Lady Emilia examined me with raised brows. Queen Narcissa looked at me coldly.

"So you've made it at last. We had given up on you, Lady Fenice." She flicked her hands at Lady Zelmira, who squeezed my arm in support before melting into a side corridor with Madrigal. We had been instructed the day before that only the royal family would be standing here at the top of the stairs once the doors were opened, ready to greet Luca.

"Where are the King? And the Princes?" I asked, still attempting to slow my breathing.

Queen Narcissa's expression turned even frostier, probably at my audacity for questioning her. "They have ridden out ahead to meet my son," she replied, letting her eye roam over my gown. "What an interesting color combination you've chosen, Lady Fenice, especially given your hair color. It certainly brings out your... freckles."

I could barely stop myself from rolling my eyes. *You can choose to be better Ella.* I didn't have very many freckles really, and although I knew they weren't fashionable, I actually liked them.

"Thank you," I said instead, shooting her a *slightly* insincere smile. "Isn't it lovely?" I couldn't stop myself from doing another little twirl, feeling almost lighthearted again at the end of it.

Marietta and Emilia had been whispering to each other, but broke off at my twirl to gape at my behavior. The Queen was frozen as still as a block of ice, and Marietta shot her a quick glance before sauntering up to me.

"Yes, that color of pink really is lovely, although I'm surprised you would venture to wear it," she said, circling me with a critical eye. I held my head high, ignoring her and attempting not to betray my nervousness.

"I heard a rumor that your stepmother is a Weaver Witch," she hissed in a low voice. I shot her a startled look, then whipped my head around as Lady Emilia's musical voice sounded close by my ear.

"Yes, and I heard a rumor that she brought you spelled lace to work yet another charm on our poor prince. Is that it here?" She reached out to touch the lace sleeve ties and I flinched away.

"Yes - I mean no. It's not charmed against Luca, obviously. But it was a gift from my stepmother."

"I won't allow you to get any more magical claws into my son," Queen Narcissa whispered angrily, her voice echoing against the empty foyer.

A sudden tearing noise sounded, and I stumbled as something tugged on my arm. I reached out to catch myself as I fell, but lost my balance completely as something tugged on my other arm. My face smacked the sandstone floor, and I heard yet another ripping noise, and felt a long strip of lace ribbon detach from the hem of my over dress.

"It's not even sewn on properly!" Marietta screeched and Lady Emilia let out a chuckle. "Then it's not fit to be seen by Prince Luca. All the more reason to remove it."

"What are you doing?!" I demanded, too shocked at their behavior to put up a fight as they ripped yet another length of ribbon from my dress.

"We are removing every stain of magic from you as possible," Lady Emilia announced, as if commenting on the weather even as her lips turned into a snarl as she ripped another bit of lace from my dress.

"If only we could remove the stain that you carry *inside* you," Marietta spat at me, tugging with surprising strength at the ribbon belt tied around my waist. Dropping to my back, I fought off her hands only to shift them to my head with a shriek. Lady Emilia had switched her efforts to the pink ribbon wound around my braids, ripping out clumps of hair as she did. Marietta redoubled her efforts on my belt, and as I tried to twist out of both of their grasp, hoping to regain my feet, I caught sight of Queen Narcissa. She was watching the entire display as coolly as she did everything, her face a mask that concealed emotion except for her eyes. My heart lurched at the pitilessness I saw there. I almost preferred the hate that had dripped from her gaze when I had first met her instead of the cool unconcern. "Stop them!" I pleaded, and she met my eyes with a blank look. I closed mine as pain seared my scalp for a moment, before blessed relief. I felt my hair tumble down my back. Lady Emilia must have had success. I put trembling hands up to my head as Marietta jerked on my belt again, finally freeing the knot, and pulling it from around my waist.

"Ladies, please," Queen Narcissa said indulgently. I saw Marietta and Emilia step back through my watery vision, and pushed up to my feet quickly in case I needed to defend myself again. *Where are Lady Zelmira and Madrigal?* My breath was coming in sharp, short gasps, and muscle cramp in my side was sending stabbing pain up my ribs.

Marietta and Emilia stood only a pace away, cruel smiles on their lips, scraps of ribbon and pink fabric littering the floor between us.

"Do you know, I don't think I approve of your choice of apparel after all," Queen Narcissa continued in a disapproving tone. "You're not fit to be seen. Go back to your room and find something else to wear. One of your old country fashions that seem to suit you so well... *Cinderella.*" I gasped at the use of Luca's nickname for me, realizing with a sudden understanding that she must have been stealing all my letters. I had signed them all as Cinderella. She continued on, reveling in my understanding of her mischief. "And don't think that I'll be allowing you to get away with your latest attempt at magic," she said glancing at the gold ribbon twinkling on the floor as she motioned to someone in one of the side corridors. The two examiners who had been present at the ball stepped forward, and a shiver of fear slid down my spine as I clutched the rags of my overdress closer. "These two will ensure your compliance, and I will alert the King to the issue." The two examiners almost floated across the floor toward me, spreading out on either side.

"I really don't think such an attack can be ignored," she almost whispered, "can you?"

My breaths came even quicker as the two examiners closed in, my eyes darting around to look at each small corridor leading off the foyer, hoping to see Madrigal or Lady Zelmira, or *anyone* come running in to help me, but I was alone.

Lady Emilia stepped up in front of me one last time, spiteful satisfaction marring her perfect features. "Oh look, we missed a piece," she said, reaching for my charm necklace and tugging it free with a vicious wrench. She realized her mistake almost immediately as the examiners screeched as one. She stumbled backward, eyes wide, just as the main doors to the grand palace stairs began scraping open. Trumpets sounded on the other side, marking the Prince's entrance to the stairs, and a roar of approval filtered through but it all faded as a golden haze overtook my vision. My consciousness was drawn inside myself, my blood roaring in my ears as a burning warmth began flooding my chest. My entire awareness seemed to constrict on that point in my heart, tighter, hotter, brighter, it burned through ever inch of my skin until it converged on top of itself. For a breathless moment I was caught in an agony of nerves and emotion and pain until it all exploded outward.

An invisible shock wave seemed to roll out from me in all directions, the force of it causing me to stumble forward even as Marietta and Emilia stumbled away from me, shrieking. *But is it invisible?* Brassy gold specks seemed to flicker in the air, eddying around on themselves and stretching out like glittering stars. I blinked, my vision blurred and hard to focus as a distracting warmth seemed to light me up from the inside out. *Are those flecks of gold? Is that my magic?* The warmth building under my skin, originating under my ribcage was distracting; beads of sweat forming on my back and neck, dripping from my hairline and dampening the sections of hair that had tumbled free from my braid. I heard myself gasping for breath and I put my hands to my chest, stumbling forward again and then stopping as I neared the top of the stairs. The sweat and tears cleared from my eyes and before me was a hellish scene.

Everywhere before me people had fallen to their knees, some moaning in agony, others with silent tears streaming down their face. Some seemed to have more self control, but even those looked in pain. I gasped under the weight of their anguish, then cried out myself as I realized I wasn't just empathizing with the expression on their face, but I could *feel* it too. Motes of golden glitter drifted through the air in front of me, and some part of my mind not occupied with taking in the connections I felt to all the people in front of me realized with a shock that they weren't flecks of gold but glowing *cinders*.

A low moan sounded from next to me and I looked over to see the Queen leaning against a huge pillar, trembling as she slowly sunk to her knees. As I focused on her, our connection became more clear and she screamed again. The longer I looked at her, the more cinders swirled around her head, enveloping her in a whirlwind of fire that coalesced over her and seemed to whisper louder, and louder in a voice that I couldn't hear with my ears but with my mind, or rather felt it brand itself on my heart. *Envy, resentment, malice,* it whispered, and as the words formed in my mind their meaning seemed to mark itself on her face, not in letters but in reality, revealing the truth of her heart on the outside, her beauty twisted by what she had hidden within.

The strength of her flaws was overwhelming and I wrenched my gaze away only to catch sight of Princess Marietta and Lady Emilia. The magic inside me latched on to them eagerly, whispering almost in delight as they writhed on the floor next to each other, just as I had been writhing away from their ministrations only moments before. *Jealousy, fear, power lust, bitterness, hypocrisy.* The voice bounced between the two of them, drawing their flaws from within and revealing them as a brand of truth on my heart. The cinders seemed to twist around and then over their heads, coalescing into a burst of flames that hovered over their brows. I wrenched my eyes away again, their vulnerability before my magic almost too much.

It was a mistake. The only other people in the room right now were the examiners and their black hearts were even darker than their robes. The cinders of magic seemed to burst over their brows with an eagerness that scared me, screaming the truth so loudly I thought I could hear it audibly now. *Murder, bloodlust, hatred, abomination.* I stumbled backwards, trying to get away from the twisted truth that was being revealed, almost stumbling as my foot hit the edge of the stairs and wobbled. I caught my balance and my eyes swept across two figures emerging out of a side corridor with difficulty, almost as if they were stumbling against a high wind. Before I could think, the cinders of my magic swirled around them. *Zelmira and Madrigal, finally!*

Zelmira's dainty face was twisted in heart wrenching pain. *Hypocrite. Fear. Magic.* The last truth drew a gasp of surprise from me, and she looked at me with eyes full of tears. *Another mage in secret?* I could feel the fear from her, the tightness it had evolved from as year after year she protected herself from discovery. My eyes flicked to Madrigal and he stumbled to his knees, not looking away even as my magic latched on to him. *Bravery, prejudice, humility.* I could almost see his struggle to accept magic before my eyes, and disappointment swept through me as I realized he had been looking at me and my magic with distrust all along. But another note sung sweeter to me under that truth. Even as he had felt an aversion to who I was, he had recognized good in me too, and had struggled to reconcile that with what he had been taught about mages. Compassion swept over me, even as I still felt raw at the suspicions he had harbored about me. Zelmira's head whipped toward him as if she was surprised, and I wondered briefly whether she had heard my magic too.

I looked away from the people around me, friend and foe alike, drawn by the pull of my magic. It urged me to go to the people on the stairs below me, to look at each one and reveal their true self. To burn away their deceits and lies and lay bare their real soul. I felt pieces of myself break off as the cinders of my magic flowed out to hover above each person's head. A cacophony of whispers spoke over my heart as the magic burned its way outward.

My eyes drifted along the crowd, finally focusing on a handful of people halfway up the stairs. *The King and the Princes,* I realized, but before I could wrench my gaze away my eyes met King Ciro's and my magic roared even louder. *Greed, pride, brokenness,* it whispered. His greed for more land, more prestige, more of everything was painful and pitiful to feel. Twining in amongst it though was something even more painful - his brokenness. Despair at the lack of love from his parents, deep pain at the indifference from his wife. The little betrayals from those he had thought loved him over the years, only to had been revealed as caring only for his power. I felt deep grief at his pain and as it welled up in my heart tears spilled over in his eyes and he hung his head.

As he collapsed on the stairs, Luca came into view, on his knees, staring at me in horror. The horror that showed on his face hit me directly in the heart and I fell to my knees in a mirror image of him. I could see myself in his mind, glowing red and gold from the inside out, the heat of my judgment like a weight on his heart, and terrifying.

Inexorably, his heart was laid bare before me as well. His insecurity rose up like a spirit, overwhelming as I sensed how he sought and failed to find his father's favor over and over again. How he tried to prove to himself that he didn't need it. Whispers of his distrust of my magic, even as he had told me he accepted me for it, licked around the edges of my mind and I curled away from that truth. *Too vulnerable.* I didn't want to know his secrets, I didn't want to face the rejection I knew I'd find there. Tears streamed down my face as I attempted to pull my magic back. It seemed to slow a bit, but not enough, and I felt it search out Luca's heart. *Courage,* it whispered. *Goodwill.* I knew that, I had always known that about him. But those things could coexist with prejudice and rejection. *Love, kindness.* As my magic ate further into his heart I tried to resist the feelings of goodness that rolled off of him. Out of the corner of my eye I saw him push to his feet, struggling and stumbling as he made his way up the steps toward me. The closer he got, the more my magic swirled around him, and the louder his love for me became. Instead of horror I felt acceptance. Instead of sundering I felt a stronger understanding. With a mountain of effort, I dragged my eyes upward as he closed the distance before me, pain on his face, but love in his heart. Even as he pushed his soul toward me, offering it freely in examination, I felt my own heart laid bare to his in rapid succession: *judgment, justice, self reliance, kindness, protective*. A cry escaped my mouth as my secrets leeched out of me. I wasn't ashamed of myself, but the rawness of vulnerability hurt, and the coppery glow of my magic shifted to searing whiteness. My need for security after the deaths of my parents and the heavy mantle of not failing the people on my estate passed out of me, and I felt Luca shudder at it. The betrayal I felt from my stepfamily, and even him wrenched my heart as it left, called by my magic to be told in truth. Luca cried out at it, and I wanted to pull it away from him so he didn't have to feel the hurt I had already forgiven him for. Beneath it all I felt a steady anchor of goodness and love from him and I clung to that, reaching for it with all my might even as my consciousness stretched too thin, reaching for more and more of the people who were there to welcome Luca home.

His hand met mine as my world went black, and I collapsed into his arms.

CHAPTER TWENTY-FOUR

Luca

I fought my heavy eyelids as I struggled to listen to Headmistress Weald's conversation with my father. Rubbing my thumb across the back of Ella's hand, I traced every vein and willed her to feel what was true in my heart towards her, not just the sense of my hand holding hers.

"Luca?" her raspy voice sounded, barely audible. The sound of it drew everyone's attention in the infirmary room.

Headmistress Weald bustled over, sitting on the other side of the bed and putting the back of her hand to Ella's forehead, as if checking for a fever. *Maybe she is. The heat of her magic had been almost unbearable.* I watched the headmistress anxiously, but her usual no-nonsense expression didn't betray anything. My eyes flicked toward Ella and she met my gaze, her eyes tight and mouth twisted in pain.

I grasped her hand tighter and leaned forward, all my weariness forgotten. "Are you alright?" My own voice was as raspy as hers had been only a moment earlier.

She nodded, but tears spilled down her face. I fought an anxious, fluttery feeling of helplessness in my chest. "Then what?" I demanded, "why are you crying? What can I do to help you?"

Her mouth twisted even harder. "Nothing, Luca. It's just - the memories of all of that pain... I'm sorry."

My heart twisted too. I had felt the echoes of that pain, the judgment her magic had made us all bear up under as our worst and most vulnerable parts were offered up for scrutiny. It all felt raw still, like my heart was a rag that had been wrung out. From what Headmistress Weald had been saying before Ella awoke, she had felt it all more keenly than the rest of us. I pressed my other hand to hers, squeezing it between my own and trying to impart all the scraps of comfort I could muster.

"I'm sorry too, that you saw all of that. All of my..." I sighed, trailing off as my face burned in shame. *My neediness, my reluctance to stand up to my father, the powerlessness I feel sometimes.* Now that she had seen it, broadcast it even to anyone who had been clear minded enough to feel it, I could face those truths head on. They were still there, but I knew about them, and at least for now, they wouldn't be mastering me again.

"No, Luca. Not you. You were beautiful. Flaws and all. And you were strong. I felt you come for me - didn't you?" I nodded, crooking a smile and relieved that she really had felt what I was trying to give to her. My love. My devotion. Even as her magic burned through me in judgment, I knew what mattered most - my choices. And I would choose her always.

"I didn't mean to do that," she continued. "My magic just - something happened when Lady Emilia broke my necklace."

Headmistress Weald nodded from across the bed. "From the report I had from Lady Red, that charm was the only thing holding back a flood of your magic being released. You say someone pulled it off of you?" Ella nodded and my blood rushed in my ears, making my tired head feel light. *It's a good thing she ran with my sister and mother before now, or I would make her -* I shook my head. No need to add one more regret to my pile of mistakes. Lady Emilia was beyond my sudden thirst for revenge, and that was a good thing.

"A foolish idea, especially considering what she unleashed," Headmistress Weald continued.

"But what *was* unleashed?" Ella asked, eyes wide and pleading. "I know it was my magic, but I don't understand it. And I had no control! I thought you were supposed to be able to control your magic…"

"Ah yes. I was just telling King Ciro and Prince Luca here about my suspicions. Easily confirmed by your last name, as it turns out. Phoenix, it means, in your country's old tongue, am I right?" Ella nodded, a perplexed frown on her brown. I perked up. This is what Headmistress Weald and my father had been discussing just before Ella awoke.

"You, my dear, are descended from a long line of mages we have long thought perished. The Phoenix Mages," Headmistress Weald almost breathed her last words, an expression of reverence crossing her face. *Ella must be a very big deal indeed.*

"The Phoenix Mages," she continued, her eyes trained on Ella's face, "were a family of magicians who passed down their peculiar capabilities to every generation. Some say they had been blessed by the Shepherds themselves for some great sacrifice, though what that was has been lost to time. We do know a little, however, at least in our records in Spindle," she shot a glance at my father. When I followed her gaze I was shocked again at his sunken expression, and the humility in his posture. I tore my eyes away, not wanting to look. "We have records of the Phoenix Mages great deeds, all in the service of their beloved Charmagne. They were the right hand mages of the Charmagnian royal family, generations ago in the wars of succession. The last great battle over the border with Spindle is the last mention of the family in our records. They held a key mountain pass from our country's encroachment, sacrificing the head Phoenix in order to do so, and ending our conflict with Charmagne forever. What happened after that, we knew not. It was enough that no more of the Phoneix mages came against us."

My eyebrows had risen with each twist in the Headmistress' story. *These are Ella's ancestors? And Lucedimora their seat?* It was situated overlooking one of the only passes into the forests of Spindle.

Ella shook her head. "But what was their magic? And why was mine sealed? Lady Red mentioned that it wasn't hidden away, but actually sealed within me, undetectable until the spell of the glass slippers broke it free."

Headmistress Weald looked thoughtful. "That I do not know, child. I can only guess. Perhaps as Charmagne turned against it's mages, the Phoenixes found a way to seal their magic and go undetected during the Mage Purges of the last few generations. They were loyal to their country to a fault, even to the death, so perhaps suppressing their magic when it wasn't wanted was the only course they could accept."

A question sprang to my lips. "What do you mean when you say they sacrificed themselves for their country. In battle?" I hoped my anxiety hadn't crept into my voice as much as it had into my heart. The thought of Ella giving her life...

"Yes, in some cases, but mostly through their magic. The Phoenix magic is the only type of it's kind. It is a sort of judgment, a purification really, of a person's soul. We all felt it today, and I daresay we won't be fully back to our old selves for a long time. And that wasn't even the full force of her magic, simply a chaotic reaction to whatever set it off." The Headmistress drew herself up and caught Ella's gaze. "It is said that the purification of the Phoenixes has the power to judge all mortals, to burn through their lies and shields until only their truest soul is laid bare, and too often, that vulnerability leads to death. We none of us are as pure as we would hope, and most of us are hiding from some part of ourselves. In battle, the great Phoenixes would overpower huge swathes of their foes, calling forth a judgment on their fears and sins, incapacitating them to a pathetic degree. The only danger was, that if the Phoenix was untrained, or if they spent themselves too far, their very soul would be given in the magic, a sacrifice that would level everything in it's path for miles, and often indiscriminately. It was a steep price to pay."

I let go of Ella's hand and stood, wobbling as my tired muscled screamed at the sudden change of position. I steadied myself on her bed, not knowing what I meant to do. I just wanted to protect her from such a fate.

"As noble as that sounds, I am hoping I am neither required to do so, nor would I do so accidentally before I can control my magic," Ella's voice sounded stronger than I would have thought given the enormity of what had been revealed.

"Indeed," Headmistress Weald agreed, eying me with an amused smile. "My suggestion would be that you come immediately with me to Deerbold Academy. We have charms there that would protect you from accidents, and access to the best magical experts to teach you control. You would be safe there, as would those around you."

Ella struggled to sit up, and I rushed to help her, putting pillows behind her back and smoothing her hair as she leaned back against them. The softness in her eyes when she looked at me calmed the nervous tautness in my heart.

"That sounds amazing. We are to be married tomorrow, and then as long as King Ciro and Luca agree, Prince Luca and I could come the day after that." I nodded in agreement even as Headmistress Weald reared back in surprise.

"Are you still going through with the wedding? I thought given what happened earlier…"

"No." My father's voice creaked across the space of the room, and all eyes flew to him. "They will marry tomorrow. If you'll have him, that is." His gaze bored into Ella, willing her to understand something. "You have pierced me, child. I am undone, and I don't know…" he coughed, the sound pitiful in my ears. I didn't want to see him like this. He had been strong and merciless my entire life, and now he was humbled. As much as I had longed to see him have an ounce of humility, the revelations of his character were still too fresh in my mind to be comfortable.

"I told you to make yourself valuable," he continued, a tired smile pulling at his lips, "and you proved to be worthy in a way I could never have imagined. I want you tied to my country, to my boy, without delay. Yes it's mercenary of me," he admitted to whatever expression he saw in Ella's eyes. "I don't deny that. It's too embedded in who I am to -" he broke off in anguish and glanced at the floor instead. "I want your strength for my side, before you go anywhere. And your promise... your promise to protect him. It would give me ease to know he has you, when I'm gone."

"Father, I don't need -" he raised a shaking hand and I broke off, frustrated that yet again he saw me as less than, someone to be protected instead of someone to lead a country in his stead.

"He is strong," Ella replied, speaking only to him. "Stronger than me in many ways."

"Yes. I made him that way - no, perhaps not," he admitted, his voice dropping lower. "He was always strong, and good. Even as a child, really. And I did my best to give him what I didn't have, to protect him as I could. But you - you would sacrifice yourself for him, wouldn't you? And remove his enemies from before his feet!"

Ella looked at him with pity and he shied away, but didn't break eye contact. "I know that you love him - why do you make me wait for your answer?"

"Yes I'll marry him. But because I love him, and for no other reason," she said gently. "I'll protect him in all the ways I know how, the small ways and the big ways, as long as I live."

"And your magic?" my father demanded, and I wanted to shake him in irritation. "Promise me you'll use it. I won't have him left like I was... friendless, and alone!"

A shock of awareness passed through me and my father looked at me only to rip his eyes away, probably hating the understanding that was dawning on my face. I had known his relationship with his parents had been fraught. And his relationship with my mother was famously cold. How they produced four children was something of a miracle. All his relationships were prickly and steeped in political machinations. I had assumed it was just his way, but now I could see it was built on a lifetime of neglect; neglect for the man that was under the crown. And although I often felt like he kept me on a short leash, his point of view suddenly aligned for me and I could see all the ways that he had provided for my own development of the man

I was. Sending me to school in a place where I was just Luca, letting me pursue my love of the sea even though he thought it a waste of time, allowing me, even pushing me at times, to pick my own wife instead of having my mother arrange something for me. Though in all of those things he had been high handed, the fact that he had allowed them had been a gift of something he had never had. Another crack opened up in my already fragile heart, and I didn't dare say anything out loud to him. It was all too sensitive still.

"Let us hope that we never need use of my magic to that extent," Ella said quietly, and my gentle understanding flipped back over to frustration as I was reminded that he had basically asked her to lay down her life for me. I stuffed that emotion down, however, attempting to focus on the task at hand.

"Well I am certainly not opposed to a quick wedding if you aren't," I told Ella, giving her a mischievous smirk. "Though I might demand that you promise *not* to sacrifice yourself for me, even if the situation does arise. But I know better than to tell you what to do. You'll do what you think is right, and you'll probably be correct." She rolled her eyes at me and I couldn't help the grin that appeared on my lips, stretching my tired skin almost too tight. I sobered at another thought. "Besides, we still have to end the spell of the glass slippers, don't we? Last I checked, they would drive us crazier and crazier until we were married, no?"

Ella laughed again. "True enough. And I think we both feel crazy enough after all that's happened. Can we truly still be married tomorrow? My magic burned through all the decorations and sent half the guests running for cover."

A grim stubbornness enveloped my heart. "Leave it with me, my Cinderella. I'd like to see someone try and stop us."

CHAPTER TWENTY-FIVE

Ella

The carriage came to a surprisingly smooth stop and I glanced across to my stepmother and stepsister. Lady Zelmira sat beside me, more docile than I had ever seen her. Still feeling the effects of my magic from yesterday, as are we all. The door of the carriage opened and Madrigal appeared. I took his hand, and he helped me down, stepping gingerly on the glass slippers I had last worn at the ball, when everything had changed. Jacqui whisking around me as I got out of the way of everyone else, adjusting my veil and smoothing out a few wrinkles on the fabric of my white and gold wedding gown.

After my display the day before, the Archbishop had flatly refused to marry us, even in the face of King Ciro, who had regained much of his bullying manner at such an affront to his orders. While they had argued, Luca had rode out in the city until he found a parish priest who had agreed to marry us. The parish was near the center of town, in a church that was probably older than the city walls, and only just larger than my guardhouse room at the palace.

It will hide the fact that many of our noble guests have either fled or are still not comfortable being seen. I didn't blame them. I hadn't wanted to know all of their deepest secrets. I didn't like my own foibles being laid so bare to Luca, even though I knew he accepted me despite them.

A scattering of cheers went up around me and I looked around to realize that what we lacked in noble guests, we seemed to have made up for in common ones. Lining the streets in a surprisingly orderly fashion were people of all social class. Children held out fistfuls of flowers, picked from their own gardens or bought from the corner sellers. I looked back at where Lady Zelmira now stood by the carriage door, holding the bouquet of flowers that had been procured for me from the palace gardens. All the lilies that my soon to be mother in law had ordered for me had mysteriously burned up in my magic yesterday. Not that I would have wanted to carry a bouquet of them even if they hadn't. As pretty as the roses that she held were, my eyes strayed to the earnest expressions on the children's faces. With a quick step, I took the roses from Lady Zelmira and walked over to an alcove of the wall that I had noticed from the carriage. It was a shrine to the White Queen, dotted with wilted flowers here and there.

"May our love be as strong as yours and the White King, milady," I whispered as I placed the offering on the altar. Their partnership was the stuff of legend. A cheer went up from the crowd, and grew even louder as I paced back toward the first of the little children, saying hello and accepting their own offerings of flowers. As I made my way down the line, I collected a large bouquet of hodge podge flowers, not nearly as aesthetically pleasing as the one I had left on the White Queen's altar, but somehow more beautiful in what it represented: a new beginning for all of us. One based on truth and togetherness. Where the nobles of the land were revealed to be the same as the commoners in essentials. Where mages could exist in harmony with non-mages. Where Princes were married by the same man who married greengrocers. It was fragile, and felt like it couldn't possibly last, but we had a chance.

As I turned onto the short gravel path that led from the street to the little chapel, butterflies started fluttering around my ribcage. Luca was there, waiting for me, his brothers standing next to him, Alessia and Anthonio guarding him. Madrigal had somehow gotten ahead of me and opened one of the doors, Aria swished her skirts as she darted around me to open the other one. My stepmother and Lady Zelmira swept through ahead of me as planned, and my butterflies threatened to soar free as I took my first step down the aisle. As I passed inside the church, my eyes locked with Luca's and my entire being shifted into place. I wanted to run down the aisle, but somehow kept my pace even.

In a flash I was at his side, an apple-cheeked priest looking at us with a smile as wide as the sky. We spoke the promises I had heard in every village wedding I had ever attended, and felt the fizzing thrill of the glass slippers' spell as it resolved itself. In it's place lay a quiet assurance of true love, and a deeper excitement at the life we would face as one when we walked back down the aisle together.

Then his eyes were on mine, his arms were around me, and somewhere nearby the priest was saying, "you may now kiss the bride." With a touch as gentle as a summer's rain, and as solid as tree of oak, our hearts collided, and he did just that.

EPILOGUE

Snowdonia

Two guards pulled open the heavy wooden doors to the audience chamber, revealing the figure of the high inquisitor, hidden as always by his hooded cape, standing next to the Queen. A sandy haired Royal Huntsman, dressed in browns and reds stalked quietly into the room and bowed. The Queen never turned from where she stared into a dark, ornamental mirror, hanging on the stone wall behind her throne.

As the doors closed, she turned toward the Huntsman, her expression as dark as her mirror.

"Huntsman Alaric," she called, motioning him to approach. Her mouth was in a grim set, every line of her posture betraying mental agitation even as her expression showed the tight lid she kept over herself. Her subject approached and bowed once again. "I am at your command, Your Majesty," he intoned, his voice low and expressionless.

The Queen twisted her hands for a moment, stealing a glance at the high inquisitor before sitting down on the edge of her throne. "I have asked you here because of your skill and loyalty, and I have need of both." She cleared her throat, and said quietly, "I have a critical mission for you, although it is a crime and will stain your honor. The High Inquisitor is here to absolve you of your sins if you take this mission, as it will be in service to your Queen and country."

The Huntsman knelt, as still as stone and silent before his Queen for a moment, prompting her to shift in her seat.

"Do you accept?" she demanded, her voice shrill.

"I am at your command, Your Majesty, as I have been since I took my oath," the Huntsman replied, not lifting his head.

The Queen leaned back against the high backed wooden throne in relief. I knew I could count on you, Alaric. And I confess, the knowledge that it *will* be you, in the end, gives me some measure of peace." She drew in a deep breath, sitting up straighter in her throne and adjusting the cut steel tiara sitting atop her graying hair. "I know you used to be friends with my stepdaughter, long ago, and will treat her with kindness. For she deserves it, even though she's turned out to be a… well." She drew in a sharp breath. "You forswore your own brother because of his evil magic, so I don't expect you will understand the concern I still feel for my stepdaughter, though she has proved to be irretrievably infected with magic as well. I only ask that the memory of your friendship makes you merciful."

The Huntsman startled almost imperceptibly, lifting his head as if to gaze directly at the Queen but stopping himself before he did so.

"Yes," she said, gripping the arms of the throne tightly. "Our 'Princess Snow White' has been manifesting signs of magic for many years now. How long I don't care to admit even to you." She sighed heavily. "I have tried everything to suppress and rid her of it, to even keep her ignorant of it, but it is now endangering the safety of our entire country."

"What is your command, Your Majesty?" The huntsman asked.

The Queen glanced over her shoulder at the High Inquisitor before turning back to the man kneeling in front of her. "The evening after she sings the Snow White song at the Winter Solstice celebrations, you must take her, along with only a few trusted Huntsman, deep into the northern forest. Use the pretext of a cartography mission ahead of our next battle with the Beasts. When you are deep into the forest, where no one can possibly observe, she must be put to death, and…" the Queen paused, her voice breathy but determined as she visibly willed herself to continue, "…and you must bring me her heart."

The High Inquisitor stirred for the first time, turning his hooded face toward the Huntsman still bowing before the Queen.

"Your own heart beats faster at the thought, Huntsman. I wonder, do you even wish for absolution for the deed you've been asked to commit?" His voice growled around the edges, sounding almost rusty from disuse.

The Huntsman stood, still keeping his head bowed in submission. "I need no absolution for my deeds. I will complete this mission, and the Queen will have the heart as she commands."

The Queen shifted in her seat, then stood suddenly, turning her back on the Huntsman and making her way back to her dark mirror with quick steps.

"Go then, Alaric. You have your orders. You are authorized for whatever it takes to complete this mission. Only, take pity on her..." the High Inquisitor whipped his head toward the queen and hissed, making her flinch before she continued. "She deserves none, for what she is, it's true. But do what you can to make her death quick. Once I have her heart, our kingdom will be safe."

The Huntsman bowed, then turned and stalked out of the throne room with silent steps.

BOOKS BY THIS AUTHOR

Belle & Beast

A war hero. A prince with a secret. A distressed damsel intent on beating the odds. They're not the fairytale characters you're used to.   BELLE: My family lost everything at the start of the Beast War. I've been waiting on my hero fiancé to come home so I can gain back what's mine. Just as the war is ending, a mysterious Prince threatens ruin not just for me, but my fiancé and our whole town too. Everything I've worked for has been destroyed, but I may know a way to bargain with this monster...

ANDRUS: I've dealt with the threat Lord Montanarte presented neatly. Now his daughter is here, complicating things with a deal I can't refuse. What began as a problem may end up strengthening my crown ... but the way her eyes haunt my dreams could be my undoing.

EDDIE: It's been a bitter struggle to drive the Beasts from our northern border. Victory secured, I'm heading home to my fiancé. But home doesn't feel like the same place I left five years ago, and the person I thought I knew best is turning out to be a stranger. Have I left a war only to enter the fight of my life?

Belle & Beast is a clean, fantasy-romance retelling of the French fairytale, Beauty & the Beast. It is the first book in the Istoire Awakens series, but can be enjoyed as a standalone.

The Red Rider

The day Red walked through the woods to meet her grandmother was the day her childhood ended. But she's not a little girl anymore.

RED: I not only survived the revolution, I thrived. I'm now sister to the Duke and Duchess of Sherwood, Captain of an elite border unit, and revered by the people as The Red Rider - the one who turned the tide from the dark days of civil war. But even though I've conquered the monsters of my past, shadows have started creeping into my present. It's getting harder to tell whether my worst enemy is the Beasts we fight in the Wasteland, or the horrors still in my head. When I'm tasked with guarding a tight-laced Pelerine soldier, his contempt for me and my country makes me want to shove his ignorance in his face. But as we start to become friends, I find myself relying on him more and more.

EDDIE: I woke up to a brutal reality after the Battle of Asileboix. Alone and wounded in a potentially hostile territory, I'm at the mercy of the intriguing and dangerous Captain Hood. She's everything I should hate, but I can't deny that I'm drawn to her. We're bound together for now, and sparks are flying as we force each other to confront our demons. It's hard for me to admit, but I'm hoping one of those sparks catches and ignites something powerful.

When Red is called upon to right the wrong of her only failure, Eddie turns out to be the one person who can stand by her side through it…. if they can trust each other first.

The Red Rider is a clean fantasy-romance retelling of the French fairytale, Little Red Riding Hood. It is the second book in the Istoire Awakens series, and although it can be read as a standalone, is better enjoyed when read as part of the series.

ABOUT THE AUTHOR

Rebecca writes clean, new adult fairytale romance in a world of magic and mystery. Everyone who deserves a happy ending gets one, and even those who don't deserve one have a chance. Whether they take it or not is up to them!

She currently lives in the wilds of rural Pennsylvania with her husband, their pint sized princess and prince, and an orange tiger cat. When she's not writing, her days are spent exploring with her kids in the woods behind their house. So far they've found a fairy circle, a witch's cottage, and several perfect climbing trees.

For a free novelette, and a peek into the Istoire Awakens world, sign up for her newsletter at:

Website: https://www.rebeccafittery.com/
IG: https://www.instagram.com/rebecca_fittery_author
Facebook: https://www.facebook.com/Rebecca-Fittery-Author-109857707463475

Made in the USA
Coppell, TX
25 March 2024